KINZURDIA

By Jason Barnum and S.Wolf

Co-Editors: Jason Barnum, R. Ann Siracusa, Jean Bottone
Book Cover artist: RebecaCovers on Fivver.

Copyright © 2016/2020 by Jason Barnum
Published in the United States of America
Published by: Jason Barnum at KDP
Original Publication Date: October 2016
Fifth Edition: October 2020

For permission requests, write to the publisher,
Jbnovelwriter@yahoo.com

Acknowledgements

I, Jason Barnum, would like to thank my family for the bouts of time given so I could concentrate on the book. Thanks To my mom Jean B. for being so encouraging and helpful along the way. Thanks to my Dad, Rick, for reading my bad drafts and giving me encouragement as well. Thanks to my Brother, Erick, who told me the book needed a redo. And in doing so, lead me to making a much better book. I thank S. Wolf for pulling me into his dream and letting me write creatively. Also for letting me come meet his family and friends. Thanks to the aid of Ann Saracusa for guiding me. And through her writing, and reading of her books, I have learned a lot more about writing. I want to thank the Furry community and friends we have met along the way. Without all your ideas our book wouldn't be as interesting. I would also like to thank everyone who has visited our site Kinzurdia.com and downloaded our preview. It means the world to us that so many of you have enjoyed only the first few chapters of our story.

I, S. Wolf, would like to thank Ann Siracusa for helping me get our story on the right track with helpful tips and editing expertise along the way. I also want to give thanks to her grandson Christian S. for helping me improve my ideas and story. Without his time and patience, I wouldn't have been able to express my ideas correctly to Jason Barnum. I thank Jason Barnum for helping me create a masterpiece over the last four years. I also thank Jessy E. for the her time over many months to help spawn some interesting ideas, drawing test covers and drawing an epic wolf for me. I thank Lisa for aiding us in the early chapter creations of the book and ultimately leading me to find Maggie C. I thank Maggie C. for having to listen to my constant discussions of this book and sticking with me through thick-n-thin times. You Maggie are my rock and you keep me going, thank you.

Thanks to Kaia H. for her valuable input on Valfens and their background. I would like to thank Floyd for inspiring a last minute character into the book and for being such a huge fan already. Also I would like to thank Robert G. for brainstorming with me and giving me many ideas for different creatures in the book. Thanks to Akito Z. for her continued support and book knowledge that helped carve the creatures into something worth reading about. I thank Gabe H. for believing in me and pushing me to finish this book. I would also like to thank Jolly Rainbow Rancher for motivating me and translating my crazy ideas into something more tangible to understand.

We want to give thanks to all of our proof readers who took time out of their month to give great feedback improving the editing of this book. Without you all we would be lost. Lastly we would like to thank our fans for sticking with us this past year encouraging us to complete our first book. We hope you enjoy the book for many years.

Table of Contents

Prologue – 13 Years Ago

Chapter 1 – A Cold Winter Day

Chapter 2 – The Next Morning

Chapter 3 – The Festival of Introductions

Chapter 4 – What About Nana?

Chapter 5 – A New World

Chapter 6 – A Mysterious Salamander

Chapter 7 – A Dark Discovery

Chapter 8 – An Unforgettable Ride

Chapter 9 – A Fond Welcoming

Chapter 10 – The Decision

Chapter 11 – The Hunt for Paracoubler

Chapter 12 – Meeting Jelina

Chapter 13 – The Rule Breaker

Chapter 14 – The Uncanny Premonition

Chapter 15 – Conversing with Nature

Chapter 16 – Deer Hunting Gone Wrong

Chapter 17 – Training with Sea Shells

Chapter 18 – A Planned Lunch

Chapter 19 – A Breezy Afternoon

Chapter 20 – Anger Management

Chapter 21 – Eight Days Later

Chapter 22 – The Zurye Ring

Chapter 23 – Last Elemental Standing

Chapter 24 – The Recovery

Chapter 25 – The Death Race

Chapter 26 – A Fiery Last Stand

Chapter 27 – Draithur's Army

Epilogue – A New Objective

Prologue

Qwinzmare Kingdom, Kinzurdia 1994
13 years ago

A beaten old hag, wearing a long, dirty, tattered gown, worn and depleted of its once-white splendor is dragged into the royal chambers. She begs and pleads to speak to the king repeating the importance of her message. Her worried face is laced and aged with wrinkles while sadness dwells beneath her eyes.

The guards toss her to the rough stone tile floor. One of the guards kicks her before grabbing her hair to lift her head up to the king, who stands from his throne with anger.

"What's the meaning of this intrusion?" He bellows as all chatter in the room falls silent. The queen shushes her three-year-old daughter who sits in her lap. The party guests stand frozen in place at hearing their king's sudden burst of anger.

The guard holding the whimpering woman's hair lifts the hag's head a bit higher, "This witch ran by our guards yelling 'King Kiel Qwinzmare will die! Queen Rosalia Qwinzmare will die! Save the child!' She wouldn't quiet down unless we brought her to you, my Lord."

The guard lets go of the woman's hair, causing the woman to fall faintly to her knees. The guard crosses an arm over his chest and kneels down before his king.

The woman starts up again, begging for the king to listen. She wails, "Please save your child! Save Rawena-Rose now; there is no time! She and all of you will die if…"

The crowd gasps and chatter rises in the room. King Kiel raises a hand for silence, standing up in front of his throne asserting his dominance.

"How dare you threaten the life of my family!? Especially my child! Guards! Escort her out of here now! She will be hung tomorrow when the sun is at its highest."

The guards start to pick her up when Queen Rosalia stands up, holding her daughter on her hip, raising a hand to stop the guards.

"Wait!" she commands. The guards freeze and look from their king to their queen and back to the king. Rosalia turns to her husband and says "I want to hear what she has to say."

Keil glares to his wife as his cheeks redden with anger. He nods, "Very well, let her speak!"

The guards drop the woman once again, and she clears her dry throat.

Standing, she curtsies slightly, showing her respect. Looking at the Queen, Agnes says, "I am Agnes. I can see possible futures – a seer of sorts. A, a few moments ago, I saw death. So, so much death. This kingdom it, it falls to ruin. Your family, you're all slaughtered." Agnes' voice falls silent and trails off as she bows her head down, her eyes weeping at the reminder of her visions.

"What? That's nonsense! I'll not hear another word! Not out of your dirty, plotting mouth!" The king rushes forward and grabs the woman by her throat. The queen frantically hands her child to their guardian nearby and rushes to Keil's side.

Rosalia puts her hand on his shoulder and whispers in his ear, causing the king to slowly release his strangling grip, setting the woman free to cough and gasp for air.

Agnes begins to whisper barely audible hisses. Keil catches the sound and bellows, "Speak up! Or heavens help me I will gut you where you stand!" He pulls out a long blade from his sheath on his right side. He points it at Agnes' belly.

Agnes repeats this time but loud enough to be heard. A mantra, threatening and foreboding,

> "The child is a wild.
> Her protectors will detect her.
> The sword will be an award.
> Her abduction is her destruction.
> The power is in her last hour. "

"Too late!" Agnes twists her head back to the entrance. "The end is near! The Lich is here!"

Clouds snuck up to the castle covering it in darkness like a thick veil. Thunder popping off nearby in rapid succession followed by a fierce light show flashing into the throne room. Rain starts to pour down the stained glass windows.

Agnes cackles as the child starts to cry; a man appears in shiny black armor and wisps of black smoke trail behind him. Smoky creatures with glowing red eyes swirl around him through the air like black ghosts. He stands motionless as a heavy wind blows, dragging leaves and debris into the room. Soon, the shadowed man begins to step forward.

King Keil backs up in surprise toward his throne. Several guards pile in front of their rulers, all with swords drawn and pointed at the intruders.

The two guards standing behind Agnes started gurgling and gagging with their eyes squeezed shut; black smoke invaded their lungs, and in seconds, the guards opened their eyes.

The room echoes from the gasps of the scared patrons. The personal guardian motioned for the king and queen to retreat. The Guardian noticed that the eyes of these guards now illuminated a bright, solid red, making the smiles on their faces all the more satanic.

7

Both guards stood at attention and pulled out their swords. The dark, obsidian armored man in the doorway looks up directly into the eyes of the king and chortles a malicious laughter.

King Keil's heart sinks and skips beats as he feels his stomach knot. "Brother! No! What have you done!?"

The armored intruder booms a loud, haunting speech, "I am not your brother!" Stepping forward, approaching the king, the armored man raises an arm, pointing at his very own brother. The guards surrounding the king are motionless and stunned, too afraid to move.

"Kill them. Kill all the humans!" Keil's brother says as he unsheathes a large, dark sword, slicing off Agnes' head, holding it by her hair. He tosses the smiling head into the crowd of guards.

Screams of agony and despair unleash as men are torn apart, limbs by limb as blood sprays onto the faces of those nearest. It is a massacre.

As more guards rush in, the king, queen and the Guardian - carrying the three-year-old girl, flee down a secret staircase and into a unique study with books lining the walls.

Queen Rosalia rushes to the book lying open atop a podium in the middle of the room. Shaking, she pulls off her pendant and whispers a few, repeated words. Soon, a portal appears.

The door from the stairs bursts open, allowing the black smoke and several red glowing eyes to come right for them. The Guardian ran through with Rawena-Rose Qwinzmare, King Keil, and Queen Rosalia quickly following. The queen begins chanting again, and the portal starts to close – letting in a few too many Dark Ones.

Keil fends off the creatures as Rosalia looks into the blue eyes of her daughter in Tate's arms. The guardian holds securely onto the child as he frantically looks between his king and queen, then about his surroundings.

They were in a study, similar to the one they recently departed. There are no candles, and the orange evening rays glint into the room through an old stain glass window.

Rosalia can only think of what poor Agnes had said: *Save the Child.*

Rosalia watched in horror as her husband tried to defend his family. Several open cuts were sliced across his face and chest, blood pooling around his feet as he forced himself to keep on fighting.

Rosalia put her pendant around her daughter Rawena-Rose's neck. A bright, warm glow radiated out from within the clear jewel as the initials "R.R.Q." were engraved into its surface. She kissed her forehead one last time whispering her love as tears streamed silently down her face.

"Keep my daughter safe," Rosalia says as she draws her silver sword, joining her husband in a losing fight.

Their Guardian, Tate Tumbleson, unsheathes his radiant sword temporarily blinding the Dark Ones long enough to take off down the stairs and out the front door, past the gates of the castle. The girl's cries grow loud and heart wrenching as a small tear runs down Tate's face; he flees with the girl in his arms.

Making it outside, away from the battle and harm behind the castle walls, Tate trips and tumbles down into a snowy bank with the child nestled in his chest, landing on his back. He swiftly stands and continues through snow piled up to his ankles. His head is light and his thoughts are racing, but he has a duty to fulfill to the queen and his lord. *Save the child.*

The guardian's breath grows shallow as he continues to get the child to safety, up and away from the castle, across a frigid river, and into the world, he thought he would never return to.

Chapter 1

A Cold Winter Day
Culbin Forest, Scotland
November 11, 2007

James

I love the cold winter. The way my boots trail through the thick snow reminds me of the good old days with my brother David, horsing around with him inside the castle gates...before the change. Watching him search for me with a snowball in hand takes me back to those days. Could it really be a year and nine months ago?

Ever since I can remember, we've always had snowball fights. We may be alone in this abandoned castle but we have each other. Even though I'm seventeen, David always knows how to bring out the kid in me. In fact, I hear him coming and instantly I feel like a kid again.

I duck behind a snow bank, I look at the snow and get the clever idea of surprising him first. *I'll start it this time. David always thinks he can get the best of me. I'll show him.* I dig my gloved hands into the softly crunching snow and form a snowball.

"James? Where are you?" David calls. Hearing him, I feel the rush. I know I have the element of surprise. Peeking up from behind the snowdrift, I hurl the snowball and finally, for once, I let him have it first!

"James! I'm going to find you!" David looks around for where I threw the snowball from. Before he sees me, I duck once more and get another snowball ready for hurling. I whip that snowball at him and — just my luck — he spots me.

"James! There you are… hey, stop!" I hit him once more with a third snowball.

"Or what?" I tease. Then I notice a grin streak his face, rosy from the cold.

"Okay, wise guy. You're going to pay for that!" David charges right at me. "I warned you! You'd better run, James!"

The excitement of our little game makes me stumble in the snow. I stand again as fast as I can, only to get my foot stuck in an icy, hard patch of snow. That's when I realize he's going to win — again. He always wins, but a large part of me doesn't mind.

David knocks me down and scoops up a pile of snow in his arms and slams it right into my face. It's freezing cold and hurts my cheeks a little, but I can't help but laugh so hard my skin turns even redder!

"Okay! Okay, David you got me!" I laugh, rolling around and trying to escape the snow piles David keeps pummeling me with. "Okay!" I laugh again, "I give up! You win! Oh my Lord, stop, it is … *way* too cold!"

Once again, David wins one of our many snowball fights. Though he doesn't exactly throw the snow, he still makes it fun.

We both stand and dust our clothes off, panting and laughing. I ruffle my brother's hair, "You're a lot stronger now. So watch the pressure, ya?"

David laughs and rolls his eyes, then looks up at me with excitement in his eyes "Oh! You ready for hunting tonight? Deer season, ya know."

Stupid question! I'm always ready. "You bet, and I'm willing to bet I'll get a deer before you do."

"Yeah, right. You need a replay of what happened?"

"Hey, you might be good at scooping snow and plopping it on someone's face, but I'm talking weapons and killing something. Want to make it interesting?" I challenge.

"You're on, but … you and I both know why I'll definitely win first," David smirked. "C'mon. Let's see how good you are with that bow. Loser has to clean the bathrooms for a month and has to act like he enjoys it." David laughs.

"You're on." I pick up my one and a half meter-long, oak re-curve bow and sling my quiver of razor-sharp, iron-tipped arrows over my shoulder. "Let's go."

We head out of the castle's main gate into the twilight. The sky is lovely, and the stars are starting to peek out above me. David sprints into the woods ahead of me, and I have to run to catch up. A few hundred yards away from the castle walls, we slow down. David perks up as he usually does in the forest and inhales a deep breath through his nose, then runs straight towards the nearest game.

It's a buck with a large rack of antlers another hundred feet ahead. It has to be a ten or twelve pointer. *Gorgeous pelt, too. It would make an amazing trophy.* Slowly, silently we creep toward the game, heading for two spruce trees, hidden low in the tall grass to avoid being spotted by our prey. The snow muffles our approach.

"I'll bet I can pierce its heart with an arrow before you can lay a claw on its fur," I whisper. "I'm feeling lucky today."

David scoffs under his breath before whispering back. "There is no way you can win this. Your arrow will hit the tree, not the buck. Ready, set, go!"

Then I see it. David sprints out of the brush, still in human form, but with fur spreading over his arms. Pointed ears poke up through his short head of hair. Soon, a beastly form takes over what was once a small teenage boy. All I can see ahead of me is a large canine with gray fur, quickly, but surprisingly quietly, running the buck into the open. A trail of torn clothing is the last remnant I can see of my brother when he zooms out ahead of me.

When he changes like this, it's still an eerie experience, and sad, but at the same time, he's my brother. I'm getting used to it. Inside, he's still David, my twin, even though on the outside he's a Dire wolf named Silver.

Sometimes I wonder what I should call him, David or Silver? But he says it's like there are two separate beings inside one body.

He's about half way to our prey now, and I'm still setting up my bow. I pull an arrow fletched with goose feathers to the string, draw the notched arrow to my cheek, and wait for the perfect shot. The deer's neck is in my sight. I let my arrow fly right as a blood curdling, high-pitched shriek fills the woods. The shriek makes David stop and stand on his massive haunches as my arrow barely grazes his fur and nicks the buck on the ear as he bounds off in fright. It whizzes past and slices through a stout tree before burying itself in a pile of snow.

I glance toward the spot where David ran off, but all I see are more scraps of his clothes and the tip of his wolf tail disappearing into the shadows, heading in the direction of the scream.

As the last of the sun's rays leave an orange glow on the horizon and the sky above dark and clear, I dash after my brother. As I run, I snatch an arrow from my quiver and close my eyes imagining the fletch igniting. *Ignis.* I blink and feel the heat of its flame warming my cheeks. The glow from my makeshift torch allows me to dodge huge roots and other debris in my path, while I do my best to keep Silver/David in sight. It almost seems like the branches and roots are making a path for me to follow.

When I catch up to him, I see a girl drenched in blood lying in the snow, clutching her face. Her low moans of pain are barely audible to my ears above David's low growling nearby. David knows something is here.

I stand still, trying to make sense of what has happened. David's silvery fur and bright ivory-colored fangs glisten in the torch light. He lowers his muzzle closer to the ground, snarling and snapping at something in front of him. A dark form is held at bay by David's crouching form, ready to spring into action.

Approaching from behind him, the light from my torch shows more of our enemy. The creature in the shadows resembles a mountain lion with short, red and gold fur and a rosy pink nose. Fresh blood drips from its fangs, and its eyes glow red as they fixate upon the helpless girl, curled into the fetal position on the ground.

David's voice enters my mind telepathically. *"Do you see it? Too big to be a mountain lion. This beast is larger than an African lion!"*

I nod toward David and look at the brute before us. It glares at us, but appears unbothered by our presence. It licks its fangs and lunges at the girl.

David leaps forward and slams it to the ground. As he does, I stake the arrow-torch into the snow and quickly notch five arrows into my bow and shoot them simultaneously. The feathers on each arrow burst into blazing torches in mid-flight before the tips sink into nearby trees, making an arena-like semi-circle. David and the beast continue to attack each other. Without losing time, I notch another arrow and, when an opening presents itself, I shoot it deep into the lion's side. The lion creature keeps attacking David as if I'd missed it completely. Helplessly, I watch as David continues to fight the lion, muscles tensed, ready to fire another when an opportunity presents itself.

***

David.

This cat is strange. My fangs rip away chunks of its flesh while James' arrows stick out of its sides and yet it doesn't weaken. *Can't it feel anything? What kind of monster is this?*

I'm not sure if *I'm* thinking this or if these are Silver's thoughts I'm hearing in my mind.

I glance at James and back at the lion again as I tilt my maw, intrigued by its behavior. Its snarl brings my mind back to the fight. I snap at the cat's face, then dodge a swipe of its claws. I hop back when the beast leaps at me. Quickly, I crouch, spring into a leap, and tackle the vicious cat in midair. My fangs drip clots of blood as they sink into the massive shoulder.

Blood spurts as I tear the lion's shoulder open down to the bone, crimson staining the snow. I leap away, feeling a tug on the fur of my hind leg. Spinning around, I realize if I had taken a moment longer, the lion could have easily taken my leg off or ripped my belly open with its claws. As the lion gets back on its paws, I throw my body against its side.

My fangs sink deeply into the soft tissue of the lion's neck. Hot, dark blood covers my muzzle and chest as I rip out the lion's throat.

I think I've finally killed it! Now to tend to the girl.

As I leap towards her, I hear the twang of James' bow. Gazing behind me, I see the lion has risen to its feet with an arrow through its skull, and is yowling like a cat from hell itself, an ear shattering, bone chilling screech of an angry feline.

"You've got to be kidding me ... that's impossible!"

Dark blood continues dripping from the lion's neck as its throat spews blood onto the snow, it charges at James. Silver inside me instantly takes over, leaps into the air, and crunches its fangs down on the back of the lion's neck. James leaps out of the way when Silver jerks our neck around like a dog playing a ruthless game of tug of war, the sound of bones snapping and cracking. Silver thrashes the lion about like a ragdoll, its blood flying everywhere. James covers his face from the showering blood spatter. Finally, Silver and I toss our head and send the lion's limp body to the ground.

I look at James, wondering if the lion creature is down for the final count.

***

James.

Notching another arrow, I watch the cat crumple, its eyes fading from glowing red to black, as if a flame inside had been extinguished. Stepping lightly, I lower the bow and approach the lion. David heads toward the girl lying in the snow, her arm over her face, curled in a fetal position, strangely quiet. Before I can replace the unused arrow in my quiver, a dark shadowy mass emerges from the beast's body.

"Watch out, David!" I holler and run toward the shadow-being, ready to shoot it.

David spins around, muscles tensed, silver fur standing on end, ready to pounce. As we approach it from opposite sides, the dark mass rising from the now-dead lion's limp body forms into a dark creature with glowing red eyes, clawed hands, and jutting jaw with sharp pointed teeth. It laughs before speaking in a strange, almost incomprehensible tongue.

"*Htaed!* You may have foiled my attack on her, but mark my words, human and pathetic beast. We shall return! *Htaed* will come! *Htaed!*"

The creature disappears in the blink of an eye.

"Is it gone?" I whisper finally.

We look around to make sure the dark shadowy creature and anything like the giant mountain lion is gone without a doubt.

"*Stay here and see to the girl. I'll check the immediate area.*" David lowers his muzzle to the ground for the scent and sprints away.

"David, see if you can find what direction that thing came from or if there are any more in the area. I hope we don't attract any of those creatures to our home."

First a statue beheaded our guest, then I found out magik exists, then a real spell created a mythical wolf and now a scary black smoke ghost threatened us after possessing a mountain lion … After meeting Zanagoth, this dark creature doesn't scare me.

I walk to where the girl is curled on a soft snow patch with foliage of the forest floor and kneel beside her. I hesitate, listening to the music of the night forest, the ordinary small sounds: crickets, breeze ruffling tree leaves, tinkling of crystal water in a nearby stream. The girl is pale, but breathing.

Good. All is quiet now. I inhale a long drag of the wintery night's air, calming my nerves, and plan what I should do. I cannot help but think, *what in the hell is a girl doing way out here in the dark all alone?* I wonder how badly she's wounded.

Carefully I straighten her legs and uncurl her body, rolling her gently onto her back. Blood, like small rivers, flow freely from under her arm across her face. I carefully grasp the arm right above the wrist and lift it to her side. Her face is covered in blood, so it's hard to see how badly she's been wounded. I'm wondering what to do when David pads over.

"All clear, Human. Creature no find. Female wounds bad yes?" Apparently Silver is in control now. David must really be exhausted.

"I'm not sure," I answer and fumble in my pockets for something to clean her. "I can't tell with so much blood. Can you wet a cloth in the stream for me? I need to get some of this blood off. Plus you may want to clean yourself up." Silver's entire front, from ears to paws, are soaked in the lion's blood.

Silver nods his head, gives himself a shake, and ruffles his fur in a wolf-like shrug.

"I'll take that as a yes." Silver watches me rip off my left sleeve, then carefully bites the cloth from my hand. He lopes away towards the northeast, toward the small stream a quarter kilometer away.

David has always told me that ever since he and Silver connected through the *bond*, he loves all the sensations Silver feels in wolf form. The rush of the wind in his fur and the adrenaline coursing through his veins pump his muscles to move faster and make him feel more alive. I don't understand how, but it must get exhausting eventually.

It's already cold in November, and the stream should be frigid, making it all the more useful to clean the girl's wounds. As I look at her, I see how beautiful she is. Her pink turtleneck sweater matches her pink and white sneakers. Her enticing curves are apparent beneath her jeans that clearly look mended. Although, now her pants have more of a glossy reddish brown color in the torchlight. She is thin. I doubt she weighs more than fifty kilograms in my arms. Her skin is transitioning from a warm glow to deathly pale.

She's losing too much blood. My heart beats faster with worry as I rock her gently in my arms, waiting for my brother to return. Then I hear David in my mind.

"Damn! I hate facial wounds, always so much blood even for a small scratch."

He lopes up and offers me the dripping sleeve. I touch her forehead with the wet cloth. My hand glows slightly as I wipe the blood away from her face, revealing the depths of the wounds. Inspecting them, I see the skin quickly knit up stopping the blood flow where the big cat claws cut her forehead. There are four slightly curved parallel lines barely visible from above her right ear across the top of her head though her hair.

Silver/David sit nearby, watching. When I look at them — it's impossible for me to think of them as a single entity — I'm staring into the eyes of a wolf, knowing that both my brother and the wolf can sense me, read my thoughts, separately, each with their own memories and understanding. How does David stand it?

"*Whoa. She doesn't look too good, James,*" David says.

"Her wounds aren't as serious as before. She's unconscious, so you'll have to carry us back home. Luckily night vision is a common trait for wolves, right? Once she's awake, we'll see exactly what she's doing out here, alone at night, and why that creature attacked her. Maybe she'll know what it was."

Propping her limp body into a sitting position, I place one hand around her middle and the other hand under her knees, and pick her up.

"*Okay, hop on!*" David crouches down for me to get on his back with the girl. Carefully straddling his back, I sit with the girl cradled to my chest and imagine blowing out the torches like birthday candles as David lopes towards the castle we call our home.

***

David.

Carrying James and this girl is a little uncomfortable, but oh well. *Why is that when there's discomfort, I'm the one who feels it?*' Turning my head, I cast a glance in their direction and notice my twin is entranced by the girl's beauty.

"*The only way you can get a girl in your arms is if she's unconscious huh?*"

James digs his heels into my sides. Still, I can't resist teasing him. "*Aww, what's wrong? Did I strike a nerve?*" I laugh at the stink-eye look he gives me as a smirk rises up my muzzle which probably looks more like a grimace.

"At least I can hold a girl in my *arms*," he rebuts. Using emphasis through our connection "How are you going to hold anything with those paws?"

"*Why hold them when they can ride me anytime.*" I turn my head to the side and wink at James over my shoulder. He smirks, shakes his head, and returns his focus to the girl.

Nearing the edge of our forest, the light from the mounted torches besides the gate in the stone wall beckon me. The wall surrounds the Kill Zone area of the castle. We even have cauldrons placed at regular intervals along the top edge.

Passing through the first and second gates, we carry the girl across the courtyard and into the main building of the castle.

"*Your turn. You get to carry her up the stairs.*"

With a nod, James slides off my back, her nestled in his arms, and I follow behind.

Silver is now tucked away inside. It feels odd being on two legs again when being on four feels so natural. I rush my way to the shower and wash

16

the clots of blood off of me. When I finish cleaning up myself, I meet my brother back downstairs before heading to bed.

"How is she?" I ask worriedly.

"She is sleeping. I bandaged her wound but it will leave a nasty scar. We should let her rest and see to her in the morning. I'll grab some sheets and sleep on the couch tonight." James says while yawning.

I say goodnight over my shoulder as I head to my room.

Chapter 2

The Next Morning
Elizabeth

Ohh, my head hurts. I roll to my side and wriggle down under the covers. The bed seems warmer and comfier than usual. I stretch out my legs and yawn as I attempt to clear the cobwebs from my brain and slowly I bat my eyelids to rid them of the blurry grogginess of sleep. My head pounds like a drum. The damp pillow slip smells of cedar wood and pine needles, an unfamiliar scent. A sense of discomfort sweeps over me. I pry my lids open, then lurch into a sitting position. I'm stunned and frozen in place.

This is not my room! I must still be dreaming. My lord, what a horrible nightmare!

My head throbs furiously. Instinctively, I reach up to touch my temple and my fingers brush a bandage wrapped around my head.

What's this? With shaking fingers, I frantically loosen the fabric enough for me to pull off. The blood coated gauze falls onto my chest. Panic rises in my stomach and surges upward to my throat. I swallow hard, realizing my recent experience with horror might not have been a nightmare at all.

I gasp loudly then quickly cover my mouth with my hand to stifle any noise. Despite the pain when I move my head, I turn slowly, taking in the giant room that could easily fit my Nanna's whole house inside.

The poster bed I occupy is fit for a king...a wrought iron frame with intricate wolves carved into the metal headboard. The glossy blue sheets are a mix between silk and velvet. There are matching, old fashioned side tables and a carved wooden dresser so dark that in the subdued light appears almost black.

Where am I? My heart accelerates as I study several area rugs with intricate designs showcasing wolves in different poses. The wall across the room is covered from floor to ceiling by heavy blue curtains, but ragged shards of sunlight peeking into the room suggest there are at least two large windows behind the drapes.

To my right, an old grandfather clock proclaims the time is one-thirty in the afternoon. Beside it, stands an elegantly carved wooden chair with my folded clothes on the seat.

The realization hits me like a blow between the shoulder blades. All the air whooshes out of my lungs. *My clothes are on the chair.*

"Oh my lord!"

I throw back the covers. I'm wearing plain gray sweats. The flash of relief that I'm dressed quickly evaporates. *Who undressed me? Where am I?*

With panic rising in my gullet, I jump out of bed and fall to the pearl-white stone floor, still tangled in the sheets. My breath comes in erratic gasps, my heart beats against my ribcage as if it will break through my chest at any moment.

I pull my legs out of the bed sheets, then sit there with my legs tucked against my chest and my arms wrapped around them, my chin resting on my knees. *What happened last night? How did I end up here?*

My memory is not with the program and sends me a big fat blank. I close my eyes and try to remember. I woke up like always, followed my routine, and went to school. I force my mind to walk through each step. It's like watching a replay of my day through someone else's eyes. I see myself in school, then walking home afterward.

Then, I'm running...

***

Why? There's someone following me.

The stalker is following me! My teeth chatter. It's that crazy guy who follows me from the edge of the school parking lot for a few blocks nearly every day. I remind myself that over and over as I run. Nothing ever happens. I always ditch him.

In spite of the rationalizations, my heart pounds. Then I see Findhorn's Coffee Shop—the most popular bakery and coffee shop in town—it's always busy. I slip around the corner and through the entrance.

Whew! Without waiting to be seated, I plop down at a table in a far corner and order an Irn-Bru from the waitress. When she brings the soda pop, I sip slowly. *He won't come inside. As long as I stay here, I'm safe.* I look up at the clock behind the counter that reads not a minute past four thirty in the afternoon.

I know that eventually my stalker will get tired of waiting and go away. I sip the last bits of my second Bru as I watch the door intently. I'm only half aware of conversations going on around me, only bits and pieces registering in my mind.

"...were you at that?" a young man seated behind me asks of his companions. "Me Da says there was some strange doings at some festival a year or so back and that the lads that live there be cursed."

That catches my attention, and my head perks up. I lean a tad in their direction.

"Yer Da is daft, then. That castle, if it even exists, 'tis nothing more than a decrepit pile of ancient bricks with vines growing amuck."

"We should look. See if them lads still there. Rumors say it's not that far from the creek in Culbin Forest," the younger man replies. "They say it's concentric. Ya know, round."

"So is a tree trunk, lad. Ya need be watchin' what you believe. Cursed or haunted? About as haunted as me left foot!" He tosses change on the table and takes the fellow by the arm, "C'mon, mate. We'd better get back to work."

I don't hear what else they say. I've never heard about there being an old castle in Culbin Forest. A concentric castle of brick with vines on it? A haunted castle in Culbin Forest? A chill skitters down my spine.

I'm positive it's the one I've been dreaming about for years. It sounds so familiar...and mysterious. I've heard about some crazy rumors of a statue coming to life and beheading a lad before. But never did I think it could be true or the location of where it might be.

Without a second thought, I pay, leave the café, and before I come to my senses, I'm hopping from one rock outcropping to another across the River Findhorn, heading in the direction of the forest. My intuition tells me this is a horrible idea but I push all rationalization to the side while my feet keep moving forward. I feel like I'm so close to finding out if this could be the same castle in my reoccurring dreams that I ignore how late it is becoming.

When I reach the shore, the woods rise around me. At first, the trees are wide-spaced with strong rays of early afternoon sun splattering the leaf-matted floor and making it comfortably warm. I know where Culbin Forest is because I've seen it on a map, so I pull out my pink cell phone and pull up an aerial map. Nothing but trees can be seen so I plunge the phone back into my jeans pocket. After half-an-hour the trees gather more densely around me, forcing me to forge a path deeper and deeper into the growing darkness. The sun has disappeared and only a few clearings are large enough to capture the sight of it. I wrap my arms across my chest and rub my upper arms. It's getting cooler, my feet are starting to hurt, and I'm tired...thirsty. At this point, I don't even know why I want to see some old castle—Scotland is full of old castles—but something inside me pushes harder and harder.

I've dreamed about it so often. There must be a reason. I have to see it. Maybe then, the night terrors will go away. I keep walking. After another half hour of pushing aside dense brush that scrapes my arms and legs, I stop and consider my surroundings. It's dark, dank and chilly, and I'm beginning to feel uncomfortable...maybe a little afraid. My internal need to see this castle wanes.

I plant my fists on my hips. "The old man was probably right." Speaking aloud gives me courage. "If there ever was a castle here, it's probably a pile of rocks overgrown with moss. No wonder no one's ever seen it on a map."

The shadows in the forest grow deeper and longer. It's harder to see. I catch the toes of my shoe on a rock and almost fall. Already darkness is descending in the woods. I stare up at the sky and see a splash of sunset colors through the tree branches. *I'd better get out of here while I can still see where I'm going. Nanna's going to be upset with me as it is.*

Heading back the way I came, the sounds of breaking branches attract my attention. I almost stop to look back, but a low growl freezes me in place like a statue. My legs refuse to respond no matter how urgently I tell myself, *Run!* Those few seconds feel like a lifetime. Fear consumes me like fire. Finally, I turn my head and stare into a pair of burning red eyes with whiskers and a mouthful of razor sharp teeth.

A gut-wrenching scream slices the air.

I realize a second later the sound is coming out of my mouth. Before I can urge my feet to respond, sharp pain slashes across my scalp, forehead and right cheek. Instinctively, I lift my arms to protect my face and warm liquid falls to my hands. I tighten my hands to block further blows while I backpedal to get away. A large root from a tree trips me, and I fall backwards onto my rear.

Blood trickles from my scalp into my eyes, blurring my sight, but still I'm acutely aware of the red-eyed beast circling me, growling louder, taunting me, and daring me to run. There is blood everywhere, my face, my hands, my clothes. *Am I going be ripped apart by the beast or bleed to death first?*

I scream inside, but nothing comes out of my mouth. The red eyed beast leaps towards me, but when I blink, he's gone from my sight. My ears, however, are blasted with growls and animal cries. Fur and leaves fly. Before me, the red-eyed beast and a giant dog or a wolf, perhaps, roll around in the dirt, fighting. My eyes connect with the glowing green eyes of the wolf right before I feel my eyes weighing like a ton of bricks and all the life going out of my limbs. I open my mouth to call out, but only a soft whimper escapes my mouth before I crash into nothingness.

***

The movie behind my eyes stops.

Sighing, I open my eyes and stare around me again. Nothing about the strange room has changed. "I must have passed out. And now, I wake up in some strange bed in some strange place."

Gently I touch what feels like scabbed gashes on my forehead and winced with pain. *It wasn't a nightmare. The animal with the red-eyes clawed me.* Bile rises in my throat, a sour taste that made me want to hurl. But what happened? Somehow I ended up here. *Where am I? What happened while I was passed out?*

I push myself to my feet and hobble to the vanity mirror. A pale image with wild hair, a swollen face and angry red gashes from scalp to chin stares back at me. Not exactly Miss Findhorn this morning.

When I reach up to touch the wound, my hand sweeps across my chest.

"Oh, Lord! My necklace is missing."

Ignoring how I look, I frantically search the room, peering under furniture, rifling through the pile of my clothes, throwing the bed pillows on the floor and sweeping back the sheets. It's not in any of these places where it might have come off by accident. Without hesitating, I jerk open the closet door.

"Ohh..." Nothing but men clothes. I'm definitely in some guy's room. "Wonderful."

There are several baggy shirts and jeans with a couple of muck covered boots, I pat down the clothes and search the bottom of the closet. Still nothing. While I'm deciding what to do next, I take a look at a picture on the dresser. Two boys, a few years younger than me, and a man, who might be their father, stand in front of a red barn, an incongruous structure out of place in a forest.

Did they bring me here?

I stumble to the window and thrust the curtains aside. A cloud of dust particles reflect in the bright sunlight as I cough and close my eyes. Then I shade them with my right hand and swipe the dust away with my left opening my eyes to a breathtaking view, as if in a fairytale. The sun, high in a blue sky, plays hide and seek with a few puffy white clouds. I look down, I must be at least three floors up. I see a thick blanket of forest towering over the tall walls around the medieval structure. *I'm in a castle!*

Below, in the courtyard, the sun's rays illuminate the small snow covered shops built into the inner sides of the walls. I see what looks like a decrepit old barn out of place in a castle setting with a few strands of grass poking up through the white blanket of frost covering the ground.

The gray stone walls have been worn smooth by years of rain and now wear a coating of thick green vines. There are several huge stone statues carved with a skilled hand into the forms of very menacing wolves that line the tops of the inner walls facing into the courtyard. The vines creeping along the tops of the walls blend in with the surrounding Culbin Forest. The main building I'm in, from where I can see, has pointed cone tops covered in green vine leaves. Everything looks to be lightly sprinkled with white sugar. The ice crystals sparkling in the sunlight.

As beautiful as it is, I need to get out of here. I turn back toward a door at the opposite end of the room. I hope that's the way out.

Wondering if I should change first, I allow my instincts to lead me across a rich, velvety-soft carpet of fur not like any bear or other animal I've seen. My toes sink into the softness. At the door, I hesitate, then twist the knob gently, pulling back slowly only to have it creak loudly. *Just my luck.*

I gather my strength and take a quick peek outside, looking left, then right. *The coast is clear. I* tiptoe into the hall. The vaulted ceilings form a semicircular radiant design. Each pillar has a star explosion design at the base of the arch. The half pillars are flush against the wall and rounded.

Fascinated, I walk along the spacious, two meter-wide hallways with small tables of dusty cobwebbed lamps and random knickknacks lining the walls. Murals depict historic tales of large wolves fighting men on horses. Expensive, antique candle chandeliers hang down from the middle between each mural. I see wax drooping down from each candle holder as a giant black spider builds its web from one hardened drip to the next.

This has to be a museum of some sort. And what's with all these wolves?

My bare feet feel long deep scratches in the tile beneath me. *What could have made those?*

Drawn by the quiet chattering of two voices from one end, I follow the corridor. It opens up to a white stone railing encasing an open square space. I glide my fingertips across the railing admiring the smooth marble until I feel more deep gashes uniformly in lines, like my forehead. I push my questions to the back of my head and gaze down to what looks like a living room with couches and a tall fireplace from the floor reaching to the roof above. A huge flat screen TV hovers above the stockings of its mantle. A large crater-like shape is next to the couch as if something heavy fell from up here. I can faintly make out the light atop the Xblocks sitting on the dark tile floor. There, on the brown leather couch sits the two boys rather grown up from the pictures in the bedroom. I can't quite make out what they look like so I set out to find the stairs down, skirting the wall to keep out of sight while I eavesdrop on their conversation.

"We couldn't leave her there," one of them says.

"I know, but what are we gonna do about Silver?" The other boy's voice is deeper and more gravelly.

"She was unconscious, David. She probably didn't even notice Silver."

"We don't know who she is, why that thing attacked her, or if there are more coming for her."

"Settle down. You checked the surrounding area didn't you?"

"Yes but…"

"I'm sure we will be fine. I'll go check on her. Maybe she's awake by now."

I turn the last corner of the stairs onto the main floor and plow face first into a rock hard chest breathing in the same cedar and pine smell from the pillow. I stumble back only to get lost in the deep blue ocean of eyes staring back at me. Butterflies tap-dance in my stomach.

A small smirk crinkles the corners of the mouth of his perfectly chiseled face. His strong jutting jaw and slightly rounded cheeks are to die for. Light from the skylight graces his curly golden hair with a squeeze of orange.

His hands grasp my arms to steady me. His biceps bulge from under his white tee, and the shade of his tanned skin rivals any lifeguard on Baywatch. When he sees me gawking, his smirk brightens into a smile.

"Good morning. I'm James Mitchell."

I 'm mortified. Heat creeps up my neck and settles in my cheeks, and my eyes find refuge by studying the floor for any tiny bit of dust or fuzz that might have escaped a vacuum cleaner. "I...I...ah..." I stammer.

He chuckles. "That goofball on the couch is my brother David. Please come and sit with us. We don't bite. Can I get you anything? Water? Tea?"

"Yes, please." I say quietly, a little shy.

I look past him raising an eye at a giant hole in the kitchen wall. I can see the refrigerator from here but keep my mouth shut. I see the start of a smirk creep up his face before hurrying out of the room. David stands and motions me to the recliner across from his seat. I notice he's about the same height and build as his brother, with the same golden tan. He's wearing navy blue sweats, and from beneath the reddish-brown curly hair, his green eyes almost glow when the light hits them at the perfect angle.

He waits for me to settle into the chair before he returns to his seat and eyes me suspiciously. Under his scrutiny, I try to act casual but fidget with my hair and tap my foot impatiently. *What's taking the other brother so long to get a glass of water?*

When James returns, my gaze locks on his like a love sick teenager only to notice a water bottle breaking my vision as it hurtles toward my head.

"Hey!" I screech and manage to duck in time to avoid being nailed between the eyes. The bottle smacks the head rest and falls down into my lap. "What the—"

"James!" David shouts and leaps to his feet. "What's the matter with you? Why'd you do that? She's probably already scared to death from last night."

"Oops!" James grimaces and shrugs at me. "I assumed she'd know how to catch."

I glare at the now smirking face of James. He tips his own bottle to his plush lips and takes a swig as I bite the tip of mine and ask, "So...who is this Silver?"

James gurgles with surprise and spits out the mouthful of water, spraying the floor and couch. He coughs hard, holding his throat while trying to recover from the choking episode. David goes from all squinty-eyed and suspicious to bleached white as though he'd dipped his head in a bucket of flour. It takes a second or two for him to regain his composure. He swallows hard, his Adam's apple bobbing, and croaks out, "Well before we can answer that question let us explain where you are. You are in our home which happens to be a castle in Culbin Forest. James and I found you last night after being attacked by a dark creature we can't even describe that well."

"So why haven't I seen you at school or even around town?"

"Well after an incident that you may have heard about at a Renaissance Festival we held at this castle two years ago, most if not all of the town has kept their distance from this place. They call us names and spread lies. When we try to visit shops for supplies we are met with closed doors. The rumors of the haunted castle destroyed our friendships. The two of us have been maintaining the castle for the past eighteen months. As for school we finished early online six months ago." David explains to me while his brother sits down next to him on the couch.

"Don't you have parents or someone to look after you?" I ask curiously.

"They're gone…"

My mouth feels dry and I gulp slowly. I blink back tears and regain my composure. I can't imagine what these two boys have gone through. "Oh…"

"So who are you, and why were you out in our woods alone so late last night?" James asks changing the subject and putting me back on the spot.

I wiggle nervously on the cushions and begin. "My name is Elizabeth Cairns. I'm sixteen years old and that is a long story."

James smiles at me. "We've got plenty of time."

I take a long sip of water and scoot forward on the edge of my seat to begin my explanation. I feel like at some level these boys are a lot like me, lost and confused but still carrying on every day. I owe them my life and I feel like I can trust these two with my secret.

"This all started in a dream I've had since I was four years old…"

Chapter 3

The Festival of Introductions
November 12, 2007
David

"So you ventured across the Findhorn River and into the Culbin Forest without any actual direction or weapons. All in hopes of finding a mysterious castle that you sort of remember from a dream you had when you were four years old. And in this dream you say your real Ma and Da were fighting black ghosts while in royal getups before some knight took you from your mother and ran from the castle into the forest…"

We sat still for a moment mentally reviewing Elizabeth's dream. I would normally think this to be odd or a pretty typical knight-in-shining-armor type of girl dream, but the way she described the black ghost with red eyes and sharp teeth is an eerie coincidence to the black ghost creature we saw last night.

"Yes it sounds crazy but the dream feels so real to me, almost as if it was a memory. But black ghosts don't exist and I haven't found any king or queen that resembles the faces in my dreams." Elizabeth says with frantic eyes darting between my brother James and me.

She reaches up to her neck and her face lights up quizzically. "Have you seen my necklace? I couldn't find it in the huge room upstairs."

"Nope, I'm sure I would have noticed a necklace around your lovely neck."

"So, I heard little bits about a beheading at the festival. Did that really happen?" She inquires timidly.

"Yes unfortunately but let me explain from the beginning. There has been haunted stories about this castle for many years, long before we became its owners. Sadly had we known of a ghost haunting this place, we would never have signed up for a lottery." A flashback blankets my eyes as I tell our story to Elizabeth.

Before I start the tale, I think back on the sequence of events that led us here and shuffle through the memories. Memories of James and I, at fourteen, pass quickly through my head. Memories of throwing tantrums and starting fights until our mother ultimately disowned us and departed, leaving us in the care of our angry, drunk, and dysfunctional Da. Small snippets of memories of my brother and I having to tend to the farm alone for a year while Da was useless. Memories of working hard to make ends meet and keep the electricity on.

Not particularly pleasant memories.

The fast memories slow down as the castle comes into view and our truck pulls up to a hidden castle in the Culbin forest.

"Let's go inside." My Da puts the old bucket in gear, and we move toward the structure at a crawl. A large wrought iron gate with sharp points reaching skyward is lowered over a dry canal about two and a half meters deep. "That looks like a driveway to the interior of the complex."

"This must have been a moat. That's the drawbridge." James points with excitement from one discovery to the next.

I only hear his babbling, but don't see what he's pointing at. My eyes are focused on two giant wolf statues on either side of the landing point where the drawbridge rests. My heartbeat accelerates. Even at this distance, I see these detailed creatures were carved by a superb craftsman. They're both in the position of a leaping wolf, its hind legs at the base with its outstretching razor sharp claws and a roaring open fanged mouth with an evil glint in the eyes. They're awesome. A chill slips along my arms, making goose bumps rise.

We roll over the lowered drawbridge and through this first gate only to see a second wall about five or six meters beyond, like a second ring of defense. It's at least two meters higher than the first wall, with only tall snow sprinkled grass filling the space between the two walls. The road ramps up and on each side there is a set of steps leading up to a second gate.

"Look." My father lets go of the wheel with one hand to gesture at the trees and bushes lining the tops of the walls as though camouflaging it from an aerial view. Once we roll through this second archway, we're in a large courtyard surrounded by buildings on all sides, with little streets angling off in odd directions.

"It's like a small city center," James murmurs.

"That's exactly what it was," I point out. "The ruler of a medieval kingdom had a whole community within the walls under his protection."

"Right, Lad," my father says and kills the engine. He reaches for the door handle, so anxious he can't seem to get a hold of it. I guess he can't wait to get out and explore. James shifts in the seat, seeming as anxious as Da.

"David, you are too far back." James interrupted my rambling. "She doesn't need to hear our life story. Get to the festival already."

"Fine…well the festival, it originally wasn't going to be held at our castle. Our Da's hobby, as a blacksmith, became a small paying side job when he decided to lower his intake of alcohol. Things started looking up. When Da bragged to his boss about our castle we won, the community took notice and became overly excited about moving the location to a real castle." The memories flood back over my eyes as I relive them again.

Early morning, I wake up to a bombardment of delicious smells wafting into my room. My stomach rumbles and I lift my nose to distinguish the pleasantries invading my nostrils. My hunger, evidently in-charge, pulls me out of my bed and pushes me out my bedroom door. A warm blanket of air wraps me in is delicious embrace as I walk toward the source of such a delightful sensation. Wave after wave of fresh coffee, bacon, eggs and cinnamon rolls! Steak! My mouth waters at the thought of such food. I almost pass up James' room, I resist the rumbles and complains my stomach creates and open his door.

I slap my forehead bringing my palm down over my face and shake my head ashamed. My brother is still snoring. How could he sleep in with all the excitement today is bringing? He knows how much this day means for our father to be recognized and important.

I walk right up to his flayed out body. He looks like a contortionist. His left arm is hanging off the bed, his face in a pillow. *How does he breathe?* The rest of his body is twisted in the other direction. It looks like he half kicked off the quilt where his feet lay tangled in the covers.

I walk up to his head thinking of all the devious things I could do to make him wake up. I take a step back and raise my voice. "James...James Wake Up!"

"Go away. I'm sleeping." he says groggily and muffled through the pillow. My stomach rumbles loudly hinting at its desire.

"Get up! Don't you smell that? It's time to eat."

He rolls over and I can see his nostrils flare out before jolting up and sniffing a few more times. He pushes me aside and dashes for the bathroom before heading to the wardrobe.

I smile thinking *I told you so*. I call out behind him as he's flinging clothes out of his wardrobe. "I'll meet you down stairs." I head out of his room still in my PJs and follow the delicious scent all the way down the stairs. Before I reach the kitchen, James rushes up beside me and stares in amazement at the disarray in the kitchen.

There are eight guests in what look like white coats and tall hats running amuck and yelling at each other. One had smoke bursting from a fire in a pan that nearly reaches the ceiling. Another is chopping what looks like carrots faster than I can say the word. Father is pacing and yelling into the phone at someone about a time delay on props that should have been here by now. *Da must not remember how long it took us to find this place.* He stops for a second gives us an ear to ear grin and points us in the direction of the formal banquet room before taking an annoyed sigh and hanging up. He follows behind us like we are escorting the king to his dining room.

"Wow!" we both gasp.

The long table before is set to seat at least thirty people. Mounds of everything piled high and platters down the center of the table. Bacon, eggs, hotcakes, bread, bowls of fruit cut and sculpted into colorful designs. The cinnamon rolls were begging *Eat me Eat me.* The potatoes are still steaming and every type of juice were filled in tall glass pitchers scattered between plates of food. There was too much to look at and I couldn't wait any longer.

"My boys have now become men, let this be our celebration for change and a new beginning." He looks at both of us staring us in the eyes. He brings out two wrapped gifts. One a long box for James and the other a small square one for me. James opens his first to find a long oak re-curve bow with twenty handcrafted brass-tipped arrows in a rich hide quiver. James looks to me wondering what I got. I open my small box to find two white oak Dirk handles carved into heads of an open maw wolf. The curved dual-edged stainless steel blade look like the wolf's tongue. The hairs on my arms stood up at the amount of appreciation and time Da would have had to put into making these for us.

Da sits down and says "Enjoy!"

We do. James and Da spark up conversations and laugh at each other's replies. I join in here and there making comments and smiling. I can't remember the last time we were ever this happy sitting down together sharing a meal and having a great time. Finally after our mom's desertion and our fathers drunkard rages, we have a happy family again. Things are looking up and I am so happy with the changes my Da has gone through all because of this mysterious castle won in that odd online contest. The bankers still stick in my mind. *They seemed rather anxious to give this property over to us. I know we did win it but something still feels off.* We finish breakfast right before the long exuberant doorbell chimes. We all stand, as a group of twenty-five townsfolk pile in. All are dressed in different garb. All carrying different sized suitcases and boxes. Our father beckons to the man in front who seems to be the leader of the group.

"Welcome to my castle and humble home. These are my two sons James and David. They can help you set up your wares. I am most pleased you made it on time." Father says with an agitated note on the last word. This leader guy must be the voice on the other end of the phone from earlier.

James looks toward me with one eyebrow raised and whispers. "These guys really let the fair go to their heads, even Da is getting into it."

"My name is Leopold and these gents behind me are my group of craftsmen, shopkeepers, and servants." The man in front says while waving his hands around for emphasis.

"Please help yourselves to some food before we begin." Father says gesturing his arm across the array of food before them.

Leopold finished early and took all three of us aside into another room to measure us. James was not a fan of some guy feeling up his leg and nearly punched out Leopold for doing so. He finally got all his measurements and scurried off to start his work and manage his men. Da assigned James to help out with the craftsmen, building stages and tables out in the courtyard. And he sent me to aid in the guidance for decorations in and out of the castle.

The hours pressed on and by two o-clock, the castle and courtyard looked like it popped right out of an Epic Renaissance Festival magazine.

More townsfolk started to arrive and were parking in the grassy area between the inner and outer walls. I could see the ring of vehicles collecting from our tower as Leopold finishes his last adjustments. I look into a wall mirror and burst out laughing. I look ridiculous with long white tights and a button-down reddish vest with a frilly collar. I walk back down the hallway to James standing outside his room with an unpleasant face. Leopold claps his hands and squeaks with excitement handing me a prince's staff made of fake gold. I feel foolish and I can't believe James even agreed to do this. Da wanted to have us take part in the reenactment but I didn't realize we needed to look like this.

James has an agitated frown. I burst out laughing because his big chicken legs look ridiculous in tights. He gives me this evil glare as I approach him.

"You won't speak a word of this to anyone!" He says angrily. "You will never see me in tights again after tonight."

"James calm down we agreed to this for Da. It is his night to shine. Let us support him even if it means wearing these dreadful tights." He takes a couple deep breaths and puts on a convincing fake smile as we walk down to meet our guests.

The first floor is thriving with laughter, shouting, cheers and loud conversations. The place is packed with townsfolk as if the entire town of Culbinshire showed up.

I push my way through the crowd before it starts to part as if I'm royalty. I look bewildered. Looking down again I remember I'm in a prince outfit. *These people are really into cosplay*. As I step outside there is a stage to one side and the shops all around the inner walls are filled with shopkeepers bubbling with conversations and excitement. Townsfolk walking every which way around attractions, many carrying chicken thighs and beer in the other hand. People are pointing and looking at all the decorations and have amazement plastered across their faces.

Time flies by and the sun starts to set. The townsfolk start to gather by the steps for a final speech from the famous blacksmith who won a castle and became king for a day.

I walk up the steps to join my father and James at the top as cheers of joy spring out into a wave amongst the crowd. Da, as predicted, is in full king's wares. He even has a golden crown. Da's favorite sword is sheathed on his side. Leopold slithers his way up next to me. I watch him wearily before he turns and steps down to join the rest at the base of the stairs between the two towering wolf sculptures.

My Da starts his speech. "Thank you all for coming and joining us in this celebration..." He continues but my mind tunes him out when I feel a slight brush pass by my arm and hear the sound of laughter. *I will never forget that voice.* I look around me but no one is there. I start shifting my feet. I look over at my brother on the other side of Da but I can't get his attention. I am getting a horrible feeling, something bad is about to happen.

I see the tails of black smoke being sucked into one of the wolf like statues at the base of the stairs. I look to see if anyone else has seen it. No one spares any attention. I tell myself it isn't real, like before *it isn't real!* I'm about to take a step forward to get a better look when a thunderous *Crack! Boom!* popped everyone's ears. A woman shrieks and points at the same wolf statue I was looking at.

Everyone went silent except for that woman for a long moment. Then there were multiple more cracks and earthshaking booms. The statue lifted its cracked body and sprang off the pedestal it stood on. The crowd parts and jumps out of the way. The head turns back toward us, its stone eyes shift into a black void. Everyone is in shock and frozen in place.

Leopold shakes and falls to the ground below the animated stone wolf. Its stone teeth scrape together emitting a high-pitched screech. A distant evil laughter ripples through the wind, breaking through our trance. People turn and flee back to their vehicles trampling over others. Women and girls cry out in pain or fright. A few younger kids are huddled close to their mum crying.

I step down to the rubble of the statue's base. The stone beast looks down at Leopold. It opens its maw about to behead him when I see my Da stick his favorite sword in the stone wolf's maw. I admire my Da trying to protect us but I'm pretty sure steel isn't gonna have any effect on stone. And in this case, the wolf flings the sword out into the crowd and we hear a loud gut wrenching wail.

"Noooo!" a woman shouts out in the direction the sword landed.

James grabs our father and pushes him back into the hall. I watch in horror as the stone beast chases Leopold to the middle of the courtyard before he trips again.

I saw it coming before it happened. I didn't want to watch but my eyes seemed to be glued on the massive size of the stone wolf. Everything shifted into slow motion as the unbelievable stone beast decapitated Leopold. The beast tossed his head towards the stairs where I stood. It rolled and came to rest at my feet. Leopold's eyes, still wide open, remain petrified in their last expression of fright.

I look back up to the stone beast as it crumbles to dust where it stood.

I look to the side where the kids were crying and a woman bent over a body lying flat on the ground. *No please Lord no!*

I ran to the woman and look over at my unconscious friend. *No he couldn't be.* The sword lay flat near the boy. No blood on the sword and no wounds other than a huge bump on the boys head.

The woman pushes me away from her child and says "What have *you* done to my baby?!" I'm taken aback because how could this be my fault? I don't recall summoning a wolf statue to kill people. That laughter, I remember that laughter coming from a ghost I met during my search of the castle. I had thought it a fiction of my imagination. *This castle is haunted! I don't think whatever or whoever it is, wants us here.*

I feel a slap across my face as my eyes focus back into my living room with Elizabeth staring at me in shock and my brother raising his hand for another smack. I put up my hands. "I'm fine, I'm fine."

"David you were shaking and had this white faced look of horror. Your skin turned cold." James said worriedly.

"Are you alright?" Elizabeth asks.

"Yeah I'll be fine. Sometimes I get these visions that feel more real than they should. James does too."

"Don't bring me into you crazy behavior." James says crossing his arms and looking back at Elizabeth. "I don't have weird visions. I'm not crazy."

"So you think I'm crazy then, having told you about my dream." Elizabeth says angrily to James.

"No, that's not what I meant…ohh David finish the explanation. I'm going to get some more water." James walks back into the kitchen as I look back to Elizabeth's unhappy stature.

"Ignore him, that's what I do. We believe you. It's hard not to after fighting off that dark creature last night. We really have no room to talk crazy when there's so much that has happened to us since we moved here from our farm."

Elizabeth seems to settle a bit and relax in her chair. "There is a ghost that calls himself Richard. He seems to have lived in this castle many years ago. He haunts this castle and we have met him occasionally trying his hardest to scare us out of here. Not too long ago we aided him with trapping a demon named Zanagoth who is out to devour him. He has since left us alone.

"Woah wait a second. First a black smoky creature, then ghosts and now demons. What are you going to tell me next that vampires exist too?"

"Vampires don't exist….that we know of." James says while walking back into the room.

"Great. I will sleep so much better…speaking of that, whose room did I wake up in?" Elizabeth asked.

"That would be mine." James puffs out his chest and sits up straight on the couch smirking at her.

"Well actually it was our Da's room before James moved into it after Silver gave my room an unplanned makeover." I add casually.

I look to Elizabeth and notice her cheeks flare up at the intense stare my brother is giving her. I roll my eyes as the flirting is thick in the air. I get up and walk to the kitchen to grab some water. Letting the two of them talk a bit. Silver sends a thankful gesture as he was feeling the need to leave as well.

"How are the two of you able to afford or even maintain this castle? I hear Elizabeth ask James.

"That's a bit of a loaded question. We haven't paid a cent on power or had much need to keep the interior clean. We mostly stick to only a few parts of the castle as there isn't much point of wandering the castle alone especially since its haunted. We did that once and it about scared my brother to death. There seems to be a magikal presence that maintains the castle and its boundaries keeping others from finding their way here. Silver has made a mess of things and we've had to clean up a lot after him."

"So who is this Silver you keep talking about?" Elizabeth asks from the living room.

The clock on the wall above the oven reads a minute past two pm. The sunrays are pouring in furiously through the windows giving the kitchen a warm glow. It doesn't take long before my brother chimes into my thoughts.

"David, she still wants to know who Silver is. I really have no way to explain it without going through the long story. Why don't you come back in here as…?"

I shut the refrigerator door and guzzle down a few big gulps of water. Silver and I are both eager to return to our wolf form. I explain to Silver that we must keep it slow and easy to avoid frightening Elizabeth.

I pull off my sweats and put them on the counter. My arms and skin grow fur, my ears nose and jaw lengthen, my back curls, legs pop and crack, and the room shrinks again as my claws tap the tile kitchen floor. We move and stretch in our Dire Wolf form. We retract our claws and slowly approach the entrance to the great room.

"What was that noise? Sounded like something fell in the kitchen. David are you ok?" Elizabeth calls out worried.

"It's okay. Elizabeth, you said you wanted to know who Silver is. Trust us, you are safe and he won't harm you. He is a bit…large but he is friendly." James explains before we walk out into the room.

We move around the wall towering our muzzle over James' head who's still sitting on the couch across from Elizabeth in the recliner. We barely see the whites of Elizabeth's eyes before she screams at the top of her lungs and flings herself back against the seat rest unbalancing the chair and toppling it over to the floor. Silver and I step over the couch and peer around the chair to see her curled up in a ball and shaking.

"Silver Get Back Now!!!" James yells as he jumps up, runs to her, and curls her up against him on the floor. Silver feels a bit hurt but I try to explain how scary we do actually look in this form.

"David, take back control!"

We can here Elizabeth's mumbling from the kitchen. "Those red eyes, those same red eyes…"

I didn't take in the fact that when Silver is in control his eyes look the same as the red eyes of the possessed lion we fought. She must have thought that it was another creature coming to kill her.

"Great Idea James." I lay on a thick line of sarcasm. *"Now she is scared of us."*

We return to the refrigerator and I apologize to Silver but we need to shift back into my human self again. Shifting has become natural now, like clenching and unclenching a fist. But there is still one problem and that's the lack of clothes I have left. I have accidently shredded most of the clothes I owned when still learning to control the shift.

The first time I was able to shift to human form, after becoming part of Silver's life, was eighteen months ago. We managed to put Zanagoth, a demon dog from hell, into a magikal glowing object. The thought of being able to fix my wound as a human, when a broken leg could kill a wolf, somehow triggered us to shift back into myself again. Sadly after two weeks in a self-made splint our leg wasn't healing.

Silver was getting increasingly uncomfortable with his dulled senses and uncomfortable perspective of hopping on one leg. He induced a shift when I was weak and asleep. The splint snapped and woke up James who ran into our room. The magik in the shift automatically rearranged the bones and repaired our broken leg instantly. For a couple days we tested this theory out. Turns out it's not only incredibly painful when hurting yourself, but it takes an incredible amount of energy to do a double shift. We quickly learned that we will only have to use this ability if we are in a dire need.

"David the only way to show her is to shift in front of her or she's not gonna believe it's you. I have been trying to tell her it's you but she refuses to believe it's possible." My brother chimes in jolting me out of my memories.

"But these are my last pair of sweats." I reply not wanting to destroy what little clothes I have left.

"Then come out here naked and give her a show…" I can feel my brother laughing when he sent that thought. That certainly isn't gonna happen. We may have been secluded from the people of Findhorn for the past

year but it doesn't mean we are animals. Silver sends and offensive gesture that I need not explain. I ignore it and tug on my sweats.

I walk out of the kitchen, bare feet slapping the cold floor. Elizabeth is still cradled in James' arms but on the couch this time. She seems to have calmed down greatly with James rubbing her back. James speaks up and says

"Here is David again. See he's in human form." Elizabeth nods silently and scrunches her body up closer to him half expecting me to change right then.

"We won't harm you Elizabeth. We saved you from that other beast." I say calmly and slowly.

She frowns at me. "Why do you keep saying we? There is only you?"

"Silver is a part of me, it is hard to explain but we are one and the same now. We share thoughts and strength. We are stronger and faster the more we work in unison." *"I don't know if this is gonna work James?"*

"What color are David's eyes?" James chimes in asking Elizabeth, giving her a small nudge.

"Uh, they are green? Wait they have a slight glow..?"

Elizabeth asks intrigued by her observation. She is staring right at me like as if she could see into my soul. See all my flaws.

I gulp hard and hear my brother again. *"Change now!"* I don't like taking orders but I am unable to look away from her. The sound of thread stretching and ripping hit my ears and I inwardly sigh over my last pair of sweats being torn apart. I am fully shifted again right in front of her. I see the white of her eyes once again but she doesn't scream. She is enthralled, amazed, maybe shocked.

"H-hi…hi…his eyes are still green… the others were red why are they green now?" Elizabeth is more concerned over the color of my eyes than the fact there is a two meter tall menacing looking wolf standing in front of her.

James takes the liberty of explaining now that I'm in Dire Wolf form again. "It's because David is still in control. When Silver, the wolf who had merged with David, takes control his eyes switch color to red. It is all part of the spell I cast on…" James tried to stop his explanation but Elizabeth wouldn't let the slip go unnoticed.

Elizabeth jumps out of his arms and turns toward him. "Are you a witch?"

James face-palms. I can't imagine trying to explain magik after my shifting into a mythological wolf. I can see the questions multiplying in those beautiful blue eyes of hers.

"So you are some master warlock with a giant bedroom and you test evil spells on your brother for kicks?!" Elizabeth's eyebrows raise, her voice heightens with every word said. She stands arms crossed with a slight pout when she finishes her rant.

I feel my legs moving back as Silver is sending images my way to retreat. I can almost see the steam coming off her head.

James peaks out between his fingers to smirk at Elizabeth's infuriated composure.

"So you think it's funny to turn your brother into a giant ugly wolf?"

Silver and I both growl deeply at the ugly comment. The sound frightens Elizabeth who happens to jump into my brother's arms once again.

My brother stares at me while tightening his jaw. *"Calm Silver down David!"* "I would be careful what you say about Silver, he has a short temper. And before you go thinking I'm a witch, let me explain a bit of our heritage.

Our Da was a drunken Scottish farmer most of the time and he dabbed a bit in metal craftsmanship. Our mother was a pure-blooded American and deserted us after we turned fourteen. Our grandparents died before we were born and we have no other living relatives that we are aware of. Our parents never talked about their parents probably because they were too busy yelling at each other all the time. I never knew magik existed before coming to this castle. I found this book one night when David and I went exploring more of this castle and I couldn't even read the languages in the book."

My brother fishes a small book, with a six pointed star incased in a circle on the cover, out of his pocket to show Elizabeth. Elizabeth takes it and sits back down on the couch.

"I have no idea how I was able to cast a spell where my brother David isn't able to. If I am a witch than David would have the same abilities as we are twins...right?" He says as a lame excuse to not frighten her any more than she is.

Elizabeth ponders over that last statement then looks at me questioningly. "Can you talk in that form?" Silver and I shake our head no, before we lay down onto the floor now that Silver has calmed down.

"But you understand what I say?"

We nod our head for a yes. Elizabeth smiles and giggles a bit at seeing our response to her questions. She turns her head back to James who is still smirking at us with his arm around her shoulder.

"So how can you communicate with him?"

My brother taps two fingers to his temple indicating his mind. Elizabeth sucks in a deep breath covering her mouth with both hands.

"Nahaah, no way, really?!"

My brother stares right at her and winks.

Her cheeks instantly turn a rosy pink. "Are you reading my mind?!" She squeaks out while covering her mouth. She crosses her legs and readjusts her sweatshirt again smoothing it out as if there was a wrinkle to straighten.

I roll my eyes and Silver is starting to get annoyed with James' constant flirtatiousness. We make a low whining sound and both their eyes snap to ours knocking them out of Elizabeth's embarrassing stare.

My brother clears his throat and gets back to the explanation. "Uh yeah um...so the spell I found was to give David more strength... and he was willing to try it out. As you can see, the spell did work…it happens to come with a few side effects that neither of us could prepare for."

"This is incredible. I still can't believe this is all real." Elizabeth says while she stands and moves timidly closer to where we are laying on the floor. She reaches out her hand but quickly jerks it back.

"May I…?" She holds her hand out again and we nod before turning our head to the side, allowing her access to our neck as a sign of trust. Her hand is soft and she gently caresses our fur.

"Oh, Wow you're so soft." She giggles as she continues to caress and scratch behind our right ear.

"So if you were carried by this knight in shiny armor, where is he now? And don't you have parents or somebody worried about you?" My brother sounds a bit jealous of the attention she's giving us.

Elizabeth stops mid caress and jumps up covering her mouth with both hands. "Nanna is going to be so mad with me. I have to change and go right now!" She turns pale and her hands start to shake. She darts past us and runs upstairs. James gets up and follows her. *We eat now, yes. We hungry.* I want to follow James upstairs but our hunger is more important to keep satisfied. We trot into the kitchen, pull on the rope attached to the fridge door handle and decide which carcass to shred meat off its bones.

Chapter 4

What About Nanna?
Elizabeth

I can't believe I didn't think of calling Nanna when I first woke up. I'm almost positive she has called the cops on me again.

I run up the stairs two at a time. I pass the second floor and bound up to the third. I can hear James running up after me, but I don't care, I need to get to my phone. I run down the hallway and almost pass the giant wooden door to the room where I woke up.

It is still open, the light from the windows lighting up the room with a magikal glow. I spot my clothes still lying on the chair, neatly folded and clean. I stop and smell the clothes, a familiar scent of cedarwood and pine needles lightly brush past my nostrils. I smile for a split second before rummaging through the clothes looking for my pink cell phone. I toss my pink top onto the bed, look around the chair, in my shoes, and on the dresser. My phone is lost. I drop to the floor and start searching under furniture as I hear slow footsteps coming closer to the door behind me.

"What did you do with my phone?!" I bark out at James while my back is facing him.

"Well, asking like that isn't gonna get me to answer the question. Did your Ma not teach you any manners?"

This boy is getting on my nerves. I swivel around on the floor and sit back on my legs. I look up, James is leaning on the door frame with his massive arms across his broad chest. I start to pout, and my eyes glisten. James snaps up straight. His demeanor completely flips, and he starts walking toward me.

"Elizabeth, I'm sorry, I'm a jerk…your phone was smashed inside your jeans when I went to wash them. It must have taken a hit when you fell in the woods last night. It wouldn't turn on, and David even tried using his charger."

"Nooo….crap! Nanna is going to send me back for sure this time." I start to cry. I don't care if he's standing right in front of me.

"You can call her on my brother's phone," James suggests with a worried tone.

"Won't matter now, I didn't memorize the number. I had it on speed dial." I cover my face with my hand peaking at this boy between my fingers.

"Who is this Nanna, and where would she send you back to?" James stands before me, being utterly genuine with a tone of concern for me.

I turn to the chair and grab hold of the armrest to stand up. I wobble a little, and I feel a warm, gentle hand rest against my middle back, holding me steady. I squeak out a tiny thanks before sitting down in the chair. I wipe the tears from my eyes and wet my dry, cracked lips. James sits across from me on his bed, waiting for my answer.

I look down at my toes before I begin. "Nanna is my guardian. Like I said in my dream, I was left here. I was adopted a few times. When I was four, I had constant night terrors, and the first parents I had didn't know what was wrong with me. They then took me back to the Orphanage. The Orphanage said I was bad, and that's why they returned me. I was adopted three more times before I turned thirteen. When I was about to turn fourteen, an older woman about sixty decided she could take one more child into her home and picked me. Over my entire life, I have been trying to keep my dreams a secret from my adoptive guardians so that I wouldn't send me back to The Orphanage." I fidget with my hair and twirl it in my fingers.

I bite the ends of my dirty blonde hair and sigh. "In the last two years, there's been a stalker following me every day after school. I told Nanna this, and she calls me a liar, she says everything I say is a lie and that my record shows it. She has her good moments and will take the other five girls and me out shopping. But we all know she only adopted us for a paycheck. Her main rule is to keep in contact with her are at all times. She threatens to send us back to the Orphanage if we ever step out of line or break her rules." I look up to see the sadness and concern darkening his deep blue eyes. He snaps his head toward the door and stands up quickly. He looks frazzled and a little worried.

"What's wrong, James?" I wonder what could go wrong now. *I'm stuck here with a fictional shifting Dire Wolf. His brother happens to be some sort of witch that isn't a witch. We are in a castle somewhere in the middle of the Culbin Forest. My Nanna is gonna send me back to the Orphanage for sure. Some red-eyed beast ripped my only pair of jeans, and my pink phone broke.*

Without looking at me, he says: "Get dressed and meet us downstairs. We have a visitor." He grabs a few clothes from his closet and his boots. He drops that same small book into one of his drawers before closing it. He starts to walk out the door, closing it slowly behind him.

"But I thought you said you two were alone out here…?" My question stops his movement for a split second before he replies.

"We are…" He closes the door, and I can hear his rapid footsteps slap the floor quickly losing sound the further he moves down the hall. I bite my lip and then my nails before snapping to and putting on my clothes from yesterday. The tears in my jeans were thankfully over my knees, allowing me to act like it's supposed to look like that.

I use the vanity mirror in the bathroom to straighten up before heading downstairs to see who their visitor could be.

A man's strangely familiar voice echoes down the hall as I exit James' room. I pad up to the same scratched marble railing. I think I may now understand how these scratches got here. David did say Silver made a mess of his room. I can only imagine how messy it is.

Peering down over the railing to see a man much taller than James and built like an ox with a sword handle sticking out the top of his long black overcoat. His deep voice echoes up to my ears, and then he looks up right into my eyes. I duck quickly behind the railing falling to the floor.

It's Him! The same stalker that's been following me everywhere. He found me! How? What is James telling him? I bite my nails before crawling back and tiptoeing my way down the stairs. I am almost to the bottom when I stop and peek around the wall at my stalker. James sees me and gives me an awkward eye glance.

"Elizabeth come on out here and meet—"

I interrupt him screaming, "Nooo! It's Him!"

James frowns, looking annoyed. "Him who? This is Mr—"

I cut him off again; he doesn't get it. "He's the Stalker I told you about!"

"Wait, what" He snaps his attention back to the stranger and takes a step back into a subtle fighting stance.

"Whoa, now that's not a nice way to treat a guest." The stranger's hands rise in the uniform sign of surrender. "There isn't time to play this childish game of who's right. I am Tate Tumbleson, Kinzurdian Guardian of the Royal Family. Elizabeth is the rightful heir to the thrown for the human kingdom of Kinzurdia." He says in a severe but rushed tone.

My jaw drops, and James looks between him and me speechless.

"I…uh…what did you..?" I stutter.

A deep growl vibrates through the walls and floor, interrupting all my thoughts. James and I look in the direction the sound came from, and he stares intently. I don't know what James told David, but the growl stops, and I hear the claws clack along the floor coming closer to me. I see the wolves' eyes fade from red to green as David brushes past me up the stairs.

"Where is your Dire running off too?" Tate, unfazed by such a creature, curiously watches David lope up the stairs.

"How do you know what my brother is?" James asks quickly before realizing he told Tate who the wolf is.

"Interesting. That explains why the wolf didn't attack either of you." Tate ponders for a moment bringing one hand in to rub the stubble on his chin.

I fidget in place, uncomfortable with the stalker so close to me. Part of me wants to flee, but the other part wants to know if what he said is true.

"Why should I believe anything that you tell me? You are the creep that follows me every day after school."

"I follow you to protect you. It is my duty to my Lord and to the vow I made to your mother." Tate says, sounding genuine. He crosses his right arm over his chest; fist clenched over his heart, and bows to me. "Please come and sit down. I have much to tell you, and we don't have much time."

I move around the wall and yell out a barrage of questions. "Wait, you know my Ma? Where is she? What did you do to her? Is she okay? Why isn't she—"

James strode over to me, gracefully took my hand, and whispered into my ear, stopping my Ma's thoughts with him so close.

Looking over James' shoulder, Tate frowns and says, "This matter does not concern you or your brother. It would be in your best interest to stay out of this situation and live out your lives normally."

James whips his head around and replies, "You think I'm gonna let you take her to Lord knows where with a few clever words. Elizabeth is under my protection in my home, and you are an unwanted guest in my castle." My cheeks feel warm with his protectiveness toward me, and I shy behind him, shielding me from the creepy stalker.

Tate clears his throat and replies, "Fair enough; I will explain the best I can. Will your brother be joining us?" James guides me to the couch, hand in hand, as Tate sits in the same recliner I fell over in not too long ago.

James goes quiet for a second. "He is on his way now. He had to change…"

Tate's eyes flash quickly, and his eyebrows rise briefly before settling back down over them. "You two are quite the pair, aren't you?"

I must have been seeing things, but I swear Tate's eyes were glowing bright gold. Tate is silent, and I look at the odd clothing he is wearing under his overcoat. He has a black turtleneck sweater with black jeans and black military-style boots.

I look to the left and see David walking down the stairs cautiously, eyeing Tate. He sits quietly next to me on the other end of the couch. He's wearing tan cargo pants, a black t-shirt, and black sneakers.

Now that we are all here let me start again. I am Tate Tumbleson. Elizabeth and I come from another realm of this world that you call Earth. The land we are from is Kinzurdia. It was a flourishing land of beasts that lived separately until humans from your earth realm used magik to breach into that realm and claim land to build on. Many of the originals were quite upset with how the humans stole the land and conquered opposing tribes.

The real enemy was not the humans but the Lich, who is from a dark realm. The humans may have only acquired a small bit of land, but when the Lich breached into the Kinzurdian world, he brought the Dark Ones cursing the land and turning anyone into the undead. The beasts looked to the humans for aid and, in turn, made the human kingdom of Kinzurdia a sanctuary. Humans taught the creatures their English language, creating the first universal language in the land. Battles with humans and beasts against the undead Lich's armies became more bearable. The humans brought knowledge and tactics, which made fighting and surviving more natural."

"The Lich disappeared for a century after gaining little ground only to return with a band of evil creations he made using curses. They became his liaisons for different parts of the world to help in taking it over. The notorious five have been an unrelenting force over the past four hundred years." Tate stops for a moment looking at my confused expression.

This is insane. Tate is insane. I look around. James is staring at him in disbelief while clenching my hand tighter. David seems to be almost salivating with the idea of such a realm existing.

"This is too crazy" I stand up, pulling James up with me before slipping my hand out of his and pulling at my hair. "You, Tate T whatever. The undead don't exist," I screech. "…there's no magik. This is all a nightmare, and I will wake up soon and go back to you, stalking me and live with an uncaring money-hungry nanny." I cross my arms angrily, leaning on my right rear leg as I stare into Tate's golden yellow eyes.

Tate gestures to James "Would you care to reassure my Princess that magik does exist? After all, you are an Elementalist."

I look to James' shocked expression.

"How do you know what I am?" James says flabbergasted at the idea of such a title.

"I have had a few earth years of experience with several types of magik that I've crossed paths with. But there is something special in you that I can't quite place." Tate stands and walks closer toward James and me.

I step back cautiously before a low guttural growl vibrates through the floor into my ankles and thighs. Our attention now focused on David. Shock spreads across my face looking into David's red eyes. I let out a small squeal and jump back against James.

David is in human form. He has his clothes on, but he is staring through us with his beady red eyes on all fours. James pulls me behind him and pushes me down onto the couch.

"Well, well…it looks like your brother has quite the bond with his wolf to manage separate soul mastery." I look at Tate's amused smiling face as he watches James deal with David's or Silver's outburst. This situation keeps getting more bizarre.

"What is separate soul mastery?" I ask Tate while James is staring down David.

Tate responds without looking at me. "It's when two souls are in one body, and either soul can take complete control of that body pushing its other soul into an imaginary cage of sorts. This ability makes it, so its other soul has no power to stop its actions. To put it frankly, it seems that your new friend David has formed a bond with a very strong-willed wolf.

James' quiet conversation doesn't seem to be working. James looks mad, and suddenly fire fills my vision as heat brushes my face.

I close my eyes and cover my face to fend off the intense heat from the flames. I squint and shade my eyes to get a glimpse of what happened.

I hear James yelling over the roar of the flames. "…you listen here Silver, you bring back David now, or I will singe off every last hair on you!"

I see James a bit more clearly now. At first, I was a bit sad that he pushed me back onto the couch, but he didn't want to hurt me. I can barely comprehend what is happening before me because James stands engulfed in flames. The orange and red glowing flames dance around him. His clothes, shoes, and hair are not scorched. His portrait is like looking through bobbing water.

Silver is unfazed by James' new threat and starts to circle us.

"Silver?" I say quietly, letting the name roll off my tongue and dropping to the floor.

Silver stops in his pursuit. His head tilts to the side, his ears erect, and his eyes dart around James to me on the couch.

"Please," I say in a voice barely audible and a bit shakily.

Silver whimpers and looks around like he's coming back into his senses, realizing what he was doing. His eyes phase back to green, and David slowly gets up from all fours. He dusts his hands on his pants before staring at his flaming brother.

"Did you have to go and threaten Silver? You know he takes that as a challenge."

I look back to James as a cool breeze passes down my arms giving me goosebumps. The fire turned blue before dissipating off James' clothes.

"Well, would you look at that. It seems you have found your protectors." Tate says while rubbing his forehead. "…Her protectors will detect her…" He mumbles quietly to himself. "It is uncommon for a Dire to have the willpower to disobey its creator but to listen to and obey you Princess…that can only mean one thing. Maybe that hag was telling the truth."

"Wait, what hag?" I ask Tate while he and the boys sit back down after all that commotion.

"There was a ragged old lady that foretold your importance to my king and queen, your parents. This prophecy was before the Lich, and his undead army stormed the castle and mass murdered everyone standing in his way. I led your parents while carrying you down to your mother's secret library. She opened a portal that brought us here to this castle. But before she could close the portal, a few of the Dark Ones followed us through…"

"Your dream…" the boys say in unison.

My dream flashes quickly past my eyes, and a tear falls down my face. "My Da?"

I look to Tate, hopeful that the dream was wrong that my Da isn't dead.

Tate bows his head and replies, "I'm so sorry, Princess; If I had stayed, you might have died."

"What about my…my Ma?" I say through sniffles and shortened breath praying she's not gone too.

"I do not know Princess. When I left her, she was strong and willing to sacrifice her life to save yours. I did not see her fall, so there is a chance she may have survived."

"My necklace…she gave it to me. We should go find my Ma then, …right now!"

"There is no time, Princess. The Dark Ones know where we are. They are on their way here. We have to leave. As for your necklace…" Tate pulls out something from his pocket. It's my necklace.

"Where did you find it?" I say, gasping and reaching for it.

Tate stands up and walks across the short gap between the chair and couch to hand it to me.
I look at James. "Will you help me put it on?" He nods and gently takes the necklace while I turn and pull up my hair. As soon as the cold metal of the necklaces chain touches my skin, I feel calmer. A small glow emanates from the white pearl gem.

"You ran into a Dark One last night who had possessed a mountain lion from the circus in town. It knocked your necklace off when it attacked you. I was about to step in, but the Dire jumped in, and then soon came James and his powers. I dared not interfere in that battle and watched you from afar."
David pitches in, "Wait a minute…I searched the entire perimeter. You couldn't have been anywhere near us."

"I have my concealment ways, plus, you were more hyped up on finding a similar scent to that Dark One. Don't they smell foul?"

David eyes his skirting answer and continues. "What about these Dark Ones? How do you know they possessed an animal from the circus?"

"Don't you boys watch the news? Turn on the TV…" Tate points to the large flat screen above the scary maw of the fireplace.

David reaches for the remote and powers on the TV. He flips to a news station, and Breaking News is flashing on the top part of the screen next to the time at 3:33 pm…

"We are live, and coming directly to you from the traveling circus in Findhorn Square. As you can see behind us, there are elephants, tigers, gorillas, and lions out of their cages and attacking their trainers and   the audience. It is a horrifying scene, but we must keep the camera rolling…"

I gasp and cover my mouth with my hands. I watch the live attacks on the screen and listen to the screams of many people.

"Oh, my Lord. What is going on?" The cameraman pans back and forth, trying to capture as much of the mayhem as possible. A tan male lion jumps from atop its cage into the crowd tearing into a woman's throat. The cameraman moves the camera over to an elephant trampling over multiple people. It grabs a red-haired man by his ankles with its snout, tossing him into the air before slamming him into the ground. The camera pans to the far right, and an ape is peeling the skin off a woman's body as if she were a banana. The reporter is a bit speechless and stutters trying to come up with something to say over the crowd of screams.

"Oh my, what is? Are you getting this? Look at their eyes! This can't be real. Wait, do you see that   tiger…no…no it sees us. Run!"

I shudder in horror, looking into those same red eyes again. The cameraman seems fixated at capturing every bit of the action as the reporter throws down the mic and tries to run.

The tiger can be seen at a full sprint, eyes full of red anger, and pounces on the reporter before running out of the camera's view. The tiger bites down on the reporter's neck and rips out his throat before the camera falls from the cameraman's hands. The screen goes black. The newscaster behind the desk appears and starts an apology for the gruesome feed.

David flicks off the TV, and we all sit in silence, still trying to take in all of what we witnessed. James reaches an arm around me and pulls me close, which helps me to stop my shuddering. David looks at Tate and asks the question we're all thinking. "How did you know that was going on? You only just arrived."

"That's not important. The beasts are heading here, so we must leave soon, or we will end up like those unfortunate people."

"How are you so sure that those things are coming here? Where would we go that would be safer than our castle?" David asks. I see where he's coming from as a castle seems like a well-built fortress to keep out enemy forces.

"We don't have time for me to explain every detail of how I know things. The Dark Ones were sent here by the Lich's Liaison known as his Spider Witch. She is a witch created from a cursed spider born from a demon to do the bidding of her master. She has dark plans for our world, and with the Lich's Dark Ones, she has been spreading darkness over our land."

"Is this Spider Witch coming here?" I ask, still wondering what Tate is getting at.

"No, my Princess, She can't open a portal, which is why you and that necklace are so important. That necklace has great power, which unlocks only for the bloodline of a special white witch. The Dark Ones were sent here for only one purpose: to kill you and take the necklace."

"Wait, what did you say…I am a witch?" My tone reaches a new high as I squeak out that last word. James looks to me and smirks.

"I knew there was something magikal about you."

David rolls his eyes. "Of course, you would say something like that, James."

A giggle escapes my lips before I fall off the couch laughing. James stands and looks down at me, quizzically.

"Are you okay, Elizabeth?" David comes to stand next to his brother.

Tears slide down my cheeks. The emotional rollercoaster I've been riding has finally crashed. I clasp my hands over my mouth to quench the uncontrollable laughter.

Tate Frowns. "This is no laughing matter, my Princess. We are in danger. The Dark Ones are here, and you are the only one that can save us." Tate stands and moves to hover over me. My thoughts turn back to the red eyes I saw during my attack. My right hand absently reaches up to feel the scar left on my head. Painful memories wake me up from my stupor, and I sit up alert and frantically look around for any Dark Ones. Tate leans down and offers his hand to pull me up.

"How can you possibly know that? I would have sensed…." David doesn't finish his sentence and stares at the front door. I look to James, and his head snaps to the front door as well. David growls low and silently moves to the window next to the door.

I take Tate's callused hand and rise quickly to my feet, wiping away stray tears. Tate lets go of me and raises his hand to the back of his head. The glass coffee table starts to rattle. Pans in the kitchen bang into other pots hanging above the island. I hear glasses shattering in the kitchen. The chandeliers above are jangling, and wax candles are falling to the floor. The Xblock looks like its hopping, and I have to steady myself up against the couch and Tate. James doesn't look much better as he stumbles forward to get a look at what David is staring at.

"We should hurry and close the gates…" James stops mid-sentence. James makes it to the window and grips on to David to keep his balance.

"It's far too late for that. We are screwed." David says, trying to stay calm. "There has to be at least twenty of them. I count five elephants, four tigers, four lions, two apes, a couple of giraffes, and one huge grizzly bear in front.

The sun hides behind the castle walls emitting an orange glow in through the open windows.

Tate pulls out his sword and slashes it through the air a couple of times, leaving bright white magikal streaks, slowly fading away in front of me. I remember that sword from my dream. It is the same sword the Guardian used to blind the Dark Ones before carrying me off to safety. Tate is my Guardian. This is really happening. I pinch myself to make sure. I look up to Tate with that realization in my eyes.

He smiles and nods. "I have always been here to protect you, my Princess." I hold on to him tightly as the floor starts to feel like we are experiencing an earthquake. Tate is utterly unfazed by the rumbling of the floor and howling of the arriving stampede. He looks ready for battle, prepared to protect me like he has been all these years. I wonder how many Dark Ones he had to fend off when they came near me. The Mitchell boys look back to me ashen-faced.

David asks Tate while staring at me. "What were you saying about Elizabeth being the only one to save us? There is no way we are going to win a battle against all of them. Even Silver is telling me to run."

"That is correct. The only way we will make it out of here alive is if Elizabeth uses her power to create a portal, as her mother did, and take us back to Kinzurdia. We must get to the secret library on the fourth floor. That is where we first came into this earth realm and should be the easiest to re-create a portal. I will hold them off until you get up there."

"But how will you get to us without bringing them up right behind you?" David asks, apparently using his wits to try to make sense of things.

"Don't question me! Barricade yourselves in. Go Now!"

I start to head upstairs, and James grabs my hand and runs up with me. "I have to grab some things from my room, come with me," James says as he pulls me along. David follows suit behind us. I look back at Tate, the once stranger who I thought was a creepy stalker, turns out to be my guardian from another world. He stands ready before a large crack, and pop sound reaches my ears.

I am pulled up to the third floor and hear the front doors snapping as they must have collapse inward. James rushes into his room, leaving me waiting impatiently at the door. He throws a quiver of arrows and a longbow over his back. James grabs two curved wolf daggers from atop his dresser and shoves them in his belt. He collects a small book from a drawer and rushes to my side. David meets back up with us carrying a backpack.   All three of us run up the stairs two at a time while we hear the echoes of roars, ape grunts, and clanging of metal on something hard.

We burst into a tiny library with books strewn around on the floor, table, and hanging off the shelves as if a twister was set loose in the three by three-meter room.

"Um, this doesn't look like much of a library, let alone a secret one…is not there supposed to be a secret door or something?" I say.

James rolls his eyes at me and unlinks his fingers from mine. He reaches under his shirt and pulls out a small brass key on a string around his neck. He snaps the rope from his neck and climbs a bookshelf to the left side of the back wall.

I look at David and follow his smirking gaze to the ladder leaning against the right back corner.

"Hey James, you know there is a ladder over there." I point across the room.

David laughs a little before he starts to hop back and forth on each foot while looking over his shoulder at the door.

"David, what are you doing? Barricade the door now!" James yells at his brother as he slides the key in. I hear a loud click sound right before the bookcase James is on swings open.

"Right!" David uses his abnormal strength, picking up a solid oak bookcase and propping it up against the door. I turn back to where the bookcase once was on the back wall to see another small area with a large black crow perched on a book podium. It ruffles its feathers and caws at us several times.

James starts to talk to it as if a bird could understand English. "We mean no harm; we are only here to use the podium. If you could back up a bit, we will be out of your way shortly.

I think James has lost it until the crow bows its head and turns to fly to a bookshelf far at the back of the room. I stare stunned. James must be some sort of animal whisperer.

"James, how do you know we need the podium?" I ask quickly still, not trusting the creepy black crow.

"For the past year and a half, I have been studying these books and this book…" He holds up the small book with a six-pointed star on the cover. "…has a portal spell that I think Tate was referring to. It mentions that, when casting a spell on a magically enhanced podium, the better the connection the caster will have when creating a portal."

"So, how does the spell work?" I ask James, who only shrugs and says, "I have no idea, I never tried it out after setting myself on fire and turning my brother into a Dire Wolf. I have no idea what I'm doing and who knows what might come through that portal."

"Are there any instructions?" I walk over to James and look down at the book, trying to read the odd symbols without translating them.

David says, "Uh guys, we have company. Look behind you."

I feel a soft wind tickle my earlobe. Turning around, I expect to see a crow, but standing in front of me is a tall bearded ghostly male with his arms crossed.

"I will not let you take my book from my reach." The ghost roars and looks over at the page James is reading. Then the ghost asks in a curious voice, "Why do you plan on going to Kinzurdia? It is much better here."

James frowns at the ghost unfazed by its presence like they have already met before.

I am a bit freaked out and move closer to James.

"You have been to Kinzurdia? Can you tell us the spell we need to get there? There are some furious beasts downstairs, and we don't have any time left."

"No, I will not let you take my book…" He pauses to look into my eyes and stops protesting. "Ah! Now I see."

The old man ghost starts to reach for me as a burst of light appears in the room. Tate walks out of it with ripped clothes and a few bloody scars on his cheek. The ghost retracts his hand and instantly dissipates from sight.

"Time to go now! Elizabeth, grab your necklace and place the other hand on the book face down."

The floor starts to rumble again as I can only imagine several massive beasts running up the stairs—the noise level increases. Tate yells to me. "Repeat after me…"

David slides up to James's other side. A loud clicking noise rings in my ears as the bookcase starts to close slowly. David watches the door anxiously, hoping like the rest of us, for the bookcase to close faster.

"Aperta portal aperta aditus terra bestias. Aperta portal aperta aditus terra bestias." Tate says, repeating the same sentence over and over louder and louder.

I can barely understand what he's saying and try my best to get it right. "Uperta portal uperta adias terra bestias!" I repeat in unison with Tate. My left hand grasping my white stone warms and lights up the room. A tingly sensation blankets me, flowing above me in a spiral pattern. My hair flies up as if being sucked up by a vacuum. Lightning snaps out of the powerful whirlwind above as thunder cracks and booms overhead. The crow caws and takes flight out of the room into the small library with the blocked door. The bookcase goes flying, and a giant grizzly bear with deep fire engine red eyes stare back at me.

"We are Drarg. We will devour your soul!" It bellows as it leaps for us only to get its foot stuck between the closing bookcase and the wall. Its eyes fade back to black, and black smoke rises from its unmoving corpse. A stench of rotten eggs and ashen charcoal infiltrate my nostrils. I plunge my nose into the bend of my left arm to quench the stink. The smoke assembles into a figure with smoky black arms and sharp claws. A mouth filled with pointed white teeth. Its eyes open to a red hue piercing its horrifying image into my retinas.

"That's not right…" Tate says quickly before getting sucked violently straight up into the black hole, disappearing completely.

"James…" David followed suit and hit a few bookshelves hard before being whipped around and into the hole.

The Drarg's clawed hand reaches for me. I look to James as I bellow out a scream holding on to him tightly.

James stares into my eyes, grabs his book, and wraps his arms around me as our feet lift from the ground. We, too, are whipped around violently knocking over the podium before being sucked into nothingness.

Chapter 5

A New World
James

A flurry of wind surrounded us as I scrunched my eyes shut, holding Elizabeth tightly against my chest. She dug her nails into my arms before her screams got drowned out by the whooshing of air gliding across my eardrums. In a moment, the rapid, forceful pressure ended, and my ears popped. I manage to open an eye.

There are hundreds of blue, yellow, and white streaks twisting and turning like a kaleidoscope. A momentary weightlessness overcomes me, then the intense pressure returns, strangling my lungs and threatening to collapse them.

Elizabeth was frozen around my left arm. Red lines trickled down my forearm due to Elizabeth's sharp pink nails digging into my skin. The buildup of pressure became too much. Warm liquid slid down my neck, tickling me under my lobes. We suddenly accelerated, like a geyser, out of a black and purple wormhole. My back hit something substantial before my vision went dark.

"Wake Up, James!"

I hear a distant female voice. I cough once. My eyelids feel heavy, and my back starts to reel in pain.

"James Mitchell, don't you die on me now…Wake up!"

I feel something shaking me before I feel sudden pain to my right cheek. That pain ignited me, and my eyes pop open, staring into a beautiful set of blue eyes. Tear streaks residing below each corner of her eyes. I want to smile but get a sudden urge to turn my head to the side.

There I vomit onto the slimy dirt under me. Mud sticks to my left ear while I hack up what's left in my stomach. The smell of my stomach bile, mixed with the noxious air of dung, infiltrate my nose and cause me to gag and cough more. My back and left side hurt a lot, but I don't feel like I broke anything, thankfully. My longbow and quiver are still in one piece but dug into my back when I landed. I sit up to get a look around. I feel a bit dizzy, but Elizabeth is behind me and helps me up.

"Don't you scare me like that! I thought you were dead!" Elizabeth puts her fists on her hips and gives me a small pout. "Oh my lord, your bleeding from your ears!" She rips off a small piece of her shirt that's not covered in muck and dabs it at my ears. She wipes away the remnants of her tears with her other hand and starts to look around.

"Where are the others, and where are we?" Elizabeth points out the two questions that I have been thinking about since I woke. We are standing on a slimy greenish-brown mud floor. Our clothes are covered in it. From the looks of Elizabeth's face, she's incredibly displeased and tries to shake some of it off her shirt with no use. The greenish-brown slime sticks to our skin and feels gritty like sandpaper when rubbed between my fingers. It's twilight out. The sky has deep purple and oranges. The stars are much different some larger than others making it impossible to tell if there is a north star here. Elizabeth notices me staring up into the sky. "Whoa, what are those?"

I see her point up and to the left of me. Following her direction, I see them. "We are no longer on our earth anymore," I say, taking a big gulp before speaking again. "They look like moons…two red moons." Both moons look full like two red Frisbees, one following the other.

My gaze focuses downward. I see misshaped stones to my left with heaps of dirt at the base of most of the rocks. Some have shallow pits with disturbed soil. Deep black and dark green weeds stick up from the ground surrounding our area of stones and mud. Red roots glint and move like worms across the muddy terrain. I jerk Elizabeth behind me quickly as two pointed roots spring forward, swiping at my toes.

"Hey, what was that for?"

I point down to my feet where the roots are still snapping left and right, looking for something to grab.

"Ahhh…ahhhh," Elizabeth screams and back petals a few feet before she drops out of my vision. She fell through a thick blanket of fog, converging on my location.

Elizabeth continued to scream. "Eeeek, James, something is moving under me!"

Her frantically waving arms pop above the fog and start to displace the surrounding mist. She stumbles while trying to stand up. She reaches for me as I move to the edge of what I can now see is a large pit at least two meters deep. Our muddy fingers touch but slip out as the mass she is kneeling on starts to shake.

I drop onto the gunk on my stomach and reach out over the ledge to try to grab her forearm. A sound like a coughing roar comes from the giant mass covered in the nasty mud grime below Elizabeth. A small head-shape mud ball starts to rise in front of the mass while Elizabeth straddles it trying to reach for my arm.

The red tint of light from the dual moons illuminates the pit, us, and the surrounding marsh-like atmosphere. My eyes have adjusted to this odd light, and I can see the red hue reflecting off the glossy slime sliding down this monster's arm as it slowly reaches up toward Elizabeth. We manage to grab each other's arms after the creature starts wobbling closer to my edge of the pit. I pull with all my might and have her climb over me. I push Elizabeth back and stand to face this monster.

"David! Where are you? I could use some help here!"

"Stay behind me, Elizabeth. I'll kill it if it comes near us." I feel the rage inside me boil as I hold out my right hand while pushing Elizabeth behind me with my left. Familiar flames ignite in my palm, illuminating the pit with a new orange glow. The mud starts to harden, and my arm becomes heavy and stiff.

A deep rumbling "Noooo" reverberates from the grimy mud glob in front of us. I pull back my arm, ready to toss the fireball at my target when the head pops up, and Elizabeth screams, "Wait!!"

I was midway leaning forward. Stopping mid-swing caught me off balance. My right foot slipped on a pile of slime sending me, and my fiery arm, face-first into the muddy swamp floor. My flame sizzled out on impact.

Elizabeth runs past me to the pit while I pull my face out of the mud. Digging the dirt out of my ears, I hear Elizabeth yell, "Tate! Tate, is that you!? You are completely covered in this nasty gooey slime stuff."

I get to one knee and push myself back up. The weight of this hardened mud feels like I'm lifting an extra forty kilograms.

I look up to Elizabeth standing at the edge of the pit, then over to the mass of mud covering Tate. He looks like the mud monster from a cartoon episode that David used to watch all the time.

"David, where are you? Silver…can you hear me!?" I know David is keen, but I can't lose him now.

Small splatters of mud hit my cheek, bringing my attention to Tate's flapping arms standing before me. He looks like a chicken trying to fly. His appendages flap vigorously to get most of the mud off his clothes. He hacks and spits out more brown slime before trying to speak.

"Why didn't you let us know it was you?" Elizabeth asks worriedly. "James was about to set you on fire."

Tate doesn't answer her but instead looks directly at me. "Don't use your fire skills here!" He scolds me as if I was a child.

"Why not? Fire has helped me out of many predicaments before."

"Look at your arm. What do you think happened to the mud that's now hardened to stone?" Tate gestures with his left hand. Elizabeth looks at me, and I can see her eyes widen as realization crosses her face.

"You mean you would have become like James' arm if he had lit you on fire? Oh my…You would be a stone statue."

"Oh," is all I can muster as the realization hits that Elizabeth understood before I did. I try punching the hardened mud with my left fist, quickly realizing how painful that idea. I ceased before I broke my left hand. After regaining my composure, I ask, "Tate, did David land near you? Have you seen him?"

He shakes his head. "No, Elizabeth woke me up when she landed on me. I didn't have a chance to look around when you were about to turn me into a stone statue." Tate said a bit smugly. He pulls himself out of the pit.

"How was I supposed to know you weren't a mud monster trying to steal my money or harm us?" I step closer to him as he does me. Our noses almost touch, my blood starts to boil again, and I almost swear I can see my own eyes flickering orange in the reflection of his.

"Boys! Stop it! We need to find David now and then figure out where we are." Elizabeth says, irritated at our squabbling.

I break my angry stare from Tate and take a deep breath to calm down while clenching my fists.

"Can't you just…you know?" Elizabeth taps two fingers to her temple while asking me the question.

"I've tried that twice, but neither of them is responding." The weight of the hardened mud on my right arm unbalances me as I walk around the pit. The fog disperses and then reemerges upon each footstep, allowing me to momentarily see the slimy floor to walk on.

The constant chirping of crickets, rustling leaves of nearby plants, and the soft howl of the wind through the thick brush give an eerie feel— Goosebumps ride up my arms and down the back of my neck. I hear Elizabeth's teeth chattering and Tate's grunts behind me. I have a bad feeling about this place.

"Oh, come on. David? David, where are you?!" Elizabeth bellows out. I turn and shush her, but it's too late. All the sounds around us cease. The quiet lurks into my gut, knotting it. I can hear my heartbeat clearly thudding against my ribcage.

A buzzing sound enthralls our ears. It sounds like a symphony of different buzzing growing louder as it approaches our location. I squint my eyes to see what looks like a cloud of glinting red graffiti floating toward us from the bushes on the other side of the pit.

"Tate!" I yell over my shoulder. "What is that?" I point in the direction of what I can barely make out as a swarm of insects the size of footballs.

"Elizabeth! James! Down now!" Tate yells out and pulls Elizabeth down to the ground covering her with his body protectively. I fall to the ground, chin in mud before turning onto my back as the swarm flies over.

I can feel the wind generated from all the flapping wings. They quickly move over us as if they were fleeing instead of attacking. Their body style reminds me of a parrot with a white beak and a colorful tail but the dual wings of a shimmery dragonfly. They have creepy spiked legs of a cockroach with antennas sticking out of their beak.

My gaze meets Tate's. He sees my confused expression and answers my previous question after the swarm passes overhead. "That swarm was a group of mimicroaches. They aren't dangerous when singled out, but in a pack, they are quite fearsome. They have this ability to mimic any sound to draw in prey and the senses and survivability of a roach to aid in aerial combat. Their beak is their most dangerous weapon, both for the vocals and the shredding of flesh. In some clans, wearing a feather of a mimicroach is said to bring good fortune."

Elizabeth stands and is even more covered in filthy mud. "Yuck, why did we have to land here instead of some dry land?" She holds her arms out at her sides, wiggling her arms to remove most of the slime.

I ignore her to commit as we are all covered in the same muck."Why didn't they attack us?" I ask, though glad they didn't stop to have a snack.

"That's a good question. There is only one reason I can think of that an entire swarm would pass up easy prey…"

"And that would be?" I say, annoyed at his placating of explanations.

"Doesn't matter, we need to get out of this swamp ridden cemetery as fast as possible."

"Eeeek… we are in a cemetery? Why are we in a cemetery?" Elizabeth squeals out and walks backward, covering her mouth only to add more slime to her cute angry face.

Tate and I both get to our feet. Tate tries to calm Elizabeth down from her momentary hysteria.

I hear a bustling of plant vines and movement coming from the tree line behind Elizabeth. The tall weeded plants shake as something approaches pushing the brush to either side. Heavy breathing and moaning snap the other's attention in my direction. Tate holds up the universal shush sign to his lips. He moves in front of Elizabeth and steps closer to me. He points as if telling me to flank from the right, and he will go left. My nerves are wrecked, my hands are shaking, and I really have to pee, but I hold it in too terrified to look away.

A dark figure steps out, leaning to one side and dragging its left leg in the muck. Zombie! I take a cautious step back.

"Zombie! Really, James….I woke up and started walking toward Elizabeth's familiar scream and you try to sneak up on me. Couldn't you at least help your brother out? I'm in pain here."

"Wait...What...David is that you?" I'm confused hearing my brother's words in my head but not matching the blob of some creature lit up under red moons. Tate pulls out his blade and shines its glowing radiance at the beast.

"Stupid human. We pain. You fix." The familiar jab of Silver's thoughts brings me out of my stupor. The illumination from the sword reveals David's pained face as he wobbles to me, cradling an arm.

"Put down your sword Tate, It's only my brother."

Tate sheaths his sword allowing my eyes to readjust to the dark red light of the night.

I haven't learned much water magik other than simple healing spells. I should have no trouble fixing a sprained ankle, but David's arm looks far worse, bent at an irregular angle.

"David, is that you?" Elizabeth squeals with joy, running up to my brother and giving him a squeeze. I cross my arms and raise a brow at her sudden need to give affection to him.

"Oww oww oww," my brother says while hissing through his teeth.

"Oh, I'm sorry, I'm so glad you are okay." Elizabeth takes a step back before wiping some of the muck off his face.

"David, what happened to your arm?" I asked, realizing that it must be the cause of his pain from Elizabeth's hug.

"After being flung out of the portal, I put up my arm and smacked into a tree. Everything went black. I woke up to the sound of your screams, Elizabeth. I couldn't move my right arm. When I tried to stand, I felt as if I was trying to balance on a plate of gelatin."

Elizabeth turns to Tate while I motion David to sit down so I can take a look at his leg.

"So, all-knowing-guardian-of-mine, why did the portal fling us around like that? You didn't mention that we would be shot into a cemetery in a dark and dank swamp. Where are we and how do we get out of this place?"

The anger in her sarcasm didn't go unnoticed. I look back over my shoulder at her. Her arms are crossed, and she leaned onto her right leg, tapping her left foot impatiently.

"Magik spells are powerful. But when said incorrectly, there are two possible outcomes. Either nothing happens, or something far less unpredictable happens. Luckily you almost said the correct incantation, or we may have well ended up in between realms. If you had said the incantation correctly, like I told you, we would have merely walked straight through to Nazereth."

A "Pffft" sound came from Elizabeth. I can almost picture her cute face flushing if the red glow from the moons didn't already turn her face crimson.

"How was I supposed to magically know how to pronounce your foreign language? All while being hunted by a possessed bear and his gang of circus freaks!" Elizabeth yells back at Tate.

While they bicker, I cup my slimy left hand into the cold swampy mud, close my eyes and imagine the water leaving the dirt behind. I open my eyes to find my dirty hand cupping a small amount of water. How clean? I wonder. Still, I use it to wash away the area around the sprain and grab his ankle firmly. I imagine his muscles and bones realigning, and a soft, warm tingling sensation spreads over my hand and into my brother's leg. The sudden intake of air from my brother tells me it is working. I pull my hand away and see my brother rotate his foot with ease.

"You realize I'm gonna have to shift to fix my arm."

"I know. You still got your bag, right? Put your clothes in it, and I'll carry it."

Elizabeth stomps over, kicking at the mud, splashing us a small bit.

"Arrg! For a guardian, he sure doesn't know how to be helpful." She smiles at David. "How are you feeling, David?" She tries to put her bitterness aside while having a general concern for my brother.

"My leg is better, thanks to James, but my arm is broken, so I will have to change."

"Why would you need to change you would only get those clothes as muddy as the ones you are wearing?"

"No, not like that. I have to shift to heal myself. So if you don't mind…."

"Oh… well, okay." She stands up from her crouching position and takes a few steps back to give my brother room. I can see her eyes go wide, expecting him to change right in front of her again.

"Tate, can you take her away, please?" I ask, knowing my brother doesn't want to strip right in front of a girl. Tate nods, understanding before smirking at David laughing with his eyes. David grips my arm painfully with his strength while I hold him back from charging at Tate. I have to hold back from laughing myself.

Tate blocks her view, and I help my brother strip down to his boxers. He walks out of sight behind a tree and reappears momentarily after holding his boxers in his fanged mouth. Tate and Elizabeth happen to start laughing at the sight of a giant menacing dire wolf holding Team Wolf boxer shorts in its maw. I tried to cover my mouth as I took his boxers and added them to his backpack's slimy clothes.

"It's not that funny, you know I can't shift with my clothes on, or I will have nothing to wear when I shift back. Shut…."

"David?" I ask telepathically, wondering why he stopped mid-sentence. David's eyes turned red.

"Stupid humans. Look." Silver has taken control, turns his head and growls at the waterline on the other side of the pit.

Metallic red eyes shine right above the water's surface. Tate moves Elizabeth further behind him, and I steady my stance in anticipation. Silver shakes out all his legs, lifts his head and howls into the air before charging at our new nuisance. Silver must know it is here to do harm. I want to bring out my fire, but my right arm is still encased in rock. I have a crazy idea and decide to go with it. I toss off my bow, quiver of arrows, and backpack to the ground. I plunge my left hand back into the muddy terrain and pull out a fist full. I ignite my left forearm, instantly hardening the mud into rock. I do the same for my chest back and thighs. I look back at Tate, who has an astonished look on his face. I must look like a human encased in rock armor.

I run forward a bit sluggishly due to the increased weight. I imagine the air around me aiding my strength to lift my feet and pushing me to move faster. The sound of strong wind blows past my ears, and I bound forward.

Approaching the waterline, I see what Silver is growling at. There is a giant four-meter long crocodile, only it looks to have parts of its flesh removed where the reddish glint of its bones protrude outward. I can see small fish swim in between its ribs like a jet ski between buoys.

I move toward Silver to aid him, but Silver snaps at me.

"No human. You fight one there."

Understanding his thoughts, I turn to my right. A similar-in-size crocodile jumps out of the water at me. Automatically I raise my arms to protect myself. I hear the grinding of teeth on stone. The crocodile pushes me back a step or two. I'm surprised to not feel more than a slight vibration through the rock.

Behind me, Elizabeth is screaming. Looking up, I see the croc's jaw clamped around my rock covered arms. I twist my left arm from side to side to release it from its grasp. The glazed over red-eye focuses on me like a snack. I wrenched my left arm free, tearing a few teeth from the front roof of its mouth. It doesn't even flinch. I pull back my arm and, aided by a fast well-placed gust behind my elbow, I upper-cut my arm into the crocodile's chest.

Dark crocodile slime splatters my face as my left-hand pops up right through the scaled back. My legs start to shake while trying to keep this crocodile from smothering me. I spit globs of black slime to the ground while simultaneously yanking on the backbone of this creature. It snapped like a twig, but the crocodile held on to my right arm as if I hadn't done anything to it. "What the heck is going on?"

"James, look to your left" David's thoughts shout in my mind. "There's another one about to spring on you!"

I turn and see the glint of the croc's eye as it leaps up out of the dark water. Both my arms are stuck in this crocodile in front of me, and I can barely keep it at bay. A bright light creeps up from my left side as I do the only thing I can do…fall down. I turn my head away, not wanting to see it chomp down on me. I hit the mud with a thud causing my ears to ring. I feel the weight and the squirming of the backboneless wrestling me for control. The bright light is shaded by a dark figure.

My eyes readjust. Tate stands to the left of me, the sword is outstretched. He slices through to the tail of the leaping crocodile. The creature falls into two pieces, split in half from head to the tip of its tail. A putrid odor reaches my nose. Wishing I could plug it, I lay there gaging while trying to breathe through my mouth. Looking at one half, I can see the organs, or what's left of them falling, into the mud next to me.

Tate turns around and comes to help me with my crocodile. He raises his bright sword and gets tackled by the other half of the crocodile. The now organ-less-bone-protruding-half next to me hops up and quickly jumps on Tate.

"Silver, help me!" I yell out, hoping he has had better luck fighting his crocodile and can get mine off me. Heaps of black goo and muddy slime cover Tate next to me as he fumbles around in the mud, trying to get a hold of either half. A cry of a wounded animal makes me momentarily pause, thinking Silver is hurt.

"Silver, are you okay?" Silver doesn't respond, but David does. *"That wasn't us, James. This thing won't die, we snapped its neck four times now, and it still advances. We will get to you soon, hold on."*

I listen again and can tell the wail is coming from behind me. I look up to see Elizabeth upside down and walking in the direction of the loud cry. I follow her path forward, and she gets closer to those same red rooted snake-like bushes.

"Elizabeth! Elizabeth! Stop, don't move any closer!" I yell back, but it's no use. She doesn't hear me over the loud scuffling of the battle. I squint my eyes and focus on what Elizabeth is reaching for.

She approaches the sound coming from atop a large stone near the bush line. The crocodile yanks my arm to the right while I was distracted by Elizabeth's choice to wander off. I turn with the crocodile and simultaneously pull my left arm out of its chest. I start beating the thing's head with a piece of its own backbone still clenched in my fist.

Elizabeth cries out. A terrified, pain-induced scream. Near me, Tate tries to run to help Elizabeth, but each half of the massive crocodile is latched on to an arm, slowing his progress. I grind my teeth and stick the bone into its eye socket while flipping it over to my right side.

I have to save Elizabeth. I have to get to her now.

Somehow I manage to squat on the croc's underbelly and, with all my might, yank my right arm out of its mouth. A few teeth stick in my stone forearm. I hobble in the direction of Elizabeth's last scream. The hardened mud slows my movement, and most of my energy is expended. *If this stone was only mud, I could get there so much faster.*

As I forge onward, I feel lighter. It is easier to move. The mud is sliding off my body. I look to my right and see Silver tear off the head of the crocodile he is fighting and toss it back into the swamp water. The body walks in circles as if looking for its head. Silver's red-eye catches mine. I see it fade back to green before I reach the large stone near the bushes.

There, a single mimicroach sprawled unmoving on the stone. Elizabeth stretches out unconscious next to the base of the rock with roots slowly crawling up her legs. The roots swipe at me, and I have to jump back from getting hit.

Tate yells out, "Don't let the vine roots touch you!"

"And how am I supposed to rescue her if I can't touch the roots!" I yell back over my shoulder, and I think I see him disappear into thin air. I look to Elizabeth and jump back in surprise. Tate is in front of me, already hacking away at the vines.

"No, No, No!" Tate whines as he grunts and hacks through the rest of the vines. The whole ones retreat back into the bush while the severed ends lay wiggling on the ground like maggots. Their openings spewed neon green liquid all over the ground. I reach down to see what it was, and next thing I know, I'm flying back through the air and land hard on my rear.

"I said, don't touch it." Tate looks back at me angrily, but worry clouded his eyes. David trots up next to me, and I use his body to lean against while struggling to stand back up. *"Are you okay? What's wrong with Elizabeth? Why did Tate push you back?"* David asks me while growling low at Tate for assaulting me.

I don't answer David because I don't have an answer for any of them. I look behind David and see the carnage from our battles. Silver's crocodile still has its head bobbing in the water while its body swims around it like a shark. Both halves of Tate's crocodile slithered their way back into the water, leaving a smelly streak of rotten flesh. My crocodile can be easily seen with a bone sticking out of its right eye socket.

David and I walk up to and look past Tate to hear Elizabeth taking quick hissing gasps of air. I pop a small fireball in my hand to light up the area better. The mud on my hand hardens, but I don't care. Elizabeth looks sick and isn't moving. Her jeans are torn off her legs from the knees down. Dark thick needle-like spikes protrude from her legs.

Tate leans over her scratched up legs and starts to pluck the spikes from her skin. When they are all out, I smother my flame and look around. The bush veins start to glow neon green in the shadows created by us and the moonlight.

Tate picked up Elizabeth and moved her to the sizeable slanted stone near the bushes. A mimicroach squawks and furiously flies off in the direction of the crocs. I look back to see Tate gently laying her down on the rock and ripping off his undershirt to wrap her legs in.

"I can heal her. Let me…" I walk up to her, but Tate holds out his arm and stops me.

"You can't heal this. It's a deadly poison, and if you were to heal Elizabeth's wounds, you would spread the poison faster."

"How do we get the poison out if we can't touch it? How do we save her?" I say frantically balling my hands in my hair.

David's ears perk up and turn to the rear of us. I can hear the swish swash of water being moved. I turn and see the mimicroach hovering over the swamp area. I see the crocodile with the bone still stuck in one eye creep up underneath it. David is looking out further passed the crocodile where there's a giant fin sticking out of the water.

The crocodile slows before it leaps out of the water, snapping the mimic roach up in its mouth. The giant fin disappears under the water and quiet sets over the area again. The mystic fog blanketing the ground grows heavier. The crocodile starts swimming further out into the swamp water. The giant fin returns, but it's moving quickly, making burgundy water waves in the moonlight. Suddenly a fish the size of a garbage truck leaps up and gobbles up the crocodile before returning back to the water.

"Tate? What the hell was that!? And what kind of crocodiles live here that don't die from broken necks, broken backbones, or even when sliced in half?" I ask while goosebumps ride up my arms. Fighting those crocs was terrible enough. To take on a fish, that size probably isn't a good idea.

"It's time to leave," Tate answers. "I will explain as soon as we get out of this swamp. There is a village not far from here. We need to get there as soon as possible. Elizabeth doesn't have much time."

Chapter 6

A Mysterious Salamander
David

Tate picks up Elizabeth and carries her across the muddy terrain and through a tall grass patch as we quickly fall in behind. Specks of light pierce through the darkness showcasing a town bustling in the distance. Above the lights are distant mountains outlined by the red sky.

I rub up against James, and in turn, he pets me on the head. He swipes his hand through our fur, down our side, knocking chunks of mud to the ground.

"Hey, drop my bag, we will catch up. I want to change into my human form before walking into a town looking like this." Mud is caked to our fur, and I can better clean up as a human. James nods his head but stays silent. He shrugs off my backpack and drops it to the ground. He looks back down and kicks a rock while trailing behind Tate.

James is taking it hard on himself. I can feel the distant waves of sorrow and self-pity emanating from his mind. He believes all this is his fault. He turned me into a dire wolf, the reason for Da's death, and why Elizabeth is close to it. I chose to go through with the spell. I decided to help cast a spell on our father, and I am as much at fault for not being able to protect Elizabeth. We should be sharing the blame, but James refuses to believe I am at fault for any of this.

I sniff the bag and look around. James and Tate are getting further ahead. The darkness doesn't bother me, and I can smell their stench a mile away. Their backs are still to me as I shift and pop my bones back into place. The adrenaline of the past fight has finally worn off, and I can feel the aches rattling my bones. I brush off all the hardened mud that's still left on me and put on my clothes. The clothes feel like sandpaper with the dirt between them, but it doesn't matter. I feel a bit more like myself, put the daggers under my belt, and zip up the bag.

Above, the reddened sky spreads over the land. The shining twin moons, surrounded by a million stars, cast their light down onto the ground. A cool breeze slithers over my arms and past my cheek rising bumps on them. Odd crickets or frogs sound behind me and to my left. I close my eyes, take deep breaths, and focus my thoughts on the fact we are in a new world, far from all we know. It's fresh, it's scary, but we have a purpose, and that is to help Elizabeth return to her kingdom safely. I must stay strong and keep my promise to her and my brother.

I open my eyes and refocus on the two dots in the distance. I better catch up, or I may lose them. I toss the backpack up and over a shoulder. I start a light jog that soon turns into a sprint.

When I catch up, I need to ask Tate about what happened back at the swamp.

"So, Tate, what was that back there that ate the croc?" I say partly still scared of its sheer size and somewhat because I am curious about what this world has in store for us.

"It's called a Skytafish. It's a lot like a mix between a Humpback Whale and a Sabretooth Fish. The size of its body and teeth grow overly large, and its best to steer clear of them than to try to fight them. They are typically the type to eat and leave. They don't tend to stay around for a fight, but we don't want to test that hypothesis out. Lucky for us that was only a baby, Skyta, or we may have had a bit more trouble if that had been its mother."

"Why, how big do they get?" I ask, wondering how much bigger a fish could possibly get past swallowing a four-meter crocodile whole.

"I have seen one be mistaken as an island. A sailboat went to dock to it, and the Skytafish rose above the surface and sucked in the boat. It practically used the sail's mast as a toothpick.

"What…" I'm speechless and hang back a bit after hearing his story.

After at least an hour of walking behind Tate who we have no choice but to trust to lead us to safety, we come closer to the lights I saw in the distance. The sky is starting to brighten as the warm glowing rays of the sun are peaking over the mountains. Sounds of a busy early market come towards us. The sizzling sounds of food on a grill and the wafting smells of deliciously cooked food entice our hunger. The aromas are a bit odd, and I can't quite place what they smell like. At this point, my belly rumbles, and I hear my brother's do the same. That fight sure worked through most of our energy, and we didn't have time to pack food before those Dark Ones, known as Drargs, came for us at our castle in Scotland.

We follow Tate into an alleyway between two buildings. Tate stops halfway in, and I collide with my brother's back. Tate turns to us with a saddened look. He looks down at Elizabeth and then to James. His demeanor quickly changed to an angered, determined look.

"Take her. I need to find someone that can help us."

James, without question, took Elizabeth into his arms while staring at her sleepy face. "Wait," he protested. "Who are you looking for, and how can you know that person will be here?"

Exasperation filled Tate's face. "He is a traveling merchant. Usually, around this time of year, he comes to this town and stays for a few months. You boys are going to have to trust me or trust the fact that I have Elizabeth's best wishes in mind."

I did not miss the fact he didn't include us in that sentence. I can see the pain under his mask and nod back to him. My brother does the same.

"Now stay close and try not to stare. David…"

"What?"

"Under no circumstances are you to shift into your wolf form here."

"What? Why…"

"Trust me. It will only put Elizabeth in greater danger."

"Fine." I didn't like the sound of that. I am a bit stronger in human form than usual but, if something terrible does happen, I won't have the strength and speed that Silver gives me in wolf form. James stares daggers at Tate with that comment. He notices how mad I get over the constraint.

"David, do what he says for now till we can find out what he means. I don't want to put Elizabeth in any more danger if we can help it."

"Yes, Master…" I say sarcastically, not liking how both of them are telling me what to do.

Elizabeth's eyes flutter open, and she yawns painfully. A few whimpers escape her mouth as James puts her down onto her feet. Tate looks back over his shoulder, and I can see his hands tighten at his sides.

"David, James. Help her walk between the two of you and stay close." With that statement, he turns back forward and starts walking.

"Wha…What's going on? Where are we? Ouch, my leg. My stomach doesn't feel too good." Elizabeth whines.

"Shh, quiet now. Everything will be okay. We are almost there. We will have you fixed up in no time." James said quietly into her ear. Elizabeth looks like she's sleepwalking. She's tripping over her own feet while resting her head on James' shoulder. James and Elizabeth look like a drunken couple. I try to do what I can to keep Elizabeth's weight from slowing down my brother's forward momentum.

We come to the edge of the alleyway as the sunlight shines down on us. I walk in Tate's shadow until he turns the corner, and the sun blinds me momentarily. I blink the light away and shade my eyes to suck in a breath of surprise. The buildings remind me of an old western village setup for a movie. There are tons of humanoid felines, bird creatures, burly furry bear things, small and tall of all shapes and sizes.

There is a couple of blob-like creatures across the dirt road from us. One fell down while another jumped on it, spewing its slime over the pathway. A crowd of all sorts of species all slipped and fell into one another. Everyone on the ground yelled out something like "Kilumizoo" before picking themselves up laughing at the blobs and going about their business like it was a typical transaction of their daily life. I turned to Tate with a massive question on my face.

Tate laughs at my expression with genuine mirth. "This world has so much you boys don't know. I keep forgetting how foreign this must be for you. Those blobs are called Kilumzu. They may look like colored gelatin blobs, but they're beings with tiny brains and three eyes."

"What sounds do they make?" I ask, trying to remember exactly what I heard.

"Actually, they can talk although they're incredibly hard to understand. It is said that slipping and falling from the slime of a Kilumzu grants good luck if you say their name on the way down. Of course, it is a myth, but some believe it is true. Believe it or not, it seems to happen often. So it's better to go with it because we could all use more luck."

"So, what about all these other creatures?" I am curious about their names and what they are. "I noticed that they are all speaking English. How is this possible?"

"There are many shifters in the land of Kinzurdia. As I have said previously, humans are of the minority. They are the ones who taught this once divided creature kingdom into a more socially optimized speaking land. The humans brought with them the English language, and by the need to find a form of communication to establish allies, they taught as many species the English language. After years of hard work and perseverance, it has become known as the universal language of the kingdom.

"Didn't they have their own languages?"

"Of course. The inhabitants made sounds and communicated among their own species, but the English spoken language allows trade and other conversations between species that could never have existed before. For example, you will see many different breeds of felines from your world, but here they are smarter and can walk upright and grow to be taller than any human. They can now talk out an issue with a neighboring clan rather than growling at them. They can form villages where multiple species can all congregate and communicate."

I take a good look around and see felines from the usual orange tabby cat to tigers, lions, and leopards.

They are all standing upright and wearing different skins. I even spot a lion wearing a zebra-striped vest.

Tate smiles at my wonder. "There are also many types of aerial shifters."

My left eyebrow rises as a response to Tate's last sentence.

"I'm talking about birds or other creatures that can take flight without the use of magik. Again, many were inspired by animals from your world. They have their own nesting grounds, but they can shift between forms like any other shifter here. You may even pick up a thing or two here if you pay attention."

Elizabeth bumps into me and knocks me out of my staring contest with a five tailed fox. The orange and white striped fox growled at me while we passed by. I opened my eyes and started to take in all the different walking and talking creatures in this village. There is a red lizard with a rack of sharp teeth chatting in a lisp while wearing a green alligator vest. It plays some type of game on the corner with a crowd of birds, feline, and reptilian humanoids.

There are small shops layered throughout the street in front of the main buildings. Smoke was sizzling off a grill to the right in front of us. I see a chef hat and the white coat rear—*finally, a human amongst all these creatures.* I turn to James.

"Let's get some food from that vendor over there." I pointed to the white hat and coat as he turned around. My arm fell to my side, and I suddenly lost my appetite after seeing what he was cooking. The cook is a three-eyed Kilumzu standing over a grill after reaching one of his slimy hands into his gelatin belly. He starts pulling out what looks more like slimy intestines before starting to fry them on the grill.

"I think I will pass. But David, don't let me stop you from that delicacy. I am sure you will enjoy it." James laughs and almost loses his grip on the barely walking Elizabeth.

I cover my mouth and hold my grumbling belly. There has to be someplace with edible food around here. "Hey, Tate, where can we go to grab a bite to eat that isn't…so exotic?"

For the past twenty minutes, Tate has been scanning the busy crowd and passers-by for his mysterious friend. He doesn't acknowledge me, but stops and stares toward a group gathered around another kiosk shop.

"Finally. There you are," Tate bursts out.

"There who is?" both James and I ask in unison.

Tate walks through the crowd, and everyone acts like he's an obstacle they must avoid. Unfortunately for us, we have to push through the crowd attracting more strange stares and now whispers among several of the shifters.

"Watch it, human!" A large rhino head yelled out before pushing me into a hard wall of a creature next to my right side.

"Who dares to run into me?" The wall of a beast stands up growing at least one meter higher than previously. It turns around, and I stare upward, horrified. It's some rock-like formation of a face. It reminded me of a cartoon I used to watch. "Huh, a puny human, Scram."

"Hey, David. Wait for us." James called out from behind, still dragging Elizabeth along. I see them sporadically between several walking creatures that pass by.

"Do you mind moving," I say to one of the creatures, attempting to clear a path for James and Elizabeth. However, this creature doesn't like my request. It is a feline looking shifter of a leopard species. Its yellow and black spotted fur coat was all that I could go by. It looks angry that I a mere human would dare tell it what to do. The crowd notices the commotion and starts giving the fierce feline a wide area. James and Elizabeth make it past the fuming feline and pass me to catch up to Tate.

"Don't you know who I am, Human? I should slit your throat for your insolence." The female feline rips its leather clothes as it shifts into a giant leopard, its head towering over my own.

I gulp. Silver pushes against my mind, struggling to break out and put this feline in her place. I hold him back and shake in my human form to keep from shifting. Remembering what Tate said not too long ago, is the only thing keeping me from shredding my own clothes.

The feline's anger boils over. The female feline's eyes go blood red. In an explosion of red flames, her entire coat color changes to blood red with black spots. Red flames flow around her as every other creature turns tail to hide in alleyways or behind the small road shops.

"Aww, the little human shakes in his petty shoes. Ha,ha,ha,ha,ha! It's time I teach you all a lesson with this pathetic human. The Lich likes humans less than all of you. If you find a puny one like this, it's best to kill it if you want to continue living under our great Lich's rule."

While she spews her death threat, Tate walks past me and right up to her fiery form.

"What is this, another human who wants to die?"

Tate pulls out his sword. Blinding light radiates from it, so bright the surrounding creatures have to cover their eyes.

"Wait, no. It's *you*," the beast cries.

I shade my eyes in time to see the large fiery beast's face etched in fear as it backs away from Tate. Tate lunges forward and stabs it with his bright blade. The flaming beast folds in on herself as if being sucked into the blade until a puff of black smoke is left. Tate sheathes his sword, grabs me by the arm, and drags me after him.

"What did I say about keeping close?" he rants. "Now, the Lich has been alerted to my presence."

"Is that a bad thing? You seem to be more powerful then you let on."

"Whoa. Did you see that?" James exclaims, catching up with us. "Tate pulled out his sword, and in a flash, the demon feline lady ran off."

"Yeah. I think everyone in this village saw … wait. What?"

Tate eyes me suspiciously.

I gulp. "Yeah, that was weird, wasn't it?" *Am I the only one who saw what Tate did? No one else?* "What was that thing, anyway?"

Tate is still staring at me. "That was Kaligula. She's one of the many demons the Lich controls. Lucky for us, I found Glizteo over here. He will be able to aid us with better clothes then the muddy rags we are wearing."

We walk up to a small shop of wares of every assortment from pans, leathers, swords, shields, maps, and skins. The carriage of the two-wheeled wooden shop cart is buried under the number of goods spread across it. I step a bit closer.

"Ouch, watch your step pal."

Now what? I jump back in fright as I look down to see a fat mutated Salamander. If it wasn't for the animal TV channel I watched growing up, I would be clueless. The creature's flattened slick head and body give it away. It has black smooth reptilian skin with red splotches of color, layering its entire body. *And I thought those crocs were huge reptiles.* This Glizteo lizard is at least three meters long and a meter wide. Its eyes are the size of my fists atop its head.

"What the …? This is the guy that can help us?"

"Let's hope so," Tate responds impatiently. "He's not only a merchant. He knows his way around these parts of Kinzurdia."

Glizteo rolls his tail under his dense mass, springs up, balances on his tail's tip, and addresses Tate. His short feet and hands elongate, and soon he stands and starts to pack items hanging on the sides. "Well, my friend, you folks have created more than a bit of commotion. Everyone's eyes are on you now. Let me close up shop, and we can do business in a more comfortable setting."

I glance around surreptitiously. Most of the strange creatures are staring in our direction. We are becoming the center of attention as the late morning sun shines over us. My belly grumbles again while waiting for this slow lizard to prepare for departure to this more comfortable setting he mentioned. Both James and I notice Elizabeth is asleep standing up while leaning against James. She is paler every time I look at her.

"Okay, this will have to do," Glizteo says while packing a few more things. I turn and look at Glitzteo as he says a few words in another dialect. The entire shop folds in on itself, precisely like the fiery demon cat lady did. A small box appeared in his hand.

"Okay, let's go to Ooshmala Inn, the finest bar and sleeping quarters in all of Ooshmala village."

I'm still eyeing the small box. Wow!

Salamander Glizteo points across the road to a narrow four-story building with a rowdy crowd pouring out of the first floor. They all have drinks in their hands and claws. Large vines shoot out from behind the bar delivering drinks to tables as we came closer. As I take in the scene, I notice Tate and Glizteo whispering to each other. Before I know what's happened, Glizteo slices the air with a webbed finger and tossed the small box into nothingness. Quickly, I turn my attention back to the strange tavern before they noticed me watching them.

My brain is already overrun with impossibilities, but my hunger distracts me and pushes me to find some food.

A flash of pink and brown streaks pass in front of my legs. I stare at it.

No. That couldn't have been... Can there really be a pig and a chicken creature? A pigken? Silver and I drool at the possibilities of how such a beast might taste. As we start to follow it, Tate catches us and pushes me into the tavern.

Inside, it's even more crowded than on the street, and too hard to see much more than a wooden stage, a bar, and several tables through the passing occupants. Tate pushes us to the back of the tavern where the Inn reception is. We don't go to the desk but straight up the steps.

"Third floor, room thirty-six on the right. Help yourselves to whichever clothes that fit you." Glizteo yells from the bottom of the stairs.

James lifts Elizabeth into his arms and starts carrying her up the steps. I follow, pausing on the first landing between floors and peer down. Still at the foot of the stairs, I see Glizteo handing Tate a small pouch that clinks as though it contains coins and a small vial of red liquid. Hurriedly, I continue up the stairs, my mind racing.

Tate catches up with us before we reach room thirty-six on the right. The Inn doesn't look more than four bedrooms across, but the walk to the room felt like forever, and there are more rooms past our door. I shrug off yet another impossibility and look forward to a nice cold shower and some clean clothes. James sits Elizabeth down in a chair inside the room and takes off her mud-covered sneakers.

"The room has three beds and two bathrooms. Each of you will get a bed." Tate says firmly.

"Well, what about you? Where will you sleep?" James asks the obvious question.

"I'm not tired, and I must watch over my Princess. If the need occurs, I will sleep on the floor next to her bed. I will tend to Elizabeth's needs. You two wash up, change clothes, and go down to the tavern for lunch." Tate says while picking up Elizabeth and taking her to one of the bathrooms.

"We don't have any money, what is the currency in this place anyway?" I say, wondering how we are supposed to pay for anything.

Tate puts Elizabeth down in a stone marble tub clothes and all before turning to me. He takes out that small pouch from earlier and pulls out a couple bronze and silver coins. "Use the silver coins for food and drinks and the bronze ones for tips. Try not to attract any more trouble. If you need something from me, talk to Glizteo, who will be at the bar.

James jumps in the shower first as I comb over the decor and wares laid out on a table in the room. It feels like a standard hotel room with off white walls and a cozy fireplace. However, the beds are only mattresses on the floor with what looks like fur skins as blankets. The table seems to be carved out of one solid piece of wood. It does feel a bit claustrophobic with the lack of windows.

The table has pants and shorts in separate leather and cloth sizes— nothing like jeans and a t-shirt that I usually wear. I choose cloth shorts with a leather belt and a leather pocketed vest. The belt aids in the size picked as these clothes didn't come with pre-sized tags. A tall mirror is sitting up against the far wall. I walk over to it and pose in my new outfit.

"What are you doing, David?" James asks, entering the room from the bathroom.

I freeze in a butt pose while looking over my shoulder.

"Ugh…looking at how weird these clothes are." I start to itch at the leather scraping my chest.

Steam floods into the room through the half-open door from the shower room, carrying the aroma of cedar and pine needles.

"Right," James says. I'm not sure if he agrees with me about the weird clothes. "Well, hurry up and take your shower while I get dressed. I'm hungry. When you get in there, just push the button. Don't worry about the rest."

James passes me with a smile leaving me wondering what he meant.

The small bathroom is mostly empty space, with a curtain of wet sagging cloth dividing it. To the left is a small table with a bowl on top and several bars of soap and towels. There is an old fashion stone tub in the center. On the tiled floor to the right, I detect water footprints leading away from a drain and the wet cloth curtain. I close the door, strip off the scratchy clothes, and hang them on a hook. After timidly stepping into the shower square and closing the curtain, I look for the faucet for the water to come out of, but it's not there. There are no handles or knobs, only a small button on the wall. There is a bright light shining down from the ceiling, making my skin glow.

Trusting my brother's word, I press the button. At first, nothing happens. I'm about to leave and yell at James when thunder erupts from overhead. I snap my head back to gaze upward. There, small clouds form and cast light rays out to the sides of the little box. I swear I saw lightning shoot through the clouds. Soon small droplets of rain start to fall down on me. I duck my head every time that thunder roars, hoping the lightning won't strike me while I reach for the soap. I may have let out a few unmanly screams because I hear laughter coming from behind the door.

After the traumatizing shower, I redressed and meet James at the bottom of the stairs. He's dressed like me with a leather vest but wears long cloth pants and sandals. He already has the coins in hand.

After greeting him, I say, "Let's get some food and try to keep a low profile, so we don't run into another Kaligula."

We walk into the ever-pressing crowded tavern on the first floor. Under the intense stares from many of the occupants, I feel like a complete outsider.

"Look," I say softly to James. "There are a couple of empty seats at that table in the corner, with the stage on the left." We head in that direction. As soon as we get close, all the other guests at the table start staring at us. Then they rise and leave, pushing us aside in the process.

"How friendly. I guess we have the whole table to ourselves." I say to James as he stares across the room. I notice he's fixated on the plant vines that are zipping across the room, delivering drinks and food.

I hear an assertive tone over the crowd that directs my attention from the vine-covered bar to the lit stage in the corner. A bird, easily recognizable as a toucan with its large beak and multicolor ringed neck, is chirping over the loud crowd. My bond with Silver intensifies, increasing our hearing and singling the bird out.

"The King and Queen will return and rid our lands of the Lich's reign. Rawena-Rose will be our savior. She has been foretold by the Council of Seers!"

A rock creature stands and voices his opinion. "You spit your Kalacuuian lies at us each year, but your proclaimed saviors never return. They won't ever return."

"I agree with the Grok," Another patron chimes in. "Humans don't care about us, and we don't need humans."

"Get off the stage!" A high pitched screech came from the other corner.

"You will all see soon, her protectors will bring her back, and she will lift the curse upon our lands!" The upset kalacuu lifts off the stage and flies to the bar just out of my sight.

I gaze at James questioningly. *"Rawena Rose is Elizabeth, isn't she?"*

I leave James at the table, reviewing the menu and head to the Kalacuu at the bar. To get there, I must pass a group of tall cats walking on their hind legs. They sniff the air and sneer at me. Attempting to ignore them, I fix my stare straight ahead of me … and stumble, bouncing off a green blob creature and falling against the stool where the Kalacuu sits. I feel the air swoosh over me as his wings flutter from the impact.

The Kalacuuian asks, "Are you okay? That was quite a nasty fall."

His concern actually sounds genuine. There's no negative tone in his voice. I get up off the floor, hoping no one else saw it.

"I'm fine. I didn't see that Kilumzu standing there." I brush off pecks of dirt I collected on the way down. "I heard what you said up there on the stage."

The toucan-looking bird's eyes go dark, and he looks down and away.

"I believe you," I say quickly.

The Kalacuu's eyes shoot up in surprise and stare at me in wonder. He looks shocked already, but I have to ask him if only to see if he was the inspiration to my favorite cereal. "Your name wouldn't be Sam, would it?"

His eyes scrunch as he looks me over suspiciously. "Have we met before? How do you know my name?"

"I saw you on a box of fruit-loops growing up." When I give him an honest answer, he only looks more confused. "It was a lucky guess, I suppose." I scratch my head, wondering if I should tell him who we are or to keep it a secret. We can't attract any more attention the way we did outside. But there is no harm in confirming his rant since the Lich already knows she's here.

"So what brings a human over here to talk to a Kalacuuian?"

"I believe you are correct. That this Rawena-Rose girl will return. In fact, I believe I saw her outside during the commotion with Kaligula."

The Kalacuu's eyes grow more prominent and appear as if they are about to pop out of the bird's head.

"Where is she now? I have to find her? There's no time to waste!"

He sounds rushed and desperate. Taking flight, he knocks over the stool he was perched on. His talons grab my forearm and drag me back through the crowd. I try, but I'm unable to pry off his iron grip with my loose hand. I knock over a towering tigress, and their whole table of tigers jump to their feet, wearing evil sneers and growling.

Just what we need. Keep it low key.

Through the fracas, I hear my brother say that he'll take care of the bird. Then the toucan drops me and flies into the wall, then swooshes out the door with smoke trails coming off his left-wing. I manage to pick myself up off the wooden floor and scramble back to our table, trying to ignore the angry group of cats heading our direction.

James had already ordered roasted pigkens wings in a sweet glaze sauce with a side of skyta eggs over a bed of sweetened seaweed. The slimy red eggs take up an entire plate by themselves. I am so hungry that it looks delicious. I'm about to dig in when our unwanted guests invite themselves to sit at our table.

"Well, well, looks like a pair of human cubs are all by themselves tonight. We decided to join you lonely folk after being so gracefully informed by your wolf shifter friend."

How can they even smell Silver when I'm in human form?

James feigns extreme respect. "I don't know what you're talking about. This is my human brother, David. I'm James. We meant no disrespect and would appreciate being left alone to eat in peace." He's trying to defuse the situation I have created.

The cats laugh, howling in a high pitch. They don't budge. "Your brother here didn't only knock over my misses, but he has the stench of a wolf, a dire wolf." The other cats all hiss angrily.

I can feel the heat waves radiating off James, and inside my mind, Silver starts getting agitated. My hands start shaking, and the cats, believing me afraid, all smile evilly.

"Why do you hate wolves so much?" I ask, trying to calm Silver down.

"Dire wolves are terrifying to us," one of them replies, appearing more relaxed than the others. "They came to our territory three cycles ago and laid waste to most of our kin, shredding them to the bone. There weren't many survivors. They always attack in a large pack making their brute force unstoppable."

I look from one feline face to the next. Many of the cats are etched with horror as they seem to relive that memory. The hair rises on their backs.

"When we smell you," another said, "we are reminded of that pain."

"But you said that these wolves run in packs," I say, all bravado now and not much sense. "Have you ever seen a solo dire wolf or one that can shift into a human?" I remember how hard it was to learn to shift back to human form and hope I am right that the dire wolves here probably don't care to change back to a weaker form. The cats look a bit puzzled and start yowling and meowing to each other.

An angry-looking male in front switches back to English. "These humans have a point, and if he was a dire wolf, he would not use words to stop a fight. Be warned, human. The wolves you may surround yourself with are evil and will not think twice to tear you apart."

One of the other male cats behind him becomes riled up and yowls at the others. In a blink, he pounced on me. He is yanked off by a vine pulling him to the bar. The salamander there catches him and winks at me. The other cats frantically rushed to save their buddy.

I breathe a sigh of relief. "Whoa. How crazy was that?"

"You have a lot of explaining to do once we get back up to the room," James says aloud and digs back into his wings. Silver and I do the same before we pay for the meal and head back upstairs. I open the door and see Tate hovering over Elizabeth while injecting red liquid into her arm.

"What the heck are you doing to her?" James screams out behind me and rushes to Elizabeth's side.

"Calm down. It's a sedative that will hopefully slow the toxins down, giving Elizabeth more time to fight it." He eyes me and says, "You sure don't know how to stay out of trouble, do you?"

"How could you know already?"

"I told Glitzeo to watch you. You didn't think I'd just let you two foreign humans wander about on your own, did you?"

I clench my fists at the thought of having a babysitter assigned to watch us eat food. Out of the corner of my eye, I see James take advantage of Tate's distraction and give Elizabeth a quick peck on the cheek. I watch his lips whisper, "Please, get better."

Finally, we sink into our beds on the other side of the room, and I try not to think about what other dire wolves have done.

Chapter 7

A Dark Discovery
James

I fall asleep to the loud snores of my brother David. The worries of
Elizabeth flutter away as I feel transported back into my deep memories.

David is hovering in the air as green smoke encircles
him. A bright white light zaps through the trees and into my
brother's mouth. Tears slide down his cheeks before
bellowing out an ear-piercing scream. He falls limply on to
the ground at my feet. *What have I done? I killed my only
brother.*
I check his pulse and hear a faint one. His chest barely rising
and falling. The fear of losing him only set aside for the
moment. David looks pale and doesn't respond to my nudges.

A loud howl snaps my attention back up to the sky
toward our castle. The moon is still full, and the fire is still
burning the last remnants of the ingredients I had thrown in
to cast the spell. *I should never have found this book.* I toss
the book to the side before looking back down at my
unconscious brother. I stomp the fire out when a second howl
announced closer this time. Dread erupted through my
thoughts now stuck out in the dark forest with a defenseless
brother. *How am I to carry him back and fight off any wolves
coming close?*

My head jerks to the left after hearing a twig snap.
Beads of sweat start to perspire down my neck. I have that
eerie feeling we aren't only being watched but hunted.
Coming from in front of me is the sound of branches
snapping. My eyes adjust in time to see a large black creature
running straight for me. My instincts tell me to run, but I
can't leave my brother here to die.

My arm hairs stand up, and a warm surge of energy
flows through my veins. I'm terrified but also have an
overwhelming feeling of anger and hatred. The creature
jumps out of the shading forest and into the moonlight. It's a

giant black wolf-like that of the many paintings in the castle. It lands before me staring at me through its glowing red eyes. It shakes its head, and a chunk of fur is missing behind its right ear. It speaks in an odd drunken slur barely understandable. The maw doesn't move, yet I hear the wolf clearly in my head. The wolf approaches slowly in a semi-circle. I can't move, frozen in place by my own fear. It pounces at me, evidently intending to take my head off. The heat in me intensified, and I stuck out my right arm into the open maw of the oversized wolf. I focused all the anger into my arm and expelled it outward.

A blue fireball thrust forward from my hand, making contact with the wolf's head, exploding it like a popped water balloon. Chunks of flesh, fur, and blood covered me and the surrounding trees and snow. The immense amount of energy left me weak and helpless. All I could do is focus on the headless wolf's corpse. The body twitched and started to fold in on itself, shifting into a human form. The human was unmistakably recognizable by his tattoos down his leg. It was our Da.

"Nooooo!" I scream as I lurch out of bed and shoot a blue fireball across the room. It smacks into a body and lays it out on the floor in a painful crack. Tate and David wake to the sound of a loud thwack and the smell of burning fur.

Tate pulls out his blade, erupting the darkness with blazing light. I cover my eyes as I hear David's complaints before the smell of rotting flesh pierces his mind. I look through my fingers to see Tate slicing the head off a sizzling tiger body. The head flips over, and I see the red glowing eyes fade out before black smoke leaves the body.

"That tiger was the same one that lunged at David downstairs," I say to Tate as he picks up the body and throws it into a bathroom.

"It's time to go. The Drargs have found us." Tate says in a commanding tone.

"But, I am still tired." David squeaks out under the glare from Tate.

"Let Silver out, and you can rest," I advise knowing David won't be able to run in his current state.

"No, you can't let others see a dire wolf here," Tate says, still reserved from explaining anything.

"It's no longer up to you, Tate. We are in danger, and my brother is too weak to run." *"Silver shift, let my brother rest. We will need your help to get out of here and to protect Elizabeth."*

David quickly undresses before Silver shifts back into his natural form. "Grab clothes, need later, yes." Silver replies and I grab my brother's backpack, stuff his clothes inside with his daggers, and throw it over my shoulder with my bow and quiver.

Tate picks up Elizabeth and carries her to the door, displeased to have a dire wolf in tow.

Silver growled at Tate when he went to open the door. Tate understood before I did and opened the door while quickly stepping aside. Another red eyed tiger leaped through the doorway, and Silver caught him in midair.

"Go now!" Tate snaps.

"Silver, catch up with us when you're done."

Silver keeps on wrestling with the tiger, trying to break its neck like he did with the mountain lion.

"Yes," I hear as I'm running down the hall after Tate. We dash down the stairs and out a backdoor. The sky is still dark with the eerie red glow of the moons. We run into some tall brush that reminds me of a lot of running through cornfields back home. Tate doesn't let up, and I have to huff and puff to keep up at his pace. I look behind me, hoping Silver is on our tail only to see a red-eyed brown blob rolling after us.

"Ahhh! Tate, we have company."

Tate looks over his shoulder then back to me. "Here, take Elizabeth, I will deal with the Kilumzu. Do not slow down for anything." I embrace her to my chest and run as fast as I can, adrenaline empowering me to keep her safe. I turn my head in time to see Tate's bright sword dicing the blob into several pieces.

My feet and legs are numb, and I start to slow down near the end of the brush. I have to catch my breath before looking at my surroundings. Ahead of me, a narrow sandy path leads to a sand dune. As I follow it, plant life becomes sparse. The night sky is still dark with the red tinge of the moons behind dark clouds. I hear someone coming up behind me. I turn and see Tate covered in brownish blobs of goo. He has a stern look while sheathing his sword.

I climb up the hill and look back over the tall brush. I see a line of parting leaves heading our way.

"Silver, please tell me that is you coming towards us." I grip onto Elizabeth tighter as I start to back up. Tate notices my defensive actions and sprints in the direction of my stare.

"Yes, we come fast. More creatures chase us."

"Tate is coming in from your right watch out." Right after I warned Silver, the line quickly broke left and zigzagged back in our direction.

A howl erupts, and Silver sends me quick images, apparently unable to form the words so rapidly. I see the flash of a sword slicing through several creatures as Silver dodged out of the way.

"Silver, get here quick. I am too tired to carry Elizabeth through the sand." I send my thoughts with an anxious feeling. Silver slides up to me, still

covered in tiger blood. Sand covers my lower body, but I'm too tired to care. I place Elizabeth, slumped over, onto Silver's back. We continue trudging forward through the sand, ignoring the screams and cries of the animals being cut down by Tate's sword.

Scanning the horizon, I see, ahead in the distance, the silhouette of a small hut in the middle of this desert—nothing else. I instruct Silver to head that way.

As we slog forward, at least half an hour passes without a sound behind us. I keep looking back, expecting Tate to appear over the last dune. Even though he's been a thorn in my side, now that he is gone, I feel lost.

How will we cure Elizabeth? Where do we go from here?

More questions fill my mind as I trudge onward, toward the hut. A sudden jerk from Silver as he stops his forward movement sends my gaze to a figure, not two meters in front of us that weren't there a moment ago. Tate slouches as he slips his glowing sword back into his sheath. He staggers a bit, and his clothes are much worse for wear with several bloody rips and tears in them.

"Hurry up, you two. We need to get to that hut up ahead before sunrise." Tate says while slightly out of breath.

"What's at the hut that's so important?" I ask, not really thinking it through.

Tate stares at me like I'm stupid. "We won't have the cover of darkness soon, and more of those possessed creatures will be searching for us. We need a place to change clothes and find safe passage through this deadly desert."

"Oh," I say, realizing how obvious that is.

"This land belongs to the Ajin. They are a secretive, deadly group of animals that don't take lightly to trespassers. But they are quite fond of rare precious metals. They consider them delicacies of sorts."

"So, you are saying they eat metal? That seems rather unappetizing." I am already picturing this type of creature as having a tiny brain … and maybe really sharp teeth.

"Yes, but the rarer the metal, the more that an Ajin will do for you. Scotland has something similar, I believe that they call it underground services."

"So the Ajin clean sewers? Why would that help us?" I ask dumbfounded that Tate would think we needed cleaning services right now. Tate palms his face and ignores me as we hurry behind his fast pace. The hut slowly getting more significant as we come closer.

Chapter 8

An Unforgettable Ride.
David

"James, how did we get to a hut in the desert?" I ask after waking up from my nap while Silver was in control.

Tate notices Silver's sudden change in attitude and stares toward my brother. "You're finally awake. Change back to human form, we don't want to unsettle the Ajin in their own territory."

Tate reaches toward me and picks Elizabeth off my back. I look to James, and he's already pulling out my clothes from my backpack. I take a quick look around and shift back into my human form. I feel the warm morning air flutter across my skin before pulling on my leather vest and pants. I manage to cover up most of the blood caked onto my skin. I rub most of the blood off of my arms and face. While I got dressed, James told me about the battle I had slept through and the sewer cleaners we were meeting at this hut.

"What did Tate say exactly, because we don't even know if there are sewers under us?" I ask, trying to understand my brother's argument.

"He said that the Ajin are secretive and deadly and that they like to eat metal for payment of underground services they provide. Tate said much like what can be found in Scotland."

I look at my brother, realizing where he's coming from and knowing my brother can be such an idiot. "I am sure Tate meant the Underground where you can go pay someone to kidnap, steal something, or murder someone else. They would be part of a group that offers gray and black services. So the payment of high valued precious metals seems like a price worthy of such an unthinkable service."

James's eyes glazed over slightly, thinking over what I said. "So we are running from otherworldly deadly creatures to seek help from other deadly creatures to obtain safe passage through a hot and deadly desert. Great."

I stretch out my limbs and pop a few knuckles before turning the corner to see Tate already talking to a hooded creature. The horizon in the distance is already getting lighter as the sunrise approaches. The small amount of light showcases a few features of this Ajin creature. It's not much taller than me, and its body is completely covered in the same hooded material. Its legs are bent irregularly then normal humans and have long skinny feet. Its snout pokes out beyond the darkness of the hood, and its slender tongue slips out when it talks. It talks with almost a lisp making hard "S" sounds.

"Passssage for four will be expenssssive. Much metal indeed."

"One gold coin should be adequate, yes," Tate said adamantly.

"Hmmm, no, that won't do that won't do. Dessssert more dangeroussss, more needed. One gold each will do, yessss one gold each will do."

"Tate doesn't look pleased in the least, but we don't really have much choice. He pulls open that same coin pouch I saw earlier back at the stairs in the Inn. He pulls out four gold coins and drops them into a skin-tight boney hand. The Ajin's snout quickly sniffed the coins deeply before its tongue jutted out and sucked in each coin. A small audible moan came from the Ajin before a slightly visible shiver ran down its back.

"Come, come, we leave at sunrise. Must get horsapeed ready." The Ajin runs off into the small two-story hut, not more than three square meters in size. The front of the shelter has an elongated arched entryway that spans past the first floor a bit. We stay outside, waiting for the Ajin to return with our new mode of transportation.

"Tate, what is a horsapeed?" I ask, confused with such a name.

"He is bringing one out now. This is the only safe way to traverse the desert without the ability to fly. For the price I paid, we best get one of their fastest ones."

I look back into the open dark archway. The head of a horse appears, and it is short, much the size of a pony. Nothing seems odd about it until it strode out past us, leg after leg with an elongated body. It kept trotting forward, and the rear was not in sight. The short legs were all close together and moving in unison. Each leg sharpened to a point like a pencil.

James' eyes were bulging, "David, what is this thing?"

A small gap separates the front legs from the rear ones. Its rear finally passed us. Creatures in this realm get stranger the longer we stay here.

"From my rough calculations, there are about fifty legs on this side alone. It's incredible." The horse's back is not far below my shoulder level. Looking past the horse to the sand dune horizon, bright purples and oranges spread through the cloudy sky. Sunset has arrived, and we now have to put our trust into this deadly long-nosed creature to traverse the hot sands of this desert. Tate is looking in the direction we will be heading. There is only more sand in view that I can see.

"Tate, what is so dangerous that we need a mutated horse to cross it? I am sure I could cross this easily." I ask, but all he does is a nod in the direction to our right.

Near the edge of where the light sand hits the darker sand is an odd-looking creature. It has the body of a gazelle with spine thorns down to its tail. The head is fleshless with a ring of dark fur down its neck. The rising sunlight shines over the sand dunes and distinguishes the two colors of sand while glinting off the obsidian black horns atop its head. The odd creature looks down at the sand and back up into the distance it plans on traveling. It looks like it is rearing up to spring forward. It jumps into a sprint. Suddenly sand balls gravitate toward it, chasing it down. More can be seen from all sides as they close in. Hands made of sand pop out and grab at its feet. The odd creature couldn't outrun all the hands. Each giant hand shaved off bits of fur and flesh while grabbing at its legs, shreds of meat thrown about until only its skeleton was left shining in the light before being pulled under.

"Oh, never mind," I mutter. "I'll take the ride."

The long-nosed anteater looking Ajin bounced upon the neck of the horse.

"Time to go before anymore giantsss wake." The creepy Ajin whispers.

"Giants... What giants? I didn't see any." .James swivels around, searching for a giant.

Tate shakes his head and hands Elizabeth to James. He quickly hops on before retrieving Elizabeth back. James looks hard-pressed to let Tate hold her the entire ride. I see my brother jump up and saddle the horse like he's done this before.

I have rarely ridden horses much at all, especially as of late. Running is faster. I jump up like my bother only to land hard on my hip and flip right over the horses back. James can't hold in his laughter and bellows out. The Ajin swivels his head around, staring at James, and a strange red glow comes from under its hood. James seemed to lose his voice and went silent.

Tate glares at both of us. "I suggest you both get on the horse and keep your voices down, or this Ajin might make his spell permanent." I saw more white in James' eyes before he mouthed several profanities that no one could hear.

I quickly dusted the sand off and carefully pulled myself back up on the horse, mounting behind James. The back is slightly lumpy as if almost like a young camel's back. There is not much to hold on to. Tate sits sturdily, one arm around Elizabeth holding her tightly and the other gripping the horsapeed's side. James isn't holding on to Tate or the horse.

That spooks me, and I begin to worry. "Tate, how fast--"

I don't get to finish my question because, at that moment, the horse shoots forward. James' head hits my jaw, and I lose my balance. My brother quickly grabs the horsapeeds skin with one hand while holding onto my right arm with his other. I am not even touching the back, bearly flying above it as the wind threatens to pull me from my brother's grasp.

The beast zigzags, and I manage to grab the top skin of a lump and pull myself back down. I clench my legs around its body like my life depends on it. The wind is deafening, and I yell, "Thanks, bro!"

James nods. *"You can't leave me with Tate. I still need your smart-ass brain to figure out how we get back to Scotland. Those giant hands will have to try harder to take my brother from me."* He looks forward, ducking behind Tate's broad back.

I glance behind us and notice several of the same sand mounds desperately trying to keep pace with this horsapeed. Looking to the sides, several more come close. Looking down, I see a few giant sand hands reaching for the legs only to be repeatedly pierced, causing a slight jerk in the body of this creature. I can feel the muscles under me tense up every time it pulls loose from another hand.

Minutes pass with the same sequence of radical turns and jolts with thunderous winds passing over us and the desert somewhat of a blur. Suddenly I jolt forward, slamming into James and him into Tate. It's as if we got pulled out of hyperdrive, and we're riding a healthy horse. I glance behind us, and a massive sand ball is gripping the rear of the horsapeed. Sand fell off the chunk, revealing a figure. Much like the rock creature, I saw at the Inn, but giant and the sand acted more fluidly filing into its proper place.

I hear James scream in my head, *"Get Down Now!"*

I swivel to the side, centimeters above other sand hands aiming for my head. A heat burst flew past my legs, and I saw the blue fireball heading straight for the giant's ugly face. Its mouth opened up, and the fireball went straight through without impact. James threw a few more, and the sand of the giant opened up into the same holes letting the fireballs pass right through. James curses a lot in my head right before the giant froze entirely and fell off the horsepeed's back. I whip my head around, almost receiving whiplash and see the Ajins red eyes fade back to darkness. It points to James, then down at the legs of the horsapeed. We are still moving relatively slow, and more giants are coming from all sides. I pull myself back up just in time for James to throw multiple small fireballs down at the gripping hands. The sand reacts similarly, allowing the horsapeed to shake off their grips and boost off toward the shoreline in the distance.

Twenty seconds later, we stop abruptly next to another Ajin hut. Waves hit the sandy beach, and I breathe in the salty air. My head still rings from running into James' back. I see the Ajin and Tate dismount, followed by James. I am a bit discombobulated and decide it's much easier to fall off. I land on my arms and feet instinctually. I look behind us and see the giants stop at the border between light and dark sand. They look quite pissed, and I sigh in relief.

The Ajin walks up to my brother and bows its head. Its eyes flicker, and James coughs out loud, clearing his throat.

"I and my pet are in your debt, human. May there be a time you need ussss we will come." The Ajin bows again and turns his back to us before disappearing into the hut with his pet. At first, I thought the Ajin still didn't remove his spell because James was utterly quiet and speechless. We both looked to Tate, who was a bit in shock at the vow the Ajin made to James.

"Why did the Ajin make that promise, Tate?" I ask, trying to make sense of things.

"Like he will ever keep it," James says, blowing it off like usual.

"Don't take his words lightly. The Ajin always comes through on their word, which is why they can be so terrifying. If they say, they will kill someone by tomorrow night that someone will be dead. So for the Ajin to make an open vow to help you, it can only mean that you saved his life and feels he owes you something worthy of his life." Tate still looks a bit astonished that the Ajin just made that statement.

Along the shoreline, a scattered row of old rowboats lay in the sand. Some look well-worn down with broken ores and others with smashed hulls. We follow behind Tate as he carries Elizabeth. He inclines his head toward a boat that looks like it may still float. On cue, I grab two sets of ores from a pile of wood, once a ship, while Tate pushes our hopefully-seaworthy choice into the shallow water.

"Get in the middle, James." Tate orders.

James is still mumbling to himself what he could possibly have the Ajin do for him and jumps into the boat, not questioning Tate. Tate hands Elizabeth over to James, sitting on the middle plank. Tate points to me and then the front. At this point, it's not worth arguing after that last ride through the desert. A calm boat ride will do us some good.

I climb in the front and sit down with both oars in my lap. Tate pushed the boat off the shore and a small distance out before rocking the boat and finding his spot in the rear. I hand him an ore. "Where we heading?" I ask, hoping for some directions.

"See that small island ahead of us? That is where we are going."

I use my bonded sight and zoom in. I can barely make out what looks to be a rather large volcano on the left side. We start rowing in unison toward our new destination.

Chapter 9

A Fond Welcoming
James

"James, David, Wake up now!"

I get startled awake by Tate while feeling our little rowboat rock back and forth by the sudden change in weight. I squint my eyes from the sudden bright light of the warm sun rays above.

Elizabeth is still curled up in the back of the boat. Her face too pale and clammy. David yawns loudly next to me, and I have to push his outstretched arms to the side to see what commotion Tate is waking us for. Tate speaks again, but my fingers are rubbing the ringing out of my ears. I see small blurry figures in the distance and hear the sound of rushing waves. It's odd because we are currently in calm water, adrift, oars at the ready by Tate's arms. The blurs start to come more into focus as David groggily wakes up next to me while using my right shoulder to distribute his weight before standing.

"Hey, why are there giant turtles on ice boards, surfing in our direction?" David says while I'm still squinting to see what the figures look like.

"How do you...wait... never mind." I start to ask before catching myself. "Dire wolves and their superior senses," I mutter under my breath, still jealous of his abilities.

David's eyes flash from green to red then green again. Message received. It seems Silver does not want to make friends with these strangers.

"Silver says he senses anger and hatred coming from them. They don't look friendly. They look to be equipped with ice spears and water tridents like out of a movie." I pocket David's wolf daggers, ready my bow, and then hoisted my quiver of arrows onto my back.

Tate frowns at my ready stance and says, "I don't think it's a good idea to show such aggression in their waters. Put down your weapons, and you, David, do not let Silver take over or shift. James, protect my princess. I will negotiate with them."

Two groups of five turtles each surround our small rowboat with their weapons pointing at us. One group is riding blocks of ice, and the other group is standing on what looks like shimmery blue dolphins made entirely out of water. The closest group, of the mean-looking turtles on ice blocks, has an assortment of ice armor, chest pieces, and helms. They have to be some sort of warrior class in their group as they are all massive and fierce.

The riders of the blue aqua dolphins, slightly smaller and wearing no armor, wave their tridents in the air while they circle us. Shouts in a foreign tongue and other high pitched sounds coming from the circling water turtles. One pink-nosed light tan shell speaks and quiets the rest down.

It must be the leader of the group. Maybe the smaller ones are female.

The smaller leader turtle points to our boat with a tall trident and says one short foreign command. Three of the five ice wielding turtles surrounding us plunge their ice spears into the water. One blink later, the rowboat is sitting in a block of ice that spreads out two meters all around the boat, making any possible plan with the oars obsolete.

Tate, David, and I steady ourselves after the boat's jolting stopped its swaying in the sea. Tate, with his hands up, calmly speaks back to them in their own dialect.

The surprise on the leader's flat-nosed face is mirrored in both David's and mine. *Who knew he could speak turtle?*

I look more closely around at the ten turtles and notice not one of them looks the same. They are shades of green, brown, tan, and black skin with round, flat, or pointed noses. Their shells have different shapes or designs like engravings in them. After a long moment of whispered chatter from a few water-wielding turtles, there was a long pause accompanied by an angry stare. The leader cleared its throat and spoke …. English.

"Humans are not welcome here. We told your king that if any humans were to cross paths with us again, they would not pass through our Keywinenyeh Waters alive. Do you have a death wish?" Her voice was majestic but stern.

A few water turtles make sounds like snickers from the back row. The leader eyes them, and they quiet down. I am shocked, and a bit stunned to see such intelligence in a turtle—one who can command with authority and speak fluently in different languages.

David attracts my attention with a worried glance. *"Brother, Silver is getting agitated. I don't know how much longer I can keep him caged up,"* David says telepathically.

I reply, with bravado but no real knowledge, "Stay calm and breathe. Tate will get us out of this."

David doesn't look so sure.

"We can't start a fight, or Elizabeth may get worse. We don't have time for Silver to show dominance," I say. *"Settle him down and don't look like your about to rip off someone's head."*

David understands. He closes his eyes and takes in a deep breath before steeling himself and nodding back at me.

Tate explains why we have come into their territory. "My good friend Glizteo, the Merchant, sent us to your island to find the cure for our companion's ailment." He gestures with one arm to Elizabeth, whom I hold protectively in my arms. "The merchant says that your island is the only one close by with the means to make a cure for what ails her. Please let us explain to your elders who she is and why she is important. Maybe then you will grant us the cure for her."

The female leader seems taken aback as if recognizing the salamander's name.

"What is your name, Human?" A small amount of spittle spews out through the leader's lips at that last word.

"My name is Tate Tumbleson, the royal guardian's leader for the human King of Kinzurdia. These three are part of my duty to my lord."

Once Tate said his name, several of the armored ice turtles moved back, one almost fell off his ice block. The back row of turtles, which – I am now sure – is composed of female turtles, gasps. Even though I'm not accustomed to reading turtle body language, these appear shocked and worried about an impending fight. What has Tate done to strike that much fear in a name? I will have to keep an eye on him.

The leader turtle clears her throat and quiets down her spooked squad. She looks back up to Tate and says her name. "I am Ula, second in command of the Keywinenyeh Tortoise tribe. How do we know you are who you claim to be? Why would the Human King's personal guardian be out here without a platoon of his guards?" The more questions she asked, the calmer and more confident her group becomes.

Tate appears agitated about the time this is taking and reaches to pull his sword. Elizabeth is in my arms, and I won't be able to get my bow in time.

"Commander. Look!" One of the ice warriors upfront points at the now-drawn sword Tate holds. Gasps and a small cry from one turtle in the back can be heard.

The blade has a bright white radiance to it even under the clear sunny sky. All the turtles look to Ula for her orders. Some I notice taking big gulps of air while looking between her and the sword.

"Well, you make your point. What is your intention with these puny hatchlings? Who is the sick one you bring with you?" Ula tries to stay stern, but I notice her waver slightly.

David chimes into my thoughts. *"Their emotions have flipped. Silver still feels small bits of hatred toward us but says most of them are now terrified of a confrontation. Silver is no longer pushing for a shift and says I can handle it."* I am grateful David is now in control and won't shift, but not because it might have caused a scene. I don't want to swim in the icy water when silver's weight may flip this little boat.

"I think its best we discuss who my companions are in a more private setting with your elders." Tate evades the questions, as usual, and tries to get the ball rolling in our favor. Looking down at Elizabeth, I see she is waking.

Her eyes open, and her gaze meets mine, then a scowl crosses her face. She coughs up blood, dips her head back, and screams, gathering the attention of everyone. I look up to see twelve pairs of eyes staring in my direction. Elizabeth grabs her stomach, gurgles, and I turn her head before she vomits onto the boat's floor between my legs.

Ula pushes through her group, touches the ice encasing the boat, and it vaporizes. The ship sways a bit now released form the ice. Ula comes close, and I glance up at Tate, asking with my eyes if she is a threat any longer.

"Let the commander see her, James. Ula is one of their best healers for their tribe."

At that, Ula quirks a smile. "I see my reputation precedes me." I nod to her, and she comes close, hovering over the water on her twin blue dolphins. She places her webbed hand on Elizabeth's chest and wheezes through her teeth. Her hand glows a light blue. "This hatchling is not ill with the disease. She has been poisoned. We must get her back to our herbalist at once."

"But commander, they are human…" one of her other female turtles' chimes in from the back.

Ula snaps back toward the sound of the questioning turtle. "Do not question my order! You know it is forbidden to harm any hatchlings regardless of race. Doing nothing will kill this hatchling, and you will be the one I punish!" With that, all the turtles are silenced. She calls out two of her ice warriors. "Ragarth…Brutus, come and push the boat back to shore. The rest of you in the formation. Now!"

Her icy tone doesn't go unnoticed. Even I got the chills from the harshness of her words.

David and Tate sit down before we are jolted forward, much like a speed boat. The icy armor of the two warrior turtles behind us glints in the sunlight. Their eyes, trained on a spot before me, are focused and determined. Their two ice blocks have merged into the others and are linked to the rear of the boat. Their ice spears are in their hands on either side of the boat. The boat lunges forward. White water spews out behind as we slice through the once-calm waters of the Keywinenyeh Island.

Ula keeps pace next to us on her twin dolphins. She looks over at Tate and asks, "What poisoned her?"

David is studying the Island as it grows in size. He is entranced by it, although I still can't make much of it out. *"James, you gotta check out this island!"* I hear in my head while trying to concentrate on Ula's and Tate's conversation.

"She was stung by the Libitina Mortis plant's thorns in a corrupted graveyard not far from the town of Ooshmala. It's been almost a day since." Tate says with worry in his words.

"And your hatchling is…still alive?" The last words are barely a whisper as if the commander is shocked.

"She is strong and has powerful blood running through her veins; I've done all I can. She has to survive, Ula. She will bring hope to many."

Ula looks back at me, cradling Elizabeth in my arms and putting fallen strands of hair behind her ear. "Who are you?" The words barely audible to my ears as Ula looks back out to the approaching shoreline.

I follow her gaze, and a shiver runs down my spine. There's a plume of smoke rising out of a massive volcano to my left with thick forests surrounding it and blanketing the island. To my right is a fantastic sight, a large lake with water falling into it from the sky. Looking up, I see a much smaller floating island where the waterfalls originate and dark clouds with lightning rumbling above. "Wow" is all that I can say.

Looking at Elizabeth, I clean off her face. I tighten my grip on her as the shoreline approaches without us slowing. I look back at the turtles Ragarth and Bruto, who look to be managing a smile at my worried glance.

"David, brace for the impact. I don't think these turtles are going to slow down."

David's ears twitch, and his eyes are still focused on the floating island in the sky.

"David!" I say aloud.

He ignores me. I hold Elizabeth in my left arm, bracing her to my chest, while my right hand has a death grip on the boat's side. We hit the shore and catch on the sand the way a fast rollercoaster stops at the end. Tate seems more prepared for the stop as if he expected it. David, however, was too lost in thought. He shoots forward like a human cannonball and lands in the sand two meters in front of the boat.

David slid on all fours and rose up to his feet covered in pearl white sand. "Pwuh Pwuh Pwuh!" David spit out clumps of sand. "Hey … Pwuh. What happened?"

"You weren't paying attention again."

I look around at some angered turtle faces as a few were pointing their spears at David. There was a deluge of foreign and English chatter amongst the turtles, trying to talk to Ula. "A hatchling … not human … part shifter … smells familiar ... evil … kill it now."

As the turtles begin to surround David, I hand Elizabeth over to Tate and pick up my bow. "I've had enough of this!" I holler, my anger starting to boil. We've done nothing to give them the impression we are hostile or evil. They seem bent on harming my brother, and if David shifts, I'm sure they won't think twice about trying to kill him.

Determined to protect David, I shrug off Tate's warnings and jump off the boat. All Tate cares about is protecting Elizabeth. We're merely pawns to him. My skin heats up as I push the turtle line and step in front of my brother.

David is shaking physically, trying to hold onto his dominance in human form. His fists clench, he takes a wide stance, and he looks back and forth between many snarling turtles in ice armor. Already I see the start of pointed furry ears through the top of his hair. The pain the turtles are causing my brother pisses me off.

I turn my back to my brother and hear the growl resonating from behind me. The turtles listen to it also and start to uniformly swirl their ice spears, causing a freezing mist to around us. I ball up my fists, one still holding onto my longbow. Rational thought escapes me as the buildup of heat is too much to hold back.

A small explosion from within ignites my skin ablaze and sends a heatwave in all directions knocking back every turtle. The female water turtles behind their faulting line gasp as all they can see now is a human torch pointing a flaming bow and arrow at the head of their leader Ula. Out of the corner of my eye, I see Tate shake his head and bite his knuckle.

My focus returns to Ula for her decision. Will she allow this threat or back her turtles off?

She looks at Tate, cocks one eye at him, and asks, "Why didn't you tell me about your gifted hatchlings? This does not bode well for either of them. Attacking us on our own island requires harsh punishment."

The turtles regroup into formation, and the water wielding turtles start to twirl their tridents in the air. Slowly whirlpools of water rise up into the air.

Tate sputters. "They are very closely bonded brothers. This one saw your initial intention to do harm to his brother. It's only natural for him to protect his own. They have more power then they even know. I would be careful about how you proceed."

That statement perks up my ears. Do we really have more power then we know, or is Tate just saying that? *How could he know how much power we have?*

The turtles hold their ground, preparing for battle, and I keep mine. When Ula does not respond to Tate, the standoff continues. For a moment, I really believe we're in a dangerous spot, and we might not get out of it alive. We are surrounded and outmanned five to one. Tate is not even lifting a finger to come to help us. Either he thinks we can handle it or he's saving his own butt so Elizabeth can get the cure.

"What in the Lich's bane is going on here?" A foreboding but still feminine voice bellows behind us. I turn my head slightly to see a group of – I do a double-take -- goats walking on their hind legs. They are more humanoid than those I'm used to on our farm, but the long-haired coat and sharp horns protruding above their floppy ears are irrefutably the same. I look down at their hooves, but they make no prints are in the sand. Strange.

This authoritative goat scans the scene. Everything seems to have frozen in place while the goat woman glares from Tate to me, to David, to Ula and back, her gaze locking on mine.

My flames sizzle out, and I lower my bow. David remains half-shifted into Silver. The turtles don't move.

A cold wind caresses my skin. A chill runs down my arms as I mentally pushed the air back to its source a bit more harshly than I anticipated—the female goat steps back as though the goat's leg is fighting for balance in a strong wind. A few of the goats around their leader look at me in surprise.

Ula bows to the female goat. "I have this handled, Salithica! You need not interfere in this matter."

I gulp when I realize I have offended another leader on this island. I sure do know how to piss off a welcoming committee.

The female goat leader, Salithica, unexpectedly looks up at me and smiles. She starts making an off sound. Finally, I realize she is laughing at me. Heat crawls up my neck, and my skin reddens once more, this time with embarrassment. Salithica takes notice and puts up a hand to quiet the turtles' surrounding commotion and her group.

She assumes a stance, not unlike a human with hands on her hips, but goat style. "It looks as though you have made matters worse, Ula … as usual." Her voice is strong and critical. "It seems you haven't noticed you have a natural in your midst … and one with great potential. Granted, he is a human, but we have not seen a human natural in some time. I want to see more of what this young human can do. But before we get to play…" She licks her chops and winks at me. The feeling of bugs crawling up my leg overwhelms me. I wonder precisely what this goat has in mind. "What is the reason these humans were brought here? It is a strict rule for no human to set foot on our land, yet you, Ula, have brought four. Explain yourself!"

Her sarcasm does not go unnoticed. My anger subsides as Salithica expels her wrath onto the pink-nosed tan turtle who, by now, looks a bit frazzled. Ula quickly orders her squad to lower their weapons and magik. Frowns and angry scowls cross the turtles' faces, but they relent and back up behind Ula, giving my brother and me space.

Salithica approached David, who is still shaking, and taps his back with her four-fingered hoof. She talks in a low calming voice. "You may shift. No one will harm you here."

Before she finishes the sentence, David's eyes turned red, and the sounds of tearing cloth breach the silence. Bones snapped and reposition, and a second later, a giant two-plus-meter-tall dire wolf stands in David's place. Salithica wisely stepped back before my brother finished.

Silver is pissed, and his open mouth exhibits sharp oversized fangs. His chest races with heavy breathing, and he darts his head from side to side to get his bearings. More chatter breaks out amongst the turtles. "… evil wolf" to "It's going to kill us all."

"Silver, calm down, don't attack anyone, at least not yet. Let's see what this leader of the goats has to say." I put my arrow back in my quiver and toss my bow back over my shoulder. I move carefully and slowly up to the agitated Silver wolf. His dark gray ears stick out with his mix of grays and

whites in his coat. Some of his slick furs shimmer in the light giving the effect of looking like polished silver strands. A low warning growl emits from his maw.

"Shh. David, you need to take back control. We need your smart-ass brain right now." I stare down Silver, and his eyes fade back to green. My posture relaxes. When I turn to Salithica, who has several of her goats with rock armor standing in front of her, she also seems to relax a notch after sensing a mood change from the dire wolf.

Ula and her squad don't look relaxed or comfortable. I detect that many are grateful they didn't attack.

Ula responds to Salithica's earlier question by saying only one name. "Tate Tumbleson."

At the mention of his name, Tate stands and carries Elizabeth in his arms to Salithica. She doesn't appear the least bit shocked at the mention or presence of Tate.

"That's right; I am Tate Tumbleson, leader of the Guardians for the human king Kiel Qwinzmare of Kinzurdia. This sick girl is Elizabeth." Salithica raises a brow in question before Tate continues.

"You all may be more familiar with her bloodline name Rawena-Rose, daughter of the Kiel and Rosalia Qwinzmare of Kinzurdia."

Shocked gasps ripple through the crowd, turtles and goats alike. Even Salithicas eyes widened. Without delay, Tate proceeds to explain the severity of the situation, that Rawena-Rose was poisoned from the Libitina Mortis plant. "She may not have much time left."

The leader of the Goat people speaks rapidly in a foreign tongue to another two goats. "The princess shall stay supervised with a few of my loyal herbalists back at my camp. However, there are grave topics to be discussed with the rest of the Council at once." She pauses for breath and turns to the turtles. "Ula, send word quickly to the others and prepare the Council for an emergency meeting. Tell your father to meet me at the base of the waterfall. Go!"

Following that command, the turtle squad runs back to the water and speeds off down the coastline. Tate reluctantly allows the two goats to take Elizabeth, warning, "Protect her with your lives."

"Wait! You're going to hand her over like that after they tried to kill us? How can we trust these things to not harm her?" My face heats up again at the thought of losing Elizabeth. David looks ready to pounce as he crouches into a snarling position. The attitudes of the goats holding Elizabeth waver as they look to their leader for confirmation.

Salithica nails me with a stare. "Do not fret young naturally. We are quite aware of who Rawena-Rose is and what she means to our future. She is the one the Spider Witch has been looking for all along.

"The Spider Witch? Who is that?" I ask.

"The Spider Witch is an enemy who has caused us much pain over the last decade, reigning terror and even corrupting one side of our island with the undead in search of her. She is a ruthless monster turning many of our tribe members into the walking undead. She takes orders straight from the Lich himself, who has taken over the Qwinzmare Human Kingdom of Kinzurdia. Rawena-Rose was assumed missing or even dead because no one has seen or heard from Keil or Rosalia since the kingdom fell thirteen years ago."

"That's not comforting me in any way. Doesn't that mean Elizabeth is the cause of all your pain?"

The leader of the Goats ponders my question for a moment. "Hmm. I do see your point. Some of us do consider humans to be the cause of much pain to us. But most of us remember the freedom we once had when the Qwinzmares ruled over Kinzurdia. "

"I thought you welcomed the humans, and they helped you fight off your enemies?"

"You are correct. The humans were good fighters and kept the Lich's minions from coming near our island. It is now an everyday battle against the corruption set upon our land by the Lich and his five powerful creations. We believe the rumors to be true that Rosalia Qwinzmare is the prophesized savior to our Kinzurdian Realm. Because of that, we will protect the princess with our lives."

She stares at me with conviction and goosebumps trail up my arms, followed by a warm tingly sensation. At that moment, I know she speaks the truth. That she would die for Elizabeth to survive. Frozen in her gaze, I can only nod to her and Tate, allowing them to take Elizabeth away.

When they have gone, Salithica calls a black-haired goat to her side. "Floyd. Escort these three to the waterfall." She turns to walk away, and David growled low.

"David, calm Silver down. She will be safe with the goats."

She captures my gaze with her eyes and holds them while she speaks sternly. "Keep your brother in human form for the Council of Elders. Otherwise, I might not be able to avoid something happening to him. As you can see, we are not fond of humans, but Dire wolves are ruthless evil creatures that we kill on sight. If I hadn't seen your brother's human form first, I would have killed him myself without questioning it. Be grateful I was here and that I am willing to take a chance on you, human." With that, she turned and floated back into the tree line disappearing from the site.

Floyd, the remaining goat in rock armor, spoke up in a high pitched squeal. "You three humans follow me to the lake." I start to step forward, but the goat didn't move.

"Uh, didn't you say for us to follow you?"

The goat looked at me, then to the giant dire wolf, then back at me. "Yes"

"But you aren't moving," I say, thinking this is one dumb goat.

The goat smirks and looks right at me answering, "Not yet."

I look around us; there's no one else on the beach but the goat Tate and David. I'm starting to redden, and it doesn't go unnoticed by the goat.

The goat sighs and says, "You humans are really dumb, did you not understand what master Salithica told you?"

I'm still clueless. Tate is standing behind me like a quiet statue. David chimes into my head using his smart brain of his. *"I think they want me to shift back into human form, but I shredded my clothes."* I slap my hand to my forehead. *Duh!*

I clear my throat and ask the armored goat: "Do you have a spare set of clothes my brother could wear?" I indicate the shreds of cloth that lay near my brother's feet. The goat realizes what I mean and makes odd-sounding snickers before looking up and around for anyone nearby.

"A shifter who can't shift its own clothes? I have the perfect clothes for him, don't worry."

I step away from David as he shifts back to human form, crouching like the terminator. He looks up and around the goat, eyeing him in front. "So … the clothes are where?"

"They are on their way." The goat raises his nunchucks and swirls them in the air. A gust of wind whips out of the forest carrying green, orange, red, and brown leaves. The wind encircles David and lifts his body up, straightening him out. The leaves are thick and stick to him and each other creating a colorful garment of sorts. The wind dies down, and the excess leaves fall to the sandy beach. I can't help but crack up at what my brother is wearing.

David looks down and around his back then back at the goat, crossing his arms. "No, no. I am not wearing *this*. There is no way."

"Well, it's your choice. It's either this or all-natural? Either way, you will be going to the Council in human form and be judged by everyone there."

My brother is pissed but has no choice but to wear the goat's selection of style given. We walk in silence as Tate and I both try to not look at him, afraid we'll crack up at his appearance. We walk down the beach in the direction the turtles went earlier. In the forest tree line to the left of us, I hear the sounds of a jungle alive with odd animal calls, bird chirps, snapping branches, all sounding in chaotic harmony.

Chapter 10

The Decision
David

I look down again at the garment made of vibrant, colorful leaves. It barely feels like I'm wearing anything, but I can't believe this is what I will be wearing to meet this island's leaders. The stupid goat assured me it is a custom look on this island, but the snickering sound from him and James's laughs make me think otherwise.

It's a dress. It even cups my pecks in an orange outline. While it's utterly ridiculous, it's better than going with my birthday suit. So I will have to swallow my pride and ignore the humiliation.

We eat him later, yes? Silver chimes in, and I actually ponder it for a few seconds.

Before the change, I would never have thought to eat any prepared raw meat, let alone straight off a breathing corpse, but this last year has proven to change my perspective. No, we can't do that, Silver. That might cause another standoff that we won't be able to get out of like last time. I can feel Silver's excitement over the prospective kill diminish.

We get back him, yes!

Silver is reading my mind since we share it. I thought that I'd find an excellent way to repay his kindness ten-fold, and Silver is learning sarcasm. My planning with Silver gets interrupted as we arrive at a crescent-shaped pond with the opening spilling out into the sea.

There is a large waterfall falling from what looks like misty clouds above. Across the pond, I see a dramatic difference in the tree line. The colorful living trees end abruptly and beyond, a devastating dark patch of broken or rotted tree limbs. The overwhelming sense of evil vibrates through my bones. Silver emphasizes his discomfort by micturating a tiny bit down my leg.

"David, do you remember the floating island … you saw…?" James inquires, then gazes upward. His words die out.

I follow his gaze. At first, all I see is the water falling from clouds. Our bond warmed up, and our dire wolf senses engaged. The sea's salty smell, the crisp fresh unpolluted air, the warmth from the sun, the velvety texture of the leaves on my body all came to focus in on our sight.

It's like looking through a scoped rifle or seeing through the eyes of an eagle. Our vision clears out the mist, and I realize we are observing the underside of a floating island. It has small rocks that orbit around its cone-shaped bottom. The rocks and dirt line end before the edges near vibrant green grass and bushes hangover. Being in the center of the island, the waterfall has a never-ending flow of water. "Whoa, it's beautiful."

This would be perfect if I wasn't wearing a dress made of leaves held together by my own sweat.

Tate, James, and I followed the rock-armored goat into the lake. We notice Salithica standing near the base of the waterfall, talking to a large shell. The shell turned toward us, and a scrawny looking wrinkled round-nosed turtle looked us over. Coming closer, I was surprised to hear Salithica talking in English to the turtle and not in her native tongue. The turtle looked as if he had crawled into a shell much too big for him. His covering had multiple engravings in it—much more than any of the recently encountered turtles. I used our bond to listen to the conversation between the two as it looked like the old looking turtle was putting up quite a fuss. One of his wrinkled hands was clutched around a staff or walking stick while his other seemed to be waving in the air frantically to show emphasis on what he was discussing. The turtle looked like it was mad, but it's a turtle; when have I ever seen one smile.

"....No Way. We will not break our rules again for more humans." The turtle had a slow grumbly voice.

"May I remind you, your daughter already has broken the rule and brought them to our island. It is now our responsibility to see this issue through. it is our duty as the leaders of our island." Salithica sternly pointed out.

"Why should we help them after they have already threatened my only daughter? They do not deserve our aid after their actions."

"That may be true, but let's see what their full intentions are, and plus, we have their princess in my hut. We can test them to see how they react. Also, it's not like our flying friends are going to lift a finger."

We start to walk up to them within the normal hearing range. "Fine, have it your … ehehemm" The elderly turtle clears his throat and looks us over before staring at me. One of his eyes goes up, and he tilts his head at me. "Human, do you not have any better attire? You look foolish in that celebration leaf dress the forest nannies wear. I hear a few snickers from the kid goat behind us.

I swallow my pride and shake my head. "Suit yourself, This will be an interesting meeting." The turtle looks at Tate for a moment longer than usual before redirecting his attention back to his daughter and her battalion of turtles. "My name is Chondro, the Chieftain of the tortoise clans and leader of all sea magik for our Island of Kywenenyeh." I feel a bit smaller now in this dress, knowing he is a major player in deciding my fate. Another turtle waddles up to his side. Chondro ushers this turtle to his side before putting a hand on his shell shoulder.

"This here is my right-hand man and my son, Konja." The turtle looks a lot like his father with green skin with scattered black blemishes, a rounded nose, and a genuine sense of calmness radiating from him. "He will be escorting Mr. Tumbleson up to our leader sanctuary." Konja nods at Tate, who follows Konja to the waterfall.

"What is Tate doing?" James asks through our connection. *"How are we going to get up to that island if that's where the sanctuary is?"*

"I'm not sure .... Whoa!" I reply while my gaze is glued on Tate as he climbs atop Konja's shell, and the turtle then shoots straight up the waterfall like a rocket.

"Brutus! Ragarth! Take the two hatchlings up." Chondro orders authoritatively. The turtles don't even blink as they come right for us. I took an attentive step back. I couldn't tell which large turtle was about to grab me.

James looks like he's about to run.

"Calm down, James. Close your eyes. We will be up there in no time."

James is still a bit terrified of heights, and this looks like no joke since we can only see the bottom of the island with our bonded sight. From James' point of view, it probably looks like Tate disappeared into the storm clouds above.

At first, I thought we would ride the turtles up like Tate did, but apparently, 'Hatchlings' have a different position. The turtles squished us to their underbelly in an awkward bear hug, and we start to twirl in a circle before the feeling of being shot out of a canon overcame me. It was quite a thrilling five-second ride if you get past the back cracking and the dizzy feeling on the way up.

James and I both puke our guts out once we're released onto the soft grass next to a free-flowing stream. James makes the mistake of crawling to close to the edge and peering down. He recoils back and dry heaves while holding his head. He is sitting on a golden glowing orb. I look down the edge and see several more at the edges of the grass.

The surrounding white structures, made of stone – maybe marble – have small openings in both the large and short rounded buildings, and thick white clouds overlap as if connecting them to each other. Some structures look as if they float on the clouds while small clouds move about like flying objects. A couple passed right in front of us, and I discovered little monkeys were riding the clouds like surfboards.

The grass is vibrantly green around the white structures, and myriads of colored flowers line the pathways to white steps. The crystal blue stream flowing through the center of this floating island glistens under the sun, but I am well-shaded by large, bushy, fruit-laden trees. Everything looked elegant and wonderful ... except for one thing.

Far overhead, a dark gray cloud sends sporadic lightning streaking through the clouds. It hovered directly over the sizeable white-domed structure to the left of the stream.

Two of the monkeys riding clouds approach us and gesture toward the massive dome. We stare. One of the monkeys pushes me forward a few steps. Altogether, James, Tate, and I follow the pathway lined with gold and white flowers to the steps.

When we reach the top, we are ushered into a large room, much like a courtroom, but instead of one judge's seat, there are four. The seats are spaced a couple of meters apart.

The white stone seems to be a common decorative trait up on this island. Each podium appears to be very different in sizes and sports a unique symbol on its front.

The one to the far right is a yellow and white lightning bolt in front of a small empty chair. Next to it, the emblem depicts a blue and white tidal wave, and the seat facing it is a much wider chair with two poles shooting up from the armrests and no back to the seat. Next, left of center, the green and brown symbol resembles a tree. The chair is much like my old computer chair at home. And finally, on the far left is a massive podium showcasing a red and orange fire symbol. Behind it, there is no seat at all, only giant double doors.

That strikes me as odd since most of the doors in the building seem exceptionally small. *What could possibly be big enough to need a door that large to enter this room?*

Silver relays a message to my brain, pointing out several species of animals that frequent this room, but he cannot pinpoint which types other than the turtles and goats. It's eerily quiet in this domed shaped room as we stand in the middle, still looking at empty podiums.

"Soooo, what are we supposed to do, Tate?" James crosses his arms over his chest and strikes an annoyed pose, tapping his shoe's toe.

Tate puffs up indignantly. "You dare ask me this question when you are the reason we're standing in the first place instead of securing the antidote for my princess. If princess Rawena-Rose dies, I will hold you responsible!" Tate raises his voice with every word to the point of almost yelling at my brother.

"Grrrrrr." A low growl emanates from my throat. Both James and Tate gape at me with shocked faces.

"David, control Silver, or we may all end up dead." James sends a quick mental message.

Simultaneously a few lemurs fly in through the large door on the puffy white clouds. Tate bites his lip to keep from spewing out whatever retort he had intended to make.

Instead, he whispers, "James, David … the leaders are about to enter. Don't speak unless spoken to." Tate eyes the lemurs flying circles around us. Their furry little smiling faces don't comfort me in the least. I doubt they were intended to.

The first leader to enter, a light-pink colored lemur, wears a long elegant white gown and a golden crown of some sort. The train of the dress is lifted above the floor by two other floating lemurs. The black and brown lemurs sit on their clouds on either side of the lightning bolt symbol on the podium.

The second leader is one we have already met at the waterfall ... the turtle whose body appeared too small for his shell. Now the poles made sense to me. A chair back wouldn't support a turtle shell evenly. He was accompanied by Ula and Konja, who we met at the waterfall as well. They held a staff and spear.

The symbols begin to make sense to me now. Turtles showed water affinities. The lemurs' emblem must mean that they deal in air or lightning affinities.

James bumps me and frowns. I read the gesture as a signal to stop staring at the floating lemurs and notice the goat entering the room.

Salithica takes her seat behind the tree podium, accompanied by two other goats. One is the starkly little goat who decided a gown of leaves was appropriate garb for me. I can't help glaring at Floyd.

The goats carry no weapons. Salithica flashes us a genuine smile and then looks at my brother and winks.

What have we here? *"Hey, James. I think that goat lady really likes you."*

"Come on. She's only being nice."

"Really. If goats could flirt, I'm sure that's what it would look like."

"I think you better worry about those lemurs getting to close to you. One might fly up your dress."

I hear my brother laughing in his thoughts and tune him out. I try not to look down at this ridiculous getup I'm wearing and swear to myself that I will pay back that goat for this.

Mentally, James taps my mind again, but I want none of his teasings. I'm still looking down at my colorful garment when James nudges me hard. I look up to shoot daggers from my eyes only to drop my jaw. Now I understand the purpose of the large doorway.

There before me, approaching the fire podium walks a humongous, real-life red dragon. Its giant wings are folded up at its sides, and the long claws scrape the stone floor as it walks. The horn-scaled face looks directly at me before blowing smoke out its nostrils. I can't tell if the gargantuan is male or female. I am entranced by its gaze, or maybe I'm fascinated to learn that dragons actually exist.

My eyes shift to a large-type creature that reminds me of a small, scaled Godzilla. The lizard stood upright with scaly skin, sharp teeth, metal armor, and swords. It captured my stare, and I hear it snicker. The more massive reptile that steps up to the dragon's right side reminds me of a fat turtle … both in a shell and in thickness. It bears the fire symbol on its shell and the metal armor across its chest. His fierce demeanor is supported by a battle scar across his face. He lugs a large sword attached to its shell next to its snapping turtle head.

"James!" I project my thoughts toward my brother. "I thought there was an obvious pattern regarding who is in which tribe, but now I'm not so sure. Why do you think that turtle is next to the dragon?"

He seemed to consider a moment, then shook his head slightly. *"I don't know. Just stay quiet, and let's get this over with. We need to get that antidote soon, or Elizabeth is going to die."*

The giant door shuts as soon as all the leaders take their positions behind their podiums. I steal a glance at Tate out of the corner of my eye and notice him bow gracefully. James and I copy his motions.

Salithica speaks up first. "We have called this rushed meeting to discuss an important opportunity and serious situation that can greatly affect our traditions and our rules on our island. I have an important guest in my quarters who needs urgent attention, so we will need to come to a decision quickly."

The dragon stares at us without blinking, not making any movement to speak.

Salithica looks to Chondro and the elegant leader of the lemurs. Neither of them move or speak. "Well, then I will start with introductions. I am Salithica, leader of the forest tribe. The infamous lemur on your right is Leena, leader of the storm tribe and owner of this fabulous floating island." Leena nods at Salithica's kind words before looking in any direction that's not us. She seems like a Verreaux's sifaka or an all-white coated lemur with a black face and pink nose. "You three have met Chondro, leader of the Sea tribe, and his two grown hatchlings Ula and Konja."

My brother nods before a "yep" escapes my mouth. Salithica frowns, and the volcanic tribe turtle rushes to me, pushing me up against the far back wall leaving fire streaks on the floor. He draws his sword and rests it against my neck. I can hardly gulp, and Silver wants nothing more than to shift and tear him to shreds. I start to vibrate. James takes a sharp breath, but he must know he can't help me.

The turtle looks into my eyes, and he takes the shaking as fear, not as me holding back a shift. Salithica's voice is heard barely over the pounding of my heart.

"Let him go, Therose. He meant no disrespect."

"He is human." He spits out the word like it fouls his mouth. "He is disrespectful standing before me. None of them should be still alive." Therose pulls back his sword as if about to slice me in two.

"Therose. Halt!" A deep roar comes from the left side of the room behind this fire turtle. The turtle doesn't want to let me live, but he must obey his commander, the now-angry red dragon. There is no room for discussion, for defiance, on this matter. I look over Therose's shoulder and see the dragon's full wingspan and fire escaping his snout's corners.

"Now that you have met Therose meet Zyerr, leader of the draconian volcanic tribe." Therose throws me to the ground. James moves to step forward, only to be held back by Tate's arm. Therose re-sheaths his sword and stands back by Zyerr's side, locking his glare with mine.

"Now that we have the pleasantries out of the way let's get down to why we have three humans standing before us. Ula! Please come in front and explain why you broke our sacred rule of no humans and brought four of them to our Island of Kywenenyeh."

When Salithica names Ula, both Chondro and Ula stand and speak in their native tongue. From the looks of Chondro's anger, he is quite unpleased with his daughter's actions.

Ula bows her head and saunters until she is in front of us. Zyerr is done being silent and speaks first. "How dare you bring such vile creatures on my island? I should have your brother roast you over a fire for this treason." Ula's head shrunk beneath her shell, further with every harsh word uttered by Zyerr.

"Enough!" Chondro stands and speaks directly at Ula. "I am sure she had a good reason to override such an important ruling.

"Be lucky your father is a leader, or I would barbeque you myself!"

"If you dare harm one scale on my daughter's shell, I will put you in a block of ice so cold you couldn't melt your way out of it."

"Enough!" Leena, the little lemur, jumps to her feet and encases both leaders in whirlwinds of air. "I want to hear Ula's reason for breaking our rule before you two destroy my building." A few of the floating lemurs on clouds guided both angry leaders back to their podiums.

"What did we get ourselves into this time?" I mentally ask my brother.

"I don't know, but I don't want to get between them in a fight." James swallows and sticks his hands in his pockets to keep them from shaking.

Salithica steps back in. "Ula, please tell us why you have brought four humans into our domain."

Ula pokes her head out of her shell and clears her throat. "It would be best if Tate Tumbleson explained in detail. I didn't want a confrontation with a royal guardian of the overthrown Human Kingdom." There is a general gasp among those present on hearing Tate's name again. What is it that Tate has done to continually have that reaction? Ula bows her head as all the eyes are now glued on Tate.

Salithica motions for Ula to return and for Tate to step forward. "Tate Tumbleson, please explain your reasoning to trespass onto our island, and tell those present who the fourth human is to the rest of us."

Tate steps forward, adjusting his clothing. He speaks clearly and with authority, like a general giving a speech to his troops.

"I am Tate Tumbleson Royal Guardian of the Qwinzmare Kingdom. You all know how the King and his family escaped through a portal thirteen years ago. At that time, I was charged with guarding and protecting their daughter Rawena-Rose Qwinzmare. I am not certain of whether or not the King and Queen survived the attacks from the Drargs, but their daughter did survive and has returned to inspire hope and regain her birthright to the throne of Kinzurdia's Qwinzmare Kingdom."

Zyerr pipes up. "If she has returned, where is she? Why is she not with you now?"

"That is a reasonable question," Tate replies. "She is not present because she has been poisoned by the thorns of the Libitina Mortis plant. She is in grave need of an antidote, and very quickly."

The lemurs in the room all hissed when they heard the name of the plant.

Leena stood up and spoke, "We know much pain from the plant you speak of. I see now why you have come to this island for such a cure. The antidote is made from the venom of a rare snake that happens to call our island home. There are very few places in the world to have this rare breed of snake. We also see the importance of why she must be protected if humans even have a chance at taking back their kingdom. A kingdom without hope is a dead kingdom. I will grant a pardon for you and your guests until she is cured."

Salithica speaks up. "I second the motion to allow these humans to have restricted access to the island."

Chondro chimes in. "I do not like how easily my daughter let you come to the island, but her reasoning was correct. I also will grant a pardon."

Zyerr lets out a few more puffs of smoke before speaking. "I will never pardon humans. But for the greater good of what may come from this decision and for my strict rule of never harming hatchlings regardless of race, I will agree to this decision to allow these humans temporary access to cure their sick one."

I let out a breath I didn't know I was holding and look to James. "*Whew. I'm glad that's over with. Now we can get the antidote and get out of here.*" Tate returns to standing next to us.

Salithica speaks again. "Since the girl is already at my hut, I will also grant shelter to these three until she has recovered. But there is one more thing that you three must do. A choice must be made for who will stay and who will retrieve the snake's venom?"

Tate pipes in before either of us get to speak. "I will stay with my princess. These two will retrieve the venom from the snake."

James speaks in my head. "*Oh, that is how he is going to play it. I think we can catch a small snake and bring it back to the hut. This won't take too long at all.*"

"*James, I don't think it's going to be that simple.*"

"You have to stop over-complicating things. Tate has always been all about 'Protect the Princess.' He decided for us so we wouldn't look any worse to the leaders."

"Sure, James, but I have this--"

"No buts. We'll capture the snake, receive the antidote for Elizabeth, and get the heck off this island."

"With that decision, our meeting is adjourned. Please leave our floating island at once. You all are no longer welcome here." Leena then dismisses everyone with a small wave of her hands like shooing away an unwanted dog.

The thought is prevalent in my mind, and Silver growls low. Stares from the lemurs made me quickly cough to cover up the mishap. James and Tate pulled me out the side door as all the leaders and their officer's exit through the other.

Chapter 11

The Hunt for Paracoubler
James

We arrive at the waterfall in time to observe the last of the turtles jumping off the island's side, leaving us stranded. That evil turtle and the other reptile hop on Zyerr's back and fly off toward the volcano.

"Well, that's great! Now, what are we going to do?" I throw my arms in the air, exasperated. "Do they really expect us to survive that fall?"

"No. Not unless you use some storm or sea magik." At the sound of a familiar voice, the three of us turn to Salithica, hovering only a few centimeters above the ground.

"How are you able to float there?" I'm amazed at the control she has over the air.

"So you are interested. I thought you might want to leave after I cure your friend."

"Uh, well…"

"Don't be too hasty to depart. There's more to our island than you can fathom. We are an island of elementalists."

Wait a minute. That makes so much sense and explains the symbols and the magik show displayed in the meeting.

"So, how do we get down from here? Can you teach us to fly?"

"No, no, no. Goats don't fly, silly. We are attuned to nature, which is why we are the herbalists on this island, but we can manipulate small amounts of the other magik to benefit ourselves. Such as the small air that pushes me off the ground."

"I'm sure this interests the boys," Tate interrupts, "but please, leader Salithica, take me to Rawena-Rose. I must see her at once." He glares at David and me with an annoyed frown and squinty eyes. He can hardly standstill.

"Yes, Yes, of course. Let us go down and see Rawena-Rose." Salinthica points one finger out in front of her, spins it around, and snaps her finger at each of our feet.

"Whoa. Oh, James!" David grasps frantically at my shoulder for balance. I'm having a hard time maintaining my own equilibrium.

It feels as though we are standing on a slippery frozen pond. Only Tate looks stable and not having any trouble. He gave the nod to Salithica and jumped off the edge.

It has been confirmed. Tate is crazy.

"Don't look surprised, young natural. Tate has had a bit more experience with magik than you two. It's time to go. The spell I cast only lasts for a short time, so I suggest you follow quickly. Oh, and do remember the air is under your feet. Do not dive headfirst." With that said, she looks at me, winks, and floats right off the edge, dropping like the turtles.

"They are both crazy," I say. *Oh, Heck, no!*

"James, you need to put trust in someone." David tries to reason with me. "So far, Salithica has saved our butts through this entire situation. Besides, she likes you."

"That is so weird. How can a goat-like a human? Besides, everyone here hates us, so that can't be true. There must be something else behind why she is so nice to us."

"There is only one way to find out," my brother tries again. "And that is to take a leap of faith … literally. C'mon, James. Let's go find that snake and save Elizabeth."

David pushes me to the edge while I try frantically to move in another direction. I think of Elizabeth. What if I lose her just because I'm too chicken to jump? That would haunt me forever.

"Okay." I try to build enough confidence to jump off a cliff when I can't see the ground below. "On the count of three, we both jump."

"Okay. You start the count."

"One… " I drag out the word as long as I can.

"Two."

"Thr…"

David jumps and pulls me with him. Wind rushes past my ears, and we are free-falling in a gray-white mist, tumbling over and around until the clouds dissipate, and the treetops come into focus, lining a crescent pond. Somehow David finds a way to work into an upright position. I'm freaking out and can't keep my feet pointed down. David shoots down faster in his narrower shape. My blood starts to boil. *I will not die like a bug on a windshield.*

Fire bursts out of my palms, and with a bit of struggling, I manage to stabilize myself in the air before floating down. I land on the ground gracefully. The air under my feet cushions the landing … I don't even feel the jolt in my knees. David's eyes widen with amazement, and Salithica smiles more than expected.

"Come, your princess doesn't have much time. I know the area where Paracoubler resides, but, as you probably suspected, this snake is not normal. It's quite unpredictable and nearly impossible to sneak up to. David can easily help you find your way back to my hut when you have the snake." She starts hovering between trees like an ice-skater. David has no idea how to control the air, and he looks back at me with red glowing eyes.

"Whoa. Don't do it, Silver."

I turn around quickly. No one is around but us. I look back to where

David stood and see a tail whip around the tree ahead of me. A colorful cloud of leaves flutters to the ground in its wake.

"That's just great!" I stare at my feet. How is Salithica able to control the air beneath her? I concentrate hard, but nothing happens … so I do what I did in the air. Flames burst out of my hands, moving me about. I instinctually lean forward and stretch my hands behind slowly.

I'm moving forward. I endeavor to keep my feet together like Salithica, but it's no use. My legs move about like a rag doll dropped from a roof. Aiming directly toward a large tree. I get that frozen feeling where you can't do anything because you know you are going to hit it. I think frantically, and a warm sensation travels through my body into my feet. Fire bursts from under my right foot, and I shot far to the left … lining up to another massive tree. I stick my left arm out and slow my trajectory in time to feel another burst of power from under my left foot, launching me up and over the trees.

Then I maneuver a slow forward flip and begin to descend. I manage to twist around and see the ground getting closer. *That's not good.* There's no time to think. I stick my arms out in front of me, but my flames have blown out. I cross my arms over my face and brace for impact.

Nothing. The pain of hitting hard never comes. Instead, soft wisps of air caress my cheeks as I look up from my arms and open my eyes to see both Silver and Salithica standing in front of me, staring. Silver is growling and in a fighting stance. Salithica looks to be slightly astonished at my entrance.

"Thanks for cushioning my fall, Salithica. That could have been pretty messy."

She blinks her eyes. "You think I would help you after you let your brother change into this hideous creature. I told you he cannot shift here. He will cause many problems for all of us." There's no question about how she feels.

Now I blink in confusion. "So, if you didn't cushion my fall, who did?"

"Stupid human, you stop you." Silver spoke in my mind while licking his chops at Salithica.

"David, take back control before Silver gets any dumb ideas about dinner."

Silver's red eyes fade into a bright green after their wolf's head shakes. Salithica's posture relaxes at the calmness now resonating from David.

"Tell him to shift back now before someone else sees him."

"He can't. He shredded that leaf gown your goat made for him."

"Ah! That explains why he was wearing that Nannie gown. Well, perhaps, for now, it's best to leave him in this state. He can help you find the Paracoubler's trail faster." Salithica has flipped direction from her previous statement. "I will warn my tribe to not kill a dire wolf with green eyes. But if his eyes go red again, I will not punish anyone for killing him."

"That is if you even could…" I say softly.

She does that hand on hips thing. It is so strange seeing a goat do that.

"Do not underestimate us, hatchling. We are more than mere herbalists. When you get back from your encounter with Paracoubler, I will show you what it is meant to be a part of our forest tribe. The snake you are looking for is black and has a yellow underbelly. It hides close to the tree line and the sands. The venom from that snake has a powerful anti-poison that cures itself of any poison it encounters.

"Is it poisonous?"

"No. It's non-poisonous, but its own venom has a nasty side effect, so try not to let its fangs pierce you. Need I remind you, this is a scarce breed of a snake, and you are forbidden to kill it. If you do, I do not have enough power to stop the other leaders from feeding you to the undead on Leena's pond's far side."

The thought of being a meal for another undead crocodile sends shivers down my spine.

"Okay, fine snake, but don't kill it," I begin recapping the mission. "Bring the snake to you unharmed, but don't get bitten." Simple enough. "Got it. Let's go, David!" I give Salithica a finger wave. "Thanks for the advice. Bye."

Silver sprints out in front of me to the shoreline. We have wasted too much time already; I hope we won't be too late to save Elizabeth.

I run to the trees' edge and see the sun slowly falling down toward the water line in the distance, reflecting its orange glow over the water's surface. It doesn't take long before I hear David speaking in my head.

"This way, James. Down the coast, I think I found it."

"Which way is this way?"

"The sun is on my left. Hurry. It's moving away!" I run down the coast flinging up sand, looking for my brother. My connection with him helps pull me in his direction. Finally, I get close enough to see the wolf crouched low, staring straight ahead. A couple of trees are blocking my view as I move in closer. I hear my Dire wolf brother speaking. I step closer, but the tree still blocks my vision.

"Why do you always get to lead? I want to go this way for a change."

"I'm the dominant one, so we always go forward."

"No, you like to go backward. It's time I go forwards."

"When you can catch dinner, you can be the dominant one."

"How am I able to do that when you keep dragging me away from my prey?"

What the heck? Who's talking?

I peek around the tree and see the snake's head rear up and hiss at the other snakehead nearby. The heads are quite large, at least the size of a football, and the same thickness around the bodies.

And its length…! I try to determine how long it is. The body leads right into the other head.

It's a three-meter-long, double-headed snake. I suck in a sudden breath of surprise.

David must have heard me because he turns his snout toward me. *"You didn't think it was gonna be a garden snake, did you?"*

He's right about that. Shifting my weight, I move closer to the tree. A small twig snaps and both snakeheads turned in our direction, hissing. David's eyes fade to red, and the snakes stopped their hissing.

"Time to run!"

"Follow me!"

The snakeheads stretched out in opposite directions and ended up not moving anywhere.

"You are unbelievable!" one head says to the other.

"I'm unbelievable? You always get to go your way, and your way lands us in these situations." The snake maneuvers itself into a U-shape. "Fine, we both go forward."

They take off quite fast, and we chase behind them.

"Silver, you can't kill it. Please let David come back."

I hear my brother's voice in my head again, *"You have a good point. There is not much we can do in this form to not harm the snake. We will go around ahead and try to trap it between us."*

"Good idea! Let's do this for Elizabeth." David takes off to the left and uses his bond to speed ahead of the snake's path. I update David through our connection in which way we are heading.

I'm gaining on the snake right as one of the heads whips around and stares at me. I see the tree they are heading for, and a smile tweaks the corners of my mouth. The snakehead looking at me isn't paying attention. They slam their midsection right into the base of the tree. The sudden stop of their fast momentum wraps their heads around the trunk of the tree. A cloud of leaves fall from above.

"I told you to go around the tree!" one hisses at the other.

"I did go around the tree at leassst three times," the second rebuts.

"No, you were supposssed to go left."

"You didn't say go left, ssso I went to the right."

"Ooh, I swear if I wasn't attached to you, I would devour you."

This snake has some severe issues. *"David, where are you? The snake trapped himself."* I get silence in return. Great! That means I have to untangle this snake and knock it out myself.

"Alright, Mr. Paracoubler. It's time to go help my friend." I walk up to the twisted snake carefully.

"We are not going anywhere with yousss!"

"Well, I asked nicely." I walk a bit closer, holding my hands carefully out in front of me.

"We don't care, Humansss are no good liars who ate our sistersss and wrapped their feet in our kin's ssskin. No human can be trusssted!"

"Well, in that case..." I lunge for one head and wrap my legs around its neck. I put it into a chokehold trying to knock it out like I saw on TV once. Unfortunately, the head I choose to grab is the stupid one. The smart head unravels its body enough to snap at me. I try to punch his head and only manage to hit the tree instead. I pummel the bucking dumb head until it goes limp and sends me to the ground with the wind knocked out of me.

"A little help here, David would be nice." I send it to David. In return, all I hear is, *"Phew! That thing sure reeks ... Fine ... bring it with us. James, we are on our way; we had a slight detour."*

"Yeah, sure. Whatever. Just get your butt back here. This snake isn't playing nice." I cough and try to get up. I look up and see the large outstretched jaw of an angry reptile. Its fangs look like ten-centimeter-long needles. I raise my right arm to fend off the snake. Two sharp fangs penetrate my arm.

"Ouch!" I cry. My muscles start to contract, and I can no longer move. I hear the snake slither away. This was my only chance of saving Elizabeth, and I failed. I blackout.

Rustling leaves greet me when I awake. Grunts come from my locked open mouth.

The fuzzy dark red night sky comes into focus. Even though my eye muscles work, the rest of me can't move. The red moon glow illuminates only my right arm that is still paralyzed above me. I reach out with my thoughts to David. "What happened? Where am I? Where is the snake?"

"Sorry, James. The snake was gone when I found you paralyzed. You look as though you're trying to block the sun from your eyes. I tried to roll you over to get you to wake up, but you rolled like a tumbleweed stuck in the same position."

"So how am I moving? I can see branches passing over my arm, yet I feel nothing?"

"Yeah, about that... Due to your condition, there was no way to carry you safely through the woods, soo ... I'm currently dragging you by your foot. Just be glad you can't feel anything. You'd probably be in a lot of pain since one of my fangs sliced right through your boot. Plus, we've hit a few bumps on the way. But don't worry. You should be fine. A few minutes with a healing spell, and you'll be good as new."

"What! Are you kidding me? I am going to kick your butt when I can move again." A pungent odor slips past my nose. *"Eww. What is that smell?"*

"Oh, that? That's ... ah, that is from uh..."

"David ... What is it?"

"Well, we picked up a helpless critter on the way back to you."

"You're telling me I'm paralyzed because you and Silver decided to pick up some helpless animal during an important hunt to save Elizabeth, the one person who is the hope for all mankind in this world?"

"He was hurt and scared, Silver smelled his fear, and we couldn't ignore him. We picked him up out of a discarded box of rotten fruit." I can feel the sincerity in his thoughts. The heart-ache both Silver and David felt for this weak little creature. The torn feeling they had to save the beast or run to aid me in battle. *"We thought he would cheer up Elizabeth when she wakes up. We didn't realize you weren't strong enough to take on that confused snake. Silver and I apologize, but not all is lost, James."*

"I am not weak! It had two freaking heads! And all is lost! The snake is probably long gone and in hiding, and I can't move a muscle! How are we supposed to make the antidote now?"

"Don't worry, brother. We are almost to Salithica's hut. We need to get past the goats at the gate first. Hold on!"

"What ... How can ...?" The words in my mind trail off as the surrounding trees and branches blur into streaks of dark colors. My body, still paralyzed, bounces off the ground back and forth. I close my eyes and wish it to be over.

My eyes open again. Above me are several angry goats studying me. David is still in his dire form. Among the angry shouts in their native language, I hear a familiar voice. At least some of my senses are working.

"Dear, oh, dear. Look at what the dog dragged in. It looks like you found the snake but couldn't capture it, could you?" Salithica says to me in English, then yells at her tribe while the other goats back off. I hear their footsteps walking out into the distance. David growls at Salithica's dog reference.

"David, I still don't like you in that form. It's very unnerving," she continues. "Drag him into my hut before his paralysis wears off. Then go in the other room, change, shower, and clean that smelly creature you brought. Clothes will be on the bed that we arranged for you."

I'll bet he's hoping for something better than leaves.

David complies, and I see hut entrance and then the ceiling made out of tree branches and twine. David pads over to me and licks my cheek. *"Good luck, I will see you in a bit."*

With that, he leaves me grossed out by his form of endearment.

Salithica comes over and berates me. "I see you failed at retrieving the snake. It's a good thing it bit you, or we would really be out of luck."

"Wh-aat? Mmhaumumwhamwhoouhm." I mumble, trying to move my lips. I mean to ask why getting bitten was a great idea?

"Of course, letting the Paracoubler strike you is not the preferred method of apprehending it, to bring back samples of its poison. But you did bring a sample of the poison. Now we have to get it out of you."

Of course! I have the poison in my blood.

She holds up a short bamboo-like stick, hollow inside but sharpened to a point on one side. I am eyeing that tapered tube like it is a long needle. I try to wiggle, but I am still paralyzed. Then I try to contact David or Silver, but they were singing in the shower.

"Don't you worry, James. I get to have you all to myself for a bit." Her eyes twinkle as she pulls up my shirt. I puke a bit in my mouth and quickly realize I can't swallow or turn my head to the side.

She puts one hand on my abs and smiles. The other, grasping the tapered hollow tube, comes close to my side. She reached up to the table and grabbed an empty clay bowl, and put it down by my right side. "This may hurt a tad bit, but don't worry. I will heal the wound right after I retrieve some of your blood. Your body will work the rest of the poison out in a few hours. On the count of three, I will push it in."

If I could just get my brother in here, I could stop this barbaric treatment.

"One."

If I could speak, I would be screaming. I can see her arm moving closer.

"Two."

Tears pool up and slide down to my ears.

"Three."

I feel a sharp pain enter my side, scraping under my bottom right rib before slowing down when coldness ripples through my veins. I hear the slushing of thick liquid filling up the bowl next to me. I am weak and dizzy. The pain fades as blackness pulls at the edges of my eyes. The last thing a see before passing out is David in human form standing over me, yelling at Salithica.

Chapter 12

Meeting Jelina
David

"What have you done to my brother?"

The smell of fresh blood drove us out of the shower. What I've done? What have I become? I left my brother in the hands of a talking goat. And now look!

Salithica and I stand over an unconscious James. I am still wet from the shower and holding a ragged cloth around my waist with my right arm. Blood from James is pooling out into an old clay bowl next to him. His arm still stuck up over his head.

"I need to get a sample of his blood; this was the fastest way. Rawena-Rose appears paler by the minute." She says worriedly.

"Who?" My memory of Elizabeth's real name left my mind when I saw my brother in such horrible shape. She points to Elizabeth on a small bed of animal furs and leaves. Two younger goats are tending to her, and Tate wipes the sweat from her pale forehead. I gulp and give Salithica a nod to carry on.

"I only need a few minutes to extract the poison from the blood and mix it with the rest of the antidote's ingredients." She closes her eyes and presses her hands over the wound she made on my brother's side. Her hands glow bright white for a second before leaving his skin, healed and smooth as if never been penetrated by such a large branch. "Now, he just needs sleep."

Salithica sits in her chair next to a table topped with an assortment of bottles and bowls filled with different liquids and powders. The air is warm and humid as I step back and let her work. James looks peaceful on the ground. Finally, for once since we left our castle, he's actually getting some sleep.

I go back into the other room to dress and find that cute ball of fur with its big eyes looking back up at me. It still emits a faintly pungent odor even though I scrubbed him three times in the shower. His little four-fingered hands can barely wrap around my thumb. It's no more than my foot's size and doesn't reach more than halfway up my ankle. It's such a tiny creature with blueish gray fur with patches of white and a pink and black nose. Its large ears make me think it could be related to a gremlin from that old 1984 movie. Who knows what fiction is anymore as we have seen so much that couldn't typically be explained. Like dragons. Who knew they actually existed and that they came from another world? Or magik, which it really does exist and can be used at will without a spellbook. My brother and these island animals are proof of that.

I pick up the little guy holding him in one hand. "Do you have a name?"

The creature makes sounds, but nothing I can decipher. I don't think it speaks any English. "We need to give you a name. Hm." I do not know what to call him, but maybe Elizabeth will come up with a name.

I put the furry ball down and got dressed, then returned to the main room. Salithica has finished. Tate holds Elizabeth in a sitting position so she can drink from a small cup.

"It will take some time before the potion works and she begins to feel better, Salithica tells Tate, "It is best to let her sleep for now. She is blessed to have such a brave and dedicated group of friends to travel with, or she may have died before receiving this antidote."

Tate lays Elizabeth down on the makeshift bed and sits beside her, still holding her hand. His whole world will fall apart if she doesn't survive. Tate usually is the strong one, the one who shows no emotion. Still, I notice a tear leak down his face before it evaporates from my sight.

"So he does feel," I say to myself and Silver.

I realize I am stroking the furball in my hand. Silver and I have already become attached to it. I walk over to the bed in the corner of the hut and place the creature between Elizabeth's neck and the hut's wall. He grabs on to my index finger, not wanting to let go. Silver stirs. He doesn't want me to leave the furball next to Elizabeth either.

"We have some stuff to do," I say to the creature. "You stay here and care for Elizabeth. You will make her feel better when she wakes up."

It still doesn't want to let go. It's hard to say no to those big eyes. "I promise we will be right back. No one will hurt you."

He nods as if he understands and chirps a high-pitched acknowledgment, then cuddles up to Elizabeth's neck like a small blue kitten. Tate eyes us and the furball. He actually smiles and nods in appreciation.

That's a first.

We walk back and forth inside the hut waiting for either one of the sleepers to wake. I'm dressed in animal skin shorts with vines as thread and a belt tied in front. I'm wearing a skin-fitting top made of animal fur formed into what could only be called a vest. Twine and small sticks double as buttons. My arms remain bare, but this is so much more suitable than the dress I had to wear that I can't complain.

Finally, Tate stops me with a hand on my arm. "Get out of the hut, David. Your pacing is making me nervous."

Salithica smiles. It's bizarre to see a goat smile. "There is a hot spring not too far from us in the woods closer to the volcano rock lands," she tells me. "Take some time and relax while we take care of your friends. Be careful not to go too far into the draconian lands, they are an angry bunch."

My eyes perk up at the thought of a hot bath. The shower is made up of a bamboo-like tube overhead that pours cold water over whoever stands below it and pulls the vine. A powder left in a bowl to the side lathered when it got wet. Even though it emitted a natural leaf-like aroma, its texture was harsh and scratchy when rubbed onto my skin. A bath in a hot spring sounded much more soothing. Glad to have something more positive to think about, I say my thanks and leave the hut.

The goats armed with sticks who guard the door allow me to pass, but with angry faces. There are several other huts in a circle, all facing to the middle of the area where a large hollowed-out tree sits over a fire pit still smoldering from a previous night. Small and large rock benches and seats were scattered around it under the large tree's canopy. There was a wall made of tall trees surrounding the camp. Only two openings in the trees could be made out. Both were heavily guarded by goats on the ground and hanging up in the trees barely visible to the eye. We walk out with the feeling of several angry eyes staring at the back of our head.

We pass large trees and bushes. Everything starts to look the same the further we go. The sun still glints in from the branches far above. A large pink flower grows by itself next to a fallen tree trunk.

"Elizabeth might like this," I speak the words aloud as I reach out to pick the flower. It refuses to be pulled out of the ground. I heave more formidably, and the head of an over-grown caterpillar-like yellow creature pops up. It gnashes sharp teeth and emits low-pitched sounds.

I let go immediately. The thing reared up on its back legs showing about twenty of its sharp pointed legs. Automatically a growl resonated from my lips, and my vision goes red. Silver speaks in my head. *"We kill."*

We drop onto all fours, still in human form, like we used to do in our living room back at our castle. I revert back into my inner cage and let Silver take over. The thing's eyes twitch at our stance. Silver leaps forward; the bug creature rears back, spins around, and clamps onto the tree nearby. It quickly runs up the trunk. Silver follows, trying to climb the tree but fails.

Settle down, Silver. Let's find the hot springs.

I sense that we are being watched, and not only by the over-grown caterpillar. I take back control and stand while looking around, sniffing the muggy air. It smells like old moss and dirt, with a few unknown odors lingering in the air. The smell of heated water is close. We angle our ear to the left and hear running water with our bonded senses.

That way, Silver says, defining our direction. We settle into a jog and eventually come to the end of the tree line. Bright light shines onto our path before we break the tree line. A massive mountain-like volcano stands before us, surrounded by scattered trees growing among the rocks and boulders. The soft, packed dirt transitions into water-smoothed stones. The sounds of the water beyond the trees beckons to us. We push past the trees and find a rock structure with water flowing down into a crater filled with white suds around the edges. The same smell from the shower soap wafts on the soft breeze.

After checking around the spring for anyone watching, we strip off the animal skins and carefully settle ourselves down into the water. We lean back against the rocks and enjoy the calming sounds of the forest. Leaves rustle on the ground and from the rubbing of branches overhead. Cool breezes wrap around our shoulders softly, and nudge passed our cheeks. Sounds of distant animals holler from beyond the cliffside as their echoes reach us from afar.

Without warning, the sensation that we're being watched comes over me. I'm sure this time, whoever it is, isn't far. A small twig snaps only a few meters away, and my head snaps forward, eyes scanning the woods around us. We hear another faint snap. We both shift our neck quickly to the right. A pebble is thrown into the water in front of us. Plop. Water splashes up to our nose. It sinks down to our feet. We stare down at the small stone as it rolls softly off our toes.

Silver takes over, and our eyes fade to red. There were sounds of bones popping in my ears as we shifted into a giant gray and white wolf. The hot water spills over the edges flooding into other parts of the furrowed rocks. We jump out and shake off the water. We growl and bare our teeth.

A strange but familiar scent of a rabbit floats past our nose while searching for the creature we are after.

We hungry, must eat. Our belly rumbles. As long as we don't eat any draconian, lemurs, goats, or turtles, we should be safe hunting anything else. I can't recall seeing rabbits in top hats or fancy dress.

We hear something small speed off from the same direction the stone was thrown. Let's hunt!

The red tint fades away as we leap between trees. The exhilaration of running again fully bonded comes over us, and our speed increases. The trees pass in a blur as we focus on a fast jumping white ball of fur ahead of us. We are closing in as tree branches poke at our thick coat of fur. We glide through bushes and leap over fallen branches and tree stumps. We snip at a bushy whitetail. Its head pops back a split second.

It is like a bunny only with two sets of noses and ears. Sharp piercing teeth protrude from its mouth. The bunny bounds around a large tree and takes us back the way we came, away from the dense forest and back into the clearing. As we break the tree line, our eyes widen, and we try to slide to a stop but tumble over the sharp-clawed feet of a fully grown white dragon.

Its pink eyes and nose peered down at us. Smoke escapes its open maw, and it bends down as if to burn us. We scramble back to the tree line and instantly shift back to my human form while using a giant bush leaf to cover my bits from the creature's view.

"I apologize to you, white dragon. We were not aware of any dragons in the area. Nor were we told of any more dragons other than the red one on the island."

"Yet, you chose to hunt innocent creatures on land that is not your own?"

Well, it speaks English. At least we can try to reason with it. Its odd facial features don't go unnoticed. It's as if it can't hold back from smiling at us. It licks its chops and steps closer. A feeling we know too well as fear strikes us. Silver wants to flee, but my clothes are behind the dragon. If we run back to the camp without clothes on, Salithica will know we shifted.

I smile and shrug. "I just need to grab my clothes, and I'll be on my way."

A loud roar of laughter explodes from the white dragon as it bends down to my human height, looking me in the eye. "A human shifter that can't shift his own clothes? What kind of shifter doesn't know how to shift with objects?" The female voice sounds more amused than a dragon ready for dinner. Its long scaly tail swipes in front of me, and the bushy tip catches my eye. It's precisely the same bushy tail we were staring at for the entire hunt.

"It was you. You're the rabbit. You are a shifter too." I look into her shocked eyes and see her for what she is.

She scrunches her eyes shut. Wind and leaves swirl around her and blow into my face. I clear the foliage away to find a girl about my age standing before me, dressed in human clothes, red slacks, and a colorful flower top. Her skin is tan and freckled. Her hair is long and red. She has the same pink eyes as both the bunny and the dragon. Her stature is slightly smaller than mine, and she's much skinnier.

"Whoa. Now that is amazing." I temporarily forget I have to hold on to the concealing leaf.

She giggles a sweet innocent giggle and points. "So is that."

I quickly cover up as blood rushes to my cheeks. She picks up the skins on the ground, still wet from the water's overflow from the spring, and hands them to me.

"What is your name?" I gather up the courage to ask.

"My human name is Jelina, You may call me by that name." She turns and starts to walk off.

"Wait. My name is David." She stops for a split second, then continues to walk away. "Hold on a minute. Please teach me how to shift with clothes."

She halts midstep and turns her head to the side. "I don't teach."

"Then help me learn how."

"I can't help you." Her head lowers as though she's studying something on the ground in front of her.

"Why are you here, then? You surely are not part of the four tribes on this island?"

"You are correct, I'm not from here, I'm looking for someone, and I'm wasting my time talking to you. Now go hunt some other helpless creature."

"But…" My ears perk up, and I hear a loud bristling of leaves. The sound gets closer.

"We are about to have company. I suggest you shift into that rabbit thing again before our company arrives." She watches me sniff the air. "It's a flying lemur. They are not fond of humans on this island." I quickly put on my wet clothes as Jelina ducks behind a tree.

To my surprise, Leena, the head snob of the lemurs, appears overhead on her flying cloud.

"Oh, it's you." Her tone makes me feel even less significant. I heard some commotion here as I was flying over on my way to check on your princess. Who were you talking to?"

"Uh, well…"

Jelina hops out from behind the tree, licking her paws. "I was talking to this bunny. I've never seen one quite like it."

"Really? Why are your clothes soaked?" She looks over to the half-empty crater with water flooding around it.

"Well, uh, I left my clothes to close to the spring. When that bunny there spooked me, I spilled a bit of the water onto the ground."

"Well, then we can't have you looking like a wet lemur." Hot air gusts spun around me for a few seconds. My skins were dry, but my hair a bit frazzled and sticking up in all directions. "Much better."

"So, what can I help you with, Leena?"

She levels a disgusted glare at me. "Have a human help me? No. I will not have your filth anywhere near me. I will, however, escort you and your new friend back to Salithica's camp, where you can be better looked after."

Jelina's eyes widen, and she hops in the other direction. A small twister of wind snatches up the white bunny and drops her in my arms.

"It's a good thing I came, or your new friend would have taken you straight into the tree trolls territory. And he doesn't like intruders. He tends to eat them." Leena says, trying to scare me. She floats next to me as I walk back toward the camp.

My new friend, as Leena put it, tries to wiggle out of my arms, but I'm not letting go. She is the first shifter I have met who doesn't care about me shifting from dire wolf to human. There is something more to her and why she's here. I know it. Plus, shifting with clothes on would be a handy skill. I hold her with one arm while I scratch behind her cute four little ears with my other hand. She looks at me with those pink eyes and settles down as we continue to walk back to Salithica's camp.

Chapter 13

The Rule Breaker
James

I wake up on the floor of the hut my brother dragged me into. To my surprise, I don't feel a bit of pain. I reached to my side, but there is no evidence of a hole or even a scar left from Salithica's barbaric methods to retrieving my blood. I look at my feet and tear off my boots. There are several small puncture holes in my right boot. I look to my right foot, and it's still a smooth tan color with not a scar on it.

David is so lucky Salithica can heal, or he would get a swift butt-kicking. I gain my footing, then shake out my limbs and stretch. Only a few aches from sleeping on the floor remain. In the corner, Tate hovers over a bundle on the bed.

"So, you're finally awake." Salithica turns in her chair next to the table of bottled liquids and cups of powders randomly placed on the surface. "How do you feel?"

"I feel fine. Just a little stiff. How is Elizabeth doing?"

"Rawena … hmm, Elizabeth is doing better. We were in time with the antidote, and all she needs now is rest."

"Good." I glance around, looking for David. He's not here. "Do you know where my brother went?"

"I told him of a hot spring nearby. He seemed eager to check it out. He will return soon." Salithica smiles. She doesn't appear worried at all, letting my brother go wonder around the forest alone.

David, where are you? I send telepathically. I don't get a mental response other than a picture of a fleeing bunny. *Great. Looks like Silver is on a hunt.* I glance at Salithica. She is actually grinning at me.

"Why are you smiling?" I ask.

"Don't you remember?"

"Uh...how about you reminding me."

"Well, then how bout I show you? You seem to be alone for the moment."

"Uh … sure, I guess." She is starting to weird me out.

She leads me out of the hut to an open area under the large tree's grassy plain in the center.

"You need to think about pushing yourself up with air," she tells me. "Put your feet together and picture in your mind that your feet are on pockets

116

of air that allow you to float."

I stand across from her and gaze at my bare feet, my big toes and heels touching the other. And I wait. I'm thinking about air pockets and my feet. I feel foolish because all that is happening is me staring at my feet.

"This isn't working. I feel no different than when I'm standing normally."

"You have such a human mind," Salithica says like she's slandering me.

"What do you mean, I have a human mind?" I ask in wonderment. "I am human. What other kinds could I have?"

"I believe the word human is stupid. Humans have done and still continue to do stupid things. We have come to label humans as stupid in general."

"I am not stupid!" My anger pumps adrenaline through me. Flames cover my arms as I clench my hands into fists.

"Well, that worked. Your brother is right about anger being your trigger."

I didn't see that one coming. "What are you talking about?"

Salithica is smiling. She moves a bit farther away from where I am standing. "Look down."

Following her instruction, I look down. *O.M.G. I'm hovering a good half meter off the ground.* My anger dissipates, and I lose focus. Immediately, my legs slide around, and I can't keep my balance. I fall backward and land hard on my back. Air escapes my lungs with a whoosh, and I groan from the impact.

The goat woman looks down at me on the ground. "Well, it's a start. You will need a lot more practice if you are going to control it." She puts out a hoofed hand; I take it and pop to my feet. I shake my shirt and brush the dirt off my shorts.

"The four magiks are centered on four main trains of thought. Storm magik is all about controlled and precise thoughts. Sea magik is more relaxed, patient, and attaining a focus where you can feel the water flow around you, whether in a large body of water or in the humid air. Volcanic magik is about strength, power, and anger, which I can see is why you come across that magik so naturally."

"Yes. I do find fire much easier to bring on command, but what about the fourth magik?"

"Forest magik is a combination of the other three. We must have precise movements, controlled strength, and lots of patience. Mix that with quick, nimble reflexes, and we can be quite the difference in a battle. We aren't only herbalists. We can control nature by communicating with it."

"So, you talk to trees?" I say, thinking she's like one of those tree huggers that go amuck.

"Yes, but not in the way you are thinking. We communicate through our minds."

"So telepathically … what do they sound like in your head?"

"No, you have such a human mind."

"Stop calling me stupid. I don't know your magik."

"It's not my magik. It's what I know best." Salithica pauses for a moment, then tries to explain in the 'human mind' talk. "For example, if you want to communicate with a tree to move a branch, you must first feel its limits. You do not want to use too much force and break the branch but not too little to not even move the limb. It takes a bit of balancing how much will power you use to move the branch. Now, if you…"

While she is explaining, all the goats walking about staring at me. A goat passes me carrying a bunch of branches to the fire pit. I do a double-take and notice the goat is not carrying them at all. They are floating above the goat's arms. One thing that sticks out the most is the goats' lack of armor and weapons. The sea turtles use ice spears and tridents with ice armor. The volcanic draconian had metal armor and weapons. But both the forest goats, and what I've seen of the storm lemurs, carry no armor or weapons.

Salithica eyes me. "Did you understand all of that?"

"Yeah sure, but why don't you carry any armor or weapons with you? I noticed that none of your tribe wears and or carries any weapons. Even the guards at the gates don't have any weapons."

She sighs. "You humans don't listen, so I will have to show you." Salithica winks at me. And disappears. I blink, but she is still gone. I look around frantically but do not see where she went.

A faint whisper drifts in from behind me as a breeze caresses my ears. "You have so much to learn, young elemental."

I swirl around only to see a few rocks by my feet move back into place before the ground looks solid again. I clear my mind the best I can and try to focus on the sounds around me. I hear laughter from young goats across the camp, the sound of crunching soil and small twigs snapping as several hoof steps walkabout. I feel a slight vibration from my right rear side and jump to my left. Salithica emerges up from the soil as if there was a secret elevator pushing her up from underneath. Her smirk not going unnoticed.

"Well, well. You are starting to catch on."

"That's a neat trick," I concede, "but doesn't explain the lack of armor or weapons."

"You mean this armor?" She snaps her arms up and out at her sides where rock and soil in mass cover her body as if she were a magnet attracting metal particles. She almost resembles the Thing from the Fantastic Four comics David used to read, except her head. Rock and hardened soil covered her arms, torso, and legs.

"And this weapon?" She picked up a twig from the ground. It grows into a meter-long staff. She stuck one side in the dirt and twirled it around to stab the other side in. When she brought it back out, both ends of her large stick are covered in rock shuffling around into place. One end shaped into a dangerously sharp spear while the other formed a massive hammer of rock and stone. The armor looked oddly similar to the rock armor I made in the swamp sludge. I remember how heavy that was, and how I called for the wind to aid my steps.

"You use the wind to make it easier to walk with all the extra weight, don't you?" I question with a knowing smirk.

"Yes, we do. It seems you know more than you think. Since you already know such an advanced technique, let's see what you can do." The rock armor grew and expanded over her head, so she looked wholly encased in rock.

Oh, no. I got lucky in the swamp. I have no idea how to remake that same situation. Salithica takes up a rather unusual karate-type stance while in thick stone armor. She then charges at me.

I dodge out of the way, tumbling into dry dirt. She brings down the hammer towards me, and I backpedal, kicking up plumes of soil. I temporarily block her from my eyesight.

Goats around our area take notice and stare our way. I fall over a bucket of water sitting next to a large root from the massive tree. Water from the bucket hits the dirt and splashes cold mud across my cheek. I grab a handful of mud and feel the same grittiness between my fingers.

Salithica picks up the hammer and swings again hard and hits the dirt between my legs. The vibration jars my head, and the thought of survival becomes instinctive. A flash of fire ignites in my right palm. Salithica raises the hammer one more time. I ignite my right foot as she comes down with a final blow. The thrust sends me quickly around the back of her, skittering over the ground. I ignite my left hand, launching myself upward toward her. I swing my molten right arm up and into her right shoulder blade, which knocks her forward a few meters. The rock collision cracked her armor, and the crack spreads through the rest of her full body armor. The armor comes to pieces, rock by rock, tumbling to the ground. When Salithica turns around, her smile fades into a scowl.

I thought I may have offended the only friend we have on this island until I heard my brother's thoughts. *"Whoa! That was awesome! But Leena, the queen of the monkeys, seems to not be as impressed. She kind of interrupted my hunt back at the hot springs earlier and insisted on escorting me back here."*

"What in the Lich's Bane do you think you are doing?" Leena says as she crosses her arms while floating in my direction.

"I … uh … well, we were practicing," I stammer like a fool. I hope it didn't look like I was attacking Salithica.

"I am not talking to you, human! Move out of my way!"

I'm really starting to hate being called human by other animals. She is wearing a long white and gold-rimmed gown that hangs off the sides of her cloud. I begin to move, then realize she intends to float over me. I duck just in time.

"I was testing the boy's skill." Salithica sounds on the defensive.

"You would have me be a fool to believe a human could possess such advanced knowledge of high-level skills, particularly at this hatchling's age. Even our new initiates struggle to perform the same skills without being taught from a master?" Her voice rose higher and higher with each word. The entire camp of goats now focused on Leena's angered words. The air became heavy with dread. I could cut the tension with a dull knife.

"Storm Leader, Leena, I did not teach him any--"

Leena cuts her off. "I will not hear your lies. You are a master of all the skills he used, and yet you deny teaching him anything while he has been in your custody? The Council will hear of this at once." She turns and floats past me so fast, only streaks of white and gold left in her wake.

Chatter amongst the goats starts to rise. I overhear the words, "Worthless human!" and "The forbidden land is calling his name." I turn back to Salithica, and she's staring at the ground. The makeshift spear/hammer weapon crumbles back to the ground, and the stick returns to a small twig blending in with the rest.

"Well, James. It appears we have much to discuss. I will be in the hut when you are ready." She didn't look at me before she spins around and enters her hut.

I turn back to my brother in his odd clothes. "What are you wearing this time? You look ridiculous."

"Hey, these clothes beat that stupid leaf-dress I had to wear before." Something moves in his arms, and I see a white and gray fur ball trying desperately to wiggle free from my brother's grip. Taking a few steps closer, I am puzzled and annoyed that he would bring another stray to the camp. I looked down and see the double ears and the bushy tail.

The rabbit thing Silver was chasing earlier. "You brought dinner to me. That's the least you could do for piercing my leg and dragging me." I step closer and reach for the odd-looking bunny. Its oddly bright pink eyes glare back at me, and it growls.

David steps back, trips over a root and releases his grasp on the hare, which jumps away. The goats are all still glaring at us. Suddenly, a few of them start shrieking. At first, I don't understand, then I see the bunny transforming into a hissing white fox-like creature with five whipping tails, each with a pink tip. Its head doesn't reach higher than my waist. And its pink eyes staring right back at me.

My eyes widen as the doubled eared rabbit completes the shift. *"David, what is that?"* I point right at the white fox, barely acknowledging it while scolding my brother.

"Isn't she beautiful? She's more amazing in that form than when she's human." David and Silver remain completely calm even though the fox rears

up and continues to hiss in my direction.

"What? She's human? How did she get on this island without being detected?" My eyes widen in surprise.

"James, she's a shifter. Wait till you see her dragon form. You will piss your pants. As for how she got here, she wouldn't say, but our conversation got cut short when Leena, the monkey queen, interrupted us at the hot spring." He stares back at me, clueless as to who and where she came from.

"What were you doing with her at the hot spring?" He grins. *"Never mind, I don't want to know. Why aren't you or Silver worried about her threatening nature?"*

"She's not scary. She's scared." He says aloud.

The five tailed white fox turns her attention on David. "What? I am not scared! I will shred you into pieces for that!"

Fortunately, Salithica hears the commotion and comes out of her hut. "I suggest you look around at where you are, young Valfen" Her voice is harsh and reprimanding. "It's unwise to make threats in my camp."

Several goats were starting to gather in a semi-circle, moving closer to our position. I notice a few picking up twigs, and a blink later, they are carrying long staffs. A few goats were there one second and gone the next. Overhead, goats slide down vines from the tall tree in the center. The branches over top of us spread out and bend to form a spotlight of the sun on this new creature in their camp. Hushed whispers are heard amongst the surrounding goats as Salithica steps forward.

"Who are you? What is your business here, and why have you intruded and threatened those under my protection?" She demands as a leader would in front of her tribe.

The Valfen seemed to snap out of her anger and glances around frantically. She slowly backs up to only run into my brother's feet.

"Jelina, don't be afraid," he says. "I won't let them hurt you."

I feel the sincerity in my brother's voice, but I don't think we could take on this entire tribe for this strange shifter.

The Valfen has nowhere to go and stands trembling at Salithica's feet. "Let me go, and I won't cause any more problems for your tribe."

"I believe we are far past that option," the goat woman rebuts. "I suggest you tell us who you are and why you are here … before my tribe shows you what we do to intruders."

The wind picks up and twirls around the white Valfen. I notice David and Silver quickly step away. In the blink of an eye, there she is … a beautiful young girl my age with freckled cheeks and orange hair. Gasps echoed through the camp at another human in their presence.

"My name is Jelina. I come to ask the draconian leader Zyerr a question about--"

"Enough! You, James, David … my hut. Now!"

Chapter 14

An Uncanny Premonition
Elizabeth

I shiver to try to open my eyes, but all I see is darkness. *Did I die?* The last I remember, we were in a dark and dank swamp, the plant entangling me. A few splotches of a town of odd creatures staring at us. A long horse ride and caving into the darkness in the arms of my savior.

"James!" I call out into the darkness. A cold breeze caresses my cheeks as a new wave of tremors flow down my arms and legs into my feet. Bumps rise on my arms as I grasp at myself to fend off the cold darkness around me. *Where am I?*

A small light in front draws my attention, and soon I'm transfixed on this light, my only hope to wake from this dreaded nightmare. The bright light shines its luminescence, pushing back the darkness, causing me to cover my eyes from its radiant glow. A human shape is slightly outlined by the light as whispers of love and hope sing into my ears. The language is foreign but beautiful.

The outlined form points behind me back, where the blackness fell from my eyes. I turn and see an outline of another figure masked in darkness. Plumes of dark smoke slither around him. The figure stands atop a pile of white bones and skulls, its form resembling that of a man, His evil deep voice echoes in my mind. I'm coming! *I'm coming for you, princess.*

He stretches out his arms, and in one hand, he carries a book much like the one James has. With a wave of his hand, the bones rise up and form an army of skeletons. Dark smoke slithers in between every bone giving life and movement to the once dead and motionless frames. The smoke returns to him, and red eyes appear above a dark mouth of white teeth.

The Drarg are back.

The dark man hidden in shadow points at me and screeches, *"Kill her,"* as his jaw drops lower with his reverberating bellow. The skeletons abide by his command. I turn and run back toward the lighted figure. I run and run, but the light doesn't appear any closer. I'm running out of breath, my heart beating in my chest like a drum, my feet ache with exhaustion. I feel as if it's useless to run any longer. My legs start to wobble as they become too tired to continue. I don't want to be swallowed by the darkness. I can barely hear a sweet soft whisper over my own exhausted heaves.

"Draithur is coming! You must survive. Now run!" With a small

burst of energy, I pick up my pace and scream.

"Aaahhhhh!" I bolt up in bed. Still breathing heavily, I wipe away the sweat pouring off my ears and down my neck with my forearm. Gradually, I open my eyes and take in my surroundings.

Frightened goat creatures scurry back, alarmed by my outburst. A small "eek" attracts my attention. A tiny furball tumbles into my hand as I sit up. It's alive. I pick up this cute little blue fur ball with big eyes and small pointed ears. It smiles at me, and I can't help but smile back, temporarily forgetting my dream. I sense several pairs of eyes fixed on me, so I roll onto my right side and look. Tate, James, David, a pink-eyed girl, and a tall goat in a leather-strapped shorts stare open-eyed back at me, their mouths open in shock, eyes wide.

The room I'm in is small, with a roof made of sticks, much like the walls. There is only enough room for a bed, two small tables, and a few chairs occupied by my friends and the humanoid looking goats. One table resembles a kid scientist's wet dream with vials and jars filled with multiple colored liquids and powders. The other table is piled with salad and what looks like a stuffed pig. Around it sit my friends James and David. It appears they were engaged in conversation with Tate, a freckled face pink-eyed girl and a goat lady.

Tate stands up and walks over to me. "Thank goodness you are alright. You are safe here."

"But my dream, it felt so real. He's coming for me. He's coming." I say, still creeped out at the thought of skeletons coming to kill me.

"Are you okay?" James steps up behind Tate and asks over his shoulder. "It was only a dream. It can't hurt you or come for you."

David elbows James out of the way. "What my brother means is, you most likely had a nightmare where you're subconscious took all that has happened recently, from the dark ones to the undead crocs, and twisted the information into a scary dream."

I look at David like he's talking in a different language. "What?" I feel groggy and try to blink the tears out of my eyes.

"Gosh, David. Now, look at what you did." James pushes David out of my field of vision. Tate picks up my hand and holds it like a precious flower.

"Let me through to tend to Rawena-Rose," the goat lady says in English and pushes through with her brown-strapped shorts. "She must still be exhausted from fighting off that poison so long." The horns atop her head and the hooved hands with the short hard fur coat sprouting all over her body proves to me she isn't a human. Not at all.

I recoil back into the wall branches holding up the soft knitted fur hides between me and this odd creature.

"What were you saying about this dream? Who is coming for you?" Tate is so severe and straight-faced.

"Who or what is that?" I point at the goat lady trying to reach for me.

"It seems you didn't inform Lady Rawena-Rose of the land inhabitants before you decided to return, did you?" The goat lady says in flawless English. "Well, she seems aware and no longer in any turmoil. I will leave you and the others to catch up. There is much to do now that James will be stuck here indefinitely." She winks in my direction but not right at me. I follow her gaze to James, and he gulps a nervous forced smile. Anger boils in me at the thought of him smiling at any other female, even if it's a goat.

Tate shakes me as I see the other two goats walk out behind the tall lady goat. I look back at Tate and ask more questions. "Who was that? Where are we? What does she mean that James can't leave? And who is the freckled girl?"

"Hi. I'm Jelina. Nice to finally meet you, Elizabeth. James speaks quite fondly of you." I look to James and could swear I see a small snippet of red coloring his cheeks. That giddy feeling of butterflies in my stomach surfaces once again.

"Where did this little blue furball come from?" I inquire. It is so comforting to hold it.

"David found it scared and alone, like he found me," Jelina responds. "But not the scared part," she adds quickly.

"We thought you two could cheer each other up." David chimes in.

Tate palms his face before speaking again. "Rawena-Rose much has hap--" I put my hand up and stop his sentence.

"My name is Elizabeth. Please refer to me by that name. I do not wish to be called by the name from a family I don't know, and from a time I can't even remember."

Tate speaks again with more reserve. "As you wish, Elizabeth. A lot has happened while you were poisoned from that plant. We are on an island where humans are typically not tolerated. The goat lady's name is Salithica. She is the leader of an island tribe, of which there are several. She helped convince the Council of Elders to give us their permission to stay a short time until you are well enough to leave."

"Yeah," James cuts in. "David and I had to find a two-headed snake to get its venom, and Salithica used it to make an antidote to destroy the poison in you."

"We've been under Salithica's protection while we're here, and her tribe has taken good care of us," David agreed.

"Yes, yes. That's all well and good." Tate shooed the boys away and pulled his chair closer. "It is true Salithica took us in and protected us, but now that you've recovered from the worst of it, we do not have much time. We have already overstayed our welcome here and must leave as soon as you are able."

The story, however, abbreviated, is a lot to take in all at once. "Where are we going?" I ask.

"We must head to Nazereth to inspire the last of your people and rise against the Lich's oppression!" Tate sounds worried and squeezes my hand harder with each word.

"Ouch! Tate, you're hurting me."

Immediately, James pulls Tate back from the bed and unlinks our hands. "What's gotten into you, Tate?" David and James say in unison.

"I saw it in her eyes. Elizabeth, tell us who is coming?" Tate says, exasperated.

"But it was a dream--" David tries to say before Tate raises his hand, cutting him off and beckoning me with his other to give a name.

"Draithur," I whisper, and cold chills ripple throughout my body.

A take a sharp intake of breath, then the sound of a chair being knocked over comes from behind James.

"Draithur?" Jelina is standing, covering her mouth and nose with her hands in a near paralyzed state from saying his name.

"Do you know who Draithur is?" James asks Jelina.

I look back to Tate, who wears a similar look of horror etched into his expression.

"He is cruel in all senses of the word. He tortures anyone or anything, even his own loyal subjects, for his entertainment," Jelina whispers and bites her fingernails. "He is a foul and wretched man who was recruited and reborn by the Lich himself. He already had ties to calling to the dead as a human necromancer in training. Once the Lich gave him the book, he became even more powerful."

"You mean the Lich gave him a spellbook?" David asks.

"Yes, but not just any book of spells. Draithur has the Necronomicon." Tate says before Jelina gets to answer.

James looks at David. "Have you ever heard of it before?"

A discussion breaks out between James, David, Tate, and this Jelina girl about the Necronomicon book. I hear tidbits from each, but they are talking over each other. Tate expresses a great desire to get me away from the island as soon as possible. James said he's not allowed to go with me, and so I must stay here to remain protected. Jelina looks into the distance as if remembering something horrible from her past.

The little blue ball of fur puts its tiny paws on my hand, and I look down at him. "Do you have a name, little guy?" I ask, wondering what to call him. He speaks small cute chirps in a high pitch and shakes his head. He ruffles out his furs and starts to lick his little feet. An unpleasant wafting smell rises up to my nose as I pinch my nose closed. "You are so stinky." He stopped what he was doing and looked up to me with big wide eyes. "I mean, I'll call you Tinky. Because you are so tiny and stinky." Tinky looks up at me and smiles, showing me his sharp jagged teeth.

"Enough!" Tate shouts over the raised voices. Everyone went silent, and even Tinky, who curled up next to my side seeking shelter. "She is going with me tomorrow, and that's final. If you pass your trials, you can come to find us after."

"Wait! Where am I going, and what trials?" I ask, completely confused. "I'm still trying to wrap my head around the fact there were three talking goats standing upright in this room and speaking English. Why can't James come with us if we have to leave so soon?"

"Salithica was caught sparring with James to test out his abilities by Leena, another elder of the island. As I said earlier, they have laws that govern this island, and humans cannot be here. Those same laws also have written to never teach outsiders any magik. Those who have learned any of the sacred magikal ways from this island can no longer leave until they become masters of the magik they wield and pledge their lives to the island's law. If James were to try to leave, he would be stripped of everything and cast into the Dead Lands at the edge of this island where the undead are located. It is a punishment viewed worse than death. Living in constant fear, lack of sleep, constant exhaustion, and inevitable turning into the undead yourself."

"Okay, so how long will that take? I mean to become a master in his magik?" I am stunned by the thought of not being able to spend more time with James. It seems as if the chaos from leaving their castle has followed us here. When my life was in peril, James and David came to my rescue. Now that James' life is in jeopardy, I can't leave him. Tate is looking at me with worry in his eyes. He shakes his head and walks to the door of the hut.

It opens before he can reach it, and the goat lady enters. "It takes years of training, and even the best in any of the classes can fall short in the trials." Tate grunts and leaves, allowing her to continue. "The trials are the ultimate test for each tribe. Each trial can either have one victor or none. This means only one tribe member can become a master during the trials from each of the four tribes."

"Well, if he doesn't make it the first time, can he take the trial over again until he does?" I ask, thinking it may only take a few weeks if we all help him learn everything quickly.

"Yes, that is possible, but there are four important issues to resolve. One, James, is a human and won't be accepted into any tribe. Two, the Trials only happen once a year."

"What do you mean only once a year?!" I ask, exasperated that James may get only one chance. "Does that mean he only has one chance to pass one test?"

"The trials are held only once a year, much like what humans call holidays. David has told me a little about how humans celebrate the first day of a new year by shooting explosives into the air. It is quite a waste of explosives, but he did say they are of different colors, which would be interesting to view. James will only get one shot to pass each test because it is unlikely he would survive long enough for next year's trials being a human on this island." Salithica said while giving me a picture of New Year's Eve.

"Wait, you said each test? How many tests will James have to pass? I ask as I continually get more upset with each bit of information given.

"That is the third issue. Your friend James is quite talented, and sadly that means he must test and become a master in all four magiks if he wishes to leave this island." Salithica bows her head and goes silent as if she thinks I can't count.

"And the fourth problem is what?" I am annoyed, no outright angry at her making me ask each question.

"The trials for this year will be here soon. Preparations have already begun." She looks right at me with sadness in her eyes.

"How soon is that?" My face heats up, and I stare daggers at her and James. James can't even look at me and turns to Salithica. He's waiting for the goat to tell me the bad news.

"Ten days from now."

"What! You said it took years for anyone to master any of the magiks! How can you think James can master four in ten days?"

"Everyone's abilities are different. James has already shown great strengths in volcanic tribal magik. The volcanic tribe uses fire, rock, and small amounts of wind magik. Their magik comes with a price of anger that could easily consume a prodigy if not mastered. He has shown he can use storm tribal magik, which is made up of wind, water, and small fire magiks. He tells me he already used sea tribal magik to heal you. Sea magik consists of water, wind, and small amounts of nature magiks. And finally, he has shown his cunning reflexes and fast adaptive abilities that we need here in the forest tribe. Our magik consists of mainly nature magik with small amounts of fire, water, and wind magik. James has shown great ability with all four elemental magiks, and thus must be tested in all four trials."

I try to wrap my head around what James must accomplish in such a short amount of time.

"So how is James even going to be able to learn these magiks if no tribes will even accept him?" I'm worried that James may get stuck on this island or worse if he doesn't find a way to train soon.

"That is the biggest issue. As the forest tribe leader, I will aid him in forest magiks as quickly as I can. Though he will still need more knowledge then what I can teach him from the other four magiks. There has been only one case like this before, where an outsider had magikal talent in all four magiks. We rarely allow outsiders to stay long enough to learn anything, and it has been many years since a human set foot on our island."

"This is such hogwash! That little monkey queen didn't even give us a chance to explain the truth. Why should I even comply with this? They can't keep me here against my will." James says furiously.
Salithica is a bit taken aback by his outburst but says nothing. Tate shakes his head while swiping his hand through his hair.

"Settle down, James. Don't let tiny lemur get to you." David does his best to convince his brother to calm down before he ignites something in a rage. "For now, I think its best not to cause any more trouble with the islanders so we can leave here without conflict. Think of Elizabeth's safety. Let's not put her in harm's way over a grudge. Plus, you have learned more magik in the last couple of days than you did during the past year. I know you can do it."

I understand the feeling James is going through at the moment. The rage he feels inside is much like how I felt when a loving family adopted me but then gave me back at the first sign of trouble. It's like being compared to a table bought from a store and then sent back for a new one once you realize that the table wasn't as expected from the picture. I want nothing more than to console him, but that feels out of place here. We are in some foreign land, and I'm in someone else's bed and abode. The way Salithica looks at him grosses me out. Maybe when things settle down, I can get to know him better. Somehow asking what his favorites are, seems a bit inappropriate now that we are no longer in Scotland.

"It is getting late, and I need to confer with Leena before the night closes. Rooms and furs have been made available for you to sleep here tonight. I will be in the next hut over if there is an issue." Salithica turns to walk out, and I blurt out the question foremost on my mind.

"Wait, what do the trials entail? I mean, what does James have to do to win each trial?"

"That question, my dear, I have already gone into great detail with your friends. It would be best for them to update you. Now I must go." She turns to James, who is looking at the floor, avoiding eye contact. Salithica winks at me after sizing up James. "See you in the morning, James."
She smiles as she walks out into the dark night sky. A cool breeze rushes in and flutters through my hair. The ocean air's sharp, clean smell with a twang of salty fish reminds me of the ocean back home.

Tate looks uncomfortable and requests a personal talk with me outside. I oblige him, leaving the new girl to converse with the twins. I pick up Tinky and put my legs over the side of the bed. When I try to stand, I wobble. Tate helps me stroll outside, leaving James, David, and Jelina in deep conversation about the trials.

Once outside, the wind ruffles my hair loose, tickling Tinky, who crawled up on my shoulder, hiding in my hair. Loud, rapid chirps squeak in my right ear. I felt his fuzzy coat snuggle up in the crook of my neck. His toenails squeeze into my skin for grip but not drawing blood, despite his claws. I study my guardian with a frown furrowing my brow. It's still weird to call him Tate because he bears the same face as the stalker who haunted me throughout my childhood. I know now it was for protection, but he still creeps me out.

Tate paces back and forth, pondering something. It must be significant for him to not say it. I stand nervously and play with my hair waiting for him to break the ice, all the while keeping an eye on the hut and avoiding the staring eyes of the goat creatures around me.

"Elizabeth, I want you to know how sorry I am about how everything has gone. This wasn't how I had planned our return to your homeland. With the rushed timetable, I wasn't able to arm myself with better details about the inhabitants of Kinzurdia. I hope you can understand that you play a huge roll in leading our people back into battle and reclaiming the human throne once again."

"What was your plan?"

I interject before he continues. I try not to sound nervous with all the weight of his words being put on me.

"The plan was to wait until you became an adult and then confront you with the truth of your parents and your kingdom. I intended to take you back to the Kinzurdia outskirts, a small town called Nazereth. We will unite with the remaining royal guard and other human survivors from the Lich's storming of the castle fourteen years ago. I did not want to put all this weight on to a child's shoulders for fear of you breaking down on me. "

"I am not a child. I'm sixteen and quite resilient from the life I was thrown into." I was actually shaking and terrified that I may be the key to another war. I steal myself again and ask. "Why didn't you tell me all this when I was younger and spare me all the nightmares?" I stare daggers at him while trying to keep from crying. I will not lose one tear. I won't let him see me as weak.

"I can see that you are stronger then I had hoped. You have been through a lot. It's too much for me to continue to burden you with more problems. I have a new plan now, one that will put the responsibilities back on to me. We shall leave tomorrow afternoon when the sun reaches its highest and sail away. I intend to take you to the last secret home of the humans in the town of Nazereth. I am meeting with someone in the morning, which can help us set our plan into motion. Now that you are feeling better take some time to freshen up and rest. We will have a long journey ahead of us." Tate says in a final tone as if expecting me to comply and let bygones be bygones.

He turns to walk back to the hut.

"What about James and David? Aren't they coming?"

Tate turns on his heel and pinches the bridge of his nose before replying. "Unfortunately not. They have to stay for the trials, but when they complete them, and we receive word of the victory, I will send a guard to escort them to us."

"No! I'm not going. Not without James!" I cross my arms over my chest and turn away. "I know you think I'm childish, but James feels like more than a friend to me than you. I can't give up on him now in hopes that he may find me later. And how much later would it be? A week, a month … years?"

"I am your guardian, Princess Rawena. You must trust me. Draithur is a mighty adversary, and he is coming for you. That means he is coming to this island. All lives of all the inhabitants will be at stake. He has no shame about killing everyone here, including James. Is that what you want to happen? By staying here, you jeopardize the lives of everyone around you. We need to leave this island so we can get to our Cloaker. He can hide you from Draithur's magik until we can make better plans to deal with him and the Lich."

I look down at my feet as my arms drop back down to my sides. Uncontrolled tears roll down my face and drip off my nose. I couldn't bear to put James or David in that situation. They are both in this mess because of me. Knowing that staying here with them would almost guarantee their death sends chills down my spine.

"Now, do you understand why we need to leave tomorrow?" Tate asks more in a demanding tone.

I have no choice but to nod, yes.

"Good. Go rest. Everything else will be taken care of by morning."

I look around. The goats are taking less of an interest in us than before. Most have gone back to whatever chores they had been doing. Some still sneer at me before leaving. It certainly feels like I am unwelcome here anyway.

I sulk on my way back to the hut with my head low, kicking at a few sticks before entering. I hesitate at the door. How will I tell James that I have to leave him here? I gather my courage and pull open the door.

"Hey, there you are. What have you two been talking about out there?" James says in one of those forced happy tones. "You aren't really planning on leaving, are you?" He looks at me with glistening eyes—a look of hope that I don't want to shatter. I look to David, who is already looking away and turning back to Jelina. I sense that he already knows.

"Not yet" is all I can muster to say aloud on this subject. "So what is in each trial? Did Salithica tell you what to expect?" I change the topic to avoid those eyes, and to find out more about these trials, James is now forced to pass.

"Yes, the four trials all take part on the day of the Blood Moon Eclipse. This day isn't like any other day of the month. The red moons fully eclipse once a month. The moons turned red when the Lich put a curse on this world."

"What's the curse," I ask. I'm not sure if I want to know or want to keep James talking.

"The curse allows the undead to thrive in this world, and the worst part is that the curse keeps them from ever being killed completely. This little tidbit of information would have been quite helpful had we known in the swamp." James' annoyed tone implies that Tate should have known and told us about it.

"That explains why decapitation and slicing one of those crocs in half didn't slow them down much." David reminds me of the gross picture I wish to forget.

"Salithica says that the red curse acts as a rejuvenation spell at night for the undead, meaning the undead are strongest at night. However, it seems that with curses, there's always one loophole."

I wait for him to continue, but he stops and stares quietly at David.

"Well, what is it?" I ask, dumbfounded.

He squares his shoulders and looks at me. "Well, the loophole occurs during the eclipse once a month. It only lasts one hour, but it covers the lands in complete darkness. Even the animals with night vision can't see but their own hands."

"I don't see how this is a loophole to the invincible undead. The undead would be even harder to spot." I say, wondering what James is getting at.

"For one hour, the curse is flipped. This transforms the undead back into their once previous selves and transforms the non-undead into the invincible undead with all the powers and memories kept intact. It is the only hour per month that the undead can be cut down in any number."

"Wait. This is too much. How is this even possible?" I grab at my skull, trying to keep my head-on. "So if the undead becomes not undead and not invincible, then killing them is a final death, right?"

"Correct. The trials are followed by what they call is the Cleansing. It's a purge of sorts where groups of their top warriors, led by masters from each tribe, cross over to the Dead Lands and kill as many of them as possible. In hindsight, it sounds fine because they are only destroying creatures that are already dead."

I am confused. "But you just said the undead turn previously back into whatever they were before they became undead. That means they aren't dead when they get killed again."

James takes a gulp, and David does the same.

"What guys ... what's the big deal? So they have to kill regular crocs and animals. That doesn't sound bad." I say, not quite grasping what they are talking about.

"Elizabeth, most of the animals in the deadlands were banished or caught by the Spider Witch. She has made several of the tribal members into these undead creations to make examples of them and haunt their loved ones. So the things that they purge will be brothers, sisters, mothers, fathers, friends, or even their own children. They will look like and act exactly as they were before they were turned."

"Oh," is all that comes out. A heavy weight presses on my chest, encasing my heart. It would be like killing any of my sisters I grew up within my home. How could I do that? Even if knowing they would turn back into an undead immortal creature lusting to kill me. The weight of the purge event finally hit me. Maybe I will be glad not to be here for that.

I ponder for a minute over this new information before lifting up my head once again. Jelina is whispering to David at the table.

I walk over to the bed and sit down. James comes and sits next to me to offer some comfort, but he's sitting too far away from me. I scoot closer and put my head on his shoulder, still thinking how horrible it would be to not only lose your own sister to a curse but then to have to kill her to break the curse on her.

James hesitates but then finally wraps his arm around me and pulls me in. I let out a breath I didn't know I was holding and fall comfortably in his grip. He moves a few strands out of my face caressing my ear. I wish this feeling would come more often but not after hearing such horrible news.

When I look up into his eyes, I see sadness. I thought I could leave him to keep him safe. But the butterflies in my stomach had twisted into a knot, and the thought of leaving him pains me. I don't know what to do now. Tate wants to leave to keep me safe. James wants me to stay to keep me safe. What am I going to do?

David gets up from the table with Jelina, calling James to come back. He walks over to our quiet moment and ruins it. "I realize we didn't actually answer your original question, and I thought you should know before you leave us tomorrow."

I sit up straight, knocking James' arm away, ruining the moment. James positions himself toward me by scooting away a bit. The look of hurt in his eyes burn into mine. Thanks a lot, David. I say to myself. Tinky felt the jolt and hissed at David. David tilted his head at the blue ball of fur before I could ask anything.

"What was the question I asked?"

"About the trials. Salithica told us what the trials consisted of and what to expect at each one. We have been discussing the rules and ways to aid James without directly breaking any rules. With only nine days to prepare James to complete all four grueling trials, he is going to need all the support he can get."

Jelina's jaw drops, shocked that David is so forward. But in this short time, I've learned that is how David is.

"So, what is the first trial about?" I ask, now newly interested again, what James will have
to accomplish while I'm gone.

"The first trial is for the Forest tribe. It requires the use of stealth magiks to steal something from the Tree Troll's home. The next trial is the Sea tribe, where there will be an ice arena, a large pool-sized hole in the middle, and a small one turtle-sized wooden platform tied in the middle to a weight holding it in place. The object is to stay on the platform for sixty seconds. Sounds relatively easy enough, but I'm sure there's more to it than they tell us. The third trial is for the Storm tribe. It is a one-lap race. They told us this involves flying in the air over land, forests, water, and volcano. There are groups of each tribe other than the wind that tries to throw up blockades or obstacles that are random, so even the fastest flyer may not even place. There are supposed to be two shortcuts allowed, but it involves flying through the Tree Troll's territory or through the Dead Lands. Each is incredibly dangerous and deadly."

"Whoa. James, can you fly?" I ask in wonderment.

"Uh, no. I hope I can learn all this stuff quickly, or I am completely screwed."

"Well, that's not exactly true," David interjects. "You did fly for a few seconds, but your landing needs work."

James' jaw tightens, and his face scrunches into one of those 'Do not say another word or I will kill you' looks.

"Okay, never mind." David looks at me and shrugs. "He can't fly yet, but I'm sure that will be the least of his problems. It's a good thing, Jelina is here. She said she saw this race last year. She can explain the route and show us where the shortcuts are."

"Actually, I plan on helping them more since I'm now stuck here with them," Jelina says nonchalantly. "I will fly up with him and be a beacon of sorts to guide him through the shortcuts.

"Wait! You can fly? Oh, this is giving me a headache. So you can teach James how to fly?" I'm excited to think he may actually have a chance.

"Yes, I can fly, but no. I can't teach James anything. I'm a shifter, not an Elementalist."

"So, you're like David. You can shift into a wolf … I don't see how that lets you fly."

"No, David is special. He wasn't born a shifter. He was created by a spell and became bonded with the other trapped soul of a wolf inside him to shift between forms. I was born a shifter and can shift between many forms at will." She says as if I can tell the difference.

"But you both shift at will, right? So, you are both the same.

Jelina stands up and sucks in an offended breath. "Don't you dare call me a hideous Dire Wolf! I am nothing like them."

David takes a step back, and his head drops down. He looks hugely hurt by that comment.

Jelina realizes what she has done. "No, I didn't mean … David, you are different. You're not like the Dire Wolves I have come across." Jelina steps over to David and puts her hand on his shoulder. David shrugs it off and storms out of the hut.

James' face is contorted into something so scary that Jelina hops back a step. I can feel the vibration through the furs and the heat waves coming off of him. James really cares for his brother even when it's pride.   Jelina is speechless, and in a blink, she morphs into a small white bird with four wings and darts out of the hut.

"Well, she can fly." But she is horrible with boys. I look at James.

He's not cooling down. I reach over and hold his hand even though it's steaming. It burns a little. I suck in a quick breath and try not to let it affect my face. James notices immediately and shuts off his internal flames. Shock etches his face with a new concern for me.

"Why would you do that? Did I burn you? Are you okay?" He frantically inspects my hands for burns.

"I don't want you to burn down this hut. I have to sleep here, you know," I say sheepishly as my excuse. James presses on a few spots of my hand, causing me to hiss reflexively with pain. James doesn't think twice. A white glow from his hands touches mine, and immediately the pain is alleviated. I pulled my hand from his and stare at my normal-colored tan hands.

I look up into his eyes and manage to squeak out: "Thanks."

He grins and says, "Any time, but don't do that again."

An odd silence comes between us while we stare at each other. James breaks it by fake coughing and says, "I think I should check on my brother."

"Yeah. David seemed pretty hurt by Jelina's words. I think he likes her."

"Is it that obvious? I hope they work things out. My brother hasn't had a girlfriend before."

"So you have, huh? How many?" I cross my arms and pout.

"Uh, um. I should really check on David, and you should get your rest. I hope you don't leave too early tomorrow. I could really use your support through this whole thing. I don't want to sound selfish, and if you have to go, I will understand. But I don't want you to go." He stood and left me speechless, sitting on the bed. James has never been so open about his feelings. For him to say exactly what I hoped he would say makes it so much harder for me to leave tomorrow.

"Good night, Elizabeth. I'll see you tomorrow." With that said, he turned and walked out of the hut after his brother.

A tear falls down my cheek onto my lap.

I lay down onto the soft furs and curl into a ball. Tinky jumps off my shoulder and down onto the fur in front of me. He sounds like he's whimpering in his high pitched squeaks. He curls up again in the crescent of my neck, breathing steadily to my chaotic short breaths and sniffles. I wish there was a better option than leaving him behind. Tate has been looking out for me for years, and I should trust that he knows best. He knew my mom and dad. He has to be right.

I keep telling myself these things to try and convince myself that I'm making the right decision. Exhausted, eventually, I worry myself to sleep.

***

I wake suddenly, and it's pitch black again. I lift myself from the floor only to feel moist soil and grass between my fingers. The smell of burnt wood and rotten flesh invade my senses. I look up, and a red glow from two moons shines down, blanketing the surrounding woods. A few trees are left standing while many are torn from the ground, ripped apart, or blown into fragments all around the stumps. Odd lumps litter the ground all around me. Warm liquid falls from my scar across my head. My hand reaches from it and pulling away, I see the thick liquid glisten in the red moonlight. My eyes start to focus more, and I realize I'm hurt. No longer am I in bed.

"Tinky?" I call out. "James? David? Where are you?" No answer comes back. I walk forward to the closest lump and reach down. The lump is completely covered in this same gooey glistening liquid. I try to flip the lump over only to scream.

It's that freckled-faced girl Jelina. She lays motionless on the ground, not breathing. As my eyes finally adjust to the red light, the lumpy forms start to take on more visible shapes like turtles, goats, lemurs, and large lizards. There is a clearing ahead of me, dark with black smoke. I start to walk forward to see what it could be.

A dark figure emerges from the smoke on a strange-looking eight-legged bear. A mysterious evil woman's voice is heard across the silent land. You could have saved all of them if you didn't leave them behind.

The dark voice comes closer, and the moonlight hits her face. She is ugly, with a spider-like torso nastily sharp pincers for a mouth and those same round eyes you would see on a tarantula. One of her long razor legs pierces something on the ground next to her and brings it into the light. It is Silver, his red eyes still bright in the light. He wiggles to free himself, but it is no use.

A large undead dragon comes up from behind and rips Silver's head from his body. I look away at the last second, but the image is burned into my mind. Several other undead creatures from turtles, lemurs, and goats are all lined up behind this creepy spider lady. She must be the Spider Witch Tate was talking about. The witch glances behind her as she laughs at my agony. A familiar shape comes from the darkness into the light holding yet another limp form. I remember him.

"Noooo!" In one hand, he's holding his book the Necronomicon. In the other, it's James' limp and unconscious form. "No! Please, no!" I cry.

Draithur doesn't care. I have my heart set on you, my princess. He takes his book-holding hand and punches right out the back of James' chest. In his hand is James' beating-heart. I close my eyes and scream at the top of my lungs.

***

"Aaahhhh!" I wake once again, scared and shaking, in the same bed I fell asleep in. Tinky screeches loudly and falls off the bed. "Aww, I'm so sorry, Tinky, I had another bad dream."

Darkness still enfolds me. It's dark outside with the smallest slither of red and yellow hidden between the trees. It must be early morning. I go to the twin's room and push open the door. James is already gone, but David is snoring away. I close the door and tiptoe my way back across the room to Tate's room. He's not in bed, but he left it a disheveled mess as if he left quickly.

Based on how seriously Tate took my previous dream, I am sure if I tell him this one, it will convince him we need to stay and warn everyone. Quietly, I go back to my bed and pick up Tinky, who curls back up to sleep. He's so cute. I'm glad David and Silver decided to bring him to me. His soft blue fur puffs up and encases his little feet and face like a baby porcupine. I know he looks tired, but this is an important matter, and I need someone to come with me to find Tate.

I pick him up. He squeaks out a tiny yawn and opens his big eyes. "Time to go, Tinky." He shakes his little body as I raise him up to my shoulder. He crawls into my collar bone and grips on for the ride. I get dressed quickly in some leather-skinned shorts and top and head out of the hut.

A few goats look in my direction while continuing to do their morning routine. A few smiles but mostly sneers greet me as I take a quick glance around the large tree. I look around and don't spot another human anywhere. I steel myself and go up to the goat closest to me. "Excuse me, but I'm looking for--"

"Get lost, human!"

I blow out a long breath. My pride is hurt slightly, but I grit my teeth, and I walk up to another goat. The goat says something – at least I received something back -- but it must be in their native tongue because I can't understand any part of it. I then remember Salithica is in the hut next door, so I hurry there and knock. A smaller goat about waist high answers the door in a childish English voice once seeing that I am human.

"Hewoah, Pwincess. What do you want?"

"Um, good morning. I'm looking for Salithica. Is she here?"

"Um… " The little goat looks around. "Nope. She went with dat uv'er fire ball hewman a while ago."

"Okay. Thanks anyway."

"Bye." The little goat closes the door as I turned around. So James must have already started training. I guess I have to find Tate myself. I reach one of the goat guards at one of the entrances to the camp.

"Do you know if Tate came by here?"

"Who?"

"A big tall male human with a shiny sword?"

"Oh. That dirty human. You missed him. He left only a few minutes ago."

"Oh, really? Which way was he heading?"

"He went that way. Follow the path. It will eventually lead to the hot springs. He was really in the need for it." The goat laughs as his buddy joins in. I ignore them and follow the stone patches on the ground, making up a small winding trail through the forest.

The sun is still not up. The ever-present moons glow turns the ground and surroundings red. The eerie sight causes me to replay my dream all over again … seeing the dead faces of Jelina and James.

For some reason, Tinky pinches my neck.

"Ouch," I cry, but I am back in the present. Ahead of me, I hear the low murmurs of a conversation—more than one voice. Steam drifts past me in the air. I must be near the hot springs. Moving closer, the bubbling sound of water boiling in the background reaches my ears. Around me, birds chirp, singing their morning songs.

The voices are distant and incomprehensible. They must be speaking in another language I can't understand. Silently, I sneak closer until I see, past a few trees, where Tate is standing. He is speaking with a cloaked man behind the hot spring. The heat waves distort his face from my hiding spot. The other man's voice sounds familiar, as though I've recently heard it.

I try to get a better look by stepping around the tree I'm hiding behind. A twig snaps loudly under my foot. The voices stop, and I see them looking around almost frantically.

Tate finally speaks in English. "Farewell, my Friend"

A bright light pierces my closed lids from where the hidden man was standing. The light shoots upward and disappears before I can open my eyes to see. I rub my eyes to get the bright sparkles out of them.

"I know you are there, princess. You might as well come out." Tate says casually, as though he wasn't doing anything suspicious. I peek out from behind the tree, and he frowns at me. "Why are you out here all alone?"

"I'm not. I brought Tinky with me." Tinky squeaks loudly when he hears his name.

Tate palms his face again and walks over to help me out from the bushes I'm tangled in.

"Who was that man you were talking to? Where did he go?"

"He's not important. Don't worry about him."

His words make me uncomfortable and even more worried about him.

"But there was this bright flash of light."

"Never mind that. Why were you out here alone with Tinky so early in the morning? You should still be sleeping in bed."

"I had to find you. I had another dream, and this time Draithur wasn't the only one in it."

Chapter 15

Conversing With Nature
James

I creep behind Salithica as she navigates through the early morning forest. Sounds of birds and snapping branches flutter past my ears as the forest wakes from its slumber. I yawn and stretch out my arms as I keep pace with her.

"So, where are we going? You seemed quite rushed to wake me up so early."

"I decided to bring you with me to the council meeting to decide what the procedure will allow you to train for the trials. It's currently against our laws to train humans, let alone have a human reside on the island. If you are to pass these tests, you will need as much training as you can get in the next nine days."

"Oh. Well, okay then." What else can I say? I follow silently as we move more quickly toward the sound of the thunderous waterfall. A familiar-looking turtle is standing in the wake of the white water. As we come closer and wade through the water up to my waist, the turtle's posture becomes clearer. It's Ula, Chondro's daughter, and she looks awfully displeased.

"What is he doing here? The meeting has already started. He won't be permitted inside."

"Fine." Salithica turns to me. "Wait here for me, James. The meeting shouldn't last long. Try practicing what you do know until I get back down here." Salithica looks back at Ula. "Let's go."

She walks toward the turtle under the waterfall. There she reaches up and starts climbing the waterfall as if it were a standing ladder.

"Okay. I guess I'll wait over there on the beach." I am not thrilled that I have to endure another wait to learn my fate in the hands of creatures that have such hatred towards humans.

"Come on," Ula sighs. "It will take you forever to climb up that way. Jump on my back, and I'll take you up." Salithica looks at her, then up, apparently reconsidering how far she would have to climb. Having decided, she pivots and jumps off the wall of water as if it were solid, landing semi-gracefully on the turtle's shell. Ula grits her teeth before shooting up the waterfall like a rocket.

How does she do that?

I watch them disappear into the early orange clouds of the morning.

138

Salithica told me to practice what I know, but that won't help me learn what I need to know for the upcoming trials. I'm sure being able to swim rapidly through the water like a rocket could come in handy.

I make my mind up and move closer to the waterfall. I have to figure this out, or I will be stuck here 'till next year. I look up at the massive waterfall, ever-flowing down into the crescent pool I'm standing in. I close my eyes as the water hits the top of my head hard, jarring my head from the impact. *Whoa. That's a lot of water.*

I grit my teeth like I saw the turtle do and jumped up into the waterfall. The harsh strength of the water pushes me down faster than I expect, unbalancing me. I land face first in the water while gulping in more. I struggle to stabilize myself, realizing, a few seconds later, I can stand.

Again and again, I force myself to try, saying out loud, "Up Up" but nothing happens. I stand soaked and pelted with hard water beating down on my face. How am I ever going to win a trial if I can even learn this on my own?

I walk back over to the beach and sit in the wet, packed sand. I take off my soaked sandals and let the water caress my toes. It's still mildly cool with the morning breeze coming off the top of the water.

What am I going to tell David? I sit quietly, thinking about the situation. I wish I could tell Elizabeth how I feel so she won't leave. It's selfish of me, but I want to spend more time with her. She is the first girl I've ever been able to connect with. We have been through some tough times in only a few days, but it feels like I've known her for years.

My trivial thoughts drift back to the present as the calmness continues to flow through me. The sound of the waves crashing onto the sand. The sensation of the waves enveloping my legs and then receding. I closed my eyes and picture Elizabeth's smiling face.

I opened my eyes and gasp. That same smiling face is in front of me, in the form of a clear-water sculpture.

"What the Heck?" I freak out and shoot back a meter. Elizabeth disappears from my thoughts, and I wonder what's going on. This results in the water falling back down onto the squishy sand below.

"Who did that?' I look around, but there is still no one in sight. I look upward and see only a slight orange tinge to the clouds above: no Salithica or Ula nearby. The echoes of bird calls and random animal sounds can be heard from the forest in the distance.

No one. I remember how calm I'd felt, all the sensations highly intensified. "I must have made that happen, but how?" My mind races, and I try to make another water sculpture appear but can't seem to figure out what I did.

Think! Think back. Think about what I was doing. I take a deep breath, calm my mind, and recall the moment. This is how I'm able to find anything I misplace. I start remembering step by step what I was doing. I scoot forward and plunge my legs back into the water, take a few more deep breaths, and clear my mind of everything but Elizabeth's smile. I remember how happy I felt every time she looked at me.

After a time, I slowly open one eye to peak, and there is a sitting blue Elizabeth smiling at me. I see my shimmering reflection as the water steadies itself. I move my head to the side, and the head of Elizabeth moves with me. I lean in, and so does she. I am about to kiss a water replica of Elizabeth when a loud splash interrupts my thoughts, and the sculpture explodes water into my eyes. The force pushes me back onto the sand, soaking me thoroughly.

"Interesting little trick, James. Which one of you is hiding and helping this hatchling trick me?" Ula scrunches her eyes and darts her head from side to side, looking around for someone other than me. She stands tall right in front of me, where she landed. When it hit the water, her shell's impact created a small wave that destroyed my water sculpture. Salithica floats down behind her on a similar ball of air she showed me yesterday. She crosses her arms, leans to one side around Ula, and clears her throat to capture Ula's and my attention. "This is what I was talking about up there. He is a natural. You know as well as I do that you're the only one here that can do that same spell. The real problem is that James here has no training, and without keeping that level of powerful magik in check, he could hurt someone unintentionally."

"Hmm, I see your point." Ula turns to me and points. "Don't you think for one second that I'm going easy on you, especially after that stunt you pulled yesterday."

"You are going to train me?" I ask, not in the least bit excited. After her actions trying to kill my brother and me yesterday, I don't trust her any further than I can throw her.

"Yes, my father is too busy. I do most of the training anyway for our tribe. Fortunately for you, the ruling went in Salithica's favor. You have been granted temporary access within each tribe to learn the four magiks to pass the trials in nine days. The ruling was made due to the unlikelihood that you could ever surpass any of the masters in training and, therefore, inevitably fail at all four trials."

Yeah. That's just what I need. Positive encouragement!

Ula continues without noticing my reaction. "The water skill you used is a conjure skill known to only the most highly trained masters of our tribe. This skill enables you to not only control water but to form it into any shape you wish and have it do actions you command. I can't believe a human could possibly figure that skill out without years of meditation practice."

"James, we must start at once," the goat leader cuts in. "You will be training with me in the mornings, with Ula before lunch, with Morty a master lemur after lunch, and finally … uh…" Salithica hesitates before he announces the final master is announced. I already know this is not going to be good.

"Oh, for Lich's sake. It's Therose! So suck it up and deal with it, little hatchling." Ula says, not caring how it will affect me. "If he doesn't kill you first, then you might actually learn something. He is the best in Volcanics right under Zyerr. He has quite a short temper ever since Kioserack died."

"Who is Kioserack?" I'm intrigued by the new name. Knowing it may be the only weakness Therose has. In that last meeting, he was so close to killing my brother, and I was so close to engulfing him in flames even though realizing now it wouldn't even affect him.

"That is a story for another time. I must go and prep my class for your arrival in a few hours. Do you remember how many turtles you threatened yesterday? I suggest you stay alert at all times." She winks at me, turns around, says her goodbyes to Salithica, plunges into the water, and speeds off like a jet ski.

The goat shrugs. "Don't mind, Ula. We are all strictly forbidden to kill you or your friends until the trials start. The punishment may include desertion from the island, and no one here wants that."

"That really doesn't make me feel any better. What's the plan for this morning?" I try to put what she told me to the back of my mind.

"Seeing how big of a wake you have made with the Sea tribe, we will start with defense skills and hand to hand combat. There is too much to learn in only a few hours, so you need to learn the basics as fast as possible. The more agile you are, the better you can dodge … even when faced with skills you've never seen before. Let's head back into a forest clearing and start."

She walks right past me. I'm still soaking wet, and sand clings to my entire backside. I spring up, put on my soggy sandals, and run after her.

As I ran to catch up to Salithica, a bright white light streaked across the sky into the distant puffy white clouds. It's strange, but so is taking self-defense classes by an upright talking goat. I disregard it and run past the front line of trees to catch up to Salithica.

"So how long will the training be? Elizabeth will be leaving mid-day, and I want to see her one last time before she goes?"

"It depends on how well you pick up on my teachings and if you can survive till lunch. You will be expected to be at the same level as all other competitors in each tribe. This means these first few hours will determine your survival. Luckily, you have me first as all my masters-in-training can practice on their own at this point." She darts her head from side to side as we near a clearing in the trees.

"Okay, so by lunchtime, I may be able to see her off then." My shoulders slouch a bit as I walk briskly behind Salithica.

"Don't worry, James, we will find a way to convince her to stay."

"David, what are you doing up so early?"

"Well, I woke up to pee and noticed it was awfully quiet in this hut. When I looked around, everyone was gone. I caught bits and pieces from you earlier about Salithica. And you training as well with Therose that bas—"

"Ahem." I clear my throat in my head, interrupting his thought. *"I will worry about that after lunch. I have to make sure the turtles don't try to kill me again after Salithica is done with me."*

"Is Elizabeth with you?"

"No, she was still in the hut sleeping when I left this morning." I start to worry, and David can feel my anxious thoughts.

"Don't worry, James, I will go find her and Jelina."

"Jelina is missing too?"

"Yeah, it may have been some of the things I said out of anger last night when she made that Dire wolf comment. It may be that Jelina and Elizabeth are wandering the camp together. You go back to training. I'll find the girls."

An odd-looking deer with ram-like horn antlers runs by me at full speed, weaving in and out of the trees.

"Alright. Let Silver know I passed a juicy-looking deer a second ago if you're hungry."

"And you have to go and entice Silver. I guess we will find Elizabeth after breakfast."

I reach a clearing where the sparse trees spread out. There are training dummies made out of twigs and several sizes of rocks up to large boulders along one tree line. There's a small pool of water surrounded by stones near the middle of the clearing. Tree branches hang over the clearing like canopies. Long rope-like vines hang down from several branches. Rock and wooden walls are scattered throughout the arena-like setting.

Apparently, this is the goats' version of an obstacle course. A cold early morning breeze ruffles my hair as I gaze around at all the stuff in the clearing.

"Alright, let's get started." Salithica moves an open area of tall grass and a few bushes near the center of the clearing. Sunlight pierces the leaves, creating multiple rays of light littering the grassy floor.

I start walking to her. "What's firs ... st?" I duck instantly as Salithica's right fisted hoof passes over me where my head was. She keeps tossing out jab-jab-swing-jab in rapid succession, barely giving me a chance to breathe between dodges. I block with one arm, and she swipes my legs out from under me with her leg. I roll away right before she slams her left hoof fist into the ground hard enough to create a crater of sand and dirt. It's as if the goats' friendly and helpful leader has been replaced with a goat lady out for blood.

I am getting pummeled. Every time I attempt a block, Salithica hits me two more times in succession before moving out of the way. Suddenly, Salithica stops all her advances, leaving me in pain on the ground with what feels like at least one cracked rib and black and blue appendages.

"Do you know what you did wrong?" is all Salithica said.

"I'm not able to block all of your attacks." I'm winded, and I grit my teeth in pain.

"No, you are overthinking. Thinking in hand to hand combat slows you down so much that you can't even retaliate. Did you notice that you didn't even strike one blow on me?"

"You were too fast. I was trying to protect my vitals and get away from your blows."

"Yes, but in doing so, you will constantly be on the defensive. Going up against any fighter, and not fighting back, will always end in your defeat."

"What am I supposed to do?"

She sighs and mutters "human thinking," then continues. You must anticipate your opponent's moves and use nature magik. Feel your opponent's movements. Feel by where they step and how much pressure they put on each leg. Knowing that you can predict the incoming assault and see where the weaknesses are. You must trust in your ability to feel your opponent's motions and let nature guide you to a safe zone. With nature magik, we don't use an element. We request the element to do what we want. For instance, we do not slide across a rock's surface. We ask the rock to slide us across. With this notion in mind, try to heal your wounds."

Standing, I am wobbly as I take a step or two, then manage to limp over to the water hole. I now realize the goats have a water hole there because they must heal often.

Holding my side with my left arm, I swing my right to help move closer to the hole. I trip on a root and fall face-first into the water. When I open my eyes, I face another pair of eyes staring back at me. They shimmer as if watching me from underwater. A strange air bubble surrounds the pair of eyes before I'm forcibly ripped out of the water. I turn my head and see Salithica's arm holding onto my left shoulder and her eyes scanning the forest with a frown on her face. I almost thought I heard laughter in the distance, but the pain waves from my cracked rib overwhelm my ears with the constant pounding in them.

Salithica looks down at me and gestures again to the water. "Heal quickly, we have a lot more to go over."

I lifted up my wet shirt and placed my hand over my broken rib. I clear my mind the best I can and concentrate by closing my eyes. A warm tingly sensation spreads out from my hand, and the bone repositions itself back to its rightful place. My bruised arms are still sore and covered with black welts the size of Silver's balls. I scoot over the well again and plunge both my arms back down in the water up to my chest. Through the ripples of water, I can still see the eyes of something looking back at me. The form takes shape slowly—the tingling sensation ripples across my skin and through my arms, followed by a soothing calmness. The pains recede.

That is what Salithica wanted to explain.

I was in no shape to request the water to do what I wanted it to do. It was as if the water knew precisely what to fix and fixed it for me. When I finally connect with water, at that moment, the odd shape becomes completely visible. It is one of the goats that stared daggers at me when I first got dragged into the camp by Silver and David. This goat has been nothing but rude and annoying since we arrived.

Anger surges through me -- he's spying on me -- and heat spreads within me like a forest fire. The water starts to boil, and the goat is startled into a panic. He swims closer to me. I send a heatwave that knocks him down further into the well's depths. Steam starts to rise.

A loud pitched squeal comes from the tree branch canopy above, then I am hit with a large gust of wind that knocks me at least ten meters from the well into a rock wall. I gather my senses, and I look to see what hit me.

Salithica is pulling a goat with several burns in his coat out of the water. My anger lessens as I realize what I did. I almost boiled that goat alive.

I lean up against the rock and stare at my arms. There is not a burn on them. I didn't mean to do that. I didn't even know how to do that. Nevertheless, this skill could be useful if I can turn water into steam. Then the water skills of the others might be less practical on me.

Or I can use it for cooking lobsters.

"How could you do that?" Salithica yells. I babble an apology, but she's not even looking at me. All her attention is on the burnt goat at her feet, and the goat she plucked from the canopy that's now wrapped in green vines. "You know he has no control, and let you play with his anger. You deserve to get burned, and you … I will deal with you later. Pick up Donny and take him back to camp, see to his burns."

Salithica looks to me with an angered face. I return a horrified look hoping she won't smite me down for attacking yet another of her members.

"Everyone, come out now!" Salithica shouts while scanning the perimeter of the tree line. I follow her gaze, and several goats, who had been camouflaged in trees, bushes, and the ground, appear—a good twenty or so.

Some are taller and skinnier then Salithica, others short and stubby. The color coats were the oddest. A few are entirely gray, tan, or black and white, but most are like marble with specks of each color mixed in.

Salithica walks up to a black and white striped goat who is a good two and a half meters tall. He towers over her, but she looks up and starts yelling at him in their natural tongue. High pitched squeals came out of Salithica and lower-pitched squeals out of the tall male goat. I could tell they were talking about me because every few seconds, that skunk pointed at me with an angered sneer. The rest of the goats draw near, encircling Salithica and the angered tall goat. I rise to my feet, not wanting to look weak in the presence of my future opponents.

I join in the group discussion with long slow strides though I can't understand a thing they are saying. The goats actually part for me to make room. I almost believe it is a gesture of respect until I realize they probably don't want to associate with me.

I steel my thoughts and cool my jets. I don't want to set fire to anyone else in this cluster before I finish my training. I calm my nerves and thoughts and focus on how I connected with the water. I put the same ideas into the sand beneath my feet. I stop walking, but I still pass the goats at the same speed. A few of them jump out of the way before I ask the sand to lie still. I am overwhelmed with exhilaration.

How awesome was that!

Behind me, the sand streaks of the path that carried me here. The skunk goat sees what I did, stops bickering with Salithica, and stares at me in shock. Salithica turns, clearly wondering why everyone is looking past her.

"Since everyone is here, how about a few sparring matches?" I say, tossing out the option.

I pan the area confronting the angered and shocked faces. Only the skunk is smirking, and Salithica looked taken aback after our recent fight.

"Okay. If you think you're ready, then Pepe here will be your first match." *Pepe? How ironic.* "He is one of our best hand to hand combatants. Let's see how much you've learned in the last thirty minutes."

The goat cluster spreads out, giving us an arena-like ring of sorts. Salithica explains the few rules, such as no killing blows, no projectiles, and a few other things before stating she will step in if it gets out of hand.

Pepe's smug smirk and intimidating manner are getting to me. A couple of days' worth of anger courses through me. I clench and unclench my fists. I can't wait to get at him. Flames started to dance in and out of my palms. I wanted to strike this guy so hard that I bit my lip before the match begins.

The pain distracts me for a split second, which Pepe takes advantage of. He unleashes an uppercut, popping me into the air, then ax chops his heel into my gut. He slams me to the ground and knocks the wind out of me.

I lie there with a throbbing head and taking in painful gasps as Pepe raises his hoofs and hollers into the sky, thinking he won. I think back to how I was able to move without moving and calm down. I listen to my heartbeat and slow the rhythm of my breathing. I ask the sand to help lift me up, and it responds in kind. Pepe's back is to me. The chants of the other goats taper off and die as they saw me rise.

Pepe turns to face me. My jaw still hurts, but I push the pain down and clear my mind as best as possible. "Oh? So you didn't have enough, human?"

This time I concentrated on what Salithica told me. Feel his movements. I focus and feel his front leg bearing more pressure than his rear. He's going to charge. The pressure and feelings come in random waves. I close my eyes and concentrate harder. I see more than feel.

In the background, I still hear the goat's taunts and laughing, but it doesn't phase me. I feel the moment Pepe's leg lifts from the ground. At the same time, I don't move but ask the sand to move me behind him.

In a flash, Pepe misses, and I push him to the ground without taking a step. Several goats around the ring gasp. Apparently, no one has gotten the better of Pepe. I think it's time to put him in his place. I open my eyes and shoot the same smirk at Pepe as he used on me.

He quickly stands and sweeps the sand off his coat. "That was a lucky dodge. You won't be able to dodge this." He lunges for my face.

Without thinking, I bend back but keep my feet planted. Pepe's hoof nicks the stubble on my chin before he recoils. I am leaning on a ball of wind that pushes me back to a standing position.

Pepe looks red in the face. "What trickery is this?" he cries. "I've had it with you." He backs up and reaches toward the forest. A warm tingling sensation flutters across my body right before a large branch breaks off a nearby tree and is flung into the hand of the tall skunk-stripped goat.

"I said no weapons!" Salithica yells and rushes toward him. Pepe is only more enraged by her intervention. His branch turns into a giant club which he swings at Salithica. An expression of surprise widens her eyes. I know she isn't prepared for him to attack her.

Instinctively, I shoot my hands outward. A wall of crystalized sand forms instantly between Salithica and Pepe's club. The club shatters on impact.

A general "Oohh!" spreads through the crowd of goats. All eyes focus on me.

Salithica snaps out of her shock first. She snares Pepe with a nearby vine and hangs him up in the canopy. Everyone hears him whimpering as he tries to loosen the vines.

Salithica only tightens them and hisses, "Be grateful the human stepped in, or I would have kept you out of the trials for good."

Another shocked intake of air emanates from the surrounding circle of goats. Knowing myself how important the trials are to leaving the island, I'm sure it's worse to be denied even a chance to move up. Pepe's whimpering stops, and his pouting face forms into a mask of pure anger.

"Alright, everyone, sparring is over. It seems the human has learned a few skills. How about we all work together and show him a thing or two?"

Snarls and grunts rumbled through the cluster of goats.

"Okay, fine! Anyone who doesn't want to help can join Pepe in the vine canopy until we are finished." Everyone gapes at Pepe and back at me. It seems like a simple enough choice, but ten minutes later, eleven goats hang from the canopy and nine goats looking a bit worried about what they should do.

"Well, James. Let's get back to work. We only have an hour left, and you still need to learn more control over nature." She looks at the remaining nine goats and calls out to one. "Nina. Would you come and stand over here next to this boulder."

Nina is a short skinny goat with a white and tan short-haired coat, a pink nose, and green eyes. She acts slightly timid when in front of Salithica, but once Salithica turns back to the remaining eight goats, she squints her eyes and sticks her tongue out at me. Apparently, that gesture goes beyond species.

When I smile and wink at her, she turns her head and snorts. The remaining eight goats spread out along the sandy path I made earlier. Four stands to the left and the other four to the right facing each other. Salithica stands next to me.

I look to her. "What are they doing?"

"Shh." She grabs my head and turns it back to the concentrating goats. All eight goats lift their hands and sway them in a synchronized mirrored form. Sand from around the clearing is picked up by the wind and twirls over their heads. I stare in amazement. Their arms swing down as if sweeping the ground. The sand lands on the path and starts to build up and up, creating a narrow path rising above the heads of the goats on either side. The four goats on both sides push their hooves against the sand as if trying to knock the newly formed wall over. The sand starts to turn a bright red color as I see smoke begin to rise. In a flash, a clear crystal narrow pathway is formed.

"That's great, but what am I supposed to learn from that?"

"A bit impatient, aren't you, James? The point of this exercise is for you to get to the other side of this walkway without leaving the top of the crystal path."

"That can't be all there is to it."

"Maybe later, we'll work on modesty." Salithica pushes me to the path. I start to climb it and find the path isn't flat but more of an arched platform, making it hard to stay upright, and on top of that, it's ridiculously slippery.

I am almost halfway across when Salithica yells behind me. "Five minutes have already passed. Let's see what you can do if something is blocking you."

"About time. I'm getting bored over here." I look to Nina as she smiles at me and then lifts up the giant seven-meter round boulder with one hoofed hand. I gulp thinking how buff that little goat is and hope she doesn't throw that at me. She does toss it in my direction, but it lands right in front of me and sinks down into the crystal. Crystalized claws grow out from the sides and latch onto the boulder holding it in place.

"What the...? How am I supposed to get past that?"

"Use that dumb human brain of yours and figure it out. The trials will be ten times harder than this. You need to learn to think outside your comfort zone if you want to have any chance of beating anyone of these goats at the trial. They are all much more skilled, much stronger, and have more elemental knowledge than you. You need to find a way that only you can solve to advance."

I push on the boulder, but it doesn't move. I hit the boulder with my fist until it bleeds. Now, that was stupid. I calm my nerves and ask the boulder to move, but it doesn't budge. I try lifting it like Nina to only pull a muscle in my back. I huff and gasp in air. What can only I do?

"David, how do I move a boulder that can't be moved by force or will power?"

"Stupid human, we hungry, you go away." Silver says like he's too busy to talk.

"Don't mind, Silver. He's grouchy from hunger. The only food we have been given is a small fish at camp. We hunt that deer thing you told us about earlier but have a hard time since it's a new scent. Anyway, what's this about a boulder in your way?"

With all that has been happening, I should have realized the few fish and salads they have been feeding us isn't sufficient for my brother's enormous appetite.

"David, it's one of the exercises Salithica has me doing. There is a giant boulder encased in hardened sand crystals on a slippery pathway. The object is to get to the other side without leaving the top of the arched path. This means I can't climb it, jump over it, or try going around it. I can't seem to move it either."

"Have you tried going through it?"

"What? It's a giant solid boulder. Heating it and pecking at it won't do any good."

"Well, you know how Silver and I watched a lot of the discovery channel. There was a part where these wolves--"

"Wolves aren't going to help me here, David." I don't know why he always thinks stories about wolves relate to my situations.

"If you'd let me finish, I will explain."

"Fine. Hurry up."

"Well, there were these wolves that lived atop a waterfall in a cave, and one of the pups went out to catch some fish but fell down the waterfall onto a rounded rock ledge. The narrator said the pup was lucky that the rock ledge hadn't been completely eroded yet and that the ledge caught its fall."

"So what, the wolf didn't die. What are you getting at?"

"Have you tried using water?" It took me a few seconds, but David sparked an idea for me.

"David, you're a genius."

"I know I am. Now, don't bother us for a while. We're are getting close to that deer."

My mind focuses back on the boulder in front of me. I pan around and up to the smirking faces of the hanging goats. I swivel in pace and slide down the arched pathway back to where I started. Random talkative commotion sprang up in their native tongue. Salithica looked at me with a tilted head, trying to figure me out. I wink at her before diving into the water well. I call the water to me and spin in place.

I stop spinning, but the water continues to rapidly turn around me, lifting me up and out of the water. White water rapids spin around me as I picture drilling through the boulder. The water drops me to the ground and spirals quickly into the boulder, boring a large enough archway through the boulder and out the other side. I use the mud under my feet to push me like the sand did earlier, right through the opening to the other side of the path.

Everyone got awfully quiet. I looked over at Nina with her shocked face and stuck my tongue out at her.

Chapter 16

Deer Hunting Gone Wrong
David

A two meter tall deer grazes in the distance by a small stream. Its thick succulent muscles bulge out of its fine brown coat of hair. The irregular S-curved antlers showcase its only difference between the regular deer we are used to hunting back in Scotland. We know it doesn't see us, but we can tell the deer is tense and ready to spring away if we get any closer. Thick and dense bushes hide our presence from our prey. Its bright out now and the suns reflection off the glistening water dances on our preys coat enticing us all the more. Even the sun agrees this deer has been chosen for us.

I think it's time for breakfast, Silver. I sure am hungry. We are both sick of eating fish and salad at camp goat land.

Hungry. Yes we eat now. Silver says before we launch ourself from the bushes.

Without any other thoughts, we jump out from our hiding spot and rush past several trees. We leap off a large slanted rock slab and soar through the air. The eyes of the deer bugged out of its skull, and the animal sprinted to the stream. We landed right on the eaten patch of grass the deer was chomping and pounce forward swiping at the tail of the deer.

A screeching "Meeeh, Meeeh" came from it as a few of its hairs slid in between our claws. This deer is faster than the ones back in Scotland, but we know it has no chance against us.

It prances and zigzags before leaping over the stream thinking it might slow us down.

Stupid deer, me hungry, you die. Come back! Silver is getting agitated.

It's okay, Silver. We need to think of a way to get a claw on him before he zags.

No think time, kill now. Run faster, kill, eat! A warm tingling rush fills us as our bond starts to kick in. A new burst of speed flows into all our appendages. Our claws extend a bit further out and our eyes fall into tunnel vision onto our prey.

We leap one last time into the air, the deer turns and freezes for a split second. He must have known this would be the end for him.

We swipe our right clawed paw downward at its neck. We feel the flesh split as our claws dig in deeper. A screeching sound pierces the air partially causing us to sway slightly before achieving the killing blow.

The screech unbalances us and we stumble as we land next to the deer. A blur to the right of us snatches the deer and rips its head clean off its shoulders. The headless carcass slumps to the ground next to us as we stare into the distance trying to make out what stole our kill. Silver is huffing and puffing and starts to circle the carcass while looking back up at the blur in the distance.

We both are more curious than hungry, more angry and annoyed that we didn't get the kill. Silver and I feel this immense anger and hatred to whatever creature decided to interfere with our hunt.

Kill it too, then eat both. Silver says. I can't help but agree with him. I never thought killing anything would be a desire of mine, but right now I can feel the anger and the hurt pride Silver feels as if it was my own. Silver truly believes that the only way to restore his pride is to kill that of which hurt it in the first place.

We leave the blood spurting headless carcass next to the small stream. Red clouds of blood filter into it as the blood is dragged downstream.

We put our nose to the ground and take in a deep breath filling our lungs with the scent of our new prey. The scent is slightly familiar, but we shrug off that thought and sprint after the creature that stole our kill.

The blur disappears into a giant bush. We weave in and out of trees attempting to catch up to it. The metallic fresh scent of blood lingers in the air. We know we are close. The creature must have stopped to feed. We slow down before creeping up to the bush. We can make out faint shadow movements through the thick brush as we hear several twigs crunch under the feet of our prey.

We need a better view point and cautiously circle the large bush until we find a low small hole between the branches. We crouch down and inch our snout in slowly to peer into the center.

The center is hollow. There's about a half meter thickness of leaves and thorny vine-like branches. In the center is another white and black splotched wolf with its back to us while bending over and licking the severed neck of the deer.

Silver and I let out an angered growl at this small wolf while creeping slowly into the middle behind the wolf that would dare interfere with our kill. The small wolf's head snapped in our direction. Recognition hit us immediately with the wolf's scent and now its eyes. Her large sharp teeth vibrated in her growl as we noticed her pink eyes staring at us.

Silver and I both stop our advance, we turn to the side while shifting back into human form. I break a branch off the shrub and hold it down in front of my bits. I turn back to look at the wolf Jelina has become only to see her fully dressed in the human form. She bellows out a laugh at our expense.

"I can't stay mad at you when you strip in front of me." She giggles and snorts.

"I didn't strip in front of you..." I look down. "Well not on purpose. It's the only way we can shift."

"That's not true you can shift like I can, so you should be able to learn to shift with clothes on." Jelina is wearing a cross strapped leather top and tight leather shorts. She looks incredibly sexy.

Silver snaps me out of it and replays the last few moments of our kill. My smile turns into a frown. Jelina notices the immediate emotional change and clears her throat.

"Why did you interfere with our kill? You had to of known it was us. It's not like there's a lot of Dire wolves that roam this Island!" I demand; my anger swelling again, hurt pride ever present.

"I uh..." Jelina looks taken aback and a bit nervous.

"Where is Elizabeth?" I ask before giving her a chance to explain.

"Elizabeth?" Jelina looks surprised and slightly hurt. "Is she all that you care about?" She shifts back into the wolf and growls.

Silver senses the danger before me and forces a shift before Jelina lunged at us. Silver managed to dodge us out of the way in time. Her claws barely graze our left thigh. Jelina looked at us eye to eye, then scrunches back. I can tell she didn't mean it, but it is too late. Silver is pissed and he is in control. She must have noticed his red eyes before she darted out of the brush.

Silver pursues with me along for the ride. Jelina's white and black fur shreds on the thick sharp thorns and a small yelp emanates from her before she bounds off ahead of us. The thorns didn't have the same effect on us. They all snapped off the branches or dug into our fur as we started to gain on her tail.

The more Jelina eluded us between trees and over large rocks, the more enraged Silver felt. The mixed emotions of anger, loss, and lust overlap each other in one big ball of emotion between Silver and me. Silver runs harder, and we bulldoze right through a small tree showering splinters past Jelina. She is puffing pretty loudly, and I know she is getting tired running at full speed.

She fakes right and sprints left toward the sounds of clashing waves on sand. The thought flutters between both of our minds of the possibility she may have a fish form and we may lose her for good. Silver nor I wanted to lose her. Our bond warms up once again, and the blur of bushes, trees, and rocks came in as streaks of green brown and gray.

The tree line of the beach is approaching fast. Jelina is almost at the water's edge. We leap and tackle her, rolling back up the sandy slant. She cries out with several yelps and tries to wriggle free from under our weight. It's no use, she is exhausted.

My bond with Silver feels like an endless supply of energy. Silver reaches down with our snout, and we inhale her scent. We lift our head back up at her. We grimace in a menacing smile and howl long and loud up into the morning's sky.

Jelina is terrified at first, but when we come down from our howl, she shifts back into her fox form with silent tears running down her face. We licked them dry and nuzzled her snout. Silver helps me realize that we claimed her as ours. That she is now our mate.

I understand more now that we needed to show dominance and to claim her as that is more an animal's instinct than that of my human upbringing. This is a world of animals and dating isn't the same as with humans. I can't deny the feelings of attraction I also have to her both in human and animal form. For once Silver and my desires are the same making this bond a special one.

We back off from Jelina and let her rise. She bows her head in defeat as her five tails sway behind her. She lifts her muzzle and lets out a short sweet howl before taking in our scent and rubbing up against us like a cat wanting attention.

After a few moments of playful nibbling and muzzle rubbing I influence Silver that I need to speak with her in human form.

We stop our movements and look into the most beautiful pink eyes on a fox we will ever see. A moment like this on a beach in the bright light of a sunny day with a light sea breeze seemed almost too good to be true. Silver and Jelina might have made up but now it's my turn.

I can feel the control being handed over to me. I can see the color of my eyes fade from red to green mirrored in the eyes of our mate. Jelina immediately notices the change and shifts into her human form.

I'm about to shift but she puts her hand on our neck and shakes her head.

"Though as tempting as it may be to see you naked again, I think you should shift into some clothes first."

I nod but realize I shifted without clothes. *How can I shift into clothes if I didn't have any on in the first place?*

As if she could hear my thoughts she said "I know what you're thinking but you can make your own clothes from your skin."

Wait. What? I tilt our muzzle and scrunch my eyes at her. She sighs.

"Just watch me." She shifts from a human wearing brown leather clothing to a white bunny then back to human form wearing a white fur coat and fuzzy pants.

A momentary dumbfounded look must come over our face as Jelina lifts up our jaw that fell. I have to keep Silvers lustful thoughts to the side as I try to figure out how she was able to make clothes from a bunny.

"You already have the power to shift to another form so you need to learn that you can manipulate that shift as you shift and form a clothing option from the previous form. All you have to do is picture what it is you want to make and keep it focused in your mind when fully shifted. Try it."

With there being only one form to choose from I have to make something out of a dire wolf skin. I think about that vest I had on before and long shaggy looking pants like the cowboys always wore. I kept those images in my mind and had Silver shift us into human form.

Jelina stands there, ever more beautifully, covering her face. I'm human again and it worked. I'm wearing a black fur vest and long pants made of short haired skin. I try to move the vest but I soon realize it's more than skin tight, it's actually part of me.

I look back up at Jelina in confusion. Jelina was looking through her fingers the whole time. She smiled at me. For the first time she looked happy.

"It's not permanent you can shift back to your regular self at any time though I'd wait for a more private venue. You can even shift certain body parts with practice and concentration. Like if you need to climb a tree but have no claws. All you need to do is concentrate." She out stretched her left hand palm up. Giant claws protruded from her fingernails.

Silver and I looked on in amazement at Jelina's control of the shift. It seems we have much to learn. I sure am glad she is ours now.

Chapter 17

Training With Sea Shells
James

A pair of howls are heard in succession in the distance. All the goats turn their heads back to camp; even the goats still hang suspended in the forest canopy. Salithica calls to her trainees.

"Everyone quickly back to camp. Those of you on the ground help the others down from the vines. I will escort our human friend to Ula."

Obediently, I follow Salithica back toward the beach while the last of the goats disappear into the tree lines.

"Don't let my smile fool you. I am amazed at how much you know, but your lack of practice will be your weakness to Ula and her trainees. Knowing her, she will try to make your training miserable. Use what you have learned and keep your mind connected with water to be able to combat any unexpected attacks."

I take her warning more seriously as I playback what happened yesterday. Ula wants us both dead.
And I am ready to kill her myself. A situation of overwhelming hatred doesn't dissipate after a day.

We walk in silence while listening to the insects and animal cries in the forest. We arrive back at the beach with the skyward waterfall parting the sky in two. Ula stands at the water's edge with Brutus and Ragarth wading in the water.

"Wait, why didn't you tell me the training with Ula would be in the water?" The thought of that freezes me in place.

"Why would I need to? That is where they live … underwater." Salithica looks at me with a horrified expression. "You do know how to swim … right?"

"Um, does doggy paddling count?"

"What is this doggy paddle swimming? I have not heard of such a thing. From the sounds of this, it seems you better be a master of this doggy paddle, or Ula may let you drown."

"Wait, I thought you said she's forbidden to kill me."

"True, but if you drown yourself, then she's not at fault. Calm down and believe in yourself."

I let out a breath I wasn't aware I was holding. *I haven't gone swimming in years, and now I have to keep myself afloat and cast magik, all*

155

while evading possible sneak attacks. Great.

Ula waves me over.

I incline my head toward Salithica and force a smile. She returns it weakly and nods. I swallow the uneasiness with a cup of uncertainty and make my way over to Ula's bright smile. She puts her arm around me and leans in close, whispering into my ear.

"I have so much planned for you today. Hold your breath, human." I gasp in air before Ula pushes me into the sea. Her two ice armored turtles grab my arms and drag me under. I am spread out between the two as they sped up. The thunderous sounds of water crushing my eardrums deafened me. I try to open my eyes, but the salty water scratches my eyes making it impossible to see my surroundings.

I feel the water slow around me and my feet start falling back down under me. I manage to open my right eye as bubbles begin to pour out of my mouth. My sight is still blurred, but there are lights of red, blue, and white. I open my other eye automatically to refocus. Pain snares at me, but the sight before me is exceptional. There are rose-bud-like pods that cluster on long vines that grow deep below in utter darkness. Turtles propel themselves between and into pods as if they were gliding through the air. Mirror-like air pockets shimmer at the openings of each pod.

I open my mouth to say 'wow' and saltwater rushes in. I gag and rip one hand free from Ragarth's hold. He has a similar shimmering bubble around his head, like that goat in the water well. He sees me convulsing and looks at Brutus, still holding on to me. Instantly we shoot straight to the surface, where I cough up a lungful of water.

"James! What's going on? Where are you? Your thoughts are echoing in our head."

"I'm fine now. I found out I can't breathe like a fish."

"Last I checked, humans don't have gills. Are you with the sea tribe? They didn't try to kill you again, did they?"

"Not yet, but I need to learn that underwater skill the goat was using earlier. Did you find that deer?"

"Yep, and found Jelina too."

"Hey David, I heard two howls clear across the island. Who was the other one howling?"

"Uh..." David leaves a long silent pause.

"If you make it back here by lunchtime, I will tell you. Until then, you should get back to training." I feel his presence leave my brain quickly, leaving me a bit lightheaded.

"...no learn anything, stupid human?" Brutus' voice brought my thoughts back to the present while staring at a fat green-faced, round-nosed turtle no more than five centimeters away.

"Uh, I didn't realize I could magikally grow gills," I say sarcastically between each gulp of air. I kick frantically to stay afloat on the surface. I turn in place and see nothing but bright blue sky and mountains in the distance. The island looks so small this far out.

"You petty, human. We gills no have. We use magik. You breathe in water quick. Now or die."

His English is a bit ragged, but I understand his point as he forces my head under the water. I freak out and grab at Brutus' webbed hands. I can hear a distant voice in my head. I stop my struggle for a second to listen to what sounds like David trying to communicate.

"James! Calm down and focus like you did with the boulder."

"Right! I can do this." Both the goat and the turtle had an air pocket bubble around their heads.

I scrunch my eyes shut and concentrate on connecting with water like before. I feel the same cool tingling sensation and quickly imagine pushing the water away from my face. A bubble expands in front of me and soon grows wider and taller to encase my head. The pressure of the turtle's hands are gone. My ears pop. I see clearly now that the water has receded to about a centimeter from the end of my nose.

I poke a finger through it without popping it, then my whole fist. I'm surprised to feel my fingers are dry when I touch my face. This is so crazy. I look up to see the turtle smirking at me before returning to his stern face. Ula comes up next to me. She pokes her bubble then touches mine, a small tube appears between our bubbles.

"Well, well, you are something special, aren't you? It's time to meet my brother before we start the class. Follow me..." She says, then breaks the tube with her webbed hand. I barely hear "as if you have a choice" before the connection servers completely. Brutus pulls me further under, and Ragarth re-clasps his hand around my arm.

This new underwater town appears more like an entire city. The brightly colored pods are scattered in a long line as far as my eyes can see. Ula swims close to us again and poked three fingers into her face bubble before throwing her hand in our direction. Tiny thread-like water spouts burrowed through the water to each of our bubbles.

"No human has ever seen our homes and lived to tell about it. So it is a secret amongst the humans that reside near these lands. I strongly suggest you keep this location to yourself."

I study the menacing faces between her two brutes and her own. I take in the stares with an uncomfortable nod. It would seem easy to throw me down some deep dark trench never to be found again.

"Okay," I whimper out before she carries on.

"This is only one of many groups of pods that surround our island. Each group has connecting vein-like seaweed to our main hub directly attached to the bottom center of the island."

"Why do you use seaweed?" I interrupt, blurting out a question. Brutus and Ragarth slow us down to an abrupt stop. Ula gets up close to my bubble.

"That information is not something a human needs to know." She turns back around, and we start moving closer to a large glowing red pod about the size of a small football stadium back home. Several seaweed strands coming from the pod's top, where the surrounding smaller pods have very few. I notice movement along with one of the vine strands. It is a little air bubble. Then I started noticing almost every vine has tiny air bubbles streaking quickly across the vines. It became pretty obvious what they are used for now. It's incredible. I see a turtle waiting outside the red pod for us. It's Konja, the son of Chondro and brother of Ula from the Council meeting.

Ula throws one more water tube at her brother and connects us to his voice. He has this grumbly nonchalant texture in his voice.

"Welcome to our humble abode, James. Hopefully, Ula has given you a great greeting before we take you to our training grounds. As you can see, we have a network of connected underwater homes that most humans, or other creatures for that matter, don't know about. We would like to keep it that way. In order to ensure our secrecy, we want to give you a friendly reminder that we are only obligated to train you for the next nine days. After that, you will no longer have access to any part of our underwater world. You are not to wander about, and you will be escorted by Brutus or Ragarth at all times. If we hear of you or your close friends spreading rumors of our lifestyle, we will hunt you down and kill all who have this knowledge. Do I make myself clear?"

I gulp slowly and look right at Konja. He says that it is so much more horrifying with such a friendly tone and a fake smile. I nod my head again, hoping not to piss off this Konja bloke. He, as well as Ula, means business. I want nothing more than to train and get the heck out of here.

I'm escorted to one of the shimmering front openings of the red pod and pushed in. I tumble to the floor of the pod, holding on to my head. The air pressure is as familiar as the surface.

I notice my clothes and skin are completely dry. I hear loud thuds behind me and see large shells roll past me before splashing down into a small pool in front of me. Arms, legs, and heads pop back out as they spring back to the surface.

"That was quite an entrance," I say boldly.

"We no walk well on dry land," Ragarth says.

"Rolling easy and fun," Brutus says with a slight smile before talking in an odd turtle clicking sound toward Ragarth.

I'm starting to recognize the differences in the ages of these turtles besides the apparent wrinkles. Their attitudes and character are much different. It seems the older they are, the better they speak English.

Ula and Konja waddle in behind me like two oversized constipated penguins. The looks on their face mirror that of disgust at their fellow turtle's entrance. It seems the older the turtles, the more serious they get.

"Well, let's begin. Brutus escort this human to the training arena."

I walk over to Brutus' flat rounded nosed face and notice a small pool of water under his feet. He starts moving forward with me but doesn't move his legs. He's using that same technique I used earlier but with sand and dirt.

"Wait," I say to Brutus. He looks at me, questioning my command.

"I can do that." I point down to his feet before walking back to the pool of water. I reach down and feel the floor. It's made out of a silky smooth, hard texture like that of a rose petal atop an ice rink. I scoop some water in my hands and throw it on the damp floor. I see the water droplets bead up and move into a raised water puddle. I remember that same tingly cool sensation like before and step on the puddle. I see the siblings stare at me with astonished faces as the water moves me back to Brutus' side.

A giant smile breaks across my face, and it is reflected on Brutus' face. I have a good feeling about Brutus. Ragarth rolls past us on the edge of his shell and in through a sizeable vine-covered archway.

"Um, English word, um he big displayer."

"I think you mean he's a showoff. He does have that rolling down pat." I agree with giving due credit to his friend.

"Who is Pat and, why is he down?"

I laugh for the first time in a while. All this seriousness is really getting to me. Now that we are away from Ula and Konja, Ragarth and Brutus show me who they really are.

"Never mind. It's a human complement, a good one."

Entering the archway, a large ice ramp structure sits in the front. A balcony of ice surrounds the outer red walls that look down upon the tall white arena. I spot seaweed wrapped around the large oval structure's edges— some of the vines connected to spots on the red pod's outer walls. I glance up to the top of the white oval, where several turtles balance on the top of this ten plus meter tall structure. It reminded me of a lot of the walls I climbed surrounding our castle back home in Scotland.

"Uh, okay. This way." Ragarth rolls up to that group over there. He points to the right side where I can barely make out Ragarth's pointed nose with reddish brown-tinted skin.

We both use the water to propel us up the steep incline to Ragarth. Brutus is in front of me, and I notice a carving on his shell near the top. It's the same water symbol I saw on the podium for Chondro at the council meeting. I look to Ragarth. He also has the same logo in his shell. None of the other turtles have any carvings on them at all.

What is that all about?

At the top of the wall, a smaller oval pool is about four meters down with ice and snow pockets all around the edges. I stand awkwardly next to Brutus and Ragarth as several turtles from across the oval pool stare menacingly at me. All the turtles are making clicking or clucking sounds to each other. Brutus remembers I am next to him and starts to attempt some translation. With his broken English, it's painfully hard to understand. Although the fact that he's actually trying to help me tells me he is probably the only ally I have here.

Ula and Konja appear atop the highest part of the ice wall and clear their throats to get our attention. Konja speaks up first in smooth English.

"As you are all aware by now, we are to aid in training a human the arts of our water magik. He will be competing alongside all twenty of you to become a master in water magik."

Several roars of clucking circulate among the others until Ula steps up.

"Enough! I will not hear any of it. These orders come straight from my father, Chondro, your leader. You will obey, or you will be removed from the competition this year."

Utter quietness falls like a blanket over the arena. It seems as though no one wants to leave the trial.

"From now on, you are required to use your English voices when in the proximity of the human. You all need the practice if you want to be a master in our tribe." Now grumbling spreads through the crowd with a few English words I can't quite make out. *Just as well.*

"As you are aware, this training ground is a miniature replica of the location for the actual trials. All of you know the specifics tests for each trial are different each year, but the arena will be similar. So learn as much as you can from this training to better your own strategy in nine days. You have been training all of your lives for this day, so put the effort in and prove to us, and your clan, who the next master will be."

A chorus of excited clucking and cheers erupt from the turtles. If this is what they call small, then I can't wait to see the trial-sized one. I noticed Brutus and Ragarth are not cheering, only quietly observing the other turtles.

Her speech ended, Ula and Konja turned their shells to me before heading down to us. Both of them have three engravings on their shells. I recognize the same water emblem that Brutus bears, a tree emblem like that of Salithica's podium, and a large letter E. I'm getting the feeling that the carvings are rank achievements. *The emblems must mean proficiency, and the letter I think means--*

"Human! James. Come, it's time to train. "Ula nods at Ragarth, who grasps both my arms and launches me into the freezing pool.

My teeth chatter instantly. The cold skewer me like a thousand sharp needles penetrating me all at once. I bob on the surface, too frozen to even dog paddle. My pride is forgotten as every turtle starts wailing in laughter.

Anger surges through my veins, followed by familiar heat waves. I thaw out instantly as steam rises, and small bubbles pop around me. The loud laughter dies down as fast as it started. Ula steps behind my competitors and pushes them all in one by one.

Several turtles are scrambling to climb back up when Ula's serious face captures every turtle's eyes. I heard several turtles behind me yell out obscenities and several loud thuds landing in the water or on the iceberg ledges along the sides. She lifts her stubby right leg and slams it into the ice wall creating a small ice crater with an ever-expanding crack splitting the ice wall apart. Its effect creates an ice avalanche taking down the remainder of the turtles, still holding on to the ledge.

"What are you turtles so afraid of?" Ula challenges them. "He's only a puny human with a few measly tricks. You all have trained since birth. Use your skills and attack him now!"

The only turtles remaining on the ice boundaries are Ula, Konja, Brutus, and Ragarth. That confirmed that Brutus and Ragarth are already masters and the carvings are now more apparent. My senses on high alert after that command, I know this will be my defining moment to show that I can be their equal.

Grunting sounds came from my left. I barely have time to move my head as three ice spikes impact the water next to my shoulder. My boiling water liquefies them on contact. *All that self-defense training, and I can barely move at all in water.*

I dodge several more ice spikes from all around, weaving and bobbing, ducking under the water, and expending too much energy. It's only been a few minutes, and I'm beginning to tire. An ice ball hits my temple, knocking me motionless. Blackness overtakes me as the water swallows me. I feel a few more balls of ice hit me underwater before feeling cold. A small bright light appears in the darkness.

"James! James, don't give up. We are here with you. Elizabeth is waiting for you. Don't give up, don't let them win."

"David? Is that you?" No answer, but I don't need one. I have my obligations to my brother and to Elizabeth. I owe my Da that much to take care of my brother and to keep my promises. I have to keep going. I have to win.

My eyes open, a bubble instantly forms around my head. I'm standing on what looks like the bottom of the pool. I use that similar whirlpool technique and spin my way up and out of the water. I land hard on an ice ledge, sliding into a snow pile. The turtles near me back up. They must not have expected me to come back up. In my momentary absence, it looks as though a full out war has taken place.

Turtles face off on each other, throwing ice balls and spears against ice formed shields and helmets. A small red snapping turtle across the pool creates a water spout at first, then shards of ice splinters swung around it rapidly until she had a saw blade-like ice disc spinning between her hands before launching it at her opponent. The other brown flat-faced turtle swings around in time to see the meter-long disc cut its way into the ice wall behind him.

The turtles near me start throwing ice spikes. I retaliate by throwing up a wall of ice behind me, blocking incoming attacks. I slide around the turtle in front of me by asking the water to move me. I place my palm down between her legs and blast a fireball into the ice, instantly breaking the platform and sending the turtle underwater. I may not be able to form ice spears or shields yet, but I know how to make fireballs. I envelop myself in flames, except my head and ankles allowing me to skate on the ice like a human torch. Ice projectiles that hit me sizzled into steam. I still feel the pummeling, but at least I won't be impaled.

All eyes are fixed on the human torch. My opponents are starting to work together against me rather than finish their own fights. Eight of them take a similar stance, the way the goats did to create the crystal bridge only this time. This time it isn't a bridge.

A giant tidal wave rises up and pushes me hard into the ice wall putting out the flames and making me puke up more water. By now, I am tired and out of breath. More ice shards zoom by me, impaling the ice wall right under the spot where Ula is standing, sneering at me. Again, my anger takes over, and I punch both hands into the ice wall. Extreme heat courses through me into my fists. The wall ice where Ula is standing evaporated instantly, and she falls into the water below. Not a second later, I fly clear across the arena where a long jutting ice pillar has materialized. The air in my lungs feels heavy and frozen. After hitting the far wall, I realized that the air in my lungs has already been forced out from the impact.

My ribs are sore. It's so bad I can't tell if they are broken or not. All turtles are too shocked to continue their advance on me. Ula disappears under the water then reappears in the middle of the pool. She rises up on twin dolphin-like water elementals towering over all of us. She bellows out a few words in her language, then again in English once she has calmed down a tad.

"The first session is complete. Take a quick break and be back here in fifteen minutes."

I look over to Ragarth's open-mouthed expression. I take it he does not see her this mad very often. Brutus makes his way over to me and picks me up. Pain strikes my right side, and I grit my teeth as I stand. She definitely broke a few ribs.

Putting my hand over my swollen side, I wait for the familiar warmth to tingle through my arm, then my hand, and into my ribs. Underneath, bones pop and crackle back into place before I can move again.

"James, do you know what you have done?" Brutus tries his best to ask a question.

"Uh, well, I guess I made Ula pretty angry, right?"

"No one has ever done to her what you did."

Okay. I take that as a yes? "Haven't any of you ever challenged her?" *No wonder they are all so scared of her.*

"You made Ula mad, really mad. She will hurt you seriously next session." I take his warning seriously. *I thought this was bad enough. I can't wait till my next beating after the break.*

Chapter 18

A Planned Lunch
Elizabeth

The sky is blue, the air warm, and several goats are up doing daily tasks around the camp. Everything seems normal enough when Tate and I enter the camp. There are a few nannies retrieving water and kids running amuck playing hide-n-seek. Tinky lies upon my shoulder against my neck when a couple billies came into the camp. Several other billies and nannies gathered to inspect a recently singed goat with severe burns and bald patches where fur once was. He smelled like a sun-baked dead rat.

The goats start some loud "Naahh-ing" before calming down and going back to their daily chores. Some nannies look over at me with malicious stares. Tate even came out of the hut during the commotion.

"What's all this about? What happened to that billy? He looks like he got cooked over a fire." He asked.

"Well, to me, that means he lost a fight with James." I grinned widely at that thought. "These goats have been nothing but cruel to us since we got here."

Not long after, the rest of the goat trainees return, and all are either worn out or still in shock from something they saw. I noticed Salithica doesn't return with them. Tinky tugs on my hair and points to his blue furry tummy. I take that as a sign to go back inside rather than stay out with more upset billies and nannies. Back in Salithica's hut, I find a small stash of purple and orange berries in a bowl on the table. I was about to plop one in my mouth when Tate snatched it out of my hand.

"Princess, what do you think you are doing?" He asks angrily. I shrink from him and nervously rub Tinky's belly.

"I was going to taste that berry before I gave a handful to Tinky. What's wrong with you?" I snapped.

"Do you not know what these berries will do to you? They have a paralyzing effect after one minute. What were you thinking?"

"I was thinking Tinky, and I are hungry. Why would Salithica leave a bowl of berries on the table if not to snack on?"

"This isn't the dining table. This is the lab table where Salithica made the cure that saved your life." He is more irritable than ever.

"Well, how in the Land of Kinzurdia am I supposed to know the difference? It's not like you are taking the time to educate me about anything.

You sneak around in the early morning. You make decisions for me that I don't understand. You tell me I'm important but don't explain anything. It's almost as if you're working for ... never mind." I cross my arms and pout. This stranger comes into my life from stalker status, then promotes himself to protector, and he's still a complete mystery to me. Tinky rubs his soft furry head in the cup of my left elbow and starts to purr, calming me down.

Tate looks taken aback by my rampage. He must have never seen an angry princess before. "I'm sorry, Princess. It is just that we aren't safe here, and I don't want to divulge any information for other listening ears. It is common knowledge that not all creatures are what they seem. They may, in fact, be working with or for the Lich and his creations. As for food, please tell me when and what you want to eat, and I will make it for you."

"Oh. So now you are a chef too? Great!" I pause for effect. "Well, I am not hungry, but Tinky is. What food do these blue fur balls eat anyway?"

While Tate makes a small fish feast for Tinky, he starts to let down his guard. He sighs and then starts explaining more about this land and some of the creatures we have encountered while unconscious.

Time flew by, and in struts, a sizable dire wolf followed by a beautiful white and pink five-tailed fox.

"Oh, David. What did you get me now?" I stepped toward this vibrant fox animal to get a better look. David blocks my path, his green eyes dissolved into red eyes, and lets out a ferocious growl. My knees buckle under me, and I fall under the towering wolf.

Tate shoots over to me in an instant and pulls out his glaring sword. The fox whimpers and hides behind the wolf. David's muzzle shakes rapidly before his green eyes came back. He shifts instantly in front of me. I shielded my eyes as Tate sheathed his sword.

"Get control of yourself, David," Tate commands. "Why did Silver take control and try to attack my Princess?" Tate looks down at the fox and back at David, now in human form. David is wearing a fur vest and pants so tight you could swear it was glued on to his abs. David looks back at the fox and smiles and then back to Tate.

"Oh. I see. Jelina, it would be best for you to shift into your human form for now."

"Jelina? Jelina, is that fox?" I ask, wondering if either one of them is going to help me up. "Why would Silver get so agitated with me over getting too close?

Jelina comes out from behind David and shifts into the human form, wearing the same leather clothing. I guess there isn't much of a wardrobe option in this land other than leather or fur.

David reaches over and takes Jelina's hand, interlocking his fingers with hers. The gesture is innocent, but instantly the heat rushes into Jelina's cheeks. She looks at Tate, then at me.

As I scramble to my feet – no help from the men, thank you very much -- realization hits me. "Oh, my Lord." You have got to tell me the details." I take Jelina's other hand and pull her toward Tate's bedroom. David lets go of her hand, but Silver emits a low growl.

Tate points his sheathed sword at David. "Control Silver, or I will."

Jelina and I leave David and Tate to discuss male issues. When I ask her to tell me what just happened, she admits to having feelings for him when she first snuck upon him in the hot spring. She didn't think he would shift into a Dire wolf and chase her. He forced her to come with him even though he held her so gently, calming her immensely. She had never felt so vulnerable before. She finished her story, and I had to recap with a few questions.

"So you stole his kill and made him super angry. Weren't you scared of him?"

"Yes. Actually, I was terrified … of David and of my feelings. How can I have such strong feelings for someone I just met? Plus, he's a Dire wolf." Jelina shakes her head in turmoil over her situation. "This wasn't supposed to happen. This wasn't part of the plan."

"What was the plan?" I ask curiously. Suspicion whips through me.

"It was supposed to..." Jelina sighs and takes in a deep breath. "Oh, nothing. Never mind. Forget I said anything."

I want to press further, but she doesn't look like she's going to offer any more information on that subject. I wonder if I should tell Tate.

I have no idea how long we chatted. I haven't seen one clock since I've woken up. How does anyone tell time here?

We walk back out to the kitchen area. David and Tate are actually cooking side by side.

"David? What's going on here?"

"Well, we got to talking after my little episode. Sorry about that. Since Jelina was so kind as to interrupt our kill earlier, we managed to save a leg to bring back here for lunch with James. Turns out, Tate is pretty handy in the kitchen."

"Is James back yet?" I glance around, anxiously hoping to see evidence that he is here, and give Tinky a few swings in my hair.

"Not yet, but he's on his way. From the workout he's had in these first two training sessions, he's going to need ample food to help him recover for the next two. You may not even recognize him when he arrives."

"Why is that, David?" I stand and cross my arms.

"He's taken quite a beating in this last hour. I know he's okay, but his ego might be slightly damaged. And don't you go repeating that, or he'll kick my butt."

"Really?" I hope James isn't disfigured.

"Well, only if I let him." David smiles, and a flash of red glows brightly in his eyes before receding back to bright green.

Sometimes I really can't tell who is talking, Silver or David.

"I don't see any games here. What do these goats do for fun around here?" David tries a diversion tactic.

Tate and Jelina shrug.

"I saw a few kids playing an epic game of hiding and seek," I say. "One kid would phase into a tree and another act like a chameleon on a rock. The kid who was "it" had these small toothpick-sized twigs that would reveal the hider and paralyze them until ... Oh! That's what the berries are for."

"What berries?" Jelina asks."

"The ones over on that table. I almost ate them, mistaking them for a snack."

"Oh, my. These purple and orange-colored berries? You would be stiff as a tree for hours if you ate more than one of these."

A loud knock on the door turns our heads. The door creaks open and in plops James, immediately dropping to the floor. Behind him stands a tall reddish-brown snapper turtle. He nods before laying ice on the ground and skating away.

James's face is black and blue. Through his shredded shirt, I see multiple bruises decorate his torso up and down. He can't even lift himself off the floor.

"Oh, my Lord! What on earth have they done to you?"

"Princess, this is not the earth you are referring to," Tate says, not understanding the human phrase.

I reach down to pick him up, and he moans painfully. David rushes to the other side of James and, together, we lift him to his feet. We drag him over to the bed I recovered on by the lab table.

"Jelina, please go find Salithica now," David ordered. "James, hold on. We'll fix you up soon."

Jelina doesn't put up an argument. She shifts into a bluebird with a red and yellow striped neck. Her sizeable black beak crashes into the door, pulling off twigs and twine as she flies past. *That bird is familiar, but I can't remember where I've seen it.*

David is staring at James again, so I assume he's doing that mind-reading thing. I walk over to the kitchen, find a cloth, drench it in cold water, and return to James to wipe all the caked blood and dirt off his face.

Salithica rushes in a minute later. "What's going on? What happened to my door?" Her eyes catch mine and reflect the same sadness I am feeling. "Ula went way too far. James, didn't you learn to counter blows being thrown at you?"

James tries to mumble an answer but sucks in a high pitch breath after trying to speak. David translates for us. "He said he did, but dodging in water slowed him down, and trying to dodge instant ice pillars was almost impossible. He says he had to outrun a Skyta fish water elemental, twenty angry ice spike throwing turtles, and still dodge Ula's fast-growing ice pillars."

Salithica looked appalled at what Ula did for her training session with James. "Well, it's over, and you are still alive. Let me heal your wounds. You will need a bit of rest before heading to the storm tribe."

She puts her hands on his bare torso. I notice her smile as she starts to rub his chest. I spring to my feet and look away. I can't believe she is taking advantage of his wounds to touch him like that. It's so wrong.

Tinky must feel my discomfort and rubs his soft head up against my neck. I pet him and scratch behind his ears. He purrs louder as I start heading toward the broken door. I look back over my shoulder and see Salithica hard at work tending to James. David moves about and is holding Jelina's hand again. Tate stares at me with a frown. I nod at him for him to follow me outside, and he complies.

Outside, between the huts, I pace nervously while twisting my hair with my fingers. I look at Tate. "Are my visions really going to happen?"

"Well, a witch's vision of the future is only one possible outcome."

"Why do they want me? I don't even know anything."

"Princess, it's not you. It's your blood they want."

"My blood? What for?"

"Princess Rawena-Rose, your bloodline dates back to the original witches who were able to open the portal connecting Earth to Kinzurdia. That was long ago, but the Lich has always wanted to be the king of all kings. He has never stepped foot into the original human realm because he cannot open the portal. With the help of a few evil witches, the Lich found out how valuable you are.

"After he attacked your father's castle, he realized you and your mother were the keys to unlocking a portal to a new world. Ever since Kaligula informed the Lich of my presence, he knows that you are here with me. He sent dark ones after you at the town of Ooshmala. They failed, and so now he's sending greater threats to capture you. That is why, Princess, we need to leave. We need to get far away from the place of the human refugees at Nazereth. We will be safe there, hidden until we can formulate a better plan of attack."

That explains a lot.

"I am not leaving James like this. And if I am going to be a queen, I don't want to be remembered as the queen who cowardly ran from a fight that leads this entire island's inhabitance to their death."

"Rawena-Rose, please--"

"No, it's Elizabeth. And we stay and fight. There are plenty of fighters here already. We will only need to inform them who is coming."

"Fine, you stubborn child," Tate says under his breath while he turns away from me. I still heard him. Finally, after a brief moment, he agrees. "We can try, but they don't trust humans here."

"Right. Now how are we going to survive the impending attack from Draithur and his Spider witch companion? Do you know anything that can help us defeat them?"

"The spider witch is a mystery. There are rumors that she's more spider than human. There's also a rumor that if you say her name out loud, she will come to kill you in your sleep."

"Has anyone said her name?"

"Yes, and of them have died from a spider bite the next day. Some, however, were a bit messier."

"Do you know her name?"

"Yes, but I'm not going to tell you. Names are powerful here. I can't risk you accidentally summoning the spider witch to your location." Once Tate released this information, it flowed out of him in a deluge.

"Draithur, however, is well known. He deals in the dark arts of necromancy. Thanks to your vision, we know he wields the book Necronomicon. He was once only a young ignorant human who believed he could use the dead to benefit himself. The darkness corrupted him, and the Lich took advantage of his potential. He gave Draithur more power and unleashed him in his old hometown. The population now consists of all his undead minions. I have a bad feeling he will be bringing a few of them with him when he comes."

"This is crazy. I need to tell James and the others. We need to make a plan."

We walk back into the hut to find James, healed by the goat woman's ministrations and more awake, sitting at the kitchen table.

"Hi, Elizabeth. I'm sorry we didn't wait for you to eat," he greets me. "I need to get back to training, and I want to be able to stand when I see you off."

He doesn't know. I haven't told anyone yet.

"James, I am not leaving," I blurt out. "We have a bigger problem. I had another horrible vision." I look down, replaying the same picture of James' death behind my eyelids. A stray tear falls silently down my cheek. "Elizabeth? Hey, don't cry." James stumbles off his chair and stands in front of me. I can smell his familiar scent of pine needles. He's so close. His warm, calloused fingers lift my chin up, and he gazes into my eyes. "I won't let anyone hurt you. I will protect you."

I want him to kiss me so badly, but his hand falls. Instead, he embraces me in a gentle hug. I cry into his shoulder for a minute before wiping my tears away and stepping back.

"I was so scared you weren't going to make it. You looked so awful." I whisper in his ear. I straighten my already-straight leather shorts. I look away. Jelina is smiling, and David winks at me. Blood rushes to my cheeks as I see how this may look. I shy away from the stares. What has gotten into me? Why do I feel so helpless and vulnerable around James?

James laughs. "So, you think I look awful?"

I balk and quickly blab out, "No, you are beautiful. I mean, you look handsome ... good." I cover my face with my hands and turn away from him.

James pulls me around to face him. "No, Elizabeth. You are beautiful." He cups my face as he stares straight into my soul. This is it! He's going to kiss me. My hands are clammy, and the seconds pass as slowly as hours. He steps closer, and I close my eyes.

"What do you think you are doing?" Tate asks from behind me, clearly agitated by the scene.

James' hand drops from my cheek, and he moves back.

I want to scream at Tate. I want to wring his neck.

I take a deep breath and open my eyes again. James returns to his seat, a little pink in the neck, and starts eating the venison left on his plate.

Tate grabs my arm. "Princess, we need to talk."

"Let go of me!" I'm infuriated with Tate and this whole situation. We don't have any time left, and James will be leaving soon to go back to training. "No. We've already talked. What we need to do is come up with a plan to get James off this island and to defeat Draithur."

I sit down with James, David, Jelina, and Salithica at the table. Tinky is still hanging on to my hair. Tate stands in the back, eyeing me, but I ignore him. I go into the vision I had and explain what Tate told me earlier. We start throwing up ideas.

Ten minutes later, after discussing the trial rules, a plan starts to emerge. "David, what do you think?"

"This may actually work, but we will need everyone here involved. Jelina, you need to scout out the locations and race paths of the trials. I will explore the undead lands.

James will train his butt off. Salithica will work her magik to convince the other leaders of an imminent threat. Tate will do what he's good at and protect Elizabeth."

"What about Tinky and me?" I am feeling left out and helpless … and just a little annoyed.

"Uh, Tinky can comfort you, and you can help Tate help keep you safe." James is sincere, and that irritates me even more. Tinky pops his head up curiously when his name is called. His big eyes on his small face are adorable.

"Wait? Are you kidding? I'm going to help," I insist, then decide to play it differently. "Please. Let me help," I plead.

James frowns, as one hand strokes his chin.

David sputters before James can answer. "Well, umm, okay. How about you do a little recon with the local non-trainees over the next week? Find out as much history and information as you can for each trial. Unearth any rumors about Draithur and the spider witch." It seems David really does have a knack for plans. "And I'll do a little training of my own with Jelani's techniques. Hopefully, I can learn as fast as my brother."

The sound of someone clearing their throat reaches from the doorway. A hush comes over everyone at the table. A small rodent stands impatiently in the archway, examining the damage to the door.

"You're late, human."

Chapter 19

A Breezy Afternoon
James

Salithica stands and goes to greet the small furball. "Morty. How nice to see you again." She flashes him a big smile. "James had a few complications that I had to attend to before releasing him into your care."

The rodent clears his throat a second time. "I will inspect him myself to make sure he is capable of attending our training session. As late as he is, Leena won't be in a good mood."

This is no lemur. He looks more like a guinea pig.

He crawls up my feet and starts sniffing. He is such a small little guy. It's hard to believe he's not a hamster. He circles my feet a few times and licks my toes.

"Eww! What the heck are you doing, furball?" I shove the midget guinea pig away from my feet.

"Morty, how many times have I told you to not lick my guest's feet." Salithica scolds him like a misbehaving child.

He looks up at her with big eyes. "Sorry. They look so white and inviting. Anyway, human, it appears you will survive. Now let's hurry and get you to practice. We all want to see if a human can fly. Plus, Leena wants to see what makes you so special. I already know your feet are."

Yuck. I think he winks at me before going back to sniffing my feet again. Bile rises in my throat, but I am able – just barely -- to keep my lunch down. That deer thigh was leaner than the ones back in Scotland.

I look to my brother in question. *"Is this for real?"*

"I will ask Salithica about him and let you know," David replies.

I say my goodbyes to Elizabeth, Jelina, Salithica, and my brother and follow Morty out of the hut. He jumps and spins into the air about knee-high before landing on a small puffy white cloud. He makes it look so easy.

I calm my nerves. *I can do this, spin and land on a cloud. Yeah, a puffy white cloud.*

I look around, and for once, I don't see anyone staring my direction other than Morty's wide-eyes and a broad smile. I plant my feet, bend my knees, close my eyes, and spring up into a 360 twist. The air current swirls around me. I lean too far forward and open my eyes just in time to see the ground before my nose hits it.

"Oh, goodness. Leena is going to have some fun with you." Morty circles me a few times as I rise to my feet and brush off dirt and twigs. He does a few figure eights between my legs, somehow leaving my feet wet.

"Follow me back to the waterfall. You are going to have to go up that way since you can't fly."

"I will fly. I just need time to figure it out, that's all." I am determined to master the flying thing. I have to succeed. That is the only way I can protect Elizabeth and my brother. A new surge of energy came over me, and I walk faster than Morty's slow hovering pace.

The long walk gives me time to absorb the nature around me, feel textures and smells odors, and bring nature inside me. The forest is alive, and its energy flows into me with every step I take. Bushes and branches bend out of the way to let me pass unobstructed. I am genuinely connected, and for the first time, I feel like an integral part of something greater. My mind is lost in my thoughts as we arrived at the thunderous sound of gushing water falling from the heavens.

Darn waterfall. The endless stream of water falling through white clouds. I'm going to fly today. To think only a few days ago, if someone told me I could learn to fly, I would have punched them in the face to knock some sense into them.

I study the white water impacting where the stream hits the pond. I remember how I failed only a few hours ago to shoot up the waterfall. Now I know I can do it.

Morty hovers next to me, anxious to see what will happen. I step into the warm water and wade under the waterfall. The hard pounding on my head slides into my ears as I tune out the world around me. I concentrate on the water gliding down and across my arms, remembering the feeling before I drilled through that solid boulder. The sensation of warmth and tingling ripples through my skin and muscles, and I ask the water to lift me.

A water bubble forms around my head as I open my eyes. The sounds of hard thumps atop my head cease. I can see clearly through the rapid water. I feel weightless, uneasiness in the pit of my stomach before I am shot up like out of a cannon. The scenery of tall trees transforms into a blue sky canvas sprinkled lightly with a few white clouds.

I make the mistake of looking down as the ground and Morty become smaller and smaller. The warm tingling sensation comes to an abrupt end as I pop up over the edge of the floating island and fall back on my bum—the stream parts ways around me, ever-flowing downward.

Morty catches up and flies in circles around me, making weird faces while tilting his head to the side. "You sure are an interesting human. Leena will be pleased. Now, get up and follow me to the training grounds."

The small island appears as it did a few days ago, with the white dome-like homes. Several cloud rings fall to the base of each home. Lemurs climb on the clouds like steps to their front doors.

Two tall, white towers stand on opposite sides of the river in the middle of the island. They seem to represent a gateway to the origin of the river. Morty and I walk along the stream past the towers. The flowing water connects to a shallow pond where steam rises, and clouds form above it like a factory production line. Morty guides me to the left, where a group of twenty lemurs stands at attention in front of Leena sitting on a floating cloud.

Leena eyes Morty and smiles. The smile melts into a frown when she sees me. She stops her discussion in her native tongue and clears her throat. "Attention class, as you may already know, a human will be joining us today. Do not let his filth or his lies taint your thoughts. Do not allow him to think he could be better than any of you. Train hard. We only have nine days left before one of you will be chosen as my new storm master-apprentice."

Approaching Leena, my wet sandals slip ungracefully on the thick grass. I'm still soaking wet from the waterfall ride.

"So this is how humans present themselves to me and my class -- wet and grungy."

"My apologies, Leena," Morty says quickly before a sudden rush of hot air encircles me. My leather skins flap vigorously in the wind, hitting my face as I squeeze my eyes shut until the current dissipates. Morty was a lot less graceful when Leena used the same technique earlier.

The hot air dries me and my clothes completely, and Morty shoos me to the backline of the class. I am a meter taller than every lemur here.

With the height advantage, I observe the rows of lemurs. It is interesting to see how every tribe has unique colors where no two look the same. The lemurs range from my hand size to about the length of my outstretched arm.

Some looked like Leena with white fur and black faces. Others were brown with black and white ringtails. A black and gray lemur stands to my right, making odd gestures with its purple face tongue. A group of similar-looking ring-tailed lemurs stares at me with big red eyes on the far side. They resemble raccoons with their white face with black rings surrounding their eyes and a black nose and mouth. They give me an eerie impression that I need to watch out for them.

Morty seems to be the runt of this litter. He could fit in the palm of my hand. He has a few shades of light to dark brown fur—the darkest on his face with big black eyes and pink toes. I am sure Elizabeth would add him to her collection alongside Tinky.

"As you are well aware, we have the best trial amongst the four tribes. We allow all other tribes to take part in attempting to stop you from finishing the race. This is to prove to every tribe that we are superior to them. You will need to make sure, from now and up until the race starts, that you know how to combat anything thrown at you or put in front of you to keep you from reaching the end. Our race is dangerous, and the years past have taken some of our fellow lemurs' lives. They were weak and unprepared. Learn from their foolishness and prove to me and everyone that you are the next master for this tribe."

Leena looks across all the lemurs and smiles. "If any of you wish to back out of the trial, now would be the time." She eyes me as she says the last words. I stand silent, provoked but determined to prove to her that I can win this stupid race.

"Fine…time to get started. Pair up and practice dodging while floating in place."

All the lemurs quickly pair up with another lemur, leaving me to stand alone. I barely recall what Salithica had said to float. Leena and Morty float over next to me.

"Since you are a filthy human who I don't want tainting any of my precious future masters, I will have Morty here train you. If you can't fly by the time the trial starts, you will be automatically eliminated from the race. The checkpoints are in the air and can only be reached by flight. You are a heavy human, so the cloud size you will need to conjure will have to be incredible to keep you off the ground."

I notice all the other lemurs have clouds about the size of my outstretched arms clasped into a circle. If that's the case, Leena is right. My cloud will need to be much larger.

"Since you have no ability yet to conjure your own cloud, I will bring you to where our youngest first learn to use a cloud."

Morty guides me back over to the cloud production line in the pond. He swings down and out of my sight while I stand in awe of how these clouds are created. Something soft, warm, and wet slides across my toes. I jerk my leg back and look down at a smiling Morty.

"Gross, you dumb bloke. Stop doing that."

"I'll make a deal with you. If you learn to fly today, I will stop." Morty giggles profusely.

"I'll make you eat those words." His lack of confidence hinders my concentration. *I'm not going to let some rat lick my feet and tell me I can't do anything.*

"He's not a rat. Salithica says he's a guinea pig. He was the runt of his litter and tossed out of his family and left for dead. Leena found him and took pity. She raised him like one of her own. Salithica says to let him believe he's a lemur as he is already a master in storm magik." My brother pipes into my head, correcting my own thoughts. I ignore my brother and try to concentrate.

"What do you do to conjure the cloud?" I ask through my teeth. Having to ask a rodent how to do something injures my pride and shrinks my self-esteem.

Morty clears his throat. *This must be a lemur thing.* "Let me begin. There is a certain posture you must hold with a level of concentration to mix the right amount of water and air frequencies to conjure up a puffy white cloud."

"What happens if you don't get the right mixture?" I ask curiously.

"Well, uh, either you don't fly, or you make something bad." Morty shivers at his own thoughts. "Don't dwell on that. It's rare that anyone can conjure up a dark cloud other than the leaders."

"A dark cloud? I want more information. "What does a dark cloud do?"

Morty looks around with others nearby and begins to shake. "Not a time to discuss such things. Let's get you started with a basic cloud.

I'm slightly taken aback at how scared Morty looked when the topic of dark clouds came up. I shove those questions into the back of my mind and follow Morty's instructions on perfect posture and positioning.

After half an hour of practicing, I can only conjure a cloud the size of my palm. Knowing I can do it at all is a relief. Unfortunately, I need a cloud a hundred times that if I am to compete in this race. My brain is tired. I sit down and lean back to rest a minute. Listening to the sounds of the water flowing and the quiet sounds of the clouds forming is soothing and comforting. I relax and try to absorb the feeling.

What I feel is Morty licking me again. I kick him off into the pond. There's got to be another way to learn how to fly. I did something different earlier with the fire, but it was precarious. I close my eyes and quickly connect to my brother.

"David, you there," I mentally think, exasperated.

"Yes, James, what's wrong?" He must sense my despair.

"How would you create a cloud of air and water?"

"I'm no Elementalist. You would have better luck knowing than me. Maybe you can think about how clouds are naturally formed. When warm air rises, it expands and cools down. Some of the warm air shrinks into tiny dust particles with a droplet of water coating it. And when many of these particles come together, it forms a visible white cloud."

"That's it. I knew you, and that brain of yours would figure this out."

"We are glad to help. Silver and I are going with Jelina to try a few new techniques ourselves. See you tonight."

David mentally pushes me out of his mind. Morty is licking my feet again. That is so gross. I toss Morty a few meters away before he flies right back to me. "Lord Morty, what were you doing?"

"You looked like you were about to pass out. I can't have a trainee of mine sleeping."

"I wasn't sleeping. I was in deep thought. Anyway, I think I figured it out." I stand up on my feet and think about what David said. I need warm air. Heat rides down my arms and into my hands, but no flames burst out. The atmosphere bends and contorts as I can see the heat waves leaving my palms. Morty floats away from me, biting his fingers.

I am aware of a large plume of hot air. I need to cool the air. I ask the air around above to come down and wrap around my plume of hot air. I feel the dust particles forming. I move them all together over and over.

A white puff emerges from the center of my concentration. It starts expanding larger and larger.

Morty's big blue eyes widen evermore. His mouth opens, and I can barely hear him whisper. "How, how can he create it with no stance, no practice?"

The loud commotion from the other lemurs behind me quiets. I ignore them and concentrate. The cloud is now the entire pond's size, and it absorbs the small clouds created by the pond. I stop its expansion and lower it down to me. I step up to climb on it only to step right through it.

I realize I must make myself weightless, like how Salithica showed me with a small ball of air. I call forth wind to hold me just above the cloud but also to the cloud. I step again and am met with a more solid feeling, so I climb up into the middle and stretch a long piece of cloud upward for a backrest. I sit down and pull a bit of a cloud across my waist. I imagine it to work much like a seat belt would hold me in place. At my request, the air turns me to face the lemurs, and I see every lemur staring bug-eyed at me. I look to Leena, and she looks furious.

Leena rides over on her much smaller cloud than mine. "Well, well, maybe there is something special about this human after all. Creating a cloud is only a small part of flying in our upcoming trial. Let's see how well you can maneuver it when under attack."

In my peripheral vision, I see Morty zoom away from me right before a large gust of air pushes my cloud barely off the edge of the island. The front half of my cloud is merely floating a meter off the ground. I haven't had time to figure out the flying part.

I reach down and collect a bit of the cloud in my hand. The water vapor comes together into an ice shard. I fall through the cloud instantly, falling to my death. By taking my concentration away from the cloud and the air under me, I created the ice shard.

That was stupid. I need to concentrate on all magiks at the same time if I'm going to compete against any of them. I'm still falling, but now I'm not worried. I push away that fear of heights and stuff it down inside me.

Closing my eyes, I envision the wind around me and smell the water below me.

I'm not in any danger. If I fall in the water, I will not drown. If I can quickly re-conjure that cloud, I can save myself from getting wet. I knit back together that cloud in my mind while I slow my decent gracefully with flames shooting out the bottom of my sandals. Once the cloud reaches a large enough circumference, I swap the fire for air nuggets and clasp myself back into the created cloud. The cloud hovers over the water at the bottom of the waterfall.

My attempt to move the entire cloud and myself upwards is unsuccessful.

Hot air rises. The thought gives me an idea.

I stick both my feet through the cloud and out the underside. I sent heat waves down my legs and out my feet. The hotter air built up underneath, quickly raising the cloud and me with it.

Wow! Now, understanding that I must change the air's temperature surrounding my cloud to maneuver it, I test it out and make a few loopty-loops in the air. The adrenaline starts rushing through my veins as I speed up in a vertical incline. Laughing, I pass the edge of the pond atop the floating island, soaring far up into the sky, leaving contrails like an airplane.

I've been up here too long. I fly down, at last, understanding what I need to do.

The shocked faces of all the lemurs and Morty add to my exhilaration. Leena twists the corners of her mouth into a smirk, and I know what's coming. This time I know what I need to concentrate on. I smile before she starts throwing several air gusts at me.

Chapter 20

Anger Management
James

I walk up to the edge of the waterfall, looking down into the sea of mist-covered treetops. Morty hovers nearby while I replay the scenes from the last hour of training.

Leena is quite skilled, but luckily she wasn't out for revenge like Ula. She knocked me out of the air time and time again but allowing me all the recovery time I needed to form another cloud. She hurled wind spirals and hail in my direction. They spun me around.

The cloud was no barrier to hard ice pellets. Every attempt to fend Leena off and better her was futile. I can't land a single attack on her with her small stature and nimble reflexes on her fast maneuvering cloud.

Sudden warm wetness crosses my toes and brings me to attention. Looking down, I see a guinea pig happily lapping up the sweat atop my toes. "Hey. Morty, we had a deal." I shake him off and wipe away his drool.

Morty floats back on his small cloud. "I know, but they are so tasty."

I scoot a bit forward-looking over the edge again. Viewing the water so far below gives me that same fearful queasiness. Knowing now that I can fly barely makes me feel any better.

Morty floats up in front of me, meeting me at eye level. "Well, since you have proven that you can fly, there is no sense in me escorting you to the volcanic tribal boundaries." Marty shakes a bit and looks around nervously.

"Morty. What's wrong? Why are you shaking?"

"We, the storm tribe, have a long ongoing agitated disagreement with the volcanic tribe. That is why Leena created this floating island -- to escape the daily torments from their members."

"Wait, how did Leena create an entire island?"

"Many years ago, we lived in treetops on the surface. The Volcanic tribe preyed on us and set fire to our homes, roasting us alive within a tree. We are more superior to them, so they had to use sneaky tactics to find our weaknesses. Leena's mother was the leader at that time." Morty looked away. I almost ask what happened to her mother when I suddenly realize what must have happened.

"So Leena lost her mother to a raid, and she became the leader, right?" My sentiments toward Leena soften a tad. I can generate more sympathy for Leena now because I can relate to losing a mother too.

179

"Yes," Morty answers. "She became the leader by an unfortunate circumstance. No matter how many patrols she put up at night, it was impossible to stop every attack. Because more and more lemurs died under her watch, she devised a crazy plan to move our home into the sky. It was the only place the lizards couldn't reach. I saw her talk to a cloaked figure one night who must have given her the spell needed to keep this island afloat."

Morty looks into the distant orange-colored clouds in thought.

"That still doesn't explain how she created an entire island?" It seemed impossible that a small lemur could carry out such a massive spell by herself. "Morty?"

"Oh, yes. Do you see that lake below us? It is the same size as this island."

"Yes?" I'm starting to get annoyed by this little Guinea pig's puzzling explanations.

"Humans…" Morty looks at the falling sun. He looks back at me. "We have talked too long. You must hurry, or you will be late in training with Therose. If you thought his sister was a mean turtle, you haven't seen anything yet." Morty floats back down.

"Sister? Morty, get away from my feet."

"Just one lick before you go. I will be quick." Morty opens his tiny mouth and sticks out his tongue, floating closer to my toes.

"No." I jump off the edge and start to plummet. Before, the rays of the sun rays shine from behind the volcano. The rush of air flaps my cheeks and rustles my hair vigorously. I take in a deep breath to push the massive knot that fear forms in my stomach out of my mind. As the wind caresses my arms, I combine the elements of water, wind, and dust to create my cloud. I pass through several misty clouds and add parts from each to my own. The tree branches start to slow down as my cloud grows under me. My cloud, a good two meters in circumference, carries me over the surface of the lake. A few goats are levitating fish out of the water at the edge. They notice me, and the fish free fall onto the sand below like a bubble holding them popped. All the goats stare at me with amazed expressions. One of them drops his gear and darts back into the forest in the direction of Salithica's camp.

I give them a wink as I float up and over the treetops in the direction of the volcano. The sun starts its preparation to set for the evening. The underbellies of clouds are changing colors from oranges to reds. *It's beautiful up here.*

"Maybe you should bring Elizabeth with you next time." A most familiar brotherly teasing voice enters my thoughts.

"Maybe, I will. I have had enough of your lust-filled thoughts about Jelina. I still can't believe she's the first girl you met, and you are already a lovesick puppy around her."

"She helps me cope with Silver, and you know how irritable he gets," David says while sending me picture reminders of that ram they shredded in

front of me.

"At least she has a cute human form too. A good eight out of ten in my book." I say, rating her looks while trying to block out those horrible images.

"Grrrrr. You no get her. She mine." Silver interjects.

"She is ours." David corrects Silver.

"I don't have time for this. I'm already running late. I have to find Therose soon for my last training session today." I relay to both of them amid their argument on who Jelina belongs to. I don't think either one heard me as I push them both out of my thoughts and concentrate on getting to the cave entrance by the forest's tree line.

I pass over the last of the trees before a gigantic pile of rock and dirt blocks out the sun behind it. Lava embers can be seen near the top of the mound spewing out small fragments like sparklers. I lower my cloud to the ground before a large opening in the rock.

The cave is enormous, at least two times the size of my castle back home. Gazing upward, many colorful reptiles in armor or leather walkabout. Loud sounds of metal clashing on metal. The sounds bring back memories of my Da making new swords for the fair. Loud foreign language and English mumbling are heard throughout this area. Reptiles, both bipedal and on all fours, walk together. Their scales are colorful in reds, blues, and greens.

Smaller caves line the walls on either side of the large opening. Almost every bipedal reptile had a mug in hand. Several groups of red lizards are laughing and falling over themselves, unable to stand vertically without help. One falls over a salamander. The Green and black slimy creature spins and slaps his tail across the fallen lizard's face before slithering off across the rock floor. My Da would easily fit in here. An odd motion attracts my eyes to my right. It's like the rock is moving, getting closer to a group of drunken geckos. A small outline starts to form before the chameleon becomes visible and steals a dagger from the orange gecko's belt. The gecko barely notices, looks around and goes back to the mug in his hand.

I step off the cloud, holding tightly onto the strap of my quiver with my left hand while the other hovers over David's daggers in my belt. My cloud dissipates, I stroll forward into the den of several angry-looking lizards. Chatter lowers for a moment before more English related talk emerges. This tribe seems to be filled with hate toward humans.

What have I got myself into?

"Do you think anyone will defeat Therose this year?" One green lizard says.

The red draconian replied, "He has had a winning streak every year for the past seven trials. It is unlikely he will lose this year."

A bulky muscular blue-tinged draconian steps up in front of the red draconian "So you call me weak. Therose has had a good run, but only due to the Kioserack sword. Once I take it from him, he will turn back into that weakling sea turtle he came crawling to us as years ago."

After inching around behind the oversized blue lizard, I achieve a better view of the group talking.

A large dark shadow blankets me and the ground around me. The visages of the smaller draconians turn pale, and their eyes widen. At first, I think they are gaping at me until they start to slowly retreat backward. Then a deep bellowing howl comes from behind me.

"Torius, you dare mock me. It is a good thing this human is eavesdropping on your conversation, or I would deal with you right now."

The large blue draconian shrinks a few inches when he hears his name called and turns toward me shakily, then he smirks and walks away. The heat of Therose's breath crawls down my neck. My automatic reaction to the angry presence behind me is to cower. Instead, I steel myself and turn around slowly. His unsheathed sword is mid-lunge toward my throat.

I lean quickly to my right, hoping I am quick enough to not get decapitated. The sharp steel blade pierces my shoulder, sending searing pain down my arm and pinning me to the cave wall. Painful, agonizing waves reverberate across my neck and pound like beating drums in my head. My eyes glaze over, and Therose becomes nothing more than a blurred figure.

Angry words are spat at me. "I thought I made it clear to your brother that humans are not welcome here! I am going to gut you like the fish I had last night. I will show you..."

His words fade as I reach up with my right hand and pull the blade out. The edge feels cool and smooth to the touch. Its curved blade making it hard to extract it. Blood gushes down my arm.

Heatwaves flutter in front of my eyes, giving me the sensation of being transported to another place. I see a figure in the distance and am pulled closer. It's a green lizard holding a long curved steel sword. The same one that Therose stabbed me with. He faces me, but there's another shadowy black figure in front of him.

Closer and closer I approach. The pain in my arm has faded and is long since forgotten. A soft sweet voice hums incomprehensible words in a songlike tone. The female figure appears familiar, tall with blonde hair, and dressed in full leather, battle-ready gear. She finishes her enchanting song, and the green lizard's sword glows bright blue as engravings flash down the length of the blade. The soft familiar voice speaks in a rushed tone, "Kioserack, hurry to kill him before my spell weakens." Both the lizard and the human female look to my right. I follow their gaze and see five of the very same dark creatures that attacked Elizabeth in our forest.

They have sharp claws and red glowing eyes in a vast black

mist. A gray-skinned human walked out from behind his black mist friends in shiny silver armor. The black smoke swirled around him and layered his creepy wrinkled skin.

"Hurry! Kill the Lich," the soft voice turns frantic. I snap my head back to her. A slightly older looking Elizabeth stands confidently tossing bright white orbs of magik at the dark creatures surrounding the Lich.

In a state of shock, I call out. "Elizabeth, Elizabeth!" It is of no use. No one can hear me. Kioserack charges at the Lich and the dark creatures move to intercept.

Kioserack is destined to be torn to shreds. I almost wanted to look away, but then a bright flash disrupted my vision. One of the dark ones disappears. Then another and another. The older Elizabeth clone is throwing white orbs of fire at the Lich, but they only bounced off his silver armor. Kioserack manages to dodge past the remaining dark ones. He flips the sword around, holding it like a dagger. He thrust the blade deep into the neck of the Lich, through the chest, and inevitably into the heart. Lich's gray skin starts to crack. Blue light shines out of the newly formed cracks until his skin exploded. Chunks of gray flesh cover Kioserack and me. The black mist shrinks down into the silver armor before glowing hot red. The armor is all that remains before boiling pain flings me back to the present.

Things in the present don't look much better.

Therose towers above me and twists the same sword into my shoulder. Hot tingling sensations ran down my neck, shoulder, and arms. I stretch out my right hand to push Therose back. A large gust of steam flings him back a good ten meters, giving me time to pull out the sword's blade and toss it to the ground.

As I recall all the wrongs I have suffered, my anger builds. The constant belittlement by every creature, plus the anguish of killing my own father, and the torment of turning my brother into a dire wolf. The thought of losing Elizabeth to some undead Lich. The energy builds up more and more. The pain of the sword tip I pull out pales into insignificance.

I have had enough! I snap.

I explode into oranges and reds, every bit of my skin covered in searing flames. Therose slides back another meter but not before he calls the sword back to him. I pull out my bow, grab as many arrows as I can, and fire into the air. They soar high and spread out. Dropping in a semi-circle around a surprised scar-faced turtle. Geysers of flame spew from each arrow. A few in the crowd leap out of the way just in time. I toss my bow and quiver down to my side and pull out David's daggers, igniting them with my anger.

Therose's sneer warps into a smile. "Well, well. The human can play with fire. Let's see if you can fight as well as you show off." He ignited his sword in orange flames and let out a battle cry before charging.

I am ready, my breathing levels out, and I focus on his approach. He is almost close enough when a giant red-scaled body lands on top of Therose, pinning him to the ground. The wind from its wings sends me and several of the crowd flying onto our backs. I look up to see Zyerr, the leader of the draconians, snarling down at Therose. His large red wings spread out, and smoke rising from his snout. I finally snap out of my rage and look at what I'm doing. My flames extinguish rapidly, as though I'd jumped in a pool of water. Cold chills run down my spine and arms. *What have I done?* The dragon isn't looking at me but more at the crowd and then focuses on Therose.

Zyerr's scaled chest sticks out as he towers over all of us, including Therose. Smoke escapes his maw with every word Zyerr roars. "How dare you go against my order! Everyone involved in this attack shall endure my wrath!"

Even I felt the need to cower. Zyerr continued in draconian, and the eyes of every reptile around popped out in fear. With Zyerr's last words, the draconians scurried away like rats.

There is no one else in sight other than Therose, Zyerr, and me. I clenched my fists and stand up to Zyerr's overwhelming presence. I saw a slight twitch in Zyerr's eyes before a small smile crept up his face.

Zyerr repositions his weight, and Therose grumbles something like, "get off me, you oversized lizard." Zyerr's eyes turn molten red. He picks up Therose and roars bluish orange flames at Therose. Therose manages to turn in time to have his shell deflect most of the blast onto a nearby hut, instantly vaporizing it.

My jaw goes slack, my fists unclench, and I take a few steps back. The heat is so intense I have to cover my face. Zyerr speaks in draconian, then stops and nails me with his gaze. A smile creeps up that intense maw of his. "Therose, meet your new trainee."

If a turtle could go pale, then it would look like Therose right now.

"But Zyerr, we hate humans. Why ... what ... No!" Therose is taken back by the news of having to train a human. He acts as though it's worse than getting sprayed with dragon fire. Therose rebuts, "I'm not even the trainer for the tribe."

Zyerr replies, "You have been the reigning champion for the last seven trials, have you not?"

Therose's disappointment morphs to pride before he nods, settling his eyes back on me and sneering.

"I have a hatred for humans," Zyerr continues, "but this one, who stands before us, shows great potential -- especially if he can get along with you for a few days. You may just see him in the final fight."

Therose took in that last statement and eyed me evilly. "I look forward to that fight if you can make it that far, human."

I gulp but try not to show the fear I feel inside.

I will have to train with the warrior. I must defeat him to win my freedom. "Bring it," I say.

Zyerr put down Therose. "You two play nice until the trial starts, or I will make whatever pain you inflict seem desirable after I'm finished with you." Zyerr takes flight and leaves us staring each other down.

"Don't think I'll go easy on you because you are a weak human."

"I wouldn't expect you to be the lenient type," I reply.

Therose's right hand becomes engulfed in flames. "Let's see how much you know." Therose throws a fireball straight at my head. He no longer has the glint in his eye to kill me but more of a desire to see what I'm capable of. My adrenaline rushes through my veins in a burst. I dodge barely to the right and gladly return the favor throwing three more fireballs back at him. This is the training I've been waiting for.

Chapter 21

Eight Days Later
Elizabeth

A loud crack sounds, and the hut door violently swings inward. The door is now slanted on its vine hinges.

Bright evening sunrays shine in outlining a dark figure in the doorway. Tate stands up in alarm and reaches for his sword. Heavy breathing is heard from the dim outline. The figure steps into the hut covered head to toe in black soot. Tate starts to pull out his sword when I recognize the intruder. I grab Tate's arm and stop his motion.

"James, is that you? What happened?" He sucks in a wheezing breath before exhaling.

"Yes, Elizabeth. It's nice to see you too." James replies sarcastically. "Therose decided to have his lackeys join in on the last training session. If you think I look bad, you should see what they look like. I think Therose did it on purpose just to let the other competitors know I'm more of a threat then they will anticipate. The problem now will be when I face Therose, he knows how I fight, and it will be harder to beat him."

James looks around before wobbling to the couch made of makeshift branches, leaves, and skins. My heart aches at the thought of what he has gone through the past nine days.

"Where's my brother and his girlfriend?" He sounds a bit smug and won't call Jelina by her name.

"Oh. Those two will be back any minute. They were perfecting a few latest techniques in the forest. I know you have been insanely busy the past week, but you should really see how much your brother has improved with Jelina's help."

Tate seems a bit bored with our conversation and goes into the kitchen to make some food. He is surprisingly a good cook.

James shrugs his shoulders and looks down. I quickly grab a cloth from the kitchen, dampen it, and walk over to the couch. I sit down next to him and start wiping the soot off his face. He jolts back at my touch, then looks me in the eye. I try not to take it personally, knowing how much he has gone through. There's something about his eyes when I look at him. It's as if they soften his hard resolve.

He leans into me as I try to get the rest of the soot off his face. My shirt, now covered in soot, is enveloped in his strong arms. I feel comfortable and happy with how much closer we have become over the last few days. Ever since Jelina mated with David, he and his brother have become more distant. I can see that it bothers James more than he lets on. I am surprised at how much I have come to enjoy James' company. He is still a jerk, but he seems to show his softer side when I am around.

"So, how has the recon been going?" James asks in a quiet tone while sniffing my hair and tickling my neck.

"Eeeek." Tinky shrieks and jumps down into my lap. I had forgotten he was on my shoulder.

"Mmmm, good." I suddenly lose my train of thought. I close my eyes and breathe in his comforting smell of pine needles. Heat blankets my face as I abruptly open my eyes to see Tate towering over us, shaking his head. I jolted back in my seat, knocking our heads together while breaking up the moment. My head is ringing. *How did he ... but he was in the kitchen?* I blinked my eyes again, and he was back in the kitchen hard at work, cooking some stew. Tinky clenched onto my leg.

"Ouch, why did you do that?" James asked while rubbing his forehead.

He looks at me with a questionable stare. The same look every adopted couple gave me before sending me back to the orphanage. I bury my eyes into my hands to escape yet again. The pain and feeling of loss consume me as I sniffle and rock myself.

He puts a hand on me to console me like every other adoptive parent before they sent me back. I tried so hard to keep my composure, to not let my past become an issue.

"What have you done to my Princess?" Tate's demanding tone rises as if he is coming closer from far away.

"I didn't do anything. She freaked out, and our heads collided." James sounded taken aback by the accusation.

"What were you doing before she freaked out?" Tate said in a sickened tone.

James let out a breath but didn't answer. He stands and steps past me. Pain clenches in my heart as he silently leaves the hut.

"Princess, are you okay?" Tate asks in a genuine tone.

I stay silent, trying to recall what took place. My senses start to replay, feeling the heat and a flash of a disapproving Tate towering over me.

"James is gone. Tell me what happened. What did he do to you?" Tate pushes again. I can feel the couch bend down as he sits next to me.

I take in a couple deep breaths. Uncover my runny eyes and look at him. "You did this!" I shout.

Tate didn't even try to hide it. "This is what is best for you. You have a kingdom. You have people that need to depend on you. There is no time for you to fool around with some boy that will get you killed. There is no place in your destiny for him. He is simply a tool you use to get you to safety."

"I feel safer in his arms than under your stare," I mumble, rising from the couch.

"What was that? Tate asks.

"Nothing." I reach down, take Tinky off my leg and place him back on my shoulder. The blue ball of fuzz is soft and comforting as I walk to the front door.

"Where do you think you are going?" Tate demands disapprovingly.

"To write a new destiny." I walk out the broken door into the cold evening air.

"Princess…" Tate calls for me. I block him out.

Most of the goats are outside, busy preparing a bonfire, fish, and festival-like decorations around the huts and down from the great tree. The sound of drums pounding out an enticing rhythm pulls me closer. A circle of goats sit around a pile of branches. David and Jelina are at the head of the circle drumming away on makeshift drums of skin stretched over hollow stumps. Some of the goats looked intrigued, others disgusted. When a young goat approaches, David hands him the sticks and shows him what to do. Several other goats have already joined in with their own drums.

I have heard the drums play the last three nights, adding music to the night's previous silence. *What have I been doing all this time holed up inside a hut? Doing everything Tate has told me. In fear of dying or being captured by Draithur and the Spider Witch.* While I've been playing house, David has been getting friendly with the natives. Nine days ago, nearly every goat showed hatred toward us. Now, only a few don't smile at us as David leads them into playing a familiar tune from the Black Bugs. David starts to sing, "we can work it out."

Life is too short to fight with James.

Jelina looks up, spots me, and smiles while holding on to David. Happiness for her fills me. A knot twits in my stomach. She nods to her right. I follow her gaze and see James sitting on a stump drawing in the dirt with a stick.

"What do you think, Tinky? Should we?" Tinky's head pops out of my hair. He looks over at James, squeaks, and hides behind my hair. He purrs, and the usual calmness descends on me. My nerves unwind as I walk up behind James. I catch David's eyes, and he smiles my way before going back to teaching the drums to another goat.

James stops drawing in the dirt the moment David smiles. My nerves tense up again, and I clench my fists. I know I need to apologize even though somehow, Tate is the one responsible.

"Elizabeth, what are you doing out here?" James tiredly asked without turning around.

"I ... I wanted to apologize for that in there. I didn't--"

James stands and puts his fingers to my lips. They are rough and warm. "No. I should apologize. It was my mistake. I wasn't thinking straight."

His plush lips destroy my ability to concentrate on the excuses he is rambling about. Life is short, and I am taking a leap. I intend to prove Tate wrong. I will determine my own fate, not some "destiny" with a preordained ending.

I grab his shirt and, pulling him close, kiss him quickly before releasing him just as fast. His surprise quickly spreads into a heart-stopping smile before he cups my face and pulls me in for a long deep kiss. When we come up for air, he wraps me in a tender embrace. Tingling sensations coarse over my skin. I look down past his shoulder and see the face he sketched into the dirt. Mine. A wet streak slides down my cheek. I sniffle and wipe away my tear. James grabs my hand and pulls me over to David and Jelina.

The last streaks of sunlight fall below the tree wall, and darkness start to close in. Salithica joins the crowd of goats around the pile of branches.

"Tonight, let us celebrate, for tomorrow twenty one of you will fighting each other to be granted the title of one of my honorable Masters. We have yet again a powerful collection of talent. May the best one win!" After the speech, the crowd cheers and roars. The goats' hoof-stomping shakes the trees, and plumes of leaves rain down on us.

"James, you have come so far these past few days. The majority of us believe that you and your friends bring more good karma than bad. We wish for you to light our beacon tonight. Join us in our celebration before you, too, are put to the test against all of my best candidates."

I'm speechless at such kind words, with only a few goats looking disgruntled by the announcement.

James looks to me and says, "Don't go running off, I will be right back."

I smile at him and regretfully let go of his hand. He walks into the middle and gets close to the branches. All eyes are on him, but it doesn't seem to affect him at all. Heatwaves float out around him right before his arms light up. The flames dance around his arms like snakes. He looks back at me and winks before he tosses several balls of fire up into the sky. Some of the goats jump back out of fright. Others are glued to the fire show he is creating before them. All the balls started turning into swirls in the air as fire particles fly down towards us. Some of the small balls exploded like fireworks.

After he stuns and delights the goats with his fireworks display, James lets remnants of the fire fall onto the dry branches and ignite the bonfire. I watch Salithica in between the explosions. At first, she was startled and slightly frightened but soon realized that these were the fireworks we had described to her previously. Chatter rises high while fish on sticks are passed out. James walks back to me and pulls me in for another heart, stopping kiss. I have to say I feel, at this moment, the happiest I have ever been.

James whispers in my ear, "We need to talk."

My face falls because I don't want the moment to end. James will be fighting for his life four times over tomorrow, and I don't want to think about it. After what I have learned, I no longer wanted him to face the dangers that lie ahead of him.

James looks toward his brother and, without a word, David whispers into Jelina's ear, and they both rise. They hand off their drums to the nearest goats and follow us back to the hut where Tate is waiting. I walk in with my head down, avoiding Tate's gaze. His disapproval weighs heavily in the small room.

"The deer stew is getting cold. Help yourself to what you want. I have one errand before the trials start tomorrow. Look after my Princess while I am gone," Tate said in a disgruntled tone before walking out right past us.

"What is his problem?" David inquires. "What errand could he need to do this late at night?"

"Who cares? We have a plan to discuss." James is annoyed at Tate's attitude. I go to lean the door back up against the wall.

"Oops. I must have broken the door when I came in. I'll fix it." James takes a breath, then scrunches his face in concentration and whispers incoherent words. Suddenly the wood mends itself and pops back into place, and the vines reattach. The door now swings better than it used to.

Chapter 22

The Zurye Ring - Forest Trial
James

I let go of Elizabeth's hand as Tate puts his on her shoulder to keep her from following me. She shrugs against it in defiance, but it's no use. That man is abnormally strong.

I slide in beside Nina in the back of the group as Salithica goes over the rules. Silence spreads across the forest as she speaks.

"The goal of today's trial is to retrieve the elemental ring of Zurye hidden in the Troll's tree and return alive with it in hand. Do that, and both the ring and the title of Master become yours! However, if you fail to return with the ring or die, you will be disqualified."

Disqualification is no problem if you're dead.

"The trial has a maximum of what humans consider one hour to be completed, or all will forfeit this year's title. There is but one main rule. None of you are allowed to kill any other candidate unless you wish to be cast out to the Forgotten Lands of the undead. That is a punishment worse than death, and by the looks, on your faces, I think we all agree."

Either it suddenly got cold, and I didn't notice, or all the goats around me were shivering in fright. One hour should be plenty of time, from what my brother found, that Troll's tree isn't more than ten minutes from here.

After Salithica finishes her speech, chatter among the competitors rises. They line up facing the direction of the Troll's tree. I looked at Nina next to me while getting in my running stance. She sticks out her tongue at me and winks before the sound of Salithica's yell pierces our eardrums.

The goats take off in a fast sprint, some already doing that chameleon thing that I can't quite understand. I'm on their heels, dodging fast approaching trees, jumping over fallen logs, and bristly bushes. All I hear is the beat of my heart thumping in exhilaration inside my chest and a few hooves stomping the ground—the adrenaline courses through me. I see one of my competitors ahead to the left. He's about to go between two narrow trees. I hear a loud pop and see the same goat impaled on a massive spike between the trees as I pass. The tip is the size of his torso. I slow quickly and start watching where my feet are landing.

I can't slow down for long. Everyone else is so much further ahead.

"You alright, James? I smell a lot of blood around your area."

"Wasn't me. Luckily, I didn't take that goat's path."

I remember back to when I was fighting Salithica and the crocodiles. The armor is bulky, noisy, and utterly unhelpful in a race, but if it keeps me from being a shish-ka-bob, then I'm going to take that chance. I fall flat on the ground right as several wooden spears fly over my head, sticking in the dirt behind me.

"David! Where did those come from?"

"Your three o'clock, up in the treetops. Whatever you're doing, do it fast. He's about to throw five more."

I quickly focus and gather the moist dirt around me. I ignite myself feeling like a clay pot in an oven. The soil crystallizes and sculpts around my body. It quickly hardens tightly against my arms, legs, and torso. My rage spikes. Someone is attempting to knock me out of the trials before even seeing the Troll.

A small explosion erupts from within me, pushing me forward and creating a little dust cloud. I use the wind to propel me. I gain momentum quickly as I approach the tree where my attacker is hiding. Rocks fall from my right palm as I imagine the dust encircling them. I swing my arm back. A long paper-thin blade heated with my rage multiplies between my ring and middle finger just before my arm makes contact with the tree. I slice that tree clean by meeting little resistance. The paper blade shatters into an explosion of rock particles. I turn and kick the tree, slamming it to the ground and launching my assailant further ahead toward the Troll's home.

I don't have time to see where the goat falls. *"James, there's a small clearing ahead, and the Troll is looking for intruders. He's already dislodged a few by swinging an uprooted tree and smashing it into smaller trees. I can smell several of the goats, but they aren't visible."*

"Thanks for the heads up. How about Jelina?"

"She's flying up in the treetops looking for more hidden goats."

Still, within the forest, I slow as I approach the clearing. I peer around a snapped tree stump and view the carnage the tree troll has amassed.

The Troll is a huge giant. Atop its head is ingrown tree branches, some with leaves still on them. He is an ugly shade of green and gray with specks of brown throughout. It's hard to tell if it's dirt or freckles. Its face is disfigured by a broken left tusk and rotting teeth, and its body is like tree bark. With four stubbed fingers, the The Troll holds the uprooted tree like a club and wheedles it around like a child throwing a tantrum. On impact, splinters of wood fly in all directions, impaling goats and tossing them in the air when struck.

I take a quick count of goats. There's one barely ten yards from me moving slowly, camouflaged by surrounding brush. Several goats jump from branch to branch overhead. I glance to my right and see a lumped figure. I make my way closer when the Troll suddenly turns and swings down quickly. His club comes down on top of a goat, making the ground rumble and shaking me off my feet. I stand and cringe when I see the bloody paste of what is left of him. Part of the goat is now stuck to the underside of the Troll's club.

At that moment, it finally hits me. *This is real.* This isn't a game the goats play every year to see who the best is. It is a game of survival. And I can't win against experts who have trained for these trials for years. I am still behind most of the goats. I see a few goats disguised in the treetops and along the ground, nearly avoiding the club. If I don't figure something out soon, I will have no chance at retrieving the ring.

"Don't worry, James. We will buy you more time."

"Wait! What do you mean?"

My brother shuts me out. A moment later, Jelina, in her toucan form, flew up behind several goats in the treetops. Between swings from the Troll, Jelina dodges back and forth before kicking at a shimmering figure. A loud cry rings loudly as goats fall from their perch atop a tree. This grabs the Troll's attention, and he hurries to investigate, swinging his club.

The club strikes the top of the tree where the goat had been hiding. Jelina falls like dead weight to the ground next to the goat. They are both about to be whacked by the Troll. Telepathically I send the picture to David.

A loud howl in the distance brings the Troll to a halt. The grounded goat scurries out of sight while three more goats leap from the tree line right in front of the Troll. I have no time to detour and see if Jelina is ok. I see the fiery red eyes of Silver amongst the tree line before he runs off.

His anger ignites my own. I know I can't beat them at stealth techniques, so I will let the Troll take my revenge on them while I run past. I survey my surroundings and spot a shimmer here and a twig crunch there. I gather water from a nearby puddle and dowse each goat I see with dirty water. The sound and visual marker are enough to further set the Troll into a rage, swinging and launching several goats in all directions. Chaos is unleashed, and goats fall over each other, trying to stay clear. Now that the goats are occupied with staying alive, I encase myself in wind and sprint forward, barreling through the clearing, between the giant Troll's stumpy legs, and into the wooded area beyond.

Ahead I see a sizeable decaying tree stump. I slide to a stop in front of the hollowed-out trunk. First, the smell hits me. The pungent odor of death and decaying flesh burns into my lungs as I gag, trying to catch my breath. The sunlight sneaks over the horizon and lights up the scene before me. A few unrecognizable carcasses lay over a fallen tree section to my right. The insects are already having a feast.

Large foot impressions on the ground lead away from the entrance, now illuminated by a sunray.

"There isn't much time left. You have to hurry." My brother chimes in with a saddened tone.

"How much time do I have left?"

"Salithica indicated when the sun hit the top of the trees, not more

than ten minutes. Do you have the ring? David asked with a sorrowful twinge to his thoughts.

"I will soon. Is Jelina ok?

"Human get ring, Troll will pay!" I push Silver's rage out of my mind and run into the foul-smelling dwelling. Silver has retaken complete control, and I'd wager that Troll has seen its last day.

The interior is worse than the exterior. Random knickknacks, bones, decaying fur piles, and animal skulls litter the floor. In the corner, a small branch with necklaces and rings hang. I quickly look over them and notice several on the ground and knocked off as if recently searched. I look to the ground and see several small hooved footprints next to the base of the branch. *No, I'm too late.*

I sprint out of there like a rocket back to the Trolls direction and the screams of several goats.

"David, one of the goats, has the ring look for a goat with the smell of decaying flesh. I am almost at the tree troll." There's no reply. I try it again. *"Silver? What is going on?"* I am left with silence. This can't be good.

I come to the clearing to see a massacre unfolding. Blood soaks in pools on the ground and covering the Troll. High pitched screams were emanating from the Troll and not the nannies or billies as I had imagined at first. Several goats lined the outer ring staring horrified at the Troll. I see a blur of fur as Silver viciously bit into and claws at the Troll. His red eyes confirmed his intent. Silver is pissed.

Jelina's limp toucan form rests against the tree trunk. I can see the bird's chest rise and fall, but she doesn't move. Several wood chunks have been bitten out of the Troll's side. Thick black goop pours out of the wounds like sap down a tree. The hand of the Troll lay apart from the Troll's body, still gripping the club. A few goats take this time to run past me to the Troll's abode. Knowing the ring isn't there, I let them pass.

I see a shimmering figure across the way, but the Troll's erratic movements and wild swings make it impossible for me to pass. The short shimmering figure dodges a swing and falls, revealing that little brat Nina, and the ring glints on a golden necklace around her neck. I can't let her win. I know I have to take advantage of her downed state and quickly send imagery to silver, hoping he helps. I close my eyes and take a quick, calming breath. I center my focus on the surrounding tree vines. I feel them bending to my will and outstretch my hands, asking them to do my bidding.

Several tree vines shoot out from the treetops snaring the Troll's legs, putting him off balance.
"Silver! Now!" I shout the command both aloud and mentally. Silver stops momentarily and then lunges at the Troll, hitting hard in its center mass, knocking him down. The Troll falls toward Nina, and she scurries out of the way, but it's too late. Her legs are caught under the Troll's massive fat belly. On the horizon, the fiery ball of the sun has almost reached the tops of the

trees. Silver thrashes back into the now motionless Troll.

I run to Nina. She looks pissed. Then she spots me coming close and screams, "Noooo! Not you. Not a human." She tries to cover the necklace from view, but I have no time to play nice with her. I ask the roots of the closest tree to aid me. Roots pop out of the dirt around Nina, encasing her arms to the dirty ground. She struggles in surprise, and I rip the necklace from her neck. I take off in a sprint back to the start.

I smell the scent of blood. I feel the aches in my joints and the heat of the rays across my cheeks. Wind pushes faster and launches me across the terrain between trees, uncaring to be stealthy or looking for traps. A whoosh of air swipes by me, and a tinge of pain is felt in my left leg. I see something sticking out of it, but my adrenaline pushes me forward. I see Salithica, a crowd of goats, and the beautiful blue eyes of Elizabeth's gaze. I stop before them, looking at the shocked faces of all the goats and even Elizabeth.

I hold up the necklace with the stone engraved ring of Zurye on it. A few of the goats I recognize from the drum sessions are cheering right along with Salithica. I limp over to Elizabeth. She still looks worried.

"What's the matter, Elizabeth? I made it in time, right?" The adrenaline leaves my body quickly, and the pain comes in sharp bursts. My head feels heavy, and my sight blurs in and out of focus. I fall to the ground, and the last thing I hear is Elizabeth screaming before I blackout.

Chapter 23

Last Elemental Standing - Sea Trial
James

I awake in a bed of soft furs. My hands explore the texture before finding a warm hand, interlocking gentle fingers with mine. My eyes open to the smiling pale, blue-eyed face of Elizabeth. The sun is glinting in the windows past several young goats, all of whom are staring at me.

"Okay. You've seen him wake up. Now, give him some space. Go on, go outside." Salithica's voice is heard behind Elizabeth. A few pouting whimpers can be heard as the door squeaks, and several hoofed feet pat their way out.

"How do you feel?" Elizabeth is still clutching my hand. I feel fine, and the memories of what happened flashback.

The premonition that I was going to lose, the sudden rage after seeing Jelina fall, Silvers enraged attack on the troll, and the poisonous spear sticking out of my hip before passing out. I sit up quickly.

"David? Where's David?" I mumble. My mind is still fuzzy as if I took too many painkillers.

Salithica walks over to me. "Take it slow. That poison came close to killing you. David is fine. We moved him to a hut outside the walls for safety concerns."

"What? Why would being outside the walls of your camp be safer? Ouch, my head." I ask in pain, trying to contact David.

Elizabeth chimes in. "Well, Jelina took a bad spill. David is not able to control Silver's outbursts, and so it's safer for the goats of this camp if the Dire Wolf stays outside the walls while looking after his mate."

"Is Jelina going to be okay?" I ask, concerned for my brother's state.

Salithica answers before Elizabeth with a slightly worried tone. "Yes, she will recover. I patched her up, but she needs more rest. You, however, don't have much time left."

"Wait. What? I thought I was fine." I say, horrified.

Elizabeth shakes her head at Salithica's comment. "You are, James. You're all right, but the next trial starts in less than thirty minutes. David and Jelina aren't going to be able to make it for obvious reasons. Tate and I will cheer for you up in the stands above the arena."

"What about Nina and the rest of the goats…?" My sentence trails off. I already know not many survived.

Salithica chokes a bit before gathering herself to speak. "Nina is

196

okay. She fractured both her legs when the troll fell on her. Twelve other goats were found either unconscious or with broken appendages and brought back to camp for treatment. The remaining seven were buried in the forest." A tear escaped her right eye before she sniffed hard and walked to the kitchen.

I know those goats felt like part of her family. Salithica had been training most of them for years before this trial. A guilty feeling shrouds me as I try to wipe my blurry vision. Elizabeth helps me out of bed, and I see Tate's glare from the kitchen, eyeing our interlocked fingers. I roll my eyes and sit down at Salithica's dining table next to Elizabeth. Tate and Salithica bring over a tray of filleted fish and salad with odd-looking vegetables and moving one-eyed purple slugs.

Tate smirks at my reaction to the slugs before telling Elizabeth, "Come with me outside. We need to let him eat quickly."

Was that a hint of him caring about my health? Or did he remove her, not wanting me to be distracted? Either way, my belly roars, and I am hit with starvation. I am glad she isn't in the room because I show those fish and slugs no elegance. I pound down the food like a caveman at a buffet. There are only remnants of food scraps on the plate, table, and floor in five minutes.

Salithica is trying to explain the significance of the slugs, but all I hear is "high in protein" and "energy replenishment." I guzzle the pitcher of water, spilling it down my bare chest and into my lap where my left thigh was still wrapped in leaf bandages. I feel much better and belch out the first ten letters of the alphabet. I pull off the twine and leaves to see a rather muscled, familiar hairless thigh. Salithica licks her lips and stares at me. Realizing what I look like, I attempt to cover myself with the plate of scraps. Red cheeks flare up on her face as she looks away from my stare. Bile pushes its way up my throat as I try to keep myself from regurgitating the food I swallowed.

Maybe David has a point. I leave the table and return to the couch next to the bed, where a new set of battle leathers have been laid out. I change quickly, and Elizabeth rushes in right after I pull up my pants.

"Come on, James. You can't be late. You have to go now! There are less than ten minutes before the trial starts, and it's far out in the surrounding water. You will need to use that speed of yours to get there before us."

I gaze into her beautiful blue ocean eyes, and she stares back with the same spark as in mine. I move close to her. Time seems to slow down. A giddy feeling erupts in my gut and travels up my spine then out to my fingertips. I cup her face with my right hand and pull her closer to me. She doesn't fight and leans in. I tilt my head, and my lips can feel the heat emanating from hers. Sudden pain erupts in my right pinky, and I backpedal away from Elizabeth, flinging my hand to cool off in the air.

"Ouch! What was that?" A small bite mark indents my pinky finger's skin. Elizabeth looks horrified. She swings back her hair off her left shoulder, revealing Tinky, the blue fuzzball that David found while I was getting beat up by a two-headed snake.

At that point, Tate entered the room. "What's taking so long? James doesn't have much time if you wish him to enter the next trial " The moment passed, and I waved off the pain, grabbed my bow and daggers, and head out past Tate.

Brutus stood in the doorway, looking displeased. "Stop human, Weapons no allowed. Must create own weapons, only magik." His broken English is enough to get the point across. I toss the bow quiver and daggers on the couch and headed outside.

"Fine, but Ula better not intervene in the trial like she did in training."

"No allowed, she watch only. You late. Hop on we go."

"Hop on what?" I ask, wondering how a giant slow turtle will move quickly over land made of dirt and twigs. Cold air beneath my feet rushes toward Brutus's spinning hands. He looks determined and in deep concentration. Water particles begin to form in the air, and a frozen center ripples out into a long surfboard made of ice. I am amazed and wish I'd had time to learn how to create one of those. Brutus smiles at me before throwing me up onto the back of his shell. I grip on and turn to see Elizabeth waving. I yell out bye as we zip crazily through the forest, weaving in and out of the trees.

This speed reminds me of the horsapeed ride we took through the desert. In less than a minute, we are already at the beach. We slide across the water's surface, hopping waves and sliding up to a massive arena with a waterfall splashing down into the water below.

The arena stands higher than our castle back in Scotland. We shoot up the waterfall and land on the cold ice ring surface. Several turtles line the ice benches around the top ring and downward like a coliseum. Giant ice island blocks float in the watery center with scattered ice ledges encircling the frigid waters below. A tiny wooden square floats in the middle.

Like in training, I learned to keep my body temperature up using the heat to resonate under my skin. I am already cold and start warming my skin for battle. I look to Brutus, and he gives me a slight smirk.

"We made in time. Announcement starting." Brutus says before Ula steps up from her ice throne and clears her throat.

"Welcome to the annual sea trial this year. As you are all aware, we have a guest human who will be joining the other twenty turtles in hopes of claiming the title of master. Do not let him win. Humans have no place amongst our tribe.

Konja steps up to her and shakes his head, then speaks to her in tortoise dialect.

"Fine! On to the rules and goal of this trial. The rules are simple. Don't intentionally kill another turtle, and only magik and magikal weapons are permitted. To be the winner and new master in the sea tribe, you must hold out on the wooden platform in the center of the arena for sixty seconds continuously. If both your feet leave the platform, the time resets. May the best turtle win!" Ula sneers at me before sitting back down.

Konja stands up in front of Chondro and announces, "All the candidates must now drop into the ring so we can start."

I walk down the steps past several turtles, goats, lemurs, and draconians. Cheers and yelling rise behind and all around me. The sun is to my back, and my shadow elongates across the entire arena. The arena bottom is a good four stories down, and there is no ladder. The familiar trainees across from me sneer at me as they jump into the frigid waters littered with sharp floating ice. I feel my legs coming out from underneath me as I get pushed hard into the arena. I look back and see Ragarth laughing.

Time slows again. Water crystals freeze into a globe above me and seal in the arena. I remember this same feeling of helplessness and push it down when I remember I can fly. I gather the air around and under me, asking the air to catch me as I plummet closer to the icy waters. My feet barely touch the water as I am lifted back up into the air and fly over the sneering turtle heads.

A loud but muffled, high-pitched cheer comes from a familiar tiny guinea pig. I fly in a few circles and finally see Elizabeth and Tate sit down close to the arenas globe top. Elizabeth's waves and my resolve to win the upcoming battle ignites.

The battle starts when several turtles materialize ice spears and tridents. Others across the arena are already encased in spiked icicle armor, throwing fast ice balls my way. I dodge and maneuver quickly, but there isn't enough room in this arena to escape the hatred Ula instilled in these turtles. I swirl my left hand, and gusts of wind diverting the approaching ice chunks to other turtles close by.

Soon I have the majority of my twenty opponents gunning for me. I take a few hits to my arms and shoulders, unable to predict or block all the ice spears and chunks aimed for my head. Cool trails of sharp ice projectiles whip by me before sudden pain breaks out in my rear. My concentration dwindles, and I feel like a rock splashing headfirst into the icy cold waters. I heard the roar of many cheers as I turned to face upward as I sunk deeper into the dark waters.

The sunlight above pierced the globe top, illuminating the water's surface. I see the small square wooden platform above being fought over by two turtles. Two more are in a heated battle under the surface, moving like serpents, slithering through the waters with lightning-fast movements.

I am no match for them. How did I ever expect to beat them in their own habitat? Bubbles slowly escape my mouth and nose, floating helplessly back to the surface. *I can't beat them. How foolish I have been all this time.*

A small group of crab-like creatures swims past. Red armor glinting from the sunlight above off the tops of their one gigantic eye atop their back shell. The pincers, one in back and the other elongated out from the tip of the eye, all open and close violently as they swim past. Long streamers of seaweed float around me and tickle my back, neck, and legs.

"You must not give up hope so easily." That same mysterious voice from earlier during my fight with Therose rang in my head. *"Fight for your friends, fight for Elizabeth. This world needs your strength."* A shimmering lizard figure appears before my eyes, the same in the vision I had with the woman that looks like Elizabeth.

Flashes of my brother alone, of Elizabeth crying over me, of Tate calling me a weakling, and of my Da's ghost shaking his head at me. *I will not let that happen. I will not give up.*

I clench my fists and scream silently underwater. An air bubble snaps around my face as my skin heats the water surrounding me to a boil. Rapid bubbles flow upward into the two turtles fighting underwater. They stop suddenly and look down at me with hatred. They nod at each other like a silent truce is formed to deal with me first.

The surrounding seaweed gives me an idea. Both turtles shoot down at me like torpedoes aimed at their target. I let them get closer before expelling my hands forward. Heatwaves flow out and upward, knocking the turtles into each other, momentarily diverting their focus from me. Several seaweed strands come to my call and stretch out around both turtles, cocooning them together on the seafloor.

Above, the platform rocks back and forth, but no other turtles are around. That means I can't let whoever is on it to stay there any longer. I propel myself upward straight underneath the platform and launch the turtle atop it up to the globe cracking his head upon the clear ice top. Several startled sounds come from the audience. I land on the wooden platform while the turtle I launched hits the sidewall and slides, unconscious, down to the icy platform.

I stand carefully, trying to balance on the rocking waves. Seventeen pairs of eyes focus on me. I know the only way I can win this is to distract the other turtles. I turn my hands into fiery torches and send fireball after fireball at every turtle around me. Turtles duck or turn their shells to me to block incoming waves of fire. A few of my fireballs land home and send some turtles flying into other ones.

Ten seconds pass. My plan is working. All the turtles are fumbling around or forced to keep blocking the fire without getting close enough to retaliate.

A turtle falls into the water. At first, I think I knocked him in, then the realization hits me … too late. The turtle sends a giant pressurized wave of water, which throws me and the platform to the globe-top like a geyser. My hands are so hot I melted the ice before impact and was launched off the platform and out of the arena, falling down into the waters surrounding the audience.

The time will be reset, but I have to think of an action strategy. What can I do to stay on the platform? I dive under the water and swim back to the center of the arena. That same school of crabs and a few schools of fish come closer to be our underwater audience. This gives me another idea that even Ula wouldn't expect.

I spin in place, much like I did during training in the forest tribe, creating suction. I spin around, gathering all the schools of odd-shaped fish and crabs. I rise out of the water, standing on a spinning waterspout as I fling large and small underwater creatures at every turtle left standing. Several turtles are already unconscious while encased in ice along the outer wall. Only ten remain, and those are the ones I concentrate on. Crabs and fish fly out, bombarding each turtle with sharp teeth or pincers. Turtles dive behind massive ice pillars or drop and hide in their shells. The turtle on the platform falls off and dives under the water below me again. I spurt the remaining sea creatures back down at the turtle under me, keeping him at bay.

The turtles behind the pillars hurl ice arrows at me. I retaliate by creating a heatwave of constant energy like that of a personal bubble. It turns the ice into steam on impact. This skill drains energy, and I can't keep it up for long. My opponents realize this and toss large slabs of ice. I can only dodge so many and keep the water rapid and the steam shield around me simultaneously.

I have no choice but to cut the ties to water and stick to what I know best, Fire and hand-to-hand combat. I request the water push me onto a ledge and retreat back down the middle hole. Several fish and crabs still lie on the ice surface, flopping helplessly.

Two grunting turtles in front of me are looking pissed. One materializes a trident, and the other slams his hand into the ice wall. The ice grows over him and encases him in transparent armor with protruding spikes in front and atop his head. They both roar and charge at me even though other turtles across the way toss spikes and lob hefty chunks of ice.

I engulf my body in flames turning my skin red hot. The ice below me melts quickly, gathering cold water beneath me. I recall my training, using the water and the sand to carry me, I slip around both turtles. The spear-wielding one catches a large boulder-sized ice block in the face and crushes against the far wall. That block nearly misses the turtle in full body armor, and he swivels in place. His eyes squint, and several ice chips float up behind and around him. A flurry of ice chips spring forward at me, sizzling on impact.

I'd think this turtle is stupid until a tidal wave of cold water dowses my flames from behind. The last few ice chips whizzed by, slicing into my shoulder, arms, and cheek. Slowly warm blood oozes down my arms and cheek. He laughs maliciously as I backpedal behind a large ice crystal.

I see a turtle standing on the platform behind him. He raises a wall of water around him and then freezes it, encasing him in a thick orb atop the platform. *Why didn't I think of that?*

"You, human, will not win. You will die by my hands." The armored turtle replies to me while preparing for his next bombardment.

"I shouldn't be the one you're worried about. That guy is about to win." I point behind him.

"What?" he turns and sees the same ice-encased turtle on the platform. He looks upward, and I follow his gaze to the side of the wall where numbers are counting down. We only have twenty-three seconds left to knock him off, or we all lose.

Even if I knock the incased turtle off, the armored one will do the same to me. I have to find a way to knock all the turtles out and stay atop the wooden platform. I spray flames out of my heels and hands, taking temporary flight—the other six turtles remaining all fling ice and water at the encased turtle. Chips break off but are quickly replenished. The six of them pound on the encased turtle with no avail. I have to do something fast. I flew above the encased turtle and surrounded the ice bubble he made with swirling flames melting the orb from all sides, tiring the turtle out from replacing all the evaporating water. The others quickly pull the turtle off the platform restarting the timer from eight seconds back to sixty—the remaining six-fight each other in the water, hoping for a chance to dominate.

I've had enough of this. My energy is waning.

In the audience is a teary-eyed Elizabeth. *She still believes in me. I can't give up now, not when I'm so close.*

Tapping that incredible energy I used against the goat underwater, I get an idea. A spark ignites within me even though it is crazy, but it might just work now that the remaining turtles are in the water. Using part of what the previous turtle did, I should keep the rest of them at bay.

I fly up high and fall back, using the air around me to accelerate my momentum and land hard atop the platform. The waves from my impact rock the water enough to send a few turtles back and the rest underwater. I put out my flames, kneel down and touch the water's edge. I close my eyes and concentrate. I open them to see a large replica of Elizabeth in front of me. I reach out, and she does too. Elizabeth's water elemental pulls the two turtles lingering on the surface under the water with her.

I tap back into the water, swaying my hands across the surface and asking the seaweed once again to aid me. The sneers on the faces snap to expressions of dismay as they are jolted downward. I stopped the swaying and clenched my fists, sinking my arms in deeper. I concentrate hard and bite my lip. Blood pools in my mouth as ice crystals rapidly grow outward from my arms. Seconds later, the entire water hole is encased in ice, its ice floor blocking the turtle's re-entry into the arena.

I look up to the timer on the wall as the last five seconds tick down to zero. Silence is widespread before I hear cheers from Elizabeth and several goats near them. The globe shatters, and everyone peers down at me. My energy is depleted, and my body is fatigued. The ice floor melts instantly, and I fall limply into the water. The last thing I see is Brutus's worried face before passing out.

Chapter 24

The Recovery
David

Jelina lays in bed, breathing evenly, while Silver frantically sends images to me of our plan going south. The gruesome images of goats getting smashed by the tree club of the troll to the unmoving, lifeless look on Jelina's feathered face.

I walk out of our small makeshift hut on the perimeter of Salithica's camp that the goats lent to us until Silver gets over his rampage during Jelina's unconscious state. After Jelina shifts back to human form, I can measure her breathing pattern. I am sure she will be alright. My emotions are still in turmoil, though, because of Silver and the worry I have for my brother as well. He barely survived most of the fights, and now I can't reach him at all. I know James is strong, and I can only hope he is too exhausted to make a connection. The other alternatives are unthinkable.

Noises from inside the hut reach our ears. Soft whimpers and a quiet couple of words cling on the wind as they travel to our eardrums.

Silver takes over my movements before I can react, and we are almost instantly at the bedside as she repeats her words a bit louder. "Silver. David."

She opens her beautiful eyes. We look deeply into them as we clasp her hands. She shakes off mine and cradles her head. "Oww, my head hurts. What happened? Where am I?"

A tear slides down my cheek, and I can't tell if it's mine or Silver's, but we both feel immensely grateful to hear her speak.

I start to explain how we ended up in this hut, but a loud crunch, followed by another and another interrupted. We all focus our hearing on what's happening outside. Several more snapping twigs and branches follow, almost as if something is approaching in a frenzy.
The smells waft in waves: Elizabeth's Sea salty aroma, Tate's unique sweaty sock scent, and a large musky smell with a tinge of pine needles. My gaze widens. I push away Silver's need to stay by Jelina's side and dart out of the hut.

My brother is being carried by a large turtle on a floating ice block, as unconscious as Jelina was not minutes before. He, Tate, and Elizabeth trail far behind. They glide over the forest floor, much like Salithica and her followers came to us when we arrived. The turtle zooms past.

"James, can you hear me? Are you okay? Talk to me!!" I run after them, guilt filling my thoughts. We spent the entire trial wading over Jelina and waiting for her to wake while doing nothing to help my brother win another trial. Silver sends conflicting emotions.

I dash back inside and study Jelina with a frown. *Does she need us right now?*

As if she can read my mind, she smiles. "I'm fine. I just want to rest. I'll catch up with you back at Salithica's hut."

I nod and turn tail, running after the ice surfing turtle. I shift back into Dire form, and Silver lets me take the lead, feeling my concern for my brother. This is the second time he's been left unconscious after a trial. I don't know if he will have the energy left to face the last two. That is more than any human can endure.

The air around me whips through our fur and knocking our tail around. Our inner bond heats, and warm sensations glide over the tips of our skin. It fills me with unquenchable energy that I use to run faster. My claws pierce the soil below and through the bark of fallen trees. I hear the rhythm of our heartbeat in unison with each ground pounce. The run is ecstatic and soothing at the same time.

A vision blurs over my eyes as Silver unconsciously takes me back to when we ran together for the first time. We had bonded with the same warm sensation energizing every cell in our dire form. We ran the length of the kill zone between the walls of our cursed castle. James had just fed us the last of the sheep while diligently looking for a spell to change me back to human and undoing the magic he had done a month prior. James had this unique expression of shock on his face when we had returned to the gate. We made it in mere seconds and even took the time to snap a low flying bird out of the air before returning.

I smile at that memory before dodging a few more trees and slowing down at the goat village entrance. The goats look skittish about letting me in as a Dire. I quickly shift into my wolf skinned human outfit of a fur vest and pants. I walk briskly past the annoyed goats and follow the icy mist left behind by the turtle's surfboard. Salithica is already inside mixing potions before turning and seeing Brutus lay my brother on Elizabeth's bed. He looks severely beaten and bruised. Guilt tugs at my heart, and Silver expresses his sympathy. Pain twinges in my mind, and a second vision springs forth.

This time I'm looking through Silver's eyes—a pack of wolves races beside him, projecting utter hatred from within. Silver sprints off ahead and sees another grayish wolf. We look into his eyes, and I know they know each other. The intense feeling is that of a brother's love. Silver's brother looks terrified that this wolf pack is here. We turn and see a large black wolf approaching. That same hatred is back, but it's mixed with fear and turmoil.

A sudden pressure engulfs my brain, and pain lashes throughout our wolf form. We are frozen in place and can't move. It hits me; this is Silver's alpha commanding him to not interfere. Silver attempts to refuse the command leaving, us writhing in pain. I am helpless, unable to do anything but watch as the event unfolds in Silver's slowed-down memory. The black wolf leaps at his brother. Warm energy spreads throughout Silver's body in an instant. Silver lunges faster than his alpha and knocks his brother out of the way.

We circle his alpha, snapping violently at him. The hatred overcomes the pain induced by the alpha.

We engage in combat, snarling, and biting. The feeling doesn't last long. As the wind picks up, suddenly, the black wolf drops dead before we can pounce. We are left silently stunned, looking at the rest of the pack backing away from us. A loud rush of wind fills our ears as we are wrenched away at wicked speeds seeing a glimpse of Silver's body fall limply to the ground.

A loud jolting snap returns me to the present.

"Hello, David. This is no time to be daydreaming. James is hurt." Elizabeth shakes me out of my short trance.

I squint my eyes and frown. It seemed so real.

Elizabeth mirrors my frown, then hurries to James' bedside. There she kneels next to him and holds his hand while playing with his hair. Tate stands motionless in the corner. Salithica is busy at her table, mixing odd foul-smelling substances.

Waves of anger pouring off me at the thought of losing my brother. Silver may have saved his brother from death at that time but still lost him in the end when James ripped Silver's soul out of his body and put him in me. I sympathize with Silver and better understand him by experiencing his point of view. He shares the same compassion for me seeing my brother on what could be his death bed. I vow to myself and Silver that I won't let anything awful happen to him again in the next two trials.

Warm, soft hands glide over my skin and interlock around my waist, pushing me against a warm body. My anger retreats when I feel our heartbeat in rhythm with Jelina's. Her scent envelops me and mends our agitated minds. She murmurs loving hopes and reassures us that James will make it through like last time. She thanks us for staying by her side while she recovered though I hear a twinge of guilt in her whisper. Tate steps past us and pushes the large turtle, Brutus, out of the way as if he is as light as a feather. Tate, wearing a determined face, stands impatiently next to his princess. He remains silent but jerks his head toward Salithica.

"Aha!" Salithica shouts aloud. "I've got it." She holds up a bowl of bubbling brown goo. I cock my head and squint, wondering what she's going to do with that mixture.

"What is it? Did you make something that will heal him?" Elizabeth asks worriedly.

"No. I can heal James's wound through touch, but he needs to replenish his energy, or he will have no chance of recovery before the next trial. This is a secret recipe I concocted to revitalize worn-out cells in the body." She halts abruptly, then continued. "I intended to use it for a goat, but it should still work … I hope." She barely whispers the last sentence.

"As long as you don't turn him into a goat, it can't hurt to try. But that bowl of goo really looks nasty."

Salithica shrugs off my comment and moves to my brother's side. Elizabeth steps back, holding her nose. Even Tinky scrunches his nose at the disgusting smell.

The goat leader spoon feeds James the boiling goo. He naturally rejects the substance and spits it out. I imagine it doesn't taste any better than it looks or smells. Salithica pinches his nose and makes him swallow. The bowl falls to the floor with a thud. With Salithica's determined face, her hoofed hands radiate a golden glow across my brother's skin.

The bumps and bruises mend and disappear. Loud pops and cracks sound as his bones are repositioned. He clenches his teeth and fists before bellowing out in pain. Memories of the past flash in front of my eyes. Back to the swamp when Silver and I landed in a tree and broke our arm. The time when I crashed into a standing clock after running from Zanagoth and broke my leg. Then back to the time, Silver first tried to take over my body. All my bones cracked and popped, growing larger and changing shape. I foolishly fought it the whole way, and it is still a painful memory.

Elizabeth rushes to his side as Salithica rises. She caresses his cheeks like our mother used to do when we were sick before she abandoned us.

James' head snaps up, giving Elizabeth a hard head-butt.

"Ow!" they both cry.

Tinky goes flying down to the floor. For a split second, I could have sworn I saw his eyes glint red. But his small screech tells me he is scared of falling that far to the ground. He climbs back up Elizabeth's side and perches on her shoulder as both my brother and Elizabeth rub their heads. James did say he could understand English. I wonder what else this little guy will surprise us with in addition to his foul stench. *How can Elizabeth stand him so close to her nose?*

Salithica gathers water particles from the air into two bags creating ice packs. Tate snatches one from her and holds it on Elizabeth's forehead, glaring daggers at James.

"How dare you harm Rawena Rose!" He bends over James. His face is etched with angry lines.

I let out a growl at Tate, who backs away.

Jelina rubs her hands over my furry vest. She distracts us from the desire to tear into Tate's throat. I smell her intent but have to shrug it off.

James will need me. James will require us both to win the next trial. He may look physically okay, but I know he feels mentally exhausted. I take Jelina's hands in mine to stop her movement. I turn to her with a determined look, and she frowns.

"Later," I whisper to her. "After the trials, we can play." She grins and purrs softly with pleasure. "But right now, my brother needs us, and I need you to help my brother. Will you help us win so we can leave this island together?"

She ponders the question. For a moment, I feared she would refuse, but then she captured my gaze and smiled. "Of course, I will help you, you big goof."

"Thank you. I am going to need you to step up your game for this one. Since I can't fly, I need your help keeping up with James over the parts of the island I can't traverse."

"I can—" Jelina started.

"Ohh," James moaned behind them and held his head. "That was a painful way to wake up. Elizabeth, are you okay?"

David and Jelina turn in time to see Tate pulling Elizabeth away from James. She struggles against Tate's action and nods to James. "Yes, I'm fine,"

James gets up and moves to the dining table to get some grub before the next trial. He starts up a conversation with Elizabeth, Tate, and Salithica.

"How did the other elders react to the news of Draither's imminent arrival?" James asked.

"They were not pleased to hear that, after harboring humans, they would be faced with the possible doom of this island. Zyerr did speak up, expressing his dislike for all of you, but having an advance warning gives him some time to prepare before and during his trial. Leena is placing sentries around the island skies. They are ordered to give a warning call to everyone on the island. Chondro has several turtle groups positioned tactically around the island for spotting any sea or air travel heading our direction. Of course, I will have many goats in trees hidden throughout the island to help locate the enemies and take out the stragglers to weed their army down. We all decided to cancel the annual blood moon eclipse ceremony. Our loved ones will have to suffer another year in their undead form, but we must protect those still alive first." Tears start to pool in Salithica's eyes.

I turn and walk Jelina outside, determined to rearrange our plan for this trial.

"Okay, what do you need me to do?" Jelina asks with sincerity.

"Do you remember when we first met? You shifted into another form that took me off guard?"

"Oh yes, the dra--"

"Shh! Don't say it out loud. Too many listening ears." I glance around nervously.

"Okay, so you need a lift. That form will definitely come in handy as fire is included."

"Really? I didn't think you could copy everything in your shifts. How are you able to learn all those magiks?" I ask, stunned at the realization of how powerful she could be.

"Shh! It's a secret. Maybe one day I will tell you when you are ready."

Ready for what? I decide to let it go. "Okay. From what we discovered during our recon, the race is only one lap that traverses all four elemental zones of the island. It starts atop the floating island and drops down to the treetops split between the undead lands and Salithica's living forest.

The path flies over the beach waters on the island's backside, then cuts through the tallest trees to the volcano. Candidates must reach the checkpoint at the top of the volcano before turning to the front beach of the island. There's is a shortcut through the troll's camp, but that's not an option for us. Then they swing around the undead lands and back up to the finish line. The other shortcut allowed is through the forgotten lands and the rumor is that no one leaves there alive."

"Can't I just fly him past everyone?" Jelina asks.

"No, the rules dictate that only the contestant can fly him or herself in the air and that no killing of other contestants is allowed by other contestants. If you notice, there's a loophole to the killing part, which we need to watch out for. There may be teams trying to kill my brother in flight, and I need your help to look out for him in the air while I'm on the ground."

I lean into Jelina, head to head, and nuzzle her nose with mine. We kiss softly before a clearing of someone's throat interrupts us.

"So, are we going to do this or what?" My brother asks all energetically. That goo really works miracles. His eyes blaze with fire, and I sense his need to prove himself during this trial.

A white blur flies past us and lands at my brother's feet. The cloud dissipates, leaving only a guinea pig licking my brother's toes again.

"Get off me, you little furball. I thought we made a deal to stop doing that."

"I know, but your feet are irresistible. It is time for us to gather before the trial starts. Are you ready, James?"

Chapter 25

The Death Race – Storm Trial
David

"Let's go!"

Morty, the guinea pig, looks around at all of us before spinning, then jumping into the air and landing on his tiny cloud. James reaches down by the door and retrieves his quiver of arrows and bow, which he swings over his shoulder. James follows Morty, jumping in the air as white wind particles spun into a puffy cloud below him. He is actually flying but very slowly compared to the guinea pig. I knew right then that our plan has to work, or he has no chance of finishing first.

I eye Jelina, then Elizabeth.

"Go, David. Keep him safe for me," she pleads. 'We will be rooting for him from here." A tear escapes Elizabeth's eye before Tate pulls her close to him.

I look back to Jelina and see the glint in her eye before allowing Silver to shift us into our massive dire wolf form. Jelina's eyes widened before she saddles our back. Her soft skin rubbing against our fur ignited our bond, flaring it to a point mixed between lust and determination. The guilt of not aiding him in the last battle molded into resolve, pushing us forward as the trees and brush whizzed by like streaks of light.

James and Morty ascend higher and higher as we near the waterfall. We slide to a stop right before the edge of the forest line. The turtles and goats' audience looks up at the misty island in the sky, waiting for something. Moments later, a loud sonic boom erupts from the direction of the island. Morty's familiar voice rings in my ears. Everyone gets quiet instantly.

"Welcome all … once again to our annual flying race of … skill amongst our … most impressive candidates. You are all invited to test our … initiates to help us weed out the weak and find the strongest … in Storm magik superiority. Directly killing any of our initiates is … forbidden. Do so, and we will give …. you a lifetime vacation … in the forgotten lands. Hold on a moment." His voice comes in waves as if sent like sonar blips. He clears his throat loudly.

"The rules of this race are simple. Our initiates must complete one full lap hitting each checkpoint in order before crossing the finish line. The first to cross the finish line alive wins. No initiate may kill another. All weapons and magiks are allowed. May our best initiate win." Morty seemed to have fixed the waves of words and made it more seamless.

Goats and turtles start fleeing in all directions. Turtles take to the water, positioning themselves for battle. Goats go full camo, jumping past us and climbing up into the trees.

"It's time, David." Jelina hops off our back and shifts in the air into a Kalacuu, a toucan-like bird. She flies into the treetops on the other side of the lake.

"You ready, David?"

"We're in place. I have your back this time," I answer.

A horn echoes in James' mind. I lunge out of my cover and sprint around the lake in the direction Jelina flew. The air whips by me, and I bulldoze through several camouflaged goats aiming blow darts to the sky while hiding by trees. There's no time to apologize. Besides, they might be aiming for my brother. A paralyzed lemur falls into the bushes to my left, confirming my thoughts of what type of darts the goats are shooting. There are still nineteen lemurs ahead of James. I hear James yell out, but it's hard to see him through the trees.

Silver, take over. I need to connect with James to see what is going on. I feel our bond tighten as Silver takes over, and I concentrate on James' thoughts. "James, show me what you see."

A wave of light flashes as my eyes come back into focus. Lemurs swerve left and right, dodging darts and icicles from below. James is avoiding them but also returning fireballs toward incoming lemurs. James glimpses to his right; Jelina is dive-bombing towards another lemur about to throw more whirlwinds at James. James suddenly lurches forward, and the treetops grow larger by the second. I'm kicked out of his sight and back into Silvers. We peer at the tree James collided with. He hits and bounces off branches on the way down.

There isn't much time. I shift back into human form, thinking back on the training Jelina gave us. I close my eyes. James is going to be severely injured if I miss him. Pain protrudes out of my fingertips, and I open my eyes to see large sharp claws. I jump at the tree, and my claws sink in. Adrenaline takes over, and we have propelled up the tree.

James is closing in, and I leap off the trunk into the air.

I catch James in midair and shift into our dire wolf form right before we hit the ground. The air whooshes out of my lungs. Above me is my brother's angry face. Jelina flies down and meets my eyes before landing.

"Sorry, James, I was so close, but that lemur got his wind spell off before I could reach him." My brother jumps to his feet, fuming, and recreates his giant cloud.

"James, wait. You're too slow on that thing to catch up. Hop on. Jelina will tell you when to fly up again to hit the first checkpoint."

James scans the sky to judge the distance to catch the lemur and sighs, "Okay, David. Let's show them how fast you are!" James starts to run forward. Jelina takes off. I catch up as James jumps into the air before landing on my back like he used to do around our castle. Silver's and my bond ignites once again, and blurs of white, green, and blue pass rapidly overhead.

We bulldoze into several more goats. Some fall into our path as Jelina knocks them from their perches. Silver's growl and sheer speed scare off those who wanted to fight back after being trampled.

Jelina calls out, "Now, James!"

James jumps high. Fire bursts out of his hands and feet before he reaches the top of the trees. The wind swirls around him as another cloud forms moments before breaking through the treetops.

James is back amid things as we leap out onto the sandy beach. Three lemurs, much further away, him and the rest of the group.

At this speed, there is no way James can catch up.

Ahead, a swarm of small slug-like insects zips across the water's surface, catching other smaller insects. This sparks a fantastic idea. If I got fast enough, I might be able to run on the water. I could catch up to the leaders and slow them down somehow.

Silver and I take a few steps back, lean back, and pounce forward, putting my all into the speed. We jumped out far into the water, splashing and falling like a brick. Sudden fear swept over Silver, which induces a shift back into human form. I swam back to the surface and called out. "Jelina, a little help here, please."

Above me, several ice pillars materialize, erected from the water. The lemurs have to swerve violently to avoid them. One less fortunate lemur hit the ice pillar head-on and falls into the water. Quickly they are transformed into bobbing ice cubes. Fiery arrows blast holes into the pillars' bases, collapsing them into the water and creating rough waves.

I duck my head underwater, which a multitude of turtles work in unison to send sharp ice spikes out of the water like mortars. Three or more turtles are working together, creating an ice pillar after ice pillar. Seaweed is floating between each group with fast-moving air bubbles. James had told me the turtles used seaweed to communicate. I need to get out of the water quickly, but James might fare better above if I can interrupt their communications.

Jelina falls in beside me. I point at the seaweed. She nods and swims deeper, turns to wink at me, and morphs into a giant fish. It looks familiar. Memories of the swamp flash quickly behind my eyes as a Skyta fish with pink eyes swims toward the ice mortars. I hook an arm around a top fin as it passes and glides through the water, watching as several turtles are swallowed whole. The large fish, the size of a house, rises higher, which allows me to stay above the water while Jelina tears through pillar after pillar.

"David. Thank Jelina, for me. I didn't think I was going to make it through all that. Four more lemurs fell while I was up here."

"No problem. We got your back. Now, go catch up to the leaders."

We steer back to the beach, and I jump off.

"Thanks, Jelina. You saved us both back there." I shift back into a Dire Wolf before landing and sprinting back into the forest. Over my shoulder, I see a pink-eyed wolf catching up to me. I allow Silver to take over again while I reconnect with James' sight.

He is flying above us. Through his eyes, I see my silver fur glinting through the passing tree limbs. When he turns, behind him, three lemurs are hot on his tail in a familiar formation. This leaves another twelve still in front of him. I feel him smile through our connection.

"Watch this, David!" He already knows I am watching his every move.

James flies down a tad below the treetops, then fires six arrows simultaneously at two trees far in the distance. All goes black for a second before branches, vines, and leaves wrap themselves around each arrow and stretch out to the other arrows making a wide barrier in front of him. He flies directly toward it. He shoots an arrow behind, which explodes and unleashes a cloud of leaves, then turns back just in time to see the branches open slightly to let him pass through.

Three solid thuds echo among the trees, followed by loud yelling. Forewarned, I shift my sight back to Silver's to evade other falling lemurs.

James flies over the treetops and beyond our sight.

Behind me, Jelina transforms into the Kalacuu bird again and flies up after James. Earthbound, I am forced to weave weaving in and out of the trees and bushes, doing my best to follow. James still trails far behind the leading lemurs.

Ahead, glimpses of the volcano appear above the tree line. Still bright, the sun is sinking low on the horizon. The volcano spews out smoke, much like it would if it were about to erupt. Plumes of ash fill the air surrounding the base of the rock walls. Our eyes burn and tear up.

"James, don't fall here. I can barely see anything in front of me." I give Silver free rein and try to see through James' eyes again. Silver isn't faring much better as we slumped over on the ground covering our muzzle next to the two colossal parallel trees. I try to connect, but instead, James connected momentarily with us.

"David, Nooo!"

I feel light-headed. I can't make out what James is saying. I don't recognize the words. The noxious fumes in the air are affecting our lungs. Our breathing is labored.

A cool wisp of air surrounds us, bringing back the memory of when Leena, queen of the monkeys, dried me off by the hot springs. This air is lighter and adheres to us, moving in a circular motion around us. The fresh air clears our lungs and reenergizes Silver and me. We cough and spit out soot. Silver and I look up and see James' worried face floating above his puffy cloud. Guilt immediately clinches our hearts, knowing he came back to save us, giving up any hope of catching up.

"David, are you okay? Silver?"

We nod our head and reply, *"Yes. Much better. Now go. You are farther behind."*

"Don't worry about that. I have a crazy idea, but I need your help." Jelina lands on our head, nuzzling our furry ears.

"Alright, brother. What do you have in mind? Oh, I see."

James calls upon the forest again, and a thick elastic vine stretches out between two trees and wraps tightly around each trunk at least twenty meters up. Smaller tree roots slither up my forearms and create a massive tree root vest with an extensive root hook atop my back. Jelina flew away in fright at the sight of it, engulfing my torso.

"James! Tell Jelina it's okay. She's freaking out."

James relays my words to Jelina. "Don't worry. Trust me, he's fine. Hop on. We're taking the express route to the top of that volcano." Jelina grimaces to me, so I smile back. She nods and lands on James' shoulders.

James creates a small bench-like seat with a large ring at the bottom. I hook myself to the ring, and a familiar warm sensation comes over Silver and me. Our bond grows in strength rapidly, and we shoot into the forest, James holding onto the seat for dear life. The vine reaches its stretching length, and my hook snaps. James and Jelina scream at the top of their lungs as they catapult toward the volcano.

I catch up quickly. Thanks to my brother's wind spell, the smoke and ash are whipped away as we bulldoze our way into the Draconian territory. I let Silver run as I quickly reconnect with my brother.

James soars through the air with a beautiful bird at his side. His rocket-flamed hands push him faster and farther up the side of the mountain. I hear his excited holler as he passes two lemurs like they were stationary. He has that same wind spell over him, and Jelina makes it easier to see where they are heading. Forming his cloud as he approaches the top of the volcano, he fires blasts of whirlwinds in front of them. They dissipate quickly in the thick plumes of smoke.

He reaches back and pulls off his bow. He fires four arrows simultaneously. The smoke surrounding each projectile gravitates to the arrow, and the four land near the top of the volcano. The massive pillars of smoke spun like four individual tornados clearing their path to the checkpoint.

Once the smoke clears, several lemurs are under heavy fire. Fireballs, lava balls, and burning arrows are flung from the top of the volcano. James passes a falling lemur whose fur singed and his skin melting off his skull. The heat from the volcano evaporated the lemur's cloud in front of me. He fell to his death.

"James, don't use your cloud. Tell Jelina it's time to use her fireproof form." She will get you through this part.

I sense his reluctance. He doesn't yet trust Jelina. To him, she is a stranger who has taken my heart. While I can understand where he is coming from, I trust Jelina, and he needs to trust me.

"Fine. Let's do this. Jelina, I need you to use your fireproof form ... whatever that is."

Jelina smiles at James, knowing I'm communicating with him. She flies in front of him and drops slightly below. Pink smoke explodes from her as white scales glinted in the sunlight below. Long wings coupled with three-clawed talons stretch out, then a large-scale body with a long tail. A white, scaled, and spiked dragon's head twists and peers at James. A pink eye winks at him, or was that for me?

Startled, James almost loses it. He's freaking out that Jelina can turn into such a massive dragon. She is as big as if not bigger than Zyerr, the leader of the Draconians.

He pulls it together, drops onto Jelina's scaled back, and holds on to one of the spikes that protrude out of her spine. Jelina easily dodges left and right between lobs of lava and fireballs. A few arrows come close, but she spews a massive pink-tinted fireball down at the draconian that shot at her. A magikal pink and white dust plume is all that James and I can see.

"James, remind me to not make her mad when she's in this form."

"I second that. Those draconians stopped their attack after that shot, and we're now on the other side of the volcano. Three lemurs are teamed up against other draconians halfway down the side. It looks like an all-out war down there."

I leave James' sight and look back through Silver's eyes. Silver head-butts a draconian lizard aiming a fire spear up in the direction of my brother. We look up and see James flying his cloud again with a beautiful white dragon at his side. Silver is a bit jealous that James got to ride her in that form before us. I try to calm him down, so he doesn't rip apart every reptile we come across.

As the trials race on, Jelina provides cover fire at the angry reptiles, although they seem more preoccupied with the three lemurs conjuring tornadoes that rip through their village. I guess what we heard about the lemurs and draconians hating each other must be true. Each seems to want to hurt the other more than they want to become a master in their own tribe. By my calculations, this leaves a couple lemurs still ahead of James.

I take over before Silver joins the lemurs and draconians in the battle for blood. I sprint back into the forest in the direction of the beach at the front of the island. I can't see where the last two lemurs have gone. James could either be first or so far behind that the two remaining lemurs may finish the race long before he gets there. We have no choice but to use one of the deadly shortcuts to catch up.

"James, have you seen any more lemurs ahead of you?"

"I can't see that far, but Jelina says she spotted the closest one

already over the beach dodging ice spears and pillars. If I don't take the shortcuts, I don't think we will catch up to that one."

"I understand, though, you may be on your own if Silver takes his revenge on the troll too far."

"That's okay. You've aided me a great deal already. I wouldn't have gotten this far without you and Jelina."

"Alright, Silver, let's go take out the troll." I let Silver take over again like I had much choice. The anger rose high, and I could see snippets of Silver's memories flashing past. Jelina lying on the ground motionless, about to be splattered all over the forest like the goat beside her. Extreme adrenaline coursed through our veins, and we howl loudly. The wind whips through our fur in a brief but firm caress. Silver's thoughts were overwhelmed with anger. *Troll tree die, Troll tree die. Must devour tree. Must kill Troll. Much pain feel.*

All I can do is aid Silver's blind heart by spotting the traps and nudging Silver out of the way. We spring one I missed, and a large log falls from the sky tied to a vine. Silver lungs in the air and snaps the trunk like a trig between fingers. Silver is the most pissed I have ever felt him. His thoughts of his family and brother filter in, and he sees red. His family was torn apart by another wolf pack, and he did nothing to avenge them. His thoughts rage on. He will get his revenge with this Troll for Jelina, for his brother, for his family.

We jump across spiked traps and zoom past darts that are too slow to hit us. We dive under a spiked limb from a booby-trapped tree. Then we catch our first whiff of the Troll. The Troll's foul stench is hard to miss, and we dial into his direction. I feel James' presence above me in the treetops. He's dodging the traps we accidentally spring as well as a few of the troll traps in the treetops like nets and paralyzing darts.

"David, the Troll is right ahead of you. I will fly out ahead and distract him."

I can barely hear what James says over a load of images. Silver keeps repeating in our head.

James tries to fake right and goes left, but the Troll reads him. He grabbed James in midair and squeezes the air out of my brother's lungs. Jelina has transformed into her Kalacuu form and is vigilantly pecking at the Troll's eyes. The Troll's other hand swats at Jelina and knocks her to the ground.

Silver and I cry out in a fury over the Troll's actions toward our loved ones. I merge my hatred for this Troll with Silvers. Our skin tingles as the buildup of loss explode around us, engulfing us entirely in searing red flames.

We leap up to the wooden neck of the Troll, chomping hard and deep before ripping out a huge chunk. Black sap-like goo spews out over the Troll and us. Moments later, the sap ignites with our fire and sets the tree toll ablaze in hot flames. High pitched screeches resonate through the forest. In the corner of my eye, I see James fall inside the melting ice sphere that protected him from the fire. James rises up slightly, out of breath, and completely stunned.

"*James! Take Jelina and run away from us. This Troll is going to die.*"

James trembles at my words before he turns, picks up Jelina and runs into the thick forest.

Our muscles bulge, and the fire ignites our desire to rip every limb off this Troll's body. My conscience is buried down inside with all rational thoughts.

The pure instinct to kill blankets our thoughts like a heavy veil. Our claws and fangs protrude even more. Our thoughts disappeared, and there was only one word that kept whispering in our ears. *Kill, Kill, Kill!*
Our strength makes us feel invincible. The segments of wood and flesh we tear from the Troll is like biting into melting butter. There isn't much left but a limbless beating stump, its wooden skin still smoldering and ablaze. Its hollow cries shattered our eardrums.

The rush is exhilarating, and the anger increases after each chuck we rip off. We are overloading on anger … anger built up until it became too much to bear. We look at what is left of the tree troll and howl the deepest, most frightening howl we have ever made. The buildup explodes out of our roar, and a wave of flames shoots out around us, and above us, the sound of a giant explosion erupted like that of a volcano -- only it came from us.

The angry-high plummets. Consciousness and rational thoughts return. Around our blackened crater, all remnants of the tree troll have disappeared. All the trees around us were flattened like a crop-circle. The closest trees are piles of smoldering ash, and plumes of black smoke rise above us in the sunlight.

I remember James being squeezed, and Jelina knocked from the sky, then. James taking Jelina away from us while we fight a burning tree troll.

"*James! James, where are you and Jelina?*"

"*We are fighting with the lemur we saw earlier at the waterfall. Are you, you again? I tried talking to you, but there was like some sort of fiery mind barrier up, and I couldn't connect with you. We also heard an explosion. Are you okay?*"

"*Don't worry about that right now. Take out that lemur, and I will catch up with you in the undead forest.*"

I take over, letting Silver rest and come back into his senses. I don't really know what happened, but there's no time to speculate. I have to catch back up and protect my brother and Jelina. The thought of Jelina brings Silver back into my consciousness, and our bond warms up. Finally, we arrive at the waterfall beach. The same spot where Morty announced the race.

Turtles are to our right and under the waterfall. Others, at different heights in the waterfall, shoot icicle darts at a lemur and my brother.

"James! Divert the direction of the waterfall!"

James freezes the top of the waterfall at a slant without questioning my command, which brings the waterfall out at an odd angle. All the turtles under the cascade fall down to us. We growl, low and vicious-sounding, and the turtles speed off on ice surfboards.

The cold water refreshes our skin and heart. I feel more exhilarated than angry. We look up at a tree across the lake and can see movement at the top of the tree. We use Silver's keen sight to zoom in and see a black and white skunk-stripped goat with a blow dart tube. He's aiming for James and puffs up to blow.

"James! Dive now!

I can only hope my thought was fast enough. My gaze follows the dart's movement. It seems as if the dart is moving closer and closer in slow motion to James, who is still fighting the lemur. His back is toward this skunk goat. As the dart closes in, James' cloud completely dissipates like the lemur's cloud over the volcano. He plummets down, startling the lemur who was fighting him. The lemur hasn't seen the dart … James was in the way. The dart pierces straight through the lemur's heart, and he drops to the water below.

Jelina and I head in the direction of the skunk. I head-butt the tree causing him to lose balance. Distracted, the goat struggles to regain his equilibrium. Simultaneously, Jelina swings down, latches her sharp talons into his shoulder, and picks him out of the tree. She flies out into the ice pillar section of the water before dropping him.

James conjures another cloud before hitting the water's surface and flies over to me.

"Thanks again, David. That was a close one," he calls to us. "You too, Jelina. Pepe has been out to get me since I bested him in training. Looks like I am going to need your speed again going through this undead territory."

"Hop on. Let's finish this," I say. Jelina nods in appreciation and takes flight.

James falls through his cloud and lands on my back. He outstretches an arm to a tree, and long slender twigs gravitate to him. I turn and scrunch my eye at him. "What are you going to do with those?"

"I needed a refill on arrows. I'm out."

He clutches my fur with shaky hands. I can't tell if he's scared of me or going through the undead forest. I take off fast again. Jelina speeds past me and goes far up and out ahead. We pass by familiar-looking crocs and grotesque abominations of what were once turtles and lizards. Luckily most of these undead creatures are relatively slow, and we glide by them without a worry.

The terrain is a muddy swampland that smells foul, and barely any sun shines in. dead trees plague the area, and tar like goop weighs down our movements.

Halfway in, the vines, of their own accord, lash out and wrap around my ankles. The sudden stop launches James into a prickly bush. The vines thorns cut deep into my legs, and we howl out in pain. My brother yells out as well as he endeavors to dislodge himself from the bush. I shift back into human form and quickly bring out my wolverine like claws. Now able to maneuver better. I slice right through the thick thorny vines.

Jelina flies back in time to see me unraveling a clenched vine that still won't let go even when severed.

"Oh, my goodness. Let me take care of those." She shifts into her valfen original form and tears into the vines with her sharp claws. My ankles get scratched, but we both know the wounds will heal when we shift again.

"I have good news. The leading lemur took this shortcut also and is fighting off a few undead up ahead of you." Jelina says while watching James finally extract himself from the bush, all scraped up.
Jelina looks exhausted. I can only imagine how much energy she has exerted to do many shifts in such a short time.

"Jelina, it's time you took a rest. Hop on with my brother." I Shift quickly back into Dire wolf form.

"But I--" She looks at me and concedes. "Fine, but don't you go thinking I'm not stronger than you." James hops back on and slaps his lap. My beautiful pink-eyed five-tailed mate hops up on James's lap. Silver and I growl lightly.

"Hey, I don't want her to fall off. Pleh! Your tails are in my face, Jelina."

We smile and take off again. Jelina digs her claws into our fur to hold on. We pass more of the same grotesque abominations. Some have heads hanging by their esophagus dangling in front of them as they walk forward. Others have holes ate out of them or chunks of flesh removed.
One has its intestines dragging on the ground behind the unfortunate goat. The goat trips on its own intestine and falls into a sludge-filled pond.

Before long, we catch up with the last lemur who is sending air gusts in every direction to fend of those same grappling vines. He sees us coming and quickly takes to the sky, dodging left and right past snapping vines as he goes. I speed up to give my brother a fast launch. Ahead, a large dead tree slants up onto a large boulder. I run up the trunk and jump up off the boulder.

James lets go of Jelina and me. He uses our momentum and springs off my back into the air. Before I even land, he uses his rocket fire to get neck and neck with the first place lemur flying up to the island. I look back to the forest and see a vine snap past me at incredible speed.

"James! Dive!"

It must be hard to listen to that command when he is so close to the end. I hope he trusts me by now. I hear the crowd of lemurs yelling and shouting atop the island. Jelina and I are out of the forgotten land on the beach, looking up at James. We see him fall at the last second. The vine snaps and latches onto the lemur's neck, which slingshot him back to the forest.

Having seen the lemur disappear back down into the forest, James creates his cloud. The floating island of lemurs falls silent when both contestants fall out of sight.

Then James rises up on his cloud and disappears past the island's edge.

Morty's loud voice echoed in our ears. "We have a winner!"

Chapter 26

A Fiery Last Stand – Volcanic Trial
James

"What happened when you crossed the finish line?" Elizabeth asks, giddily listening intently to my retelling of how the race went. We are all sitting around the campfire.

"Well, there was a bunch of lemurs floating and standing up in shock. A few that were flying ran into other lemurs and fell to the floor. Morty was the only one cheering for me before he announced me as the winner. Leena looked more than displeased that I, a human, bested all her masters in training. But I did see a glint in her eye. I'm not sure what that was about. There wasn't much of a celebration, only Morty licking my feet to show how happy he was that he trained the winner."

The sun is hiding behind the horizon, and there isn't much time left until my next and last trial. A cool breeze dances around us before evaporating into the fire. It makes my arm hair stand on end.

I have a terrible feeling that Draithur may be close.

I look over at my brother, who is smiling at several goats shivering in the corner. *"Stop scaring them. We will need them when Draithur arrives."*

"I know, but they were aiming to take you out in the race. They deserve to be scared of me."

"Brother, no one deserves to be scared all the time. I'm fine. We won. Let's not torment the group that has aided us and given us a place to stay on an island with such hatred toward our kind."

David looks back across the fire to my side, where Elizabeth is curled up under my arm, watching the fire cinders fly up into the air. Jelina is nuzzling David's chest. I find it uncomfortable to look at those two.

Tate stands by Salithica's hut with a sneer etched on his face. He seems to be in an argument with Salithica.

"When does the Volcanic Trial start?" Elizabeth clenches onto my left arm. I know she doesn't want me to go, and, truthfully, I am not looking forward to it. I am mentally and physically exhausted. I am unsure if I will even make it to the center of the volcano.

"Very soon, unfortunately, " I answer. I glance at my right hand, which holds the half-eaten bowl of goo Salithica gave me. The Summoning ring of Zurye has its six gems reflecting the flames in them. As I stare, the red gem starts to glow.

For no particular reason, my attention is drawn to a blue fur ball eyeing my food. Tinky is perched on the side, torn between his hunger and the smell of it. He takes a small handful and chokes it down. His eyes bulge out, and he starts to vibrate the bowl. He whisks up and around Elizabeth, making her giggle. The laughing is contagious as Tinky runs between and around all of us at the campfire. The lovely sound of Elizabeth laughing gives me the courage to finish the last of the goo in my bowl. I will need every bit of strength I can muster to defeat the Volcanic's tribe champion, Therose.

A loud gong sounds in the distance, coming from the direction of the volcano. Elizabeth goes from laughing to teary-eyed face. She remains silent, and I can pretty much read her mind to be safe and come back to her. I stand, pat along my belt to make sure my brother's daggers are on me, and check my quiver to be sure it is full of arrows. I watch Tinky zoom back up to Elizabeth's shoulder, puffing out his small blue chest. I know Tinky will look after her while I am in battle. David and Jelina mirror my determined look as we head to the edge of the camp.

"I will be back for you, Elizabeth, I promise." She covers her face as a sneaky tear streaks down it.

"Be safe. You promised." Elizabeth tries to stand firm to see me off. Tate appears behind her, wrapping his arm around her and pulling her to his side. Tate really freaks me out. He is no longer the same polite human that arrived at our doorstep.

David lets Silver shift as I stare into red eyes before fur coats his body, and his muscles snap into position. David's shifts have become more flawless since we have been here. If I had blinked, I would have missed the transformation. I run and hop on Silver's back as Jelina shifts into her Kalacuu-Toucan form. We race off through the forest, past the hot springs, and arrive at the edge of the volcanic tribe's village.

Silver and Jelina hide amongst the rocky terrain while I look upon the utter destruction left in the wake of the tornadoes the Lemurs summoned during the race. Woodcrafts and weapons litter the ground. Several lizards are still collecting the scraps of their belongings as their reptilian children cry over broken toys. An unannounced tear falls on my arm. The village is devastated.

No wonder there is such hatred between these two tribes. The volcanic tribe is made out to be a ruthless, arrogant tribe, but right now, they look like a helpless tribe trying to pick up what's left of their life to survive. Up ahead is a gathering of lizards, salamanders, and other reptiles. A profound toned speaker is talking in Draconian tongue.

I push my way through to the base of the volcano cave opening. My twenty opponents are lined up and facing Therose.

I walk up to the end of the line and stand at attention.

"I was beginning to think you were going to chicken out of this competition, human. It would have been a shame to not have a chance to end your life in battle." Therose mocks me before continuing the announcement of rules in English.

"This is a trial of the fittest, the strongest. Those who dare to take on this trial must fight for themselves as teamwork may only get you killed. There is only one victor, and that is if any of you can best me in battle. This is a fight to the death! Those of you that are too weak to handle it may leave now with your tail between your legs!"

Silence answers his challenge. No one leaves, and every draconian in the line has a rage-filled sneer aimed at Therose. *Looks like I'm less hated here than Therose.*

"No wimps this year. Good, then this might be a fun battle in the end."

Everyone looks up, and I follow their gaze. Zyerr, the red dragon leader of the draconian, swoops down and lands on Therose. Zyerr rocked on the turtle's shell before speaking.

"Think outside the box, and you may have a chance at beating Therose this year. He is one of my most powerful masters, but he is thick-headed. You will need to use your magik in a way that Therose won't expect. Killing others is not a penalty as it is part of a real battle. If you fall, only you are to blame. The goal of this trial is to be the last draconian standing in the arena. Do this and win Kioserack's sword and title of master."

"Get off me, you ugly red lizard," Therose says as he struggles to climb out from under Zyerr's claws.

Zyerr breathes in deep and bellows out a magikal red glowing flame into the sky. He takes flight and soars to the top of the volcano. The group of draconians gathered around us is now climbing up the sides to join Zyerr at the top. Therose rolls up to a standing position. Flames spin-out from beneath his feet as he speeds into the cave, leaving a fiery trail in his wake.

The draconians around me appear frazzled, then one of the blue lizards follows Therose. We all follow suit, and flames erupted between us all. Fireballs and flame swords flew and clashed against each other before even making it into the cave's entrance. Growls and roars of anger spew from the throats of every reptile. Dusk has settled, and the fiery torches around the cave entrance glowed fiercely. I dodge a few fireballs thrown my way before speeding off after a yellow salamander slithering its way into the cave.

A group of four draconians still fight behind me, not even caring to enter the torch lit cave. Fiery explosions shake the mountain as plumes of smoke wafted past me to escape the inferno left behind. I sweat profusely due to the extreme temperatures inside the confined walls of rock and stone. I slow down, coughing, and gagging after inhaling too much smoke.

"Brother, it is no use. It is too hot in there. We can't venture further in without frying our skin."

"David. Don't come in any further. Just update me from the top of the volcano."

I knew my brother and Silver wouldn't be able to follow me in here without water magik. I calm my nerves and collect my thoughts. How did I create Elizabeth's clone out of water? I think about the frigid water I had to overcome in the sea trial. My perspiration begins to move around my skin, layering me with a thin cooling shield of protection against the constant waves of heat. I wave my arms and ask for the winds to help in clearing the smoke around me. A wind bubble forms encircling me as my lungs fill with cleaner air.

I push off the wall and run forward, feeling that same rush I had back when Silver was chasing me through the castle. My feet ignite, and I'm propelled forward faster than I thought I could run. *"So, this must be what you feel like running with your bond."*

"Whoa, how did you learn to run so fast?" David sounds shocked. He is looking from behind my eyes again.

"Race, yes. We race later, yes" Silver challenges.

I'm barely able to turn left or right at these speeds. How does my brother manage to not hit anything? *"I ... Ahhh."*

A fiery boulder comes at me too fast, and I can't avoid it. I stop the fiery speed and drop to the ground, instinctually calling rock to me. All that training with Salithica is really paying off. The boulder flattened me, but not before I am fully covered in harder stone. The boulder cracks and then shatters into tiny fragments falling all around me.

"James! James, are you ok?"

"Only a minor headache, I will take care of it. Keep Jelina safe and give me a heads up on the arena battles."

"You got it. No one has reached the arena other than Therose. He looks bored, spinning on his shell. The view of the Blood moons is clear from up here. They are close to overlapping."

"We don't have much time. I have to finish this before the curse hits the Island." I steady my resolve and toss several fire coated rocks back in the direction the boulder came.

A loud yell bellows as I hear a loud thud echo through the tunnel. This cave system is more like a maze of tunnels. It will be more challenging than I thought to find the right one that leads to the middle of the arena.

I come to a fork in my current tunnel—three paths to choose from, three directions, and no time to backtrack. I grab three arrows from my quiver, summon forth my wind speed, and fire them, one down each tunnel. The fletches ignite after leaving the bow. They leave a fiery trail behind. Two explode when colliding into dead ends, and the third exploded further down. Its explosion comes with lizard shrieks. I run down the right path with the aid of the wind pushing my rock armor forward.

There is a fiery red glow emanating from the distant end of this tunnel. Yells from draconians grow louder as I approached—metal clashes against metal. Boulders explode and shake the very walls that enclose the tunnels. Dust and rock particles fall from the ceiling on every collision. A flurry of fireballs hit the wall right in front of the opening, stopping me in my tracks.

I peek out of the cave at the vast opening in the interior of the volcano. I see Therose in the distance salivating at the arrival of so many draconians. He stands atop a large floating island of red rock. Lava pushes it around, making the ground unstable. Large dragon bones enclose the platform like a cage. Twelve or so draconians are on the rocks surrounding the platform in firefights of their own. I see two lizard skeletons sizzling in the lava at the far side of the arena.

I don't see any of the draconians even trying to jump into the arena with Therose. The realization strikes me as odd that some of the draconians are pulling their killing blows at the last second. I don't have time to figure out why. I have a score to settle with Therose and a promise to keep. I dodge my way past a few snickering reptiles and jump of a cliff, landing into a roll inside the bone caged arena.

"So, you dare to be my third challenger? Did you not see what happened to those two?" Therose points in the direction of the lizard skeletons swimming in the lava. "Do you think a puny human could hold such a powerful sword as the late Kioserack's? Only those truly worthy of this power can wield it, and you are not worthy."

"Are you done talking, or is this how you win your fights ... by boring your opponent until they throw themselves into the lava?"

"You pesky little human. I will destroy you!"

"Bring it." I crack my knuckles and take a boxer's stance. I grip the rock with my feet and feel for Therose's movements. He lunges forward, and I quickly step out of the way while he slams into a bone. He reaches up and grabs at the ends of two bones, snapping them off and igniting them in orange flames. I pull out my brother's wolf head daggers, covering them in blue flames.

We dance around each other's jabs, and slices ducking, dodging, and sweep kicking at the other. I catch Therose off balance, and he falls back on his shell, rocking helplessly. I step up close, and he spins around, firing fireballs like a machinegun. I throw up a fiery barrier letting the fire absorb into it before pushing the heatwave into him, sending him flying into the cage of bones.

The surrounding noises fall silent as Therose rose slowly with anger etched in his face. I look to see some astonishing draconian faces and other sneers. That same blue lizard from earlier speaks out to my left.

"Now, do it now."

For a second, I thought he was talking to Therose, but then a storm of fiery boulders and fireballs are thrown toward the caged platform. Flaming shards of stone and metal weapons fly in all directions whizzing by both my and Therose's heads. The other draconians set a trap for not only me but also

Therose. Was this what Zyerr was hinting at in his speech. What better way to win than to take out both of us at the same time and then fight each other for the sword.

Therose's look of anger has melted into a worried expression. He, too, knows there is no way to fend off twelve other fire-wielding draconians and me. I am too tired to fend off this many enemies alone. I was expecting a more one-on-one fight in the end, but this is ridiculous.

I am dodging left and right, jumping over and falling under multiple fireballs. All I can do is block and dodge to stay alive. This reminds me of when Salithica nearly beat me to a pulp, and I couldn't lay one attack on her. She pushed me to think outside of the box.

In the past, during the race, when I couldn't do it alone, I could count on my brother, my team, to pull me through and win a battle. I look over at Therose, getting hit and beaten down by multiple hits. This is not how I wanted to win our fight.

I quickly encase Therose in a cold wind that causes every fireball to sizzle out when it hits. I do the same for myself and start blowing back the giant boulders to their throwers. My gaze connects with Therose's. There is no longer a glare of hatred for me in them, only a glint of relief. We nod at each other, and for the moment, we had joined sides. He manages to return to his feet. I block an attack and deflect projectiles. Therose swings around me and fires attacks back at the draconians. We swivel and turn and maneuver around each other in a graceful battle harmony, covering each other's backs from attacks and firing back at draconians. The draconians started to dwindle until we were the only ones left standing or alive.

Therose backed up. "Now it's your turn, human. Did you think that our little truce would last?"

"Of course not, but I could not claim that I'm better than you if you died fighting against your own tribe."

Steam spewed out of his nostrils. But a warning sound rolled past both our ears.

"James! They are here. Get out here quick!"

Therose gazes at the top of the volcano, worry lines on his face.

"C'mon Therose. I'll take you up. We are going to need everyone's help with this battle."

"I am going to murder you."

"Yeah, yeah. You can do that later, but right now, we need to save your home." His expression is one of bewilderment.

"Fine. As long as you don't drop me in the lava to end our battle."

"There's no more time; let's go. Use your fire to give us a boost up."

I gather the wind around me to steady myself as I jump on to Therose's shell. I grab him by the top of his collar and thrust fire out the bottom of my feet. Therose does the same, and we shoot up to the top of the volcano.

There, Therose and I can see movement along the darkened tree line. I take five arrows from my quiver and send them flying, igniting them before hitting the trees. Light spreads, and I continue my barrage of arrows until I'm all out. The line extends from beach to beach. A fiery arrow missed a tree and struck the back of a huge dracanian head. Its fumbling movements reminded me of my brother covered in mud from the swamp and the undead we saw in the race.

"David, how many are there?"

"Jelina flew up to get a better count, but there are way too many. It's like they brought all of the undead from the forgotten lands with them." My brother sounds worried.

"How could they do that? Those things all had a mind of their own and went after their own tails. How could they all be lined up in some formation like soldiers taking orders?" I am stunned by the sheer size of Draithur's army.

"It's the Necronomicon. It has to be what's controlling them."

"Where is Elizabeth?"

"Tate escorted her to the base of the volcano to await your victory. I see her and Tate climbing up the face of the volcano now."

"I will meet up with her. Any sign of the spider queen or Draithur?

"Not yet, but I imagine they aren't far behind."

A dark presence emanates from the forest's edge. I climb down to Elizabeth and hold her hand as Therose looks on ahead of me, taken aback by what he sees.

Then a dark figure steps out in front of us.

Elizabeth screams.

Chapter 27

Draithur's Army
Elizabeth

Chills slide up my spine. My nightmare unfolds in front of me. Snapshots of Jelina dead on the ground, Silver decapitated, and James' beating heart-throbbing on Draithur's Necronomicon. A scream penetrates my ears, bringing me back to reality, to the army standing before me.

James pushes me behind him in a protective motion as Tate unsheathes his bright sword illuminating the battlefield closest to us.

The tree line is filled with staggering slow-moving bodies. Some are dragging limbs, others crawling to the edge. The forgotten lands are presenting the horrors that lurk inside. Grotesque lizards with their flesh ripped off, showcasing glistening redbone beneath. Holes in a goat could clearly be seen through much like holding up a piece of Swiss cheese. A lemur-like creature sits on the top of a turtles shell licking the blackish goo pouring out of the turtle's skeletal face.

The foul stench hits my nose, and I quickly turn, pinching my nostrils closed and gagging. No use. I retch and barf my dinner onto Therose's feet. He gasps with disgust.

He isn't even paying attention to me. He holds up Keoserak's sword and swings it overhead. With each swipe of the blade, his face turns more from scared to angry. Therose ignites his sword. Yells and shouts come from the draconian ranks behind him.

I wipe my mouth with some leaves. From behind the tree line, I sense a cold dark presence looking at me. Draithur struts out in front with five Drargs on either side. The spider witch is not with him nor the bone dragon from my nightmare.

"Hello, Princess. I have been dreaming of the day that you will be mine. Today is the day that you will be my beloved by my side. I brought a few friends with me to make our union special."

"You can't have her. I won't let you touch her." James barks out while David joins us atop a rock cliff looking out over the forest below. David looks at me, and Silver's eyes glow red as his attention snaps back to the uprising of undead. Another warning sounds overhead but is drowned out by the hollers and yells of the draconians.

"I'm taken," was all I could muster in his presence. I don't know why that slipped out. I don't even know where James and I stand on the matter. We haven't had time to discuss a relationship. Draithur moves closer, bringing my attention back to him.

"Tsk. Tsk. That isn't acceptable. I guess that leaves me only one choice … to kill that puny human and his friends so that we can be together. Their heads will make great decorations for our wedding." Draithur chortles an evil laugh.

My stomach turns with revulsion, and I want to vomit again. I can't help imagining James, David, and Jelina's heads on sticks on a wedding table. The imagery looks so real as if Draithur is sending images to me mentally. I push them out of my head and wipe away the tears with the back of my hand.

James cups my face in his hands. "Elizabeth, that will never happen. I won't let it. We will protect you. Stay with Tate." His quick short orders give me confidence, even knowing that he and the others may die protecting me.

Jelina flies overhead, transforming from a Kalacuu into a large white dragon with a slight tint of red from the moon light. Her pink eyes glowing vibrantly in the night as she blows pink fire out of her nostrils.

"Tate, protect her! Jelina, pick what you can in the air and cover us on the ground. David, use that bond of yours with Silver to dismember as many as you can. We have to stop them from reaching this cliff."

Therose is done waiting. His actions had riled his draconians, and several, if not all, of them behind me raise weapons. A draconian yell comes from Therose as he and his fellow draconians charge into battle. Movement in the trees attracts my attention as a few goats positioned themselves overhead the mass army, Salithica, in the front.

Sudden darkness falls over the moon as though a cloud blocked its light. A hoard of lemurs, each on their own small clouds, arrive overhead and spread out. Leena leads in front, ever more pissed at the intrusion. The turtles aren't here yet, but Therose isn't waiting.

James and Silver fall in line behind Therose and make their way to the battle's front lines.

Draithur unleashes his ten Drargs onto the first ten lizards that surround Therose, James, and Silver. Jelina shoots pink fireballs one after another in Draithur's direction. Undead creatures near Draithur jump in the way at the last second, providing him with unlimited body shields. The undead creatures that sacrificed their beings are blown apart, splattering black blood all over Draithur. He smiles at me, unfazed while wiping his face and licking his fingers. Bile rises again, and I have to force myself to keep what little food is left in my stomach.

Leena fires lightning bolts that cause exploding body parts to fly across the battlefield into other lizards. Wind gusts through several in the air and back into the forest. Some were pulverized by goat spears. The forest looked as if it was raining arrows as several hundred were shot up in the air before landing on to targeted undead below. The draconians lit the front of the battlefield up with fire and smoke. Fireballs fly across and around draconians. Explosions in the distance produce spires of smoke rising and glinting in the red moonlight. A large red dragon, Zyerr, swoops down, engulfing the entire front line of the undead in red flames.

Draithur barely moved, if only to dodge a large boulder or a flying limb. He winks at me before gazing at James. I followed his gaze back to James, David, and Therose backed up against themselves, fending off eight of the ten Drarg possessed draconians. A black goat jumps from atop a tree down into the circle. He whips around in some martial arts style and strikes the enemy with his nunchucks while dodging every slow attack made by the Red-eyed draconians. Blood and flesh rip off each possessed draconian, showcasing their skeleton below.

No amount of damage slows these monsters down.

Jelina sees Silver trapped in the circle and swoops down. She brings her head back, and James quickly pops up a fiery shield around Silver, Therose, the black goat, and himself. Pink flames spread over all of the possessed draconians melting their skin off, leaving glinting redbones in the moonlight. The dark black smoke oozes between each bone as the joints still move as if unfazed by the lack of tendons. The two remaining red-eyed draconians return to either side of Draithur.

James sends a heatwave out, pushing back the surrounding skeletons and giving them more room to fight. Therose eyes Jelina, his surroundings, and then James, who nods at him before lunging at a skeleton closest to him. Draconians in the distance launch a few undead up in the air. Wind cyclones toss them further up as barrages of arrows fly into them before being electrocuted by lightning and impaled by large ice spikes.

Large rolling objects thunder down both sides and knock over undead in their path like bowling pins. Turtles hurl ice waves, hail, and icicles into the mix. Chondro stuck out with his wrinkled figure and charging in first with Ula and Konja on either side. The scene before me is nothing but chaotic. I hope with all my heart that James survives the battle. He has been through hell all day to gain acceptance by the leaders to leave the island. And now he's exhausted and worn out yet giving all he has gone to protect me.

I see Draithur walk up behind Therose and James. "James, look out behind you!" I yell, hoping he can hear me.

Draithur raises his Necronomicon book, and a lightning black orb surrounds it as if it's sucking in dark magik. I quickly remember that barely audible whisper of a command I gave Silver when he took over David's human form. "Silver, Attack Draithur!"

Silvers's head immediately pops up from the battle. He snaps his head toward Draithur and pounces toward him. James notices at the last second and jumps in front of Therose as a dark lightning bolt springs forth from the book. Silver knocks Draithur over, but the bolt had already left, hitting its target.

James flies into the back of Therose … hard … getting the turtle's attention. Therose sees James' limp body at his feet.

"Nooooo!" I scream.

Tate holds me back as I try to run to James. I ball up on the ground as my heart feels like it's going to shrivel up. Tinky snuggles up against me, trying to comfort me. Silver howls a scornful howl. The rock cliff I sit upon darkens as I look up to the moons and see them finishing the eclipse.

A bright blue explosion sends a wave coursing over and through all of us. The moons are now one and glow bright blue in the night sky. Tinky jumps back.

I look at my arms. The skin is rotting off. Bones protrude out from beneath them, and I scream.

The battle is temporarily suspended as all our allies look like the undead and all the undead turn back into the original creatures they were before. I spot Draithur backing up and looking around for his bodyguards. The Drags have all disappeared, leaving ten draconians fumbling around in front of Silver and Therose.

I run to James, escaping Tate's grasp.

James stands upright with his back to me. He turns around.

I suck in a breath and cover my boney face. James's entire face has melted off, leaving black bone beneath. Black goo slides down his chest and a hole where the bolt of dark magik hit him. His jaw swings loosely, and he smashes it back up into his skull, welding the bone back into his face. He looks down at his boney hands and fleshless legs. Fire ignites his hands and feet. He flies up into the air before landing on a cloud, floating over to me. Inaudible words escape his mouth while he caresses my cheek. A glob of black goo spurts out of my eye onto his face. His jaw loosens again, and flails as black liquid streams out of his mouth.

Tate pulls me away from him, grabbing James' attention.

Tate still looks like Tate, unaffected by the moons' curse and still holding his bright sword in his other hand.

"There's no time to explain my appearance. Take advantage of this and kill Draithur. He no longer has control of the undead, and the Drargs are unable to reappear until the eclipse ends."

Don't you think you could have told us this earlier? I want to ask the question, but my mouth won't move correctly in this form. Only odd noises emerge. Tate drags me back up the hill.

The surrounding Draconians, lemurs, turtles, and goats seem much less affected by the transformation. Lemur skeletons ride on clouds zipping in and out of the battle tossing air gusts and throwing lightning bolts. Goats use the trees' vines to pull up all the now-normal-looking creatures up to them before decapitating them without mercy.

Jelina overhead, once a beautiful white dragon, is now a horrifying skeleton dragon. Not an ounce of skin is left on her as pink flames erupt around her, covering her bones in a pink glow. She spews more flames down on the crowd, no longer holding back. She burns the once-undead-but-now-normal creatures alive.

Therose, and his now undead draconian army, started wreaking havoc on all the familiar creatures that were attacking them. Cries and begs for mercy fill the battlefield. The tables have turned, and the islanders are winning.

James dives back into the fight.

Silver howls a familiar sound. He pounces on Draithur's undead skeleton body.

Draithur drops the book and fights to free himself from a hideous red-eyed, half skeleton-spiked Dire Wolf. Silver snaps his neck and tosses Draithers head into the air. James catches it midflight and sets it ablaze, but Draithur's body searches for his head, moving without one.

What am I missing? Something isn't right. I'm missing something!

For one thing, Tinky, my blue furball, isn't on my shoulder. He's always on my shoulder, particularly at times like this. A horrible feeling that something is wrong hits me like a blow to the solar plexus. Very wrong. They have to know this night is the eclipse. After all, their master created the curse on these lands throughout Kinzurdia. I look around for Tinky, hoping he's not hurt or, worse, eaten.

Tate swings his sword, frantically at something behind me. I jump back and see a swarm of knee-high spiders surrounding Tate. A large plumb dark figure starts to come into focus in front of me. Familiar sad eyes stare back at me. Large ears twitch in the red light, and glinting white sharp fangs protrude from the corners of its frown. It's Tinky!

Tinky is the size of a professional sumo wrestler. His big arms spread out.

I hop back, away from him. He opens his mouth, and … speaks to me.

"Elizabeth, I'm sorry, but I have to do this."

I'm frozen in place by the sheer size of him and that he actually spoke to me. A shadowy silhouette of a large spider stands behind him. Evil laughter vibrates my bones.

"Come to me, child. It's time to fulfill your destiny." A spider web drops from overhead and lands on me. It wraps around, cocooning me. It tightens until it is impossible to wiggle a centimeter. Tinky picks me up and carries me on his shoulder back to the Spider Witch. Despite the bindings, I see her clearly now. She is as ugly as I remember her from my dream. Her bottom black spider half includes eight horned spider needles for legs. Her midsection is humanoid. Spider webs are intricately placed, covering up her breasts, and her eyes are disconcerting.

A lightbulb finally clicked in my brain. This entire battle was nothing more than a distraction to grab me.

"Princess! Noooo!" Tate yells out behind me. Tinky stops and turns to face Tate, allowing me to connect my gaze with his. He is held down by thirty or more of the giant spiders and their webs. He tries to swipe at the onslaught of approaching spiders. His eyes turn pure gold, just like the flash I saw of them back in the castle. The Spiders explode outward from him in all directions, and he is left floating in midair. A bright white glow emanates from him, much like the white light I saw surrounds him when he talked to someone in the forest. He falls back to the ground, shaking his head before looking back into my eyes with his normal ones. A frown is pasted across his face, soon replaced by anger as the surrounding spiders tackle him. Tinky whips me back around and carries me up to the Spider Witch.

"I have her, my queen, as promised," Tinky says sorrowfully.

I still am shocked that Tinky could betray me like this.

"James! David! Help!" I scream inside my head as loud noises come out of my mouth that sounds more like a dying rat being dissected alive.

A large blue hand covers my mouth, muffling the remaining noises as Tinky follows his Queen and her minions into the forest below. I try to wiggle and kick, but it's no use. The spider witch stops and bows down to my face. I can see her hand grab dust off of her legs and hold it out in front of me. She blows it into my face until I cough and gag. My head goes light, and then everything begins to turn black.

"James! Please come for me before it's too late."

Epilogue

A New Objective
James

"That little blue furball took Elizabeth! That is your excuse for not protecting her," I yell at Tate while looking across the now-silent red battlefield. The moons now passed each other, and my human body is returned to normal. I am furious!

The residents of this island are outraged and seized with sorrow over comrades' loss and having to kill their own family and friends during the eclipse. Zyerr flies overhead, casing the remains of the battlefield, probably counting his losses. Leena gathers her dead, and the group passes them back up to their island. Morty sees my glance, stops his flight, and heads in my direction. Many turtles alongside Chondro and Ula spread out among the bodies, hovering their bright glowing hands over any they could save. Salithica is barking orders at trees and bushes where her goats are camouflaged, still on high alert for any undead that may be lurking nearby.

I stare at Draithur's severed head and punt kick it into the crowd of bodies. I yell out a slur of intangible words toward anyone and everyone near me. Losing Elizabeth is not an option. I can't let the only girl I've ever really cared about die at the hands of some evil power.

Heat builds up more and more as I go through all the brief moments I've had with Elizabeth. From the moment I saw her lying on the ground curled up in Culbin Forest, a small flame ignited inside me. The more I got to know her, the more that flame burned inside.

Its flames only recently danced across my heart, but now her loss sparks another part of me. A more profound, raging fire consumes my heart, stoking in me a desire I have never felt before. I now know my path, which is to save Elizabeth from the evil that curses these lands. My drive is absolute, and I don't care if I have to go alone. I will find her and bring her back.

"You will not be alone, brother. I will be by your side every step of the way. Jelina and Silver agree. Let's go save Elizabeth!"

My brother's words hit home, and I finally let go of my emotions. Hot rage pushes against my walls until I finally let go. A massive heatwave burst from within my heart, expanding out, knocking over healing turtles, and making the Lemurs fly evasively. The trees bend back as the leave shake loose. Goats fall from trees, and the draconians cover their faces from dirt being kicked up. Everyone's eyes now stare at me.

"Tribes of Keywinenyeh Island. My brother and I came to you as intruders, as refugees, seeking aid for our friend. We obeyed all your rules, endured all your treatments, and passed all your tests. Though we were treated as outsiders, we still felt some connection to you and this island. Over the short span that we have been here, we learned some of your traditions and values. You all care for your kin, as do we. And Elizabeth has become part of my kin, part of our kin.

She has been proclaimed to be the savior of this land. But she cannot do it alone. She is still young and still needs protection.

I failed her today, but with our combined strength, we will not fail her again. I fought alongside you all today, not for myself, not only for Elizabeth but for this island, for all of you. I ask that you lend us your strength, like we have for you, to help us take down the Lich and free Elizabeth from a deadly fate."

I stare out and around at many faces that represent everyone inhabiting the island. The air thickens, and many mumble in their native languages. The few snickers and angered faces are upon several draconians and turtles. Zyerr landed breathing smoke out of his nostrils, looking over at Therose. I stare at his face, etched in anger. The silence makes it that no one will step up to the plate and help us. Silver pads up to my left side as Jelina lands on his back in her Kalacuu form. She jumped down and shifted into her Valfen form. Showing me some support for my speech.

I look over at Salithica. She looks down, avoiding eye contact with me. The black goat swirling his nunchucks looks worried for his leader. I shake my shoulders and turn around, facing Silver and Jelina.
"Well, I guess it's only us," I say more loudly than necessary.

"Hold it right there," a deep, commanding voice says behind me. "We didn't get to finish our dual. You can't leave this island… unless I come with you and watch over you until we get to dual again."

I smirk at Therose's reply, and for once, I am glad he will be joining us. I stare into his stern eyes.

"You stupid human. You went and threw yourself in front of me two times, getting in my way, so now I will have to show you what that means." He raises the blade up in the air and brings it down, stopping before it reaches my neck. Gasps are heard behind him, but the anger in his eyes diminished. He flips the blade around and offers the sword to me. I am stunned but not nearly as shocked as Zyerr and the rest of the draconians.

"I have never dueled a warrior in battle as strong and determined as yourself with the heart to protect other draconians over your own kind. I owe you my life, and I will repay it fighting at your side."

"Therose!" Zyerr steps up to us as I reach for the sword. I manage to grab it right before Zyerr unleashes a golden tinted red flame engulfing Therose. I thought he had been incinerated much like that hut during training.

The flames lifted, and Therose stands strong like he is rejuvenated.

"Therose, you thick-headed turtle. You finally learned the last of my teachings. Use that flame wisely when battling against the Lich." All the draconian eyes are bulging out, shocked at the first draconian to receive Zyerr's dragon fire. Therose stands chest out and smirking at all the angry faces.

"Go with the humans, protect them, and when you are ready, call for me, and we will come to join the battle to rid this world of the Lich."

Therose glanced at me and smirked. Then he walks over and whispers, "I can't wait to test these flames out on you."

On the sideline, Salithica and the black goat whisper enthusiastically. Salithica notes my glance and nudges the black goat in my direction. The black goat straightens his leather vest as Salithica walks purposefully up to me.

"I, too, wish to join your group and fight by your side. You have shown us great strength and kindness. It is time I venture out and aid you in the battle to save all of our kin."

Her statement amazes me. "But you are a leader of the Forest Tribe. Aren't you needed here?"

"Yes, but I have been training a master to take over my position someday. I'm getting old. This would prove a great training opportunity for him. I have lots of knowledge of the other lands that may come in handy for you if I'm with you. Floyd, come here."

The same black goat with his nunchucks floats over to us. He is exceptionally skilled in battle. David chimes in, *"I remember him. I owe him for that dress he gave me."*
Salithica turns to the crowd of goats in the forest. "From this day forth, Floyd will be acting as the leader of our Forest Tribe until I return. Listen to him and train for battle. We will need everyone ready when the time comes to fight for our kin once again."

I glance upward at Leena. She stares back at me and lifts her nose to the sky. She might as well say, "Don't look at me like that. I want no part of your war." She turns and takes off. All of her lemurs turn and follow. *That isn't surprising. I wasn't expecting them to lift a finger.*

I feel wetness on my feet again. Looking down, I see Morty slobbering all over my toes. "I take it you will be joining us?"

"Yes, I can't let these delicious feet out of my sight that long." I roll my eyes and kick him off my feet, but he keeps flying around my kicks and latching back onto a leg. From the corner of my eye, I see Ula and Chondro watching me. Neither one looks particularly eager to help out. I'm surprised when Ula walks up to me.
"I don't like you, human. But we want the Lich gone, so we are sending Brutus and Ragarth with you. They will not protect you. They are simply going along to collect intelligence and to learn more English. As new masters,

they need the training."

Brutus and Ragarth roll up to me. Brutus reaches down for an official handshake.

I peer around him and see the angry faces of both Ula and Chondro. I shake his green hand with a smirk winking at Ula. She snorts and turns away from me.

That looks like it.

I look around at our little posse of warriors. I am happy.

For the first time, I feel like we may have a chance at rescuing Elizabeth. Then Tate walks out and ruins the moment. Looking at him spurs hatred within, and flames dance in my palms.

"Let's go. You are making us late," Tate orders.

Just like that, he commands authority and takes charge. But I can't argue. I have no idea where to even start. I don't like him, but we need him to take us to the castle.

Kioserack's sword heats up in my hand, and a vision fills my mind. I grab at Silver's fur to steady myself and can feel David peeking in. Swirls of red smoke disperse to the edges of my sight. A familiar voice rings in my ears from a distance. I see a single silhouette of a lizard standing in the distance mouthing the words: *"It's time."*

About The Authors

Please take the time to check out our website: kinzurdia.com
Also check out our Facebook and Twitter: #Kinzurdia. Discord, Reddit,
Become a Patron
Please take a few minutes and review this book. Let us know what you like
about it or what could be improved. If you enjoyed this book please tell a
friend about it.

Jason Barnum, lives in Tampa Florida. He works full time and manages to
write in his spare time. He enjoys reading fantasy novels on his kindle or
nook, but still has a small private collection of great paperback books. He has
a love for animals and especially cats. Jason also spends some spare time
helping tutor students in math. He is also a gamer, who loves technology. The
book series that started Jason's passion for reading is called Maximum Ride
by one of his favorite authors, James Patterson. This book, Kinzurdia, will be
his first written work other than a few poems he wrote back in 2001 and the
preview of Kinzurdia.

S. Wolf, lives in the Mideast of the United States. He has a love for dogs and
wolves. He is a wolf collector. He collects just about anything you can find
whether an avatar in a game, a stuffed animal or a rare collectible. Some
games have even made characters in their games from his wolf ideas. He is
known well amongst the Furry community and has plans on being the mascot,
Silver, later down the road when he gets the wolf suit. He has a disability but
he doesn't let that stand in his way to convey his ideas to creating this series.
This is his first written publication.

Made in the USA
Las Vegas, NV
29 August 2021